TRACKER

C.J. CHERRYH

THE FOREIGNER UNIVERSE

FOREIGNER
INVADER
INHERITOR

DESTROYER
PRETENDER
DELIVERER

INTRUDER
PROTECTOR
PEACEMAKER

PRECURSOR
DEFENDER
EXPLORER

CONSPIRATOR
DECEIVER
BETRAYER

TRACKER

THE ALLIANCE-UNION UNIVERSE
REGENESIS
DOWNBELOW STATION
THE DEEP BEYOND Omnibus:
Serpent's Reach | Cuckoo's Egg
ALLIANCE SPACE Omnibus:
Merchanter's Luck | 40,000 in Gehenna
AT THE EDGE OF SPACE Omnibus:
Brothers of Earth | Hunter of Worlds
THE FADED SUN Omnibus:
Kesrith | Shon'jir | Kutath

THE CHANUR NOVELS
THE CHANUR SAGA Omnibus:
The Pride Of Chanur | Chanur's Venture | The Kif Strike Back
CHANUR'S ENDGAME Omnibus:
Chanur's Homecoming | Chanur's Legacy

THE MORGAINE CYCLE
THE COMPLETE MORGAINE:
Gate of Ivrel | Well of Shiuan | Fires of Azeroth | Exile's Gate
New omnibus edition available September 2015!

OTHER WORKS:
THE DREAMING TREE Omnibus:
The Tree of Swords and Jewels | The Dreamstone
ALTERNATE REALITIES Omnibus:
Port Eternity | Wave Without a Shore | Voyager in Night
THE COLLECTED SHORT FICTION OF CJ CHERRYH
ANGEL WITH THE SWORD

C. J. CHERRYH

TRACKER

A Foreigner Novel

DAW BOOKS, INC.
DONALD A. WOLLHEIM, FOUNDER
375 Hudson Street, New York, NY 10014

ELIZABETH R. WOLLHEIM
SHEILA E. GILBERT
PUBLISHERS
www.dawbooks.com

Jacket art by Todd Lockwood.

DAW Books Collectors No. 1685.

DAW Books are distributed by Penguin Group (USA).

Book design by Stanley S. Drate/Folio Graphics Co., Inc.

First Printing, April 2015

1 2 3 4 5 6 7 8 9

DAW TRADEMARK REGISTERED
U.S. PAT. AND TM. OFF. AND FOREIGN COUNTRIES
—MARCA REGISTRADA
HECHO EN U.S.A.

PRINTED IN THE U.S.A.

To Willow, especially Irene.

Table of Contents

1

The sun touched the end of the bay, the end of a good day. A ragged streak of cloud lit up gold with a shadowy attempt at pink.

Jaishan ceased her leisurely tacking toward the sunset and turned for port with an experienced hand at the helm. Gold sunlight swept her deck, cast shadows down the planks as the massive boom swung over.

The sail thumped and filled with the shoreward wind, a purposeful course, now homeward bound for Najida estate.

"Fascinating system." Jase Graham, spacefarer, turned and took a firm grip on the rail as water began to rush and foam under the bow.

Bren Cameron leaned easily beside him, elbows on the same rail. He loved the sound and the feel of the sea. They could have had a bit more speed, but that wasn't what they wanted now. This was the last bit of sailing they'd get before Jase went back to the space station overhead, and good-byes were in the offing.

Tano was at the helm, enjoying the job—atevi, native to the world, as humans were not: black-skinned, golden-eyed, a head taller than most humans. Tano's partner Algini was close by him; and their teammates, Banichi and Jago, were lounging on the equipment locker, against the rail, enjoying the wind and the absolute absence of threat.

Bren was glad to see it. Rare that his bodyguard got an hour off, let alone whole days, let alone a week of such days. His bodyguard was still in uniform—Assassins' Guild black happened to be all they owned. But they had shed their heavy leather jackets in the sun today, and gotten in a little fishing.

Banichi was certainly moving far better than he had a week ago. He was zealously keeping up with the exercises on his arm and shoulder. He was also getting impatient with the rehab schedule and entirely ready, Banichi assured them all, to resume ordinary duty.

Being on the boat meant security enough that Banichi and the rest of them could relax. Ordinary duty out here in the wide bay need involve nothing more strenuous than watching the horizons and casting a line.

There was hardly anywhere on the planet more secure than where they'd been the last number of days. The aishidi'tat, the Western Association of the atevi, was at peace—still in shock from the loss of two lords, the investiture of an heir, and the return of the *old* leadership of the Assassins' Guild—but at peace. Banichi, of that Guild, had been no little involved in the event—which was why he was under doctor's orders not to push anything, and why it took being out in the middle of all this water, with a navy ship out across the bay—to make Banichi admit there was indeed leisure to relax.

Banichi laughed at something his partners had just said. That was a very good thing to hear. It unwound something in Bren's own gut.

"First vacation in a long time," Bren said to Jase, beside him. "You've got to come down to Earth more often. You're good for us."

"My duty-book's going to be stacked and waiting for me," Jase said with a sigh. "Anything the senior captains don't want to handle, *guess* where it'll go in my absence. Right to my desk. —But it's worth it. I've enjoyed this."

"Even the gunfire?"

"Well, I mostly missed that part."

"Not all of it."

"It was an experience," Jase said. "And your own duty-book's going to look like mine, I'm afraid. You've still got the chaff from that mess up north to deal with. Wish I could help with that."

"Minor," Bren said. It said something about recent months, that he could call the ruin of an historic atevi clan "minor." But it *was* minor—now that the Kadagidi clan's influence had diminished.

And diminish, yes, it had. The aishidi'tat, the Western Association, was in fact down *two* clan lords since the start of Jase's visit, and politics was certain to surround the replacements, but Bren had *some* hope there would be a quick, sensible solution—as yet unthought-of—but it was not his job to think of it. The aiji in Shejidan, Tabini, was firmly in power. The Assassins' Guild, the core of the judicial system, was functioning as it had not in years. And Bren, paidhi-aiji, translator to the court, intermediary-at-large, could now draw a deep breath and hope all the agreements he'd pinned down stayed put.

They were both human, he and Jase. Bren, born to the planet and Jase, to the starship *Phoenix*. Jase had been a special child—born of long-dead heroes, destined to be something a dead man had known and Jase had never learned. That he'd come early to a captaincy—one of the four who held that post—was destiny, maybe; genetics and politics, certainly—"But I don't know what I was for," Jase had put it.

"Does anybody, really?" Bren had answered that one, and Jase had thought about it and laughed.

So here they were—Jase a ship's captain, visiting a planet that had so much history with his ship; and Bren himself—wielding a power he'd never remotely planned on holding, disconnected from Mospheira, and inextricably involved in Tabini-aiji's affairs. But alike. Intermediaries, both, trained to mediate, to communicate—*both* of them grown into an authority neither of them had planned to hold and a job nobody had imagined would exist. Mediators. Negotiators. Translators not just of language, but of mindsets and cultures.

Humans were the cosmic accident on the planet, involving *Phoenix* and a desperate human colony, centuries ago. *Phoenix* had arrived at the Earth of the atevi, crew and passengers destitute and dying, an unknown world their last reachable hope.

But the world already had a population. Atevi had been chugging along in their steam age, having achieved railroads, having achieved a reasonably peaceful government long before humans had ever appeared in their heavens.

Phoenix built an orbiting station for a base, manned it, and left in search of another home for its colony. But the humans left behind saw what they wanted, and reached for it, flinging themselves earthward, desperately, on what atevi called the petal sails, one after another, until the station could no longer sustain itself, and the final handful left, shutting the station down, leaving it to drift silent, abandoned.

And the descendants of those desperate colonists now formed a terrestrial nation: Mospheira. The island of that name lay a day's sail away, too far across the strait to spot from this vantage, even as a haze above the sea. It was a large island, tag-end of the massive monocontinent on which atevi dwelled, easily within reach of any determined individual with a rowboat and a mission.

But it was isolated by atevi law—excepting one appointee: the paidhi, the human interpreter to the atevi court.

These days, that would be him.

The paidhi's original job, as Bren had undertaken it, had been, first, to assure an accurate flow of information between humans and atevi; and secondly to turn over human technology to atevi at a measured, studied rate, so as not to upset the peace of the world. That was how the original humans had bought their safety, having lost the War of the Landing.

And humans, Mospheirans now, had locked themselves in technological synchrony with the atevi of the mainland, turning over the safe parts of their precious Archive, not accelerating the pace of development, not pushing atevi into change that might turn dangerous, that might cause upheaval, and war.

Mostly the paidhi's job had been to collect words—whatever atevi words the sitting paidhi judged humans could accurately and safely use, in the University-controlled interface. It was a glacially slow process. The paidhiin had handled the careful, meticulous phrasing of official communications, but held no control over the content.

That was what Bren *had* started out to be—a maker of dictionaries, a court functionary who sat on the steps of the aiji's dais, when court was in session, and who spoke only rarely, on direct request. The utmost ambition of Bren's life in the first year had been to avoid a second War of the Landing on his watch. He could not, in the beginning, even edit a document. He could only say: excuse me, sir, please, take no offense, but that word has a connotation . . .

But he'd had to deal with Tabini-aiji, who wanted to *talk* to him, and wanted verbal answers. Fast.

He'd slipped over into actively speaking the language the first week. Tabini had pushed that situation.

Pushed him until he'd begun to operate outside the rules—begun to *speak* the language. Now he primarily *thought* in it.

Tabini-aiji wanted more technology. Under Tabini, planes became jets, radio became television, and industry proliferated. Atevi took to computers and improved what they were handed, finding their own path, making their own discoveries.

Then *Phoenix* turned up, back from centuries of absence, bringing a wealth of old history, old human quarrels, and a single question: which government on Earth had the industrial power they needed? Cultural kinship linked the ship, for good or ill, to Mospheira. Need linked them to Tabini-aiji.

The job of the paidhi-aiji instantly changed. More, the ship appointed its own paidhi—Jase, who'd parachuted down the way the colonists had—to build a relationship with the continent, which had the range of earthly resources a space program needed. It had meant Jase learning Ragi. It had meant atevi building a space program while Mospheirans argued about it. And ultimately it had meant getting atevi and Mospheirans to cooperate—because control of half the orbiting station had been the price of Tabini-aiji's cooperation.

Everything had changed, like so many snowballs headed downhill. Atevi were in space now, equal partners with Mospheirans on the station in a fifty-fifty arrangement which had two command centers and two stationmasters, cooperating together in a three-way arrangement with the four *Phoenix* captains—of whom Jase was now third-senior.

And Bren Cameron had ceased to represent Mospheira at all, in any regular way. His personal loyalty—his man'chi, in the atevi way of putting it—rested on the atevi side of the straits, and not just because that was the job he could do best. He represented Tabini-aiji's interests not only to humans on Earth and aloft, but to atevi lords on the continent, and he held a district lord's rank in order to do it.

So he'd come a long, long way from Mospheira, mentally speaking—a long way from human allegiances and human politics. He'd not visited the island in nearly four years—two of which he'd spent in deep space, remote from the world, one of which he'd spent down here, trying to patch the damage the push to space had done to the balance of power on Earth.

Of human contacts he still kept active, there was his brother Toby. There was Barb, who had been his lover, and now was Toby's partner.

And there was Jase, now third-senior of the starship's four captains—but still technically ship-paidhi, too. Jase knew atevi customs and he spoke Ragi, the principle atevi language, passably well.

And being ship-folk, a stranger to any planet, Jase's mindset was *not* Mospheiran. Jase's instincts might biologically match Mospheiran instincts, but his native accent was ship-folk, and he had never set foot on Mospheira, nor cared to go there.

Well, that was all right, in Bren's thinking. There was still no one he had rather see in a position of influence among the ship-folk. Jase wanted the survival of Mospheira *and* the safety of the ship and the station aloft, and he wanted the survival of the atevi. They shared the same set of priorities.

And if there was one person on the planet who truly understood what he was and how he thought—it was Jase.

That was why, in Jase's company, at the rail of a moving boat, Bren could draw breath right now with an ease he didn't feel with others, even the atevi lords whose survival *he* fought to ensure, or the Mospheiran president he tried to keep generally abreast of whatever atevi were doing—or, for that matter, with the aiji he served. They shared a job. They shared the same worries. They served the same interests.

So perhaps it was a little selfish of him to wish his area of the world could float along in the lazy way it had been going for a few more days, just one or two days more, before he had to go back to what Jase called his duty-book.

By tomorrow evening he'd be back in that highly securitied apartment in the privileged third floor of the Bujavid, the great fortress and legislative center above the capital city. There'd be no duty-book, no computer files waiting for him on his return, but there would certainly be a message bowl sitting in his apartment foyer, a bowl overflowing with cylinders from people wanting a slice of his attention—lords and department heads with agendas that had been suspended for the last few weeks while the Assassins' Guild had a meltdown and the aiji's son celebrated his fortunate ninth birthday.

Missing from that bowl, to be sure, would be the unwritten problems—a determined handful of people who *wouldn't* write to the paidhi-aiji politely and officially advising him they wanted him dead, and who wouldn't be Filing Intent with the Assassins' Guild. Oh, no: a legal Filing would never pass muster with the Guild, let alone Tabini-aiji, and his enemies couldn't gain any partisan following to demand it. So they couldn't succeed above-board. That meant anything that might come at him would not follow the rules.

That problem went with the title, the estate, the boat. He'd gotten back to the world a year ago from a two-year voyage into deep space—to find the aishidi'tat in chaos and Mospheira bracing for war.

He and the aiji-dowager and the will of the people had set Tabini-aiji back in power, a movement carried on the shock of their arrival and the revelation that neither Tabini nor his young heir was dead.

Well, things were better. He'd actually been able to take a vacation—give or take a few stitches in his scalp, and Banichi's need for rehab on that shoulder.

And now . . .

Now *Jaishan* had put her stern to the setting sun and her bow toward the end of the bay. Her sail had filled with a golden sunset, and the west wind was carrying her home with the hum of the rigging and the rush of water under her white hull.

And that was all he needed think of for the better part of an hour.

"Want to take the helm for a while?" he asked Jase.

Jase laughed. "They never let captains take the controls up there, you know. Helm won't have it."

"Well, there's that island over there to port. That's the only thing in this part of the bay you have to miss. Want to do it?"

"Love to," Jase said, and they left the rail and crossed the deck. Tano was perfectly content to turn over the wheel and instruct a novice how to handle it. Easy job, with a perfect wind carrying them and not much to do but keep *Jaishan*'s bow headed for home.

She nodded a bit as Tano demonstrated how she was handling. Then she cut through the water with a steady rush, fast under sail, beautiful in her spread of canvas. And Jase had the helm now, delighted.

Perfect day. Perfect finish.

"You can feel the speed pick up," Jase said. "Amazing how it feels in your hands."

No readouts, no numbers here, no helmsman nor navigator, nothing like a starship's bridge at all, just the wind aloft and salt water running under her keel. The sounds and vibrations all around them were like nothing else in the world, readout without a dial or a blinking light. Bren would have taken *Jaishan* in himself—he got few chances to enjoy it. But Jase should have this run, something to think back on when he got back to his own reality, up in space.

Maybe this last outing would be a lure sufficient to bring Jase back to the world. Jase hadn't been so much for fishing. The notion that they were going to kill and immediately eat a creature was just more than Jase liked to inspect too closely, much as Jase appreciated fish when it appeared from a kitchen, spiced, plated, and sauced.

So they'd just sailed this day, skirted the picturesque if hazardous offshore rocks off the end of the peninsula, and at least gone far enough from shore to see the haze on the horizon that was the island of Mospheira.

His aishid, his personal bodyguard, had done all the fishing on the other side of the boat, and brought back a sizeable catch for Najida's cook to deal with.

But the fatality to fish needn't trouble Jase, who had happiness on his face and the wind in his hair.

They were dressed atevi-style: trousers, boots, and, since the sun had started down, warm outdoor coats. The bay could be chill. One wanted to keep hands in pockets when *Jaishan* was moving like this, and Jase's bare hands would be quite cold, gripping the wheel, but the air was clean and good.

The wind played little tricks as they came past the jut of the Edi headland that sheltered the little fishing harbor there, and Tano anticipated it, turning up by Jase's shoulder as the wind first fell off and then came back stronger. Jase coped without help. *Jaishan* steadied, a thing of beauty in the dying light, chasing her own shadow on the water.

And when the shore loomed up in the twilight, and the lights of Bren's own estate at Najida showed on the hill above the landing, they had a feeling of real homecoming, a sense that they had indeed sailed away from the world today, and were coming back to a lingering fantasy of country life and rustic warmth.

They were arriving too late for dinner at the house, however: that had happened early, before sunset. Bren had asked the youngsters and Jase's two-man bodyguard to pack for their return, and his staff had intended a special early supper for their guests, with all the youngsters' favorite dishes.

Bren hoped that affair had come off well, and that the youngsters were having the time together he had intended. He and Jase had had their own light supper at the first of the twilight—sandwiches, nothing extravagant—and they were holding out for wine and dessert once they got in.

They *could* have been out on the boat all day if he had really pitched a fit. Cajeiri knew that.

They *could* have been. But nand' Bren had hinted, quietly and hopefully, that it would please him very much if he could have some time to talk to Jase. Nand' Bren had offered Cajeiri and his guests a dinner party instead, just themselves as the sole focus of the Najida staff, and Cajeiri had not argued, because nand' Bren was seeing *his* guest go home tomorrow, too, and of course he wanted some time. Nand' Bren had done everything in his power to make their visit the best it could be, and nand' Bren had taken them all out on the boat every day but this one.

So all in all, and largely thanks to nand' Bren and Jase-aiji, the birthday had been excellent, and Cajeiri was sure his auspicious ninth year had had the very best beginning it could have. His guests were here from the space station and his baby sister was born safely and his father had named him officially his heir, in front of the whole aishidi'tat.

Not to mention the Guild had gotten rid of the people who were causing the trouble, and was now doing what it was supposed to do, which was to keep peace in the aishidi'tat. The Marid, the district to the south that had made war not so long ago, was peaceful, and that meant they were safe enough to be out at nand' Bren's estate, sailing whenever they wanted and without any great worry about enemies.

Everything would have been perfect this evening, if only there could be endless days in front of them.

But no, Gene and Artur and Irene were going back to the station, leaving on the shuttle tomorrow with Jase-aiji and his bodyguard.

That meant he would not see his guests for another year, and maybe longer than a year if stupid grown-ups got to feuding, again, as grown-ups were always apt to do.

Or if his mother got her way and his guests could never visit the Earth again.

But no feud and none of his mother's objections was going to stop them meeting forever. He had made up his mind to that, and he was sure his father, the aiji of the whole aishidi'tat, was on *his* side this time.

Besides, his mother had his new sister to take care of. That meant she was spending less time worrying about him. And when she was not thinking about him, she was surely in a much better mood.

"This time you will have to write," he said to his guests, as they were sitting in their suite, well-fed, with all their belongings and souvenirs strewn on the master bed. His valets and his bodyguard were doing the actual packing. They were better at it. Boji, small, furry, black, and large as a baby, was traveling with them, and he was bounding about his cage, keenly aware of the packing, and upset about it. He wanted to be out. And that would not be a good idea, in case the door should open.

"We will write," Gene said in Ragi, and added: "I *did* write."

"You did write," Cajeiri agreed.

"We all tried," Artur said.

"This time my father *will* give me the letters you send. I am sure he will. And I shall write as often as I have something to say."

"My mother may not give me the letters," Irene said, also in Ragi. "She can be happy. And then she is unhappy. One does not know what will happen when I am back. She will surely be angry that we stayed more time."

Upset mothers were not in anybody's control. Cajeiri understood that very well. "We shall meet next year. Don't worry."

It was conniving, that was what Great-grandmother would call it, and Irene would do what she promised she would do, no matter what Irene's mother said. They could be sure of that. Irene was much braver than anybody might think.

So they connived together. And planned their next meeting.

It felt, on this last night, a little like the old association again, except that Bjorn was not with them—Bjorn had decided to stay with his tutor, or whatever people had up there: *school* was the ship-speak for it. Gene said Bjorn had had to stay in the program or he could have lost his place with his tutors, and his parents would have been really upset. A place in tutorage was not easy for a Reunioner to get—and Bjorn was smart, and older, and it was a program that, right at the start, just after they had arrived on the station, had let in just the best and smartest of the Reunioner young folk. And now that program was on the verge of being phased out. Cajeiri understood how desperate life was for Reunioners, how short supplies were, and how important it was that Bjorn stay where he was and not be dismissed and lose his chance.

His father being aiji, Cajeiri thought, *might* have negotiated something that would have let Bjorn come down and not lose his place—but his father had already been extraordinarily accommodating in allowing his guests at all, and he had wanted to create no extra problems with station politics.

They had resolved they were going to be sure that Bjorn could come next time.

And they had set up in detail how they were going to get around obstacles during the next year, arranging for messages to get where they needed to go, and when they should expect the first one, and how he was always going to mention a number in the ending that would tell them what the number of the letter was. That way they would always know whether all the messages were getting through.

They would do the same for messages to him.

He was too young to use the Messengers' Guild on his own, and there was a scarcity of paper for printing things on the station, so the messages he sent would be real letters on paper, which would go up in packets on the shuttle missions. That meant his packets would go first to Lord Geigi, on the atevi side of the station—that was how it would work. And their answers would all come in the same packets as Lord Geigi's reports home, on stationery that was part of the souvenirs going with them.

Along with his own little packets he could send any little light thing, if his father allowed and if it fit within regulations. So he decided he would always pack in some fruit sweets for Lord Geigi. He was sure Lord Geigi would appreciate the gift, and send the letters on to the human side of the station. Lord Geigi knew very well how his mail had gotten held forever, this last year. And Lord Geigi was on their side, and he *would* do it, and make sure things happened.

"Tell Bjorn, too," he said. "Tell *him* to write to me. Often. One wishes to hear about his program."

"We tell him," Irene said. "*I* see him sometimes. Not often. But I shall tell him everything we did. He will be—" She changed to ship-speak. "He wanted so much to come. But the rules say no. He cannot be absent."

"Next year," Gene said. "Next year for sure. And you keep in touch with *me*, Reni, do you hear?"

Irene lived in a different section than Gene and Artur. Reunioners were divided up in residencies by sections, and Gene was not allowed to go where Irene and Bjorn lived, which was some sort of special place.

But they had set up their ways to deal with that, the same that they had had on the starship—tunnels, just like on the starship, that ran beside the public corridors, or over or under them. They had mapped them on the ship. They had mapped them on the station, and Gene had explored all the way to the place atevi authority started. They had made maps together, and added a whole new section to the little notebook that Cajeiri always kept close—the little notebook that had always helped him remember, and now helped him imagine places he'd never seen.

He could imagine now where they lived, and how their place related to the atevi side. And before, all last year, politics had gotten in the way of their even getting letters to each other. But now they had an ally, and if someone tried to keep them from writing, the tunnels meant ways they could get to the atevi side, where atevi made the rules.

"Lord Geigi will definitely always help us," Cajeiri said. "And if people try to stop us from writing to each other, just get to the atevi side. Just walk right up to the doors and say my father said so and they should let you in."

"*Did* he say so?"

"Well, he *will,*" he said, and they all laughed a little, which was disrespectful, but he was also determined it would be true. "And do *not* tell your parents any sort of things that may scare them!" Humans and atevi might be different, so very different they could have very dangerous misunderstandings. And if one added parents into the numbers, one could only imagine what sort of misunderstanding could happen. "Whatever your parents ask about the trouble, always say, That was very far from us, or . . ." He put on his most innocent face. "Was there something going on?"

Artur laughed, and they all did.

"We never saw the gunfire," Gene said with his most innocent expression.

"Never!" Irene said. "We just had nice food and pretty clothes and we went to parties and met your parents. How could there possibly be a problem?"

They laughed. There had been scary moments, particularly at Tirnamardi, when nand' Bren and nand' Jase had gone to deal with Lord Tatiseigi's neighbor; and that had been a scary time. They had ashes drifting down onto Lord Tatiseigi's driveway, and there had been bullet holes in the bus when nand' Bren and nand' Jase had come back.

It had been even worse, when Great-grandmother had had to send nand' Bren right into the heart of the Assassins' Guild to take down the Shadow Guild. They had had to pretend everything was perfectly normal that evening. But they had not known whether they might all be running for their lives before morning.

That had been an extremely scary night, and nand' Bren and Banichi and several of Great-grandmother's guard had come back wounded. But Father had had Cajeiri and his guests inside the tightest protection, and they had had Jase-aiji and his bodyguards with them as well as Father's and Great-grandmother's bodyguards around them. Jase-aiji's bodyguards had weapons that could take out half the apartment and maybe the floor under them, and he was very glad *those* had never come into question.

So, no, they had never been in that much danger.

And right after that, while everything was still in confusion, his father had turned his birthday into a public Festivity and he had had to make a public speech and be named, officially, his father's heir.

His associates had been there when he had becomc "young aiji," not just "young gentleman," so they knew what had happened, and how everything had changed. And so far the title had not been a great inconvenience, but that was, Cajeiri feared, only because he still had his foreign guests. When they left, tomorrow—when they left—

He feared there were going to be duties, and more appearances in court dress, and that his life for the next whole year and forever after was going to be just gruesome.

But he would do it.

He would do it because behaving badly could mean his guests could not come back. Priorities, his great-grandmother called it.

He would definitely have to go back to living in his suite, inside his father's apartment, with his mother—and his very new sister, who was a baby, and who was going to cry a lot.

He would have his bodyguard for company. And he would have his valets, who were grown men, but they understood him and they were patient. His little household was his, and no one would take that away.

He was sure he was going to have to go back to regular lessons. His latest tutor was not a bad one—even interesting sometimes, so it was not too awful. And he was coming back with a lot of things to ask about.

But he had still rather be out at Najida or Tirnamardi.

He would not get to ride his mecheita until the next holiday, and that only *if* he could get an invitation from Great-uncle Tatiseigi and *if* he could get permission from his father to go out to Tirnamardi. And all that depended on whether there were troubles anywhere near. It might be next year before he could go, because there *were* currently troubles in the north. During the whole year, there was still going to be the question of the succession to the lordship of the Ajuri *and* the lordship of the Kadagidi, either one of which could break into gunfire or worse and just mess everything up in Tirnamardi, where his mecheita was.

Worse, Ajuri was his mother's clan, and the upset in Ajuri was going to keep her upset all year.

But maybe being "young aiji" meant even his father would be more inclined to listen to what he wanted.

And what he wanted was to go riding for days and days; and what he wanted even more than that was his guests back again—*before* next year if he could somehow manage it.

But third, and what he wanted most of all, and had no power at all to arrange—he wanted his guests to live safe from politics up on the station. The situation up there, the Mospheirans feuding with the Reunioners—that quarrel really, really worried him.

There were over twice as many humans on the station as there were supposed to be, and the half of them, who had come up from the island of Mospheira, hated the other half, who had arrived last year from Reunion, out in deep space. There was not enough room. So things had become crowded and difficult.

More, a treaty said that there would always be as many atevi up there as there were humans—and *that* agreement was thrown out of balance, with the Reunioners arriving. Now there were twice as many humans as there ought to be, but only the same number of atevi. Maybe it would have been kind for atevi to give up some of their room to make things better, but for some reason they were not doing that. He had to ask his father why. It was possibly because they did not want the Reunioners staying there and fussing with the Mospheirans. Or possibly just that they did not want to interfere in a human feud.

And then there was the accident with one of the big tanks that grew fish and such that fed the station—when the station had already had trouble feeding everybody before the Reunioners had come. Atevi were not willing for humans to be short of food, however. So they had helped with that, with workers and metal to repair the damaged tank. And Lord Geigi had sent workers and materials that modified a number of public areas into living spaces. But it was all still a mess.

And there was no easy way to fix it. The ancestors of the Mospheirans had had a disagreement with the ancestors of the Reunioners, and now, just when the Mospheirans had gotten themselves through a very scary and dangerous time, and built everything to make themselves comfortable and well-fed again—the Reunioners showed up to overcrowd them.

Mospheiran humans on the station wanted to pack up all the Reunioners and send them out to go build a completely new station at the barren ball of rock that was Maudit, far across the solar system. Mospheirans wanted never to see them again.

He did not agree. His three guests were Reunioners, and he did not want them sent out to Maudit.

So if the Mospheiran stationers won and the Reunioners were set to leave, he intended to get his guests and their parents over into the atevi section of the station, under Lord Geigi's authority, where no human order could reach them. He had not gotten his father's agreement that that was what they would do—but that was his intention, and he intended to do what he could to arrange that, quietly, so as not to upset adults.

He intended to write to Lord Geigi, for one thing, and get Lord Geigi to agree to protect his guests. And their parents. He would ask it in principle, first. That was one of his great-grandmother's words. In principle. Nand' Bren would say, getting one's foot in the door.

And once he knew *that* was set up, and given that they *could* reach Lord Geigi by the secret passages Gene had mapped, then he could at least feel easier about his guests. They might have to go back tomorrow. But tomorrow he would set about getting them back down to Earth for his next birthday.

Nobody was going to take them away. Nobody was going to threaten them because of some stupid quarrel their ancestors had had.

Nobody was going to stop him.

If being heir of the aishidi'tat meant anything—he was going to get his guests back and keep them safe from stupid people.

2

Three people waited on the dock as *Jaishan* came in: Saidaro, who cared for *Jaishan* most of the year, and Saidaro's two assistants, elderly fishermen from Najida village, the Edi community just down the hill from the estate.

On an ordinary day, Bren would have stayed to shut down the boat and talk and do whatever maintenance might have come up, but not this evening. *Jaishan* was going to be rejoining Lord Geigi's yacht, going back to her ongoing task of ferrying passengers and supplies to a new construction going on, a new Edi center on Lord Geigi's peninsula, keeping a promise to the Edi people. The sea offered the best and most direct access to the site, for heavy loads, of which there were several waiting.

So Saidaro would be at work late into the night preparing her for that run, putting up buffers to shield her paint and brightwork from the loads of lumber and stone, coils of wire and pieces of pipe that would be her routine cargo through the rest of the good weather.

And by fall—the new Edi administration would have a focal point, a place where the Edi people were the law.

The sail came in as they passed the point, and Jase surrendered the helm. Tano *could* bring her in on sail alone, but the current was tricky here, and it was far easier to turn on the motor for the approach to dock, and not rely on a slightly fickle wind. *Jaishan* motored in sedately under Tano's hand, and as they neared the buffers, Jago tossed the mooring loop.

Saidaro, on shore, caught it and dropped it neatly over the post. The two old fishermen waited aft to catch a second line from Algini. Banichi usually did that cast, but Banichi, under strict orders to protect the arm, simply cradled it and stood frowning but compliant.

And with *Jaishan* snugged in, Saidaro and his helpers ran out the rustic gangway to its buffered catching-point.

From there, Jase and Bren could walk down to the steady, weathered boards of the dockside, with Jago and the rest to gather gear and follow . . . they would not let Banichi carry a thing.

"My feet always expect the dock to move," Jase said with a laugh.

"We'll probably both feel the sea moving all night," Bren said. "I know I will." He gave a nod to Saidaro and his crew. "Daro-ji, thank you! She is in your hands!"

"Nandi." Saidaro bowed, the fishermen bowed, and Bren collected his bodyguard and his guest and headed down the few steps from the wooden dock to the flagstone path.

Three of the staff from the house were coming down the zigzag path among the low evergreens, hurrying to assist them with such baggage as there was. Banichi and the rest became all business ashore, even here at Najida, even on this easy walk up the winding path to the driveway. Banichi and Jago went in front and Tano and Algini walked behind, leaving the local lads to gather up the catch from the onboard storage and bring along the smaller baggage. Tano carried only one sizeable case personally—the black leather bag that non-Guild were never supposed to touch. But the mood was easy, all the same.

They walked up a turn, and the beautiful, restored window—recent gift of the aiji-dowager—shone in the twilight above a dark row of evergreen shrubs, red and blue and gold glass lit from within the hall.

The aiji-dowager, who had weathered a serious attack at Najida, did nothing by halves. She had ordered, additionally, two stained-glass windows for the new dining room, a frame for the central window that would look out on the setting sun. It would be a defiant expanse of bright-colored glass, surrounding a window that would give that room the most glorious view on the coast. The windows were a security hazard, but they had their defenses.

And the world they would overlook, one hoped, was more peaceful now than it had been in living memory.

Three and four bends of the path brought them up beyond sight of the window, up to the drive and the portico—an area likewise restored from recent disaster. Construction there was finished. The new west wing's roof, a skeletal shadow beyond the portico, out where the old garage and the old garden gate had used to be, was actively under construction. The crew wanted to have the complex roof sound and the interior protected before the good season ended, so even with guests in residence, there had been constant hammering during the day, with workmen from Najida village coming and going on the graveled road.

The Reunioner youngsters, who had never seen wood and stone in their lives before their visit, had been fascinated by the process. So had Jase been. They had gone out more than once to watch the work . . . even climbed up to see how the structure was made.

But the crew had gone home to their suppers, down in the village. Hammering had ceased for the night, and would not resume before they left, early, early in the morning.

"You'll remember to send me pictures when it's all done," Jase said as they headed toward the door.

"Deal," Bren said.

The house door opened for them unasked. Najida's major domo, Ramaso, welcomed them in, staff waited to take their outdoor coats, and to provide their indoor ones. Other servants deftly took away the day's catch from those following, and whisked it off to the kitchen—it would likely reappear as the staff breakfast in the morning, once the lord and his offworld guests were safely out the door and away.

"A pleasant trip, nandiin?" Ramaso asked.

"Entirely, Rama-ji," Bren said. "The young gentleman and his guests have retired?"

"They are still awake in their suite, nandi," Ramaso said, "well-fed and happy, by all report. Do you still wish only the cakes?"

"Jase-ji?"

"Certainly that will be enough for me," Jase said. The sandwiches they had had for supper had been more than they could eat. "A glass of wine, the cakes, and I shall be very content."

"The sitting room, then," Bren said, and led the way, Banichi and Jago attending. Tano and Algini went on toward their own quarters, there being a little packing yet to do.

He and Jase had their dessert, wine chilled so that moisture frosted the glasses, and a plate of spice cakes still so warm from the oven that the icing melted.

Banichi and Jago took cakes, too, but not the wine, and after sending an order to the kitchen, uncharacteristically informal in this very safe house, they took a second plate of little cakes with them and retired to quarters to help Tano and Algini pack up. Jase's bodyguard, Kaplan and Polano, were likewise off in Jase's suite, packing for a much longer trip.

So he and Jase had this one last evening to themselves, no duties to think of . . . locally speaking.

"My hindbrain's already starting to add up what's waiting for me," Jase said ruefully, feet propped on a footstool, and a second glass of wine in hand. "And top of the stack is my report to the captains. *And* to Lord Geigi." A lengthy pause. Then: "And Tillington. Bren, we two need to *talk* about Tillington."

"In what regard?"

Tillington was the Mospheiran-side stationmaster, human counterpart to Lord Geigi.

Tillington had been all right, in Bren's estimation: Tillington had kept his half of the station running fairly well—cooperating, generally, with Lord Geigi, getting along well with Ogun, who ran the ship's affairs on station.

Tillington had had a hard situation. *Phoenix*, under Captain Sabin and Jase, with Ilisidi, Cajeiri, and Bren aboard, had gone off on its voyage to deal with a remote station in deep space, a lone human outpost that had been supposed to be dead—but which had been left with records they didn't want lying there for any other entity to find: those, the human Archive, needed to be destroyed. That was the mission. Ogun, senior captain, had stayed behind, with half the crew, to maintain the ship's authority on the station.

Then, no fault of anyone aloft, so far as he knew, the disasters had multiplied.

A conspiracy on the mainland had unseated Tabini-aiji, seized the spaceport, grounded all but the one shuttle which had happened to be at the space station. The paidhi-aiji *and* the ship-paidhi being absent on the mission had meant translation between humans and atevi was down to Yolanda Mercheson, who suffered a breakdown. The shuttles no longer flew and pilots and crews went missing. Supply to the space station stopped.

Geigi had refused to move the one shuttle he had left from its station berth. Geigi had kept it ready against the return of the ship—with the paidhiin, the aiji-dowager, and Tabini's heir.

Tillington had argued long and hard about that shuttle. He had wanted to use it to build up Mospheiran technology and launch a human force to unseat the conspirators on the mainland—not a happy prospect on the atevi side of the station, and Geigi, who had the shuttle *and* the only crew able to fly it, said a firm no.

Geigi, meanwhile, had launched his own program to deal with the mainland's new rulers. He had shut down construction on the atevi starship, diverted all its labor and resources to the construction of a satellite communications network, hitherto lacking, and to the production of sufficient food in orbit, which would render the station independent of Earth.

Tillington had cooperated with that—not happy, no, but cooperating, while the Mospheiran government had pushed its own shuttle program into production. They pushed training pilots of their own—and struggled with supply delays. The mainland, in hostile hands, no longer supplied certain materials, and the Mospheiran space program made progress only slowly.

In the midst of it all, *Phoenix* made it back—bringing in five thousand Reunioner refugees—when the station had thought at most there might be a hundred or so.

The aiji-dowager lost not an hour. Geigi, discovering *Phoenix* was coming in, had the shuttle and crew up and ready, and Bren, and the aiji-dowager, and Tabini's son—had headed straight for the shuttle dock. They'd landed on Mospheira, and crossed the strait to deal with the conspirators in a way a human invasion never could.

The ship, in the exigencies of prolonged dock, and with supplies at rock bottom, refused to house the refugees any longer. It began disembarking the refugees—five thousand souls, all turned out onto the station, skilled workers, without jobs, without housing, and with no prospects, in a station with no jobs, not enough housing, and no plan for their numbers to double. The ultimate issue was—what voice should these new people have in anything? What were they going to demand, if they were given any vote at all?

And if they had to increase atevi presence to balance the numbers of humans—the newcomers would still be a majority of humans aloft, and *they* included people with children. *They* were going to increase in numbers, and *they* didn't have to pass screening to get into orbit—they were born there.

On Earth, things were much better. Murini's regime, the conspiracy, had held power on the continent only by force and assassination. Now Tabini was back in power, Murini was dead, and there was peace on the continent.

Mospheira likewise prospered. Trade resumed, and their shuttle program now regularly sent a vehicle into orbit. Atevi shuttles were in regular service. Vital supplies reached the station, so one had assumed there was progress on the situation aloft. *Geigi* had said nothing negative about Tillington, except the complaint that the man always sided with the senior captain, and that humans had dithered along with a decision about the refugees. But then—well-bred atevi were not inclined to complain until they were ready to call on the Assassins' Guild. So to speak.

Evidently—it was *not* all under control up there.

"So what's going on up there?" he asked Jase. "What's Tillington doing—or not doing? I understand his workers aren't happy. I know *somebody's* got to make his mind up and find a solution for the refugees, and *they've* been divided as to what. But is it worse than we know?"

Jase took a deep breath. "As of five days ago, it turned decidedly worse. I talked to Sabin last night, and I have clearance to say this. From her. Not from Ogun."

Secrets and division between the two senior captains. That didn't sound good.

"Here's the problem," Jase said. "Tillington's been agitating to get the Reunioners to go to a new construction at Maudit. You know that. But when the news got out three Reunioner kids were coming down here, the rhetoric got significantly nastier. And apparently when we called asking the kids' time down here be extended, Tillington stepped over the edge. He's now claiming that Sabin and Braddock made a deal so Braddock would agree to evacuate Reunion Station."

"We had to haul him out by force. That's ridiculous."

"The alleged deal puts five thousand refugees, some of them with knowledge of critical systems, behind Sabin taking over the human side of the station, putting station operation entirely in Reunioner hands, and Sabin taking over as senior captain."

An ugly scenario unfolded instantly. If one wanted to view Sabin in Mospheiran terms, with the knee-jerk Mospheiran assumption of self-interest and territorial interests over all, Sabin had been, for the last two years, in a position to dictate life and death for the Reunioners, and five thousand refugees constituted a large potential subversive force, on that scale.

The fact was—if Sabin had wanted, last year, to take *Phoenix* and all five thousand Reunioners and go establish another station somewhere, she could have done it with no hardship to herself and no permission from anyone. If she were aboard *Phoenix,* as she had been, nobody could have stopped her, and the world might never have seen the ship again.

But Sabin had done as she had proposed to do. She'd lifted off all survivors from the station, even Braddock—she'd destroyed the problematic human Archive and brought the refugees—numbering vastly more than anyone thought—safely to Alpha Station.

True, she'd put them off the ship and onto the station as beyond the ship's ability to sustain any longer. That would have upset Tillington, but the ship would *not* attach itself as a permanent hotel for residency. None of the captains would agree to that.

That had suddenly made the refugees a Mospheiran problem—Tillington's problem and Captain Ogun's problem.

No, Sabin hadn't made herself highly popular with Mospheiran stationers, and hadn't been high on Ogun's list of favorite people before she'd taken the ship to Reunion. Ramirez, who had been senior captain, was dead. Ogun had been second-senior, Sabin third, when an alien species had come down on Reunion ten years and more ago. And there remained, behind Sabin's voyage back to Reunion, deep questions about command decisions and why the possibility of survivors had been hushed up. Captain Ramirez' deathbed confession about Reunion had left nothing safe or sure between Ogun and Sabin.

But the fact was, despite the personal differences that had arisen between Ogun and Sabin, Ogun had stood by while Sabin took the most precious thing ship-folk had, *Phoenix* itself, and headed out where (one now suspected) Ogun damned well understood there was an extreme danger.

Had Ogun ever fully briefed Sabin about what had really happened out there?

Two hundred years ago, human beings had planted their space station in territory an alien species claimed—had evidently passed unnoticed—until *Phoenix* had poked deeper into that species' territory and triggered alarms.

That species, the kyo, had blown Reunion Station half to ruin—then vanished, only to pop out of the dark again when Sabin arrived.

Monstrous expediency might at that point have said to hell with human survivors *and* the Archive: save our own skins—but Sabin hadn't done that. Sabin had calmly stood her ground with the kyo and gotten all the survivors off.

Sabin *might* have promised the Reunioners any sort of thing while they were in transit, just to keep peace aboard.

But Sabin hadn't done that, either. Bren had been there. Jase had been there, second in command. So Bren knew with certainty that Sabin had never made a deal, never made promises of power—never given the refugees anything but adequate food and a way to survive.

"All right," he said to Jase. "Lay it out for me. Who stands where in this mess? Who's on whose side and why?"

"One." Jase held up his first finger. "Sabin and I. We backed these three kids coming down here. Ogun didn't want that. It wasn't going to happen. You saw what happened to me when I landed—sick as hell for weeks when I came down. All sorts of theories as to why, with me as the living proof of why spacers don't adapt. The medics had their notions. But taking Reunioner children down there and having them sick was not a popular idea, politically speaking. Then Tabini-aiji insisted on it. Sabin and I—and the senior medic—won the argument once atevi politics weighed in." Jase held up a second finger. *"Two.* From the moment the Reunioners walked onto the station deck, Tillington has wanted to send the Reunioners off to mine Maudit and build a separate station where he never has to see them again."

Third finger. "*Some* Reunioners, notably Braddock, actually want to go do that. You can guess why."

No question there. Braddock, accustomed for years to being absolute authority on Reunion, had new ambitions.

Fourth finger. "*Sabin* wants them landed on the planet where they'll be swallowed up forever in a sea of Mospheirans." Thumb. "The *majority* of Reunioners want to build new space onto this station and integrate with the Mospheirans, who don't want them to be there."

"*Six,*" Bren said, holding up his own thumb. "*Mospheira* has an opinion in this affair. Mind, I haven't consulted on this one—I'm a long way from representing Mospheira at all, these days—but Mospheira won't want a rival government setting up out at Maudit any more than they'll want Mospheiran-born workers outnumbered and outvoted by Reunioners on the station. They won't want Reunioners settling in atevi territory, which atevi would never permit, anyway. But they also know, like it or not, that five thousand Reunioners aren't going to go away."

"Whatever happens," Jase said, "however we resolve the question, disposition of the Reunioners can't wait another year. It *can't.* The station had to surrender three entire sections to their residency, piecemeal, and jury-rigged. We have people living in what used to be workshops, partitioned-up, but extremely bare bones. Singles are still in barracks—that's a minor problem. But no jobs. No cooking facilities: you get food at kitchens, just like on the voyage. There's a flourishing black market, and theft we haven't had to cope with on the Mospheiran side. Fights break out, and Braddock's people swagger about attempting to say they run things, even holding trials. It's not tolerable long-term. And Tillington's just gone over the edge, accusing Sabin of conspiracy, stirring things up on the Mospheiran side. So this is a quiet request, just an advisement. Can you do something about Tillington—move him out, move him up or down, no preference, but get him somewhere he can't cause more trouble? And is there *any* way to look at getting the Mospheiran legislature to bring the Reunioners downworld?"

Bren drew a deep breath. It was a sane proposal. With the new med, the fact there'd been *no* such sickness as Jase had experienced before, either in Jase or the children—yes. It became possible. That didn't mean it was going to be an easy proposal to advance in the Mospheiran legislature. But yes, if the ship had come up with something to enable an easier transition to the planet—if it had found a way to prove the Reunioners could live and thrive down here—

"I'm doing all right down here," Jase said. "I'm adjusting. Those Reunioner kids have no problems. *Nothing.* They've skipped pills. Two have been off them more I suspect than they admit. They're not sick, so they forget. So Reunioners *can* adjust to being down here. We supply the population with meds for a few months . . . and their way of looking at the world will adjust. Maybe a few will have to go back, for medical reasons that haven't turned up yet. But right now—if the Mospheiran legislature hasn't been getting the word from their constituents up there—we're still fragile. Damned fragile. We've got water, we've got basic protein and carbohydrate, but there are shortages of things we need. Diet's not what it was. And I waited to bring this up now because I didn't want to be debating it while we were trying to deal with the kids and everything else that was going on. Then the Sabin and Tillington matter blew up, making it impossible to put the problem off any longer. I'm sorry to tie the two together. But they tie themselves together, unfortunately. Tillington doesn't want the Reunioners, and he apparently doesn't want any Reunioner kids on the planet."

"Landing does become possible." They'd been consistently hearing only two solutions for the refugees . . . Maudit, or a station expansion. There were serious objections to both. Now . . . "Where do the captains stand? You want me to propose this as a program?"

"It's Sabin's position. And mine."

"Not Ogun's?"

"Ogun wouldn't be unhappy to be rid of the problem."

"The logistics are impossible. Five thousand people, going down by shuttle, between cargo runs."

"Easier down than up."

"It still takes the passenger modules."

"There's light freight you could pack into that config on the return."

"That's still a lot of shuttle loads, while you're having shortages."

"The more people we shed, the less pressure on the system. Mospheira's program's looking to launch a second shuttle next year. And we can build a second shuttle dock, granted Geigi will give us the resources. That doubles our ability to handle freight."

"We can't double the shuttle schedule—they take the time they take."

"We could build more shuttles. In space. So no unneeded ground time."

Resources and construction gear tagged for the starship under construction had already been diverted to Geigi's robot landers and the satellite system. Resources *would* have to be diverted to a Maudit expedition or a station expansion: that the Reunioner problem was going to absorb resources was a given. And a second dock was safer, did conceivably speed turnover . . . increased options. There were ground holds because of a problem in orbit.

"Have you mentioned the idea to Geigi?"

"Not yet. But he's already contributed supplies, just in housing the refugees. He did say—which I certainly relayed to the Council—that the aiji will not permit the station to increase permanent human occupancy space without a corresponding increase in atevi population; and that if there *is* a decision to build a station out at Maudit, the same principle will apply."

"That would be correct."

"Tillington's also said he'd demand a Mospheiran presence at Maudit, whether or not he's gotten an official position on that, which also slows down any movement of the Reunioners elsewhere, because if we don't have shuttle space to spare, we definitely don't have transport for three different construction crews going to Maudit, let alone materials and habitat. I tell you, Bren, the damned thing just accretes parts and pieces, and most of them add to the problems rather than solving them. Everybody wants to control it. Nobody wants to actually do it. Whatever *it* is. And we can't go putting it off. This last year's been difficult. We're entering a second year with these people in temporary housing, on a diet that's bland beyond description and supplemented with pills. We've got to do something. And the anti-nausea med *works*. And human senses adjust. It's our best option, Bren. It's entirely possible."

"It does change the picture. I agree. The logistics remain a problem."

"The *politics* are a problem. And they're becoming a worse one. It's not anything analogous to the old situation, but both sides, at least at the administrative level, are treating it as if the old feud is alive and well."

Mospheirans had fled to the planet in the first place because they'd fallen out with the ship and station administration. And Reunioners were the descendants of the old admin and the loyalists who had taken off and deserted the Mospheirans, only to return in *this* century, tail between their legs, having stirred up a worse mess than the War of the Landing.

Reunioners, in the person of Louis Baynes Braddock, wanted to dictate the future of humanity in space?

Packing the lot down to Earth became an increasingly attractive solution. Possibly it was going to be more attractive to the *majority* of the Reunioners.

"They've never experienced a planet. It won't be the same for them."

"The kids had no trouble," Jase said. "And these people aren't their ancestors. Reunion was gravity-anchored to a lump of rock and ice, not really a planet: there was no attraction there. But there *is* a natural attraction to this planet. The past isn't the present. Once you tell the Reunioners that the planet is a possibility for them—minds will change. And those kids just *proved* they can live down here. That's the point."

"It's a better alternative than we *have* had."

"Economically and logistically."

"And politically. Mospheirans can make controversy out of siting a shuttle port they *do* want. Room for five thousand people they envision as the ancestors—"

"Versus an expansion of the station that's going to upset the Treaty. Or a separate state with a history of hostility."

"The Reunioners won't all favor it," Bren said.

"Braddock chief among that number. He wants his own station, out there, out of reach, with his hand-picked officers running things again."

"He can still cause trouble. God knows, Mospheirans are always ready for issues."

"Up there—there's no shortage of *issues.* Being short of food and living space is productive of *issues.*"

"Mospheirans down here don't know Braddock's name," Bren conceded. "Most don't have a clue about the Pilots' Guild. Nor, for that matter, do we actually care."

A slight grim laugh. "The fact Louis Baynes Braddock still thinks he should order the Captains' Council doesn't impress them?"

"Not in the least."

"Maybe we can bring Tillington on board, get him behind the notion of landing *all* the Reunioners, setting things back the way they were. . . ."

"I sincerely doubt it. For other reasons. Bren, the man poses a problem apart from the Reunioner issue."

"He was a good administrator through the Troubles. He and Geigi worked out a system to communicate without us . . ."

"Which has become a problem. He doesn't want *me* involved and he certainly doesn't want Sabin. He's all snug with Ogun. And so far as his great achievement—that neat little system that doesn't require humans to communicate with atevi in anything *but* code, it's just a longer list of the code the shuttle program worked out, and Tillington's so devoted to it he doesn't call on *me* at all, or ask me to interpret the soft tissue of the answer. Geigi will ask me in depth. I have a good relationship with Lord Geigi. But with Tillington—no. With him, yes is yes, that's the end, and he'll read it according to what *he* thinks yes means. And if it later doesn't turn out to be the precise yes he wanted, then he says Geigi broke his promise. Communication staff to staff is cordial, accurate, and makes things run. Communication between the two stationmasters is another matter."

It was a complete right turn from the information he'd gotten from Geigi, even in prolonged exchanges. But—dealing with atevi—sometimes silence was another kind of information. Atevi completely avoided problematic humans, rather than collapse a useful situation. Humans didn't always figure that out.

They'd gone to war, humans and atevi, as an outgrowth of such a situation.

"I'm listening," he said.

"He doesn't like Reunioners," Jase said. "And yes, the shortages and the crowding are a problem, but it wasn't the personal choice of the Reunioners. He complains to his subordinates and crew chiefs, sympathizes with their problems, blames the Reunioners for all of it. He was massively upset about the kids' visit, called it special privilege for the Reunioners, didn't want it to happen, said they were short of supplies and the kids' visit was taking up a shuttle flight—an exaggeration. We used the smallest passenger module and we'll carry cargo both ways. Ogun wasn't in favor of it—he was siding with Tillington's view until the aiji's request came through. But that wasn't the end of it. He said Tabini's government was still unstable, he said the children would be in danger and if anything happened the Reunioners would riot. Well, Sabin fixed that. She proposed I go down as interpreter and run security. So that happened, and we came down. But when we called up to the station to advise the kids were going to stay through another shuttle rotation— Tillington started saying he had information that the kids were a setup, that they'd always been a setup, and that Sabin had arranged their meeting the young gentleman on the ship."

"That's ridiculous."

"It gets better. According to Tillington, Sabin's plan was to get Reunioner kids linked to the young gentleman, to get in tight with the atevi, to get an agreement with Braddock and the Reunioners, that *she* was going to be their ally. That it was all cooked up on the voyage back."

Bren's pulse ticked up a notch. Two notches. "He actually said that."

"That's as Sabin reported the statement to me, which she had from Ogun—who usually doesn't restructure information. Ogun asked her what the truth was. She naturally said hell, no, it was entirely atevi business what the young gentleman did. She didn't *stop* it, because atevi security was watching over the situation. She said she'd as soon space Braddock, given a choice; she'd done everything she'd promised Ogun she'd do, and she'd handled a refugee situation they hadn't planned for. *And* she'd brought the ship back, what more proof than that could he want?"

"Saying the aiji-dowager might have an ulterior motive is like saying the sea has tides. But involving her as your captain's ally in a special deal, as putting emotional pressure on the aiji's son, in her care—at his age—and to take—" Neither ship-speak nor Mosphei' had a word for it. He changed to Ragi. "—to institute a new aijinate aboard that ship, far from the aishidi'tat, to involve herself and the aiji's son in foreign politics and foreign ambition— No." He dropped back into ship-speak, for another logic. "First, you and I know it didn't in fact happen. The aiji-dowager deals from her own hand. No one else's. And certainly she wouldn't use her great-grandson as anybody's ally in some human power game. No. First, it's false. She allowed the association with the Reunioner children for her great-grandson's sake—a boy who'd scarcely *seen* another child—of any sort. And secondly, if word of this accusation reached her, she might well File Intent on Tillington. Mind, she *does* have Guild personnel on the station. He'd better not repeat this theory, anywhere outside Ogun's office."

"We have no way to stop him. It's not mutiny. It's opinion, and, all said, he's *your* official. In the *Mospheiran* sense."

"No question he's Mospheiran," Bren said. "But he's not on Mospheira."

"He's opened a wide gulf with Sabin. I don't know how he can retreat from this."

"I don't know how he can retreat from it either, given the situation. I'm serious about the dowager's position. She will be serious, if she takes notice of it. If Geigi hears it, Geigi won't work with him."

"Geigi already won't work with him. I *know* Geigi can speak a little Mosphei'. It doesn't happen."

True. Basically true, during all their absence from the solar system and all the troubles, with all the building, Geigi had been communicating using the supply system codes they'd developed for that interface in the space program, in shuttle guidance, in all the places where numbers and codes could carry a meaning.

"So he's become a liability. A serious liability, driving a program that's going to divert materials for years. And the Reunioners remain a problem driving every decision we make. If we propose moving the Reunioners down, that process is going to take time, and new construction, with politics all the way. If we remove Tillington now, he'll have an opinion. If it's political power he's courting, I can foresee which party will back him. Damn. Is *nothing* ever simple?"

"We've got Tillington on one side, Braddock on the other, up there, and theoretically we're not in charge of Braddock, Tillington is. Tell the President this: when you chose the crews to come up to the station, you *screened* people you sent. They're all certified *sane.* The Reunioners were all born on Reunion. They've been through hell in the last ten years. And we took all the survivors. There was nothing like screening. There still hasn't been. We've got theft we never had to deal with. We have a shadow market we never had to deal with. You wouldn't believe what you can turn into alcohol. We've likely got some seriously confused head cases in that population. And we've got Braddock, who thinks the Pilots' Guild is in charge of the universe. We're one psych problem short of a security nightmare. And *we're* fragile. *Phoenix* is. Tillington's politicking between Sabin and Ogun is bringing live *our* old issues. My people *still* haven't answered all the questions about *why* Ramirez pulled us away from Reunion and stranded those people out there in the first place. It's *not* a dead issue with the crew *or* with the Reunioners. It may never be. Damned sure nobody in the crew is on the side of the old Pilots' Guild, and Braddock's claims to speak for that ancient organization get no handhold with us. But now Tillington's shooting sparks into a volatile atmosphere. I don't think he understands how what he's saying translates to us *or* to atevi. But he's the wrong man in the wrong place right now."

He'd been busy since he'd gotten back. He'd been fighting for Tabini's return, fighting to keep Tabini in office, fighting to defuse issues that had nearly taken the aishidi'tat apart. Tillington had been a name to him, and he'd trusted Geigi to tell him if there were things that needed attention. Of course there were disputes. There were issues. Those had seemed distant, someone else's problem.

Then three kids wanted to come down to the planet for a birthday party, and three political systems exploded?

"Understand," he said, "I have *no* standing with the Mospheiran government any longer. I haven't been back there since before we left the planet."

"The President *is* still an old friend of yours."

"He is. And I can still talk to him, on that basis—and as what I am on the *atevi* side of the strait. I *will* try to talk to him. But, damn, Jase. I wasn't paying attention up there. I let this one get past me."

"You've been just a bit busy. Sabin knows that. It's why we've said nothing until now. So Tillington doesn't like Reunioners. His wanting to ship the Reunioners out to Maudit was understandable. Everything was understandable—down to the point where he decided he still wanted Ogun's ear all to himself, everything the way it had been—and Sabin and me out of his way. That's my theory. He doesn't want Sabin back any more than he wants the Reunioners. In his head, it's all one event that's messed up his little world."

"Damn, Jase." He looked into the half-empty glass, as if it held an answer. Jase said he wasn't as good at persuasion. But this was beyond persuasion. Massive changes had to be set in motion. "I hope the kids are safe going back up there."

"They'll be safe. I have no question of that. All the official craziness has been behind official doors. And best we keep it that way."

"I hope so. I'll get on this. I may need to fly over to the island, see if I can get a quiet meeting. Limit the number of outlets for this information, if you can. Last thing I want is Tillington's theory of what happened debated in the legislature. One thing I *will* send up with you. Tabini-aiji wants those kids officially protected, by ship command. Wants them kept out of station politics. In any sense. He demands their free access to the planet, protection from political exploitation or political mention, and if that is threatened, he wants them on the atevi side of the wall up there. I have the wording. It's that treaty clause—persons under protection of the aishidi'tat to be treated as citizens *of* the aishidi'tat."

Jase drew in a breath. "I don't think it was ever envisioned as three kids from Reunion."

"The wording stands. As associates of the young gentleman, they have standing with the aiji. You don't need to publicize the document. It's just there if the Captains should need it. And it will be *here* if Tabini decides he needs to invoke it."

Jase nodded. "Got it."

"My personal seal as the aiji's voice is no problem. I'll have the document for you tomorrow, in case there's any problem. I'll get the aiji's official seal on a more specific document to follow, shipped up to Geigi's office by the next shuttle after yours. Keep them under lock and key, so to speak. But know they're there."

Jase stared into his own barely touched glass for a moment. Then:

"Come up there, Bren."

"I'm up to my ears. Negotiations are at a make-or-break point . . . things we've been working on all year, that *have* to work. Things that can make the peace last."

"Your help—would be invaluable."

"I'm out of touch. I haven't had time—"

"One shuttle cycle. You could make a difference."

"Is this from Sabin?"

Jase shook his head. "From me. I'm asking you. None of the rest of the potential problems want a compromise. But trying to find a solution, convincing the Senior Captain to take it . . ."

"Down here, I know the issues. Down here, I have a role. Up there—I risk becoming one more issue. I'm *not* a Mospheiran official anymore."

"You've been up there. You were part of it. I'm asking, Bren. Calling in a favor."

Favor.

Gut-deep, he hated the ride up and down.

He needed to call the President—Shawn Tyers was an old friend, an old ally. He could be frank and honest with Shawn, make him understand, tell him the situation . . .

Shawn, who'd come up through the State Department, dealing with atevi—Shawn would understand it was serious. That something urgent had to be done, before atevi had to take notice of Tillington's statements.

But what Jase said . . . what Jase described . . . was not *one* problem. Was not one man. There were problems up there. There were five thousand problems, outnumbering the Mospheirans on their own half of the station.

Five thousand problems and a situation that had gone unaddressed for the last year he'd been trying to pull the threads of the aishidi'tat together, and keep Tabini alive and the shuttles flying and the system functioning . . .

He'd left problems aloft to the four *Phoenix* captains and the two stationmasters—and knew they'd had troubles.

Geigi and he had been in close contact, and Geigi hadn't complained—but Geigi's priorities had been, the same as his, the survival of the aishidi'tat. Up on the station, Geigi held most of the robotics, and the construction stockpiles, controlled all but one of the shuttles that supplied the station, and kept order, presumably, on *his* side of the station.

On the Mospheiran side, however, there had been a year of stress, a year of overcrowding and some shortages and a stationmaster who wasn't bearing up under the load—a year when there'd been planning to ship the Reunioners out to another construction, as yet only blueprints, even for the transport to get them there.

Nobody had committed money to the plan. Nobody had laid supplies on the table. A full year, now, and nothing had advanced except more blueprints, and Reunioners themselves were divided, some wanting to stay, some wanting to go. Braddock had inserted himself into the argument and pushed to go start the building, with himself in charge.

That had stalled things. Nobody outside the Reunioners wanted Braddock in charge. Most of the Reunioners didn't want Braddock in charge, but there weren't any others stepping forward.

Go up there?

Talk to people?

Get Tillington *and* Braddock out of the picture?

He was tired. He was exhausted. He had the tag ends of the year's work lying on his foyer table back in the Bujavid, things that *enabled* the solution to the aishidi'tat's problems. He'd taken a couple of weeks off to handle four kids and a birthday party.

"All right," he said to Jase. "All right. I'll come. I'll get started on the Tillington matter as soon as I get to Shejidan. And when I do get up there, I'm not coming in on Sabin's side, understand. I'm far more help that way."

"Understood. I know how you work."

"But I'll get there. Soon as I can get the decks cleared down here. A few weeks."

"You take care of yourself doing it. No more taking on the Guild bare-handed. None of that sort of thing."

"No more," Bren agreed fervently. Stitches notwithstanding, the back of his head still gave a phantom ache when he thought about it, and his valets feared he would have a lasting scar. "I'm confining my near-term activities to the legislature. Paper cuts will be my only hazard. And committee meetings. Not my favorite thing, but they'll be the limit of my travels for the next few weeks."

"Definite, however, that you're coming?"

"I'll be there. Don't break the news yet. But tell Sabin I'll get Tillington out of there, one way or the other. And in that matter—do me a personal favor, will you?"

"Sure."

"Pay a visit to Lord Geigi for me, would you, among first priorities? Tell him I didn't have time to get over to his estate, this trip, but I do have his staff reports. I could computerize them. Or you could hand-deliver them. And polish the contact. Just in case other routes get political."

"No problem with that. I happen to like Geigi—I know, I

know, not a word to use. But I *like* the man. He's good company. I like his cook, too."

"You've gotten a taste for the food, have you?"

"Kaplan and Polano even like the eggs. We don't get enough *flavors* in our diet. Nicely balanced, all the right vitamins. But, *God,* send us up some pepper sauce."

Bren laughed. "I can manage that tonight. Personal stock. If we expand the shuttle fleet—we can consider exporting some. Tell Geigi, too, that the Edi manor now has walls. They're racing to finish the roof before the autumn rains. Same here at Najida." The servant, long statue-still, offered another round of spice cakes. "Thank you, nadi-ji," Bren said, declining. "One has had sufficient of the teacakes."

"Indeed," Jase said in Ragi, likewise declining. "One more glass, however." And in ship-speak. "I'm not constrained to be responsible tonight. My head's stuffed with agendas I don't want to sleep with."

"The same," Bren asked the servant, to match his guest. "Thank you, nadi-ji."

The servant poured, one and the other.

Jase gazed at him, and lifted the refilled glass. "To fixing this."

3

The bus was coming. Standing in the foyer, with staff and baggage all about them, Cajeiri could hear the tires rumbling down the gravel road, and all too soon he could hear the bus turning onto the cobbles of the portico.

There was no way to stop it and no way to gain another hour at Najida. Nand' Bren and Jase-aiji and their bodyguards were saying their good-byes to the major domo, Ramaso; and the house staff who had come to see the guests off had now started to move their baggage out into the dark, at the edge of the cobbled drive. That included, with both the big house doors now open, Boji's rolling cage. That cage, ancient brass bars and filigree, made an enormous racket on the stone, which set Boji to jumping about and screaming. A truck would be coming behind the bus to take the big items, like the wardrobe crates, and Boji. And his valets were going to ride the truck and the baggage car both to keep Boji calm.

Cajeiri had no personal luggage to carry. House staff did that, and would not let his bodyguard or his guests carry luggage, either. The bus, the very same red and black bus that had served them up north in Tirnamardi, at Great-uncle's estate, entered the drive and pulled up under the lights—a beautiful huge bus, red and black, his father's clan colors, though it belonged to nand' Bren; and they had patched the bullet holes before they had shipped it to Najida.

He was usually very glad to see it.

But not this morning. He wished he and his guests could run

away to the hills, or out to the forest, or most anywhere they could gain another day down here. But that was not the way things were going to be. The baggage truck pulled up under the portico light, right behind the huge bus, and the servants rolled Boji's cage out to it as the lift-gate lowered with a racket of its own. One attempted conversation with one's guests. One tried to keep conversation light and happy.

Meanwhile servants loaded Boji and his cage onto the lift-gate and got him aboard. Their big clothing crates trundled out on their carts. Behind those, nearer the door, smaller bags piled up. Most of that size belonged to their guests, and staff would stow those in the luggage compartment under the bus.

Their belongings went aboard far too fast.

Then it was their turn.

"Thank you very much, nadi," Cajeiri said, correctly bowing a good-bye to Ramaso as they filed toward the bus. "Thank you for taking care of my guests."

Gene and Irene and Artur likewise made little bows, and thanked Ramaso, as they should.

Then while nand' Bren and Jase-aiji waited, they boarded the bus, Irene and Artur being helped a little up the tall steps.

He and his guests and his own bodyguard had the whole back of the bus to themselves, and nand' Bren's two valets followed them back a moment later, immediately asking whether they wanted cold drinks or hot tea this morning.

Nand' Bren had said there was going to be breakfast on the train. Cajeiri was not sure he could eat breakfast, and he had no desire for hot tea at the moment. They had all stayed up late, since no one had come to ask them to go to bed, and it had been their last night together. So late into the night they had laid all their plans and made all their arrangements to get together again. And his stomach was upset now.

He wished that Gene, hindmost in boarding the bus, and who had the most initiative of all his friends, had just bolted for the open land, dashed off across the fields and lost himself in the woods for a few days. In his wildest imagination he told himself if Gene just decided he was not going, then they might all miss the shuttle and have to stay and find him.

Or if Artur and Irene absolutely had to go back to their parents and only Gene ran and missed the shuttle, the staff would just have to send Gene to Shejidan once he turned up. And maybe Gene's mother would just say it was all right and Gene could just stay for a while. Gene said his mother never cared what he did, and anything he did was all right.

Gene could survive in the woods until he was found—Gene knew how to dodge searches.

But even before they had landed on the planet, Artur had said, Jase-aiji had warned them all that he and his bodyguards had the means to track them, and that if they broke one little rule or got into trouble—he would have to report it officially.

So if Gene ran now—they might never get permission to come down again.

It was a little mean, to tell them they could not make a move without the ship tracking them.

But he understood. His own situation had begun to be exactly like that. He knew his aishid would have to find him. He knew their lives could be at risk if he misbehaved.

So the notion of any one of them running now was just an empty dream. His guests all *had* to go back to the station when they promised, to prove they could, and would.

And once they got home, they had to tell the right story to everyone who asked, assuring them that everything on Earth was perfectly safe, and never admitting there had been a danger of any sort.

So they all settled, obedient and quiet on the bus; and Cajeiri's bodyguard sat in the seats across the aisle.

They waited, with no choice now, no wild escape possible. They had been lucky once: they had had one extension of their visit, which was probably because of technical stuff with the shuttle, though grown-ups could claim it was a favor to them.

He hoped he was going to get his guests back, next year at least, because they *had* done well.

Let them come every year until they were all just about grown—Irene being the oldest. He and his guests would behave so well, and they would not do anything against the rules next year, or the one after that—

But when it was the right year, if Irene could just wait until they all were of age, they could *all* just refuse to go back. And if he supported them in their request to stay, they could win. Three humans would never be welcome living in the Bujavid: there was too much jealousy over those apartments. But they could very easily live here at Najida. Najida had hosted nand' Bren's brother when he was here; and he was sure nand' Bren would agree if he asked.

They might do that—when they were grown.

It seemed a very long time of behaving.

But his guests were a favor that he could always lose, to politics, or to his father's displeasure.

When you get back to the world, Great-grandmother had told him, just last year, *when you are back among atevi, among people who act properly, you will find atevi feelings in yourself, and you will have a much surer compass than you do right now.*

That meant a needle would swing to the world's north, no matter how one tried to turn it somewhere else. That was what mani had meant when she said that.

And sometimes his feelings really were like that: he did feel an attraction. He felt it toward mani, of course, and toward his parents. But he did not think mani had ever expected he would have such a strong swing of that compass toward three humans, who, as mani had explained it, had compasses of their own, which might eventually swing to a very different place.

Mani had said his internal compass would get stronger and surer as he grew.

Well, it had done that.

It had done it, even during this visit of his three guests. He had gotten far more determined about his own future, and he had thought matters through. He had no question at all that his internal compass swung to his father, and to mani, and to nand' Bren and even to Great-uncle Tatiseigi, who had really surprised him; but there was no question either that Gene and Irene and Artur had a very necessary place in that arrangement, and he was not going to lose them.

Humans can change loyalty, nand' Bren had told him once.

"Will *you* change, nandi?" he had asked nand' Bren right back, and nand' Bren had looked a little distressed.

"I could not," nand' Bren had said. "No. I would not."

He thought about that, as the bus began to roll.

If nand' Bren could be so absolutely certain of himself, could not these three?

And if it was a feeling nand' Bren had, could not these three have it?

Gene wanted to come back. Artur worried about his parents, and tried to find what made everybody happy—which was why Artur was so quiet, and thought so much; but at some time in the future Artur had to make *himself* happy, and Artur was going to find that out. He was sure Artur could be happy here, with things to investigate, like rocks, and thunderstorms—

Irene, now—

Irene was the one who was not going into a happy situation, back on the station.

Irene and her mother—like Gene, Irene had no father—did not agree. He certainly understood not agreeing with parental rules, but Irene followed them only because she had to. That was what Irene said.

Gene had gotten arrested by security and gotten a bad mark on station. He did not so much defy the rules as ignore the ones that inconvenienced him. Cajeiri understood that.

Artur would ask permission and then try to reason his way through the rules. Artur was fairly timid-acting, but that was because Artur was thinking how to get past the problem and still not break any rules.

But if Artur ran out of time, Artur would do what he felt he had to.

Irene, however—he feared Irene would just explode someday. That was what he always felt, dealing with her. Irene would reach a point she would just explode. She had changed her hair before she came down, gone from dark as atevi to fair as Bren, and her frown when they asked said they were not to ask about it. She had cut up most of her station clothes with scissors the second morning in Tirnamardi, and thrown the pieces away, very upset with them, saying only that she needed room in her baggage. She had been collecting writing paper, even scraps, and he had given her whole fresh packets of it, so there was a lot of stationery in her personal luggage right now, along with two picture books he had given her, and her prettiest clothes from his birthday festivity. She was going to wear her riding clothes to go to the spaceport. Irene was very, very smart, smarter than any of them, he suspected. She was certainly the best at languages, and she was, of all of them, a little scary, possibly because Irene herself was always a little scared. What she was scared of, Cajeiri was not sure—maybe she was scared of her own questions. She was a little unlike the others. Her skin was brown. Her eyes were dark. Her frown was like a sky clouding over. And she was so scared of flying she got sick and probably would again.

He so wished he could help her.

He'd said that to Gene, last night, about Irene needing the rest of them, about Irene just exploding someday, and Gene had understood him.

"We can't always get to her apartment," Gene said, and tried to explain, saying, "Like the Bujavid. Like the third floor. Not everybody comes there. Security zone, where Irene is."

So Irene's mother had to be somebody more important than Gene's mother and Artur's parents. And if Irene lived in a security zone, then *he* was worried for her. Irene's mother had been against her coming down until the very last moment. And then Irene's mother had changed her mind for no reason they really understood. If Irene herself knew why, she had not told them; but at least she had gotten to come.

There could be a problem, a very big problem with Irene, on the next visit.

If her mother was important, then politics was involved.

And he *knew* what that meant.

It was a fair long road from Najida to the train station, one Bren had traveled more often than most roads—and it was a faster trip these days, thanks to peace in the district. Najida cooperated nowadays in road maintenance with the township to the south, with Geigi's estate, and with the township to the north, so Bren had found himself the unlikely owner of, to date, a fire truck, a yacht, an ambulance, a road grader, a large truck, a dump truck, and a formidable earthmover that could variously hammer a large rock or pick it up in a bin. Combined with other districts, Najida could do substantial jobs for the district, like road repair, employing no few locals in the process.

So he was somewhat proud of the local road. Not so fine as some, but good enough for market traffic, all the way to the township in the south, and again to Geigi's estate.

Najida district was his home, in a sense. It had become that. He cared about the people. He cared *for* them. Whenever he was here, he heard their problems and solved them if he could, whether with application of his personal income or by hearing both sides of an argument and sorting it out as fairly and sensibly as he knew how. He maintained the few roads, he lent transport at need. He paid medical bills. And when he was not here, the Najidi could write to him in the capital, and he would do what he could for the district from the Bujavid—which very often was enough to handle the difficulty. It made him extraordinarily happy, being able to do that.

But now he was traveling back to a different existence, to do a wider job, while Najida disappeared behind them in a cloud of dust. In that other job, there was far less thanks, but it mattered far more to the outside world.

And now Jase wanted him to expand that endeavor.

He and Jase sat and talked while the sun rose and the dawn landscape ripped past the unshielded windows of the bus.

They weren't using the window shades this morning. The youngsters and Jase had so little time left to see the world, and it was an hour void of other traffic. Trucks might come later today, picking up or delivering goods or, rarely, passengers. But now the road was vacant and they had an unobstructed view of grasslands and small groves of trees.

It was a special train they were meeting, at a very early hour, and indeed that old-fashioned train was waiting as the bus climbed the barely perceptible rise. The engine sat steaming a plume into the pink morning light, ready to roll.

The station where it waited was a modest and rustic place. There was a newly painted little office, next to a small plank-sided warehouse, a wooden loading platform and the requisite water and sand towers of more modern vintage. The venerable and elegant steam engine had only two cars at the moment—one a standard baggage car, the other an old-fashioned passenger car with windows that only looked like windows.

In point of fact—it was the elegant Red Train, the aiji's own, with the baggage car that usually attended it. Tabini routinely lent it to the paidhi-aiji on official business—and in this case it was here to convey honored guests to the spaceport and bring the aiji's son back home. It had run from Shejidan, crossed the Southern mountains and the chancy district of the Senjin Marid last night to be here this morning.

It would not be taking the same route home.

The bus rolled slowly to a halt alongside the platform and opened the doors.

Tano and Algini were first out onto the platform, and other armed, black-uniformed Guild appeared from both train cars.

Those would be the aiji's men, who would have ridden out from the capital, and who now would ride back in the baggage car.

Clearly, from the easy manner on both sides, they were people Tano and Algini knew, and Bren himself recognized two who served in the aiji's own apartment.

Algini gave the all-clear. Banichi and Jago got to their feet; Bren and Jase did, and they exited first.

Then the young folk came out, joined them in crossing to the waiting train, a short walk with a living shield of Guild bodies, to a second, assisted climb into the waiting train car.

Inside that car was red velvet from a prior century, fake windows with fake shades that didn't work but looked elegant—two areas of small tables, ordinary seats, then a bench seat at the rear, near the galley. The youngsters took the reverse of their seating on the bus. Bren and Jase and their bodyguards went to the rear where there was a bench seat and galley, while the youngsters and Cajeiri's young bodyguard stayed at the two table and bench arrangements nearest the door.

"Tea?" Bren's senior valet asked as they settled in. The water in the tea service was already hot, no surprise there. The containers with their breakfast arrived aboard from the bus, handed up by the aiji's men, who were out on the platform seeing to the baggage.

There was the sound of another vehicle outside: their baggage truck had arrived, with the young gentleman's baggage, and his. Jase's bulkier baggage, and the youngsters' one large case, had gone to the port last night.

They would take tea while the crates loaded, he and Jase. The youngsters declined.

Boji's screech was audible even with the car door shut. No question he was part of the operation, first loaded, last off.

And toward the end of the first cup, came the thump of the baggage car door slamming shut.

In a moment more, the Red Train began to move, a barely perceptible motion.

Bren's valets, Koharu and Supani, began the breakfast service with a professional flair. Ramaso and Cook had provided absolutely everything they could ask, hot and chill, and spicy and sweet and savory, from the insulated cases. A liquid storage held an abundance of iced fruit juice.

Even the youngsters stayed in a cheerful mood so long as the fruit juice held out.

But as Koharu and Supani cleared the service away, a glum quiet descended on the young company at that end of the car. Heads came close together up there, secrets exchanged.

"They're exhausted," Jase said quietly, over a last cup of tea. "They were up all night. They're running entirely on nerves this morning. Irene's scared of flying. Absolutely terrified."

"Poor kid," Bren said. And added: "They've been running hard for days. And it was a given they wouldn't sleep last night until they fell over."

"If they did sleep at all, it was about an hour toward dawn."

He and Jase shared a second pot of tea. Banichi and the others, in rare relaxation, sat at the other end of the bench, in their own conversation. Jase's bodyguards, Kaplan and Polano, in green fatigues, had the side bench seat, backs to the false windows, talking together as the valets cleaned up and put the dishes away.

Jase, like the youngsters, had opted for atevi dress all the way to the spaceport. Just when they'd change clothes, or whether they'd all change before the launch, Bren hadn't asked.

Maybe the clothing choice was a courtesy to their hosts. Maybe it was a way of not saying good-bye yet.

But Jase, Bren thought, was already mentally going home, already thinking about problems aloft, business that had to be done—and Jase was clearly less happy this morning.

Truthfully, he was going through exactly the same process. He'd have liked to have more days at Najida.

He'd have liked to have time to handle some local matters.

He'd have liked to make a personal visit to Kajiminda, Geigi's estate, just down the main road, to take a leisurely walk through Kajiminda's ancient orchard. He'd have liked to take the bus out to the new construction the Edi were building at the end of that peninsula.

He'd even more have liked to have a week to himself on his yacht, to feel the sea under him. He dreamed of four or five days to pretend to fish, but he absolutely couldn't afford any more time away from the capital.

And he found himself, in the quiet moments this morning, already thinking about the legislature: already thinking about the dowager's agreement with the Marid, and about the next things that had to be done.

He wasn't thinking, quite yet, about the problems on the station.

He was doggedly not thinking about that.

That resolve failed. He urgently had to do something about Tillington. A letter to Mospheira was a start. The President, Shawn Tyers, was indeed an old friend. And he had to make that letter say what needed saying. He *might* have to go to Mospheira, to say what needed saying. He just didn't know.

He'd been up well before dawn composing one document—in two languages.

Now he quietly picked up his briefcase, opened it, and handed them to Jase.

"What I promised," he said. "Take the copies for your own files. I have a translation for the aiji."

"Exactly what I need," Jase said, as he read, and gave a deep sigh. "Excellent. Thank you."

"There'll be a statement with the aiji's own seal, next shuttle."

Jase drew his own traveling case from the floor near his seat. "There was a little lingering question up there, whether Tabini-aiji would stay in office or whether, if he did, his power would ever be what it was. I have no doubts now that it's probably greater than it ever was. And I'll convey that impression to the Council."

"I'll report to the aiji, in turn, that Sabin remains his ally."

"Ogun isn't the aiji's enemy, understand, if I've given any other impression. Ogun's just keeping all the connections polished. And right now, and since Yolande's resigned, he thinks he needs Tillington. So he gives him maneuvering room, and tries to encourage the right maneuver. Does he know the man is flawed? Probably. Ogun's no fool."

"I'll be thinking about Tillington. I'll do something."

"To the great relief of all of us."

"Given what you said last night," Bren said, and let that trail off in very dark thoughts. "God. God. Why can't people get along? We—meaning you and I—right now—we two could sort out the Reunioner business and get everybody half of what they want—if we could get one *hour* of honest compromise out of both sides."

"I'd settle for five minutes. But we have done good things on this trip, the two of us."

"We should arrange an annual Official Fact-finding," Bren said. "Bring the kids."

Jase laughed. "I'll use that argument."

"Next year. The official birthday."

"Another Festivity?"

"Ten is a less felicitous year for the young gentleman, so there'll be no public celebration entailed. A much quieter event. No public access. You've never seen the mountains. We could take that train trip to Malguri. With the window shades up. Snowy mountains. Glaciers."

"The kids would like that," Jase said. "*I* would."

Came a burst of laughter from the front of the car, where the youngsters gathered, laughter far louder than usual, and not involving Cajeiri's bodyguard.

Nervous laughter. Desperate laughter. The kids were trying their best to compress everything good into a last few hours.

It was like that with him and Jase—tense. Keenly aware of imminent parting. They'd had weeks to say everything they could think of. They'd cleaned up the loose ends last night.

But they *would* be seeing each other in the immediate future, in a much more serious context—and he didn't know how he was going to exclude Cajeiri from that trip, on the one hand.

Or get permission from his parents, on the other.

It would be an excuse for Cajeiri to get access to the kids.

But did he want the boy to become a presence in station politics?

The Red Train gave a little jolt as they shunted onto the northern route, bound for the spaceport.

4

It would have been a lot smoother, at the spaceport train station, just to say their good-byes at the door of the Red Car, let their guests cross the rustic wooden platform to the waiting bus, and let the train continue on to Shejidan with no more delay.

But that just wasn't going to be satisfactory for the kids, and Bren didn't even suggest it. The Red Train could safely sit where it was for an hour: the spaceport spur, off the main north-south line, didn't have anything incoming or outgoing for at least two hours.

So they all—excepting Tano and Algini, who stayed with the train for security—walked out onto the platform, where uniformed spaceport personnel were offloading the few pieces of carry-on baggage from the baggage car—Boji's shrieks of protest about that process were loud and frequent.

The spaceport bus was waiting alongside the baggage truck—but this time the kids delayed crossing the platform, gazing at the horizons all about them, sweeping from the high metal fence of the spaceport, to the rolling hills and grasslands that surrounded the train station in the other directions.

Trees. Grass. Everything had been a miracle to them. Artur was taking home his little collection of pebbles, little brown and gray rocks from every place he'd visited. A spaceborn child from a metal and plastics world, he'd never handled bare rock before.

Never seen a sky cloud up and rain.

None of them had.

The kids needed to move on and board the bus now. And Cajeiri wasn't urging them and he wasn't watching the scenery, either. He was watching them, utterly ignoring Boji's muffled shrieks from the baggage car. Bren gave them all a minute more, in the relative security of the place.

"Got to move, kids," Jase said then. "Sorry. Have to go."

They did move, not without looks back. They dutifully boarded the bus and went all the way to the seats in the back—where they immediately took peeks under the drawn window shades.

Bren, standing in the aisle, said to Jago, "Tell them they may raise the shades, Jago-ji."

It was more of a risk here, but it was still a very small risk, now, counting an area with security all about. And if raising the shades made the youngsters feel less confined and compelled in their leaving—he judged it worth it.

So they all settled, leaving their hand luggage to the spaceport crew, all of it set aboard the bus, down in baggage.

The bus door sealed. As the bus startled to roll, the youngsters scrambled to raise the window shades on both sides of the bus, seeking a panoramic view. The driver turned the bus about on the broad graveled parking area, then took the gravel road along the security fence at a brisk clip.

Bren tried to think of any last moment thing he needed to say to Jase, something he might have forgotten.

Likely Jase was thinking just as desperately, going down a mental checklist. They'd reached their agreements. They'd planned their course. Matters belonging to the world were rapidly leaving Jase's interest.

Matters on the space station, Bren thought, were invading Jase's agenda hand over fist.

Jase's security team, Kaplan and Polano, were talking idly behind them, saying they'd be glad to get back to friends in the crew, and wondering if there would ever be an atevi restaurant on the human side of the station.

The kids—there was noise back there. There was nervous laughter. There were periods of heavy silence.

Leave the boy behind, when he made his own promised trip up to the station?

That wasn't going to be easy.

But there was the matter of domestic peace, too—and the boy had new ties to Earth. A new baby had arrived in the aiji's household, and Cajeiri needed to bond with his new sister, and needed to firm up the bonds with his parents.

That bond mattered, to the atevi psyche. It mattered desperately. And they'd disrupted that, in the boy's life. Two years of separation at a young and vulnerable age. And Cajeiri was just getting over it, *finding* his parents again, with his emotions all fragile with being parted from his associations on the ship and being forced to find what he had lost on the planet.

No. Not a good idea, a trip up to the station right now, with hard politics potentially at issue up there.

But how on earth did one tell the boy no?

The final turn. They pulled up at the guarded gate, and port security let them right on through, the armored doors yawning open on another, more modern world.

In the front windows now, the shuttle—it happened to be *Shai-shan*—rested sleek and white, looking like a visitor from the world's future in a gathering of mundane trucks and tankers of this present age, the whole area blinking with red warning lights and blue perimeter flashers.

Closer sat the administrative and storage buildings. The freight warehouse and preparation area loomed on the right, and, low and inconspicuous in the heart of the complex, sat the passenger terminal—a modest two-story building, of which shuttle passengers generally saw no more than the sparsely furnished lounge.

But they didn't go to the terminal. The bus drove past the blue flashers, straight for the edge of the runway, and there the bus stopped.

They would board directly: Jase's prerogative. That was the word from the port. A starship captain could waive customs for himself and his companions, where it came to personal items. And Jase had done it.

There was no more time. Cajeiri got up, and his bodyguard did, and his guests did. He looked at them all—he looked hard, trying to remember every detail of their faces, their relative height—that was going to change. By their next visit, and forever after, he would very likely be the tallest of them, and the tallest by quite a lot, once they were all grown.

The bus doors opened, and it was time.

They had to behave now. They had to follow all the regulations. Most of all things in the world, they had to keep nand' Bren and Jase-aiji firmly on their side.

Cajeiri had only one immediately chancy intention, however: to go just as far as he could with his guests, and not to have to say good-bye at the bus door. He led the way up the aisle, up to the door, as Jase-aiji's bodyguards were going out, and as Jase-aiji was taking his own leave of nand' Bren. If he got onto the steps, he had to go down them to let his guests out, and his bodyguard had to go out, and he would *be* outside with them.

But Jase-aiji *and* nand' Bren went on out ahead of him. So he was able to go outside with his guests, just behind Kaplan and Polano, and stand with them under the open sky. They were so close to the runway they could hear the address system from trucks attending the shuttle, voices talking about numbers, and technical things.

Jase-aiji had lingered to talk with nand' Bren and their security. But nand' Bren was going no farther, so this, now, was where they had to say good-bye, having gotten at least this far together.

His guests understood, too. Irene's eyes started watering, and she kept trying to stop the flood, and trying to make her face calm.

"One regrets," Irene said in good Ragi, wiping at her face. "One tried not to do this, Jeri-ji. It's *stupid*."

"You have to go," Cajeiri said, "but remember what we said last night. We are associates. Forever. And I *will* get you back, so long as you want to come back. If everything goes well—I shall get you back for my next birthday. Maybe sooner."

"We stay connected," Gene said.

"I have my notebook," Irene said. She sniffed and her voice shook.

"Just be careful what you say to everybody," Cajeiri said. That was his greatest worry. "Tell only the good things. Be careful. And remember you should not have to pay anything to send letters or to call me on the phone. Do not let anybody say you have to pay. Nand' Geigi will send the letters for you if you cannot reach nand' Jase. Just get the letters to him if you have any trouble. And go to him first if anything goes wrong."

"We shall write," Gene said. "A lot."

"Come along, kids," Jase-aiji said, waiting with his bodyguard. "Sorry. They want us aboard. They're going into an unscheduled hold for us."

A moment of panic came down then. They looked at each other. Irene took a deep breath and managed to steady herself. Artur and Gene gave a little bow, very proper.

Then they walked away, all three.

The youngsters all three were very polite, very proper in their leaving, bowing as they passed on their way to Jase, and Bren returned the bows very gravely, in silence.

Irene was the last.

"Nandi," she said properly.

"Reni-daja," Bren said. That was Cajeiri's name for her. "Have a very good flight."

"Get me back!" she whispered suddenly in ship-speak, looking up at him. "*Please* get me back, sir!"

Then she spun around and ran the few steps to catch up with Jase and the two boys, wiping tears as she went.

God, Bren thought, a little shaken by that. He stood watching as Jase and the kids walked on their way to the shuttle, along the safety corridor painted on the pavement. Jase had his hand on Gene's shoulder, and the boys had Irene between them, holding her hands.

He turned then to see how Cajeiri was taking the departure, and saw a forlorn figure, as tall as he was, back already turned, boarding the bus with his own bodyguard waiting.

Damn, he thought as he headed back to the bus. He wasn't sure whether Cajeiri had seen or prompted that exchange with Irene, but he was relatively sure Cajeiri's young bodyguard had seen it.

When he boarded, Cajeiri had gone to the rear of the bus with his bodyguard, and they were all talking to him, heads close together.

The adult world that made good-bye necessary just wasn't going to have any welcome advice for the boy right now. And he and Jase had planned as much as they could plan to be sure the kids *would* come back next year.

It was bound to hurt.

It *had* to hurt. But it was part of the boy's growing up.

He settled behind the driver with Banichi and Jago for the trip back, sighed sadly, and leaned back. The driver started the bus, took a broad turn, and headed back the way they had come.

"How is the schedule, nadiin-ji?" he asked them.

"We are well within the window," Banichi said. "One freight is inbound for the port, but we have plenty of time."

They would have no trouble getting off the spaceport spur before then. The shuttle would launch before then.

And it was significant that Cajeiri hadn't asked to stay and see it go.

"One cannot read the young gentleman at the moment," he said to his aishid. "One is concerned for him."

"He is making every effort," Jago said, "to bear this in a dignified way. He has done very well today."

So Jago thought the boy was handling it well enough.

But making the boy happy to go back to the confines of his life in the capital, making him content, there—

That was not going to happen.

They reached the platform, they left the bus in silence and crossed to the train. Tano and Algini waited for them at the steps.

The boy, first inside, with his bodyguard, just settled where he and his guests had sat, in the empty seats, at the now lonely little table. His young aishid stood, uniformly long-faced, in the nook beside him.

"Young aiji," Bren said, pausing by the table, "if you should wish to join me at the rear of the car, you would be welcome. One does not insist, however."

A muscle jumped in Cajeiri's jaw, a little effort at self-control. The boy looked up. "I shall prefer to sit here, nandi. Thank you."

Fragile. And so wishing not to give way right now. Bren gave a little bow and with a movement of his eyes, advised his valets, who were in charge of service on the train, and poised to offer tea or anything else desired, also to let the boy be. The boy's own bodyguard would do anything the boy wanted. Cajeiri just asked to be alone, and one had to respect that, in a boy who had, overall, done very, very well and behaved bravely in recent weeks.

So Bren went back to the bench seat at the rear of the car, with his bodyguard, and with his valets following closely.

"The household might have tea, nadi," he told his valet quietly, including Supani and his partner Koharu in the suggestion—and he settled into his place on the corner of the bench seat, where he habitually sat. His bodyguard settled with him, and the train began to roll.

Quiet again. Devastatingly quiet. No Jase. No kids' laughter.

In another half hour he had the word from Tano that the shuttle had started its takeoff.

Within the hour he had the word that the shuttle had cleared the atmosphere and was in space, safely past the most dangerous part of its return.

"Advise the young gentleman's aishid," Bren said and Tano did that, via Guild communications, just the length of the car.

The young gentleman settled after that, over against the wall, head down, arms folded, apparently asleep.

Despite the adrenaline from the launch and the climb to orbit, the youngsters on the shuttle would soon be ready to fall asleep, too, seatbelts fastened, for the next few hours.

They'd certainly earned it.

They'd all earned it. Jase and his bodyguard, too.

The paidhi-aiji, however, who had been up before dawn composing documents for Jase, had two reports to outline while the details were fresh in his mind, and another set of documents to translate.

The train was headed home, on an eastward route right back around to the Central Station. They would come into the capital, then take the ordinary route along the edge of the city, to the Bujavid train station.

Tatiseigi had returned to the capital some three days ago. Ilisidi was back from business in the East.

And the letters waiting for him in his Bujavid residence were surely overflowing the message bowl by now, business postponed as long as it could be.

Aiji-ma, Bren wrote to Tabini, *the guests have gone home with many expressions of gratitude for their visit. The young gentleman is exhausted, and sleeping as I write. His comportment was exemplary in these last days. I am very glad to have had him as my guest at Najida and he is welcome at any time to return. He is a great favorite of my staff.*

I had opportunity to speak with Jase-aiji at some length.

Last night he conveyed a request that I visit the station in the near future, to become acquainted with the station's current situation and more specifically with the performance of Tillington, the human station-aiji, Lord Geigi's counterpart. Lord Geigi himself has not, in my hearing, complained of Tillington, but I am alarmed at recent statements, which are problematic for our political allies on the station.

The difficulty springs from an ancient disagreement, in which the Reunioners, who were the aijiin of the station in past times, lost the man'chi of the population, and then left the world to pursue settlement elsewhere.

During the two years of the recent Troubles, Mospheirans on the station, in anticipation of a much smaller number of Reunioners returning, worked hard to enlarge the living space and also to repair damages done to the food production factory by a stray piece of rock, this during our mission to Reunion, and during the two years when Murini, of unfortunate memory, had grounded the shuttles.

The arrival of a much larger than expected number of Reunioners has crowded the human section of the station and shortened supply. The station is divided into two territories. And the Reunioners came with families. Mospheiran workers, for whom families are forbidden, have been crowded into less space, and have a very limited ability to return to Earth for family visits. For various reasons, including scarcity of employment, the ancient antipathy of Mospheirans toward Reunioners has resurfaced, creating tensions.

The Mospheiran folk wish to be rid of the Reunioners who have disrupted their lives, and indeed, the population of the station is oversupplied with humans so long as the Reunioners remain. But any plan to have the Reunioners go apart and build another station risks the eventual rise of an opposition group of humans. I most strongly discourage that as a solution, aiji-ma. First of all, there is the treaty requirement of numerical parity, which would require atevi presence in equal num-

bers. It is likely that if the Reunioners stay on the station under current conditions of shortage and overcrowding, there will be conflict. It seems clear that if they cannot stay where they are and we cannot send them elsewhere, the Mospheiran government has it incumbent on them to bring the Reunioners down to Earth. In the general population of Mospheira, five thousand Reunioners will become a minority population and they can be integrated into Mospheiran society.

Unfortunately two human aijiin have risen in opposition to each other, station-aiji Tillington, appointed by the Presidenta of Mospheira; and Braddock, about whom I have previously reported, who has appointed himself aiji of the Reunioners, though currently unrecognized by the Mospheirans.

Tillington's activities in promoting a new station for the Reunioners have produced a division of policy even among the ship-aijiin, with Ogun-aiji favoring Tillington and Sabin opposed to his proposals.

Lately, however, Tillington has made false statements regarding Sabin-aiji, which are destructive of the peace and which cannot be tolerated.

Jase-aiji has asked me first to contact the Presidenta by letter regarding Tillington's behavior and seek his dismissal and replacement. He has also asked me to come up to the station to acquaint myself with the current situation. I shall contact the Presidenta. I hope to see the appointment of a new official who will work toward a settlement of the Reunioners and a relief of pressures on the station. Of course I cannot go aloft without your permission, aiji-ma, but it seems to me that peace in the heavens does well serve your administration, and I hope you will grant me leave to do this, so I may bring back useful information.

I have several urgent Earthly matters before me in the meanwhile, and I shall be working on those with a view to settling all issues in the current legislative session before I undertake anything else.

I look forward to a meeting and discussion at your leisure, aiji-ma. I am happy to report I bring you no other crises whatever, and that our guests are now safely in space again.

To Ilisidi he wrote:

Aiji-ma, the guests are safely in space and by the time this letter reaches you, your great-grandson will be safely home with his parents as well.

I was greatly surprised to see the magnificent windows at Najida, and to see the first one in its permanent place in the main hall. They are extraordinary, and I by no means expected such an extravagant honor. They will be treasured not only by myself, but also treasured by the people of the region.

I remain indebted to you as well for your continued support, and notably to Lord Tatiseigi for his gracious hospitality on his estate.

I shall immediately address myself to the matter of the railroad, and hope for an early conclusion favoring all your plans.

I look forward to giving a more detailed report at your convenience, but I can safely report there is no urgency involved on any matter involving our guests or your grandson, whose deportment was impeccable throughout.

He is now at home with his parents and new sister and I hope will enjoy the memories of an extraordinary visit.

He was, he began to realize, exhausted. And he had just kept silent, in the dowager's letter, about a very dangerous situation, and glossed it over in his report to Tabini. He didn't like the position he was in.

He sat there, staring at nothing at all, and hoped for an early night, his own bed, maybe the chance to sleep in tomorrow.

It wasn't altogether likely, but one could hope.

5

Cajeiri drew a breath, waking. The train was making that strange sound it did, slowly puffing up the incline in the tunnel under the Bujavid, a sound he had heard, oh, many times before in his life, on good occasions and bad.

His bodyguard was near him.

But his guests were not.

He knew it just in the air, before moving. His guests had a kind of perfume about them that was not atevi, and that was gone. They were gone and their belongings were gone, as if they had never been here at all.

He had had so strong an impression in his sleep that everything was all right and they were with him—that he had thought things should be that way when he waked.

And he knew now they were not.

He did not lift his head immediately. He composed himself, carefully settled his expression, decided how he should behave—as if nothing in the world were wrong—and began to do that, waking, and stretching, and saying, conversationally, to his aishid:

"I believe we are about two turns from the platform, nadiin-ji. Are we ready?"

"Yes, nandi," Jegari said, and added: "Nand' Bren says the shuttle is now safely in space."

That was good. He was glad to know it. But the sympathetic look his aishid gave him nearly unraveled him.

They knew how upset and how sad he was. They absolutely knew it.

He gave his head that little jerk his father used when he was giving a silent order to behave, and kept his face expressionless. They knew that gesture, too. He meant to give no acknowledgment of his distress, no outward admission, not even for nand' Bren.

And he desperately hoped nand' Bren would not shake his composure with any expression of regret.

He could not avoid nand' Bren's company, however. He just said, when the train had stopped, and nand' Bren came down the aisle— "I am doing quite well, nandi."

"You are indeed, young aiji," nand' Bren said, giving his greater title, very courteously, and, to his relief, not treating him at all as a child.

"Mind," nand' Bren added, "that your parents will be anxious about your impressions of your guests, and their influence on you. They will be forming their opinions about the effects of their visit. Trust that I shall be giving them a very favorable report, as Jase-aiji will give to his associates."

Practicalities. Politics. That was a relief. That was what he had to think about. Nand' Bren was very sensibly warning him to think clearly.

"And well done, young aiji."

That—jarred him a little.

"Nandi." He gave a little bow. He already knew his parents would be judging him, and listening to those reports—and to some reports less favorable, probably, by busybodies he could not control. Any bad report worried him. But there could not be too many of those. "I shall be very careful," he managed to say. "Thank you, nandi."

He was to leave the train first, these days, being his father's heir.

Being no longer *just* a child.

Tano and Algini went forward and opened the door, and

stepped down to the platform first—senior Guild, as his aishid was not. Cajeiri followed, disembarked under their guard.

And everything was ordinary. The train was at its ordinary spot. Some of his father's household staff were on the platform to meet them and handle baggage, and likewise some of nand' Bren's staff stood by as the baggage car began to open up. He heard Boji give a shriek. It echoed eerily and lost itself in the high darkness of the station.

But his valets, and nand' Bren's, would be taking care of all that detail, so they need not be delayed by that.

Should not be. Dared not be. He had learned that from infancy, that he was not safe standing anywhere in a public place for too long, because *some* people, probably including, at the moment, his mother's own clan, wanted to kill him.

They crossed the platform, he, and nand' Bren and their bodyguards, a much smaller party on their return. They reached the lift in company with nand' Bren, and Tano keyed them in.

The familiar ride up was not an easy few moments. Cajeiri stood and looked at the lights on the panel, and tried to clear the lump in his throat as the car rose up, up, up through all the levels of the Bujavid's sub-basements.

When the car reached the third floor above ground, and the doors opened on their own hallway, he exited the car with his bodyguard, turned and bowed to nand' Bren, and said, with good control: "Nandi, thank you *very* much. One is very grateful."

"One thanks *you*, young aiji. Well done. *Well* done, today."

Oh, if that *today* were not there, he might have held it better. *Today* was not a happy word.

But nand' Bren simply bowed and said not another word, just headed off toward his apartment, regardless of precedent.

Cajeiri was grateful for that. Nand' Bren's was a door that he must pass to reach his own, one apartment farther down the hall. But he could concentrate now on gathering his dignity.

He would not, at least, have to face his father immediately;

he could say hello to the servants, change coats, get to his own suite, *then* report to his father. He could do that.

He stood there a breath or two, then quietly nodded to his aishid, and Jegari and Antaro, each with letters to carry, departed in the opposite direction.

He and Veijico and Lucasi walked on, as nand' Bren reached his own apartment door.

Antaro was carrying a letter he had written to his great-grandmother; and Jegari carried a similar letter to his great-uncle Tatiseigi—both resident just up the broad, ornate hallway, with its plinths, its vases, its antique silk carpets.

His guests had thought it very beautiful. He had never noticed so many things until they had marveled at them.

He did not want to talk to his great-grandmother or his great-uncle yet. He had no wish to talk to his parents, either—but they were a duty he could find no way to escape.

I am well, he had written in those notes to mani and to Great-uncle. *Thank you very much for entertaining us. My guests were very happy and they thank you very much. I thank you for the wonderful things we enjoyed and also thank you very much for my presents. I look forward to the next time I can ride.*

I am going back into my parents' apartment now. I understand that I have new responsibilities to my father and I am very grateful that I have had more time with my guests than I expected.

Thank you very much.

And to both letters he had added another line, in hope that there would be an interruption in his boredom—or a safe place, should his mother and father be having one of their arguments.

Should you wish to invite me to dinner or lunch or breakfast soon, I would be very honored.

Narani was waiting at Bren's door to open it as they arrived—of course Narani was waiting, alerted long since to their arrival at the train station, and having been in contact with Banichi or Jago all the way up.

And, standing now in his own apartment foyer, with household staff crowding the inner hall and the smell of fresh baking and festive pizza in the air, Bren gladly handed off his outdoor coat and the bulletproof vest—Jago had insisted he wear the heavy, hot garment today, just in case.

Now he could wear a comfortable light coat; his bodyguard could shed their own armored duty jackets for more comfortable light leather, likewise offered in staff hands.

Here was safety and very familiar faces. Narani was beaming. So was Narani's assistant and understudy Jeladi, while the staff farther back in the hall was all but standing on tiptoe to get a view and their share in the homecoming. They had a personal stake in recent events, after so many weeks of upset and absence, and their personal efforts in caring for young humans.

"Everything went well with the young visitors, nandi?"

"Very well, Rani-ji. Nand' Jase and the young people are now safely up in space, and it will be an easy journey home for them now. The young gentleman is bound for his own door, at the moment, safe and well. We have finished our mission with honor."

"Excellent," Narani said. "Truly excellent, nandi. There is pizza. There is every delicacy. And chilled wine."

Home. He was definitely home, and safe, with all obligations discharged.

It had been a while since he had been home with no guests, no emergencies, no crisis. The staff had justly declared itself a party in celebration of the event, and there in the doorway, like a barge making its way through crowded waters, came stout Bindanda, the master of the kitchen, his dark arms dusted with flour, clearly fresh from work, very dignified and very happy.

There stood, on the table beside Bindanda, a less welcome sight—the overflowing message bowl, a sight almost obscured by the press of bodies in the hall. Message cylinders not only filled the figured porcelain bowl; a second, less elegant brass bowl held the unprecedented overflow.

Oh, not everything therein could possibly be felicitous—or simple. Simple letters his secretarial staff handled. They sent up the problems, the puzzles, the security threats, and the high-ranking ones. And all those were waiting for him.

It was, however, a homecoming party, Bindanda and Narani could not be denied, and his staff, who had coped with their comings and goings and their emergencies and communications throughout a chain of problems, certainly had earned it. His valets, still laboring with the baggage downstairs; and most of all his bodyguard, who had been more than once under fire and on duty with only scant letup—they certainly deserved it.

The mail could wait.

It was expected and ordinary that the major domo should meet Cajeiri at the door.

It was not expected *or* ordinary that his father and mother did.

That was entirely disconcerting. He was not ready for them. He was not ready to be questioned or required to report. He froze in place, too tired, too confused to know what to say or do first.

Then Great-grandmother's teaching took over. Manners. Manners gained a person time. Manners let one gather one's wits, decide what to do, and above all, calm down.

"Honored Father," he said, bowing once and again. "Honored Mother. Thank you."

"Welcome back, son of ours," his father said. "I trust it was an enjoyable trip."

"It was." He was being examined for signs of distress: he knew he was. "The train was on time. Thank you very much for sending it."

"Was it a pleasant stay at Najida?"

"Very pleasant, honored Father." That was entirely true. "We went out on the boat three times."

"One would think," his mother said, "that your guests would be missing their families by now."

That was a test, too. His *mother* had not been one to miss her family. She had run away from her father, then run away from Great-uncle, then had another feud with her father and run away again, and lately she had had another feud with Great-uncle and Father both—but she had not run away.

She was still difficult and quick-tempered, and she challenged him with that question. What she was really wanting to know right now was whether his guests were traditional, proper people who had proper respect for their parents.

Or whether they were foreigners with, as she was already sure, defective upbringing and no proper respect.

Nobody could win, with his mother.

"We were busy," he said. "We were all busy all the time. We went out on the boat and we walked down to the village, and everything—" He was running off his train of thought, going nowhere useful. He was exhausted, and control was difficult, especially dealing with his mother. A servant stood behind him. He slipped his coat buttons and slid it off his arms. The waiting servant took it, and the major domo slipped another on, the bronze brocade, one of his three better ones that he had not taken with him. "Thank you, nadi."

It was a better coat than someone ought to choose, who was simply going to go to his room, take it off again, and take off his boots and rest. So the major d' knew something.

"Staff has made a special supper," his mother said.

He could hardly bear the thought of food. His stomach was empty, except for breakfast. He had wanted to throw up, all the way from the lift to the apartment.

But he was suddenly on the edge of mad, now. He was not entirely sure what he was mad at. His father seemed to be on his side, and stood there to defend him. His mother was being nice, at least on the surface. Everybody was being nice. But his temper surged up, the instant his mother said supper—not that there was a thing he could do about it, because everybody had made their plans, Cook had made dinner, and that was the way it would be. He hoped there were no invited guests he had to please—but there usually were when there was any formal supper.

"A private supper," his father said. "Just the three of us."

Well, that was better.

And maybe the bronze brocade coat just meant they were treating it as a sort of occasion: himself, his mother, his father—

He belatedly remembered there were *four* of them now, and suddenly guessed what would be very politic to ask his mother on his homecoming.

"How is my *sister,* honored Mother?"

"Very well," his mother said, and looked pleased, as if he had guessed right and finally done the right thing.

"Go wash," his father said. "Supper is about to be served."

"Yes," he said. He *thought* about saying that his servants were coming upstairs with crates—but they were also coming with Boji, who was going to be upset and probably loud about it, and he really hoped Eisi and Liedi could get Boji quietly into his room before dinner started.

Boji, however, was definitely not a happy topic with his mother, and he had no wish to forecast trouble before it happened. "I shall wash and be right back," he said, and bowed again: bowing was always a way to change the subject without having to look at anyone.

And washing gave him a chance to give private orders to his aishid.

He escaped down the hall with them in attendance. He was so tired, so very tired he was shaking. But he had told himself all the way home that his best way to get his guests back next year was to make his parents happy, and the best way to do that was to go back into the household and follow all the rules.

And he was doing that, so far.

But before he even could reach the bath, there was a rattle and rumble down the outside hall that would be his valets bringing the baggage to the door, and bringing Boji back. One of Boji's earsplitting shrieks echoed in the huge hall outside. He looked back toward the door.

His mother had come back into the foyer, looking upset.

"Nadiin-ji." He appealed to his bodyguard, who were right behind him. "Help them. Please keep Boji quiet. *Hurry!*"

Antaro and Jegari were best with Boji. They headed back to the foyer and Veijico headed down the side hall—to the kitchen, he could guess, urgently looking for an egg, boiled or otherwise, in case his valets should have run out.

That left just Lucasi to attend him, and they went down the hall to wash, both of them. He reached the washroom, heard the outer door open as Boji's cage came rattling in.

Lucasi properly should not leave him alone right now, but he said, "Go be sure," and Lucasi went to have a look and be sure Boji got to his suite.

Cajeiri washed his hands, splashed water into his face, wiped back the stray wisps of hair about his face, and headed for the dining room as Veijico passed him, headed out to the foyer, carrying an egg. Boji was setting up a loud fuss out there despite all his staff's efforts, and they were still bringing in baggage, which involved noisy crate trolleys.

He let all that happen as it had to, trusting his bodyguard and his valets, who knew as well as he did how to handle Boji. He slipped into the dining room alone, sat down, as his father was seated, and listened, worried.

A closed door did not entirely muffle the sound of Boji's cage rolling across the mosaic floor of the foyer.

And it did not at all muffle the sound of Boji shrieking out—or of a baby crying far back in the apartment, where his mother had her rooms.

The racket of Boji's arrival reached a high pitch, then quieted.

"One is very sorry," he said. His stomach was upset. He heard his mother chiding staff in the hall outside.

"Are you well?" his father asked, a clear diversion of topic.

"Yes," he said, doggedly determined not to look around. "Everyone was well. Nand' Bren is well."

The baby's crying came clear for a moment. A door had opened and closed. Likely his mother was going back to see to his sister. It was hard to think of anything but that.

"One very much regrets the racket, honored Father."

"One trusts Boji will settle soon," his father said. "And were your guests glad to go home?"

He thought about politely lying, and decided on the actual truth. "No, honored Father. We were all sad."

"Indeed," his father said, but offered not a clue what he thought about it. His father picked up his spoon. "We may as well have the soup."

The polite thing was to ask all the courteous questions. And he should want to ask. But he was afraid of the answers. Two more sips of a tasteless soup and he gathered up his courage and did ask: "And are you and Mother well? And the baby?"

"We have all been very well," his father said, as if they were at some official function with hundreds of witnesses, and they were obliged to give only felicitous answers.

But unlike his human guests' habit of saying absolutely everything and anything at dinner—manners insisted there be no unpleasant talk and no business discussed at his parents' proper table. He pretended to eat. He wished he just could go to his suite and go to bed.

His father laid his spoon down with his soup half-finished, and servants hastened to remove that dish, and hovered over Cajeiri's. Cajeiri carefully laid his spoon down on the spoon-rest, and his soup likewise went away, replaced by a dish of pickle.

His father made no move. He made none.

The servants left the room.

"Did your guests enjoy their visit?" his father asked.

"Very much," he managed to say. "*Truly* very much, honored Father. Thank you."

"You will want them to visit again, I suppose."

"Yes," he said. There was a knot in his throat so extreme he could hardly keep his voice steady. "*Yes,* honored Father. I do."

His father nodded.

"One promises," he said desperately, and then thought that tying one thing to another immediately might not be the best idea, and maybe the subject was too close to discussing business at the table. "One wishes."

His father said, wryly, "We shall make a judgment closer to the time, and for reasons *of* the time, son of mine. Please make your mother happy, and do *not* let Boji escape near the baby."

"He—"—would not hurt her, was instant to his lips, but Great-grandmother would say, Never stand surety for a scoundrel, and Boji was, admittedly, a scoundrel when it came to escapes. "I shall be very careful."

"Excellently done, on your part, these last days," his father said. "And your mother also says so. Eat your pickle. Or had you rather have the meat course?"

His stomach was beyond uneasy. The knot would not go away. "I think I had rather the meat course, honored Father. We were up all night. No one could sleep."

"In such distress?"

"It was the last time we would be sure to have, honored Father. We wanted to talk."

"One understands," his father said, and tapped his bowl with his knife, summoning the servants. "We shall have the meat course," he said, "and a little carbonated juice with it."

Fruit juice was all that sounded good. He was glad to see the strong-smelling pickle go away. He never wanted to smell it again. The seasonal meat arrived: fish, and bland. The fruit juice was the best thing.

"Very good," his father said, and just then Mother came back in. It was, one was glad to note, quiet in the hall, from the direction of his own suite, and quiet from the farther hall, where his sister was.

Mother settled quietly into place, saying nothing about the two courses missed. A servant provided the meat course, and the fruit juice, and she took both.

"Our son was just saying," Father said, "that he had a very good time. His guests were sad to leave, and that, being as young and impractical as youngsters may be, they stayed up all last night talking. I believe our son will wish to go to bed soon."

"Will you wish to see your sister first?" his mother asked, and oh, he was not his great-grandmother's great-grandson for nothing.

"Oh, yes," he managed to say, though by now everything sounded distant to his ears, and he only wanted to lie down. "Thank you, honored Mother. Father." He drank all the juice, and ate two bites of the meat dish; and managed a spill of gravy onto his collar lace.

"One regrets," he said, mortified.

"No matter," his father said. "I think our son may better do with rest than food, daja-ma. Shall we not all have our dessert and then go visit Seimiro?"

"We shall," his mother said.

There was a light dessert, frothy and tart. That tasted good. Cajeiri had that, all of it, and as his father signaled an end to the service, and thanked the cook, he pushed himself up from the table, and went with his father and his mother to see his baby sister.

Seimiro's crib was in the room with the windows he so envied, with the windows all shut and curtained. She was darker than he remembered, a much healthier color, and tightly wrapped in blankets. She looked content, asleep with her thumb in her mouth.

"She is very pretty." It was not a lie, but it was certainly an exaggeration. She was a baby. Nobody knew what she would look like. But there she was, all new and the object of Mother's attention. There he was, with a spot of gravy on his collar lace.

But he was indisputably his father's heir. His father had

seen to that, just an hour before Seimiro was born. And Seimiro had years and years to go before she would be any threat to him at all.

He *felt* no strong man'chi to her. He noted that in himself. When he had parted from his guests, he had felt as if some piece of him were torn away. For Seimiro, he had only the dimmest of feelings—simply an awareness that she was his mother's baby; and relief that, because Seimiro existed, he was not *obliged* to belong that closely to his mother and not obliged to feel strongly attached. He had honestly hoped to feel something a little more for his sister than he did, one way or the other. He had thought he felt something the night Seimiro was born, but all that had faded now, strange to say. He was exhausted, fresh from company he deeply cared about, that he could not have—and she was just this sleepy little lump that, in possession of a room he would like to have, kept her eyes shut and her thumb in her mouth, and ignored him.

Disappointing. Great-grandmother said he would waken to certain feelings, and that right feelings would be automatic because he was atevi.

So—why did he feel robbed of his human associates? And why did he have no proper feeling right now where it regarded his sister-of-the-same-parents?

Was he angry that she existed?

He thought not.

Was he disappointed that she turned out to be just a baby, who would be a baby for years, and probably live in this room with the windows he coveted, getting favors his mother would not give him, until she was older than he was.

That was stupid. There was no way she could be anything other than a baby—though before she was born he had imagined teaching her and running about with her, and showing her all the fun things to do. He had felt very warm and good about *that* Seimiro, who in his head had been something like eight.

Well, there she was, and there she would be for months and

months, just a blanket-wrapped lump, who would grow very slowly into Somebody who probably would take his mother's side whenever there was an argument.

Eight was years away. And by the time Seimiro was old enough to do stupid things with anybody—he himself would be too old and responsible to do them.

Time worked far too slowly at Seimiro's end of things and far too fast at his.

"Very pretty," he said sadly, and put out his hand to touch his sister's tiny hand. "When she can play games I shall be too old for them."

There was a little silence around that. He had been very stupid to say it.

"Your life will not end with your fifteenth birthday," his father said, seeming amused. *"Believe* me."

Seimiro wriggled about and clenched her other fist, eyes still tightly shut.

He finally felt something toward her, then. He felt *sorry* for her, because she was going to be far more lonely than he had ever been, certainly having no chance of flying on a starship and meeting other children. Nobody unauthorized would ever approach Seimiro—unless she somehow got the chance to escape and travel with Great-grandmother. Or with him.

Mother was telling him how strong Seimiro was, and how she had to be watched, because she could wriggle right off her blanket, and how even now she was trying to turn over.

It was a very small beginning on misbehavior. Maybe she was doing her best.

But it was going to be forever until she *could* break free.

She was going to need encouragement.

And that would not make his mother happy. But it might rescue his sister, and make her much happier in her life.

"To bed, young gentleman," his father said, which was, given the way he was thinking, a very welcome escape.

* * *

Bren had barely had the chance to change his coat for an old favorite, and his traveling boots for comfortable house wear.

Staff, absent any order to restrain themselves on his return, had prepared a meal from which nobody had to refrain, not even his bodyguard, on this rare occasion of universal peace and celebration. Supani and Koharu arrived with the luggage cart and, on orders, the cart and its crates simply stood blocking the foyer, while the hard-working pair mingled and exchanged gossip they'd brought from Najida and Kajiminda. Bren was glad to see it.

Staff asked no questions of him personally. But one felt obliged to render some sort of account about recent events, the young gentleman's guests, and about nand' Jase—since they had all been guests on the premises at one time and another.

"The children," Bren said, "are very grateful for their visit. They are back in space, headed for the station. They learned how to ride, they sailed out into the straits, they visited Najida village. They did everything we could think of for them to do." He realized the staff had not heard about the new window at Najida, they had not seen the new wing about to be roofed—so he made a far longer report than he had intended, finding his voice a little thready by the time he finished. But staff provided him another glass of wine to keep him going, and it was very pleasant to sum up a thoroughly happy several weeks.

"And there are letters," he remembered to say: he had brought a whole bundle of them, from the families and neighbors of most of his staff—letters that would make the rounds to everybody, because those who were not from Najida village or estate still had ties there. Letters from home began to go the rounds: a wedding, the birth of a new cousin, a trip to the Township—

And once the letters came out, then there was the gift crate to open. Staff at Najida had sent various items to staff here in the Bujavid. There were gifts, sweets of all sorts, shared all around.

"Rani-ji," Bren said quietly to Narani, in a breathing space, "is there any word from the aiji? Should I go there this evening?"

"The aiji has just sent word that you may rest, nandi, and he will see you tomorrow, unless there is some urgent news."

"None." He was vastly relieved. He wanted to get his thoughts organized on paper before he forgot some important detail, and, God, the prospect of sleeping a little late in the morning was—

"The aiji-dowager," Narani added, "has invited the paidhi-aiji to breakfast."

The dowager's breakfasts were crack-of-dawn.

"Thank you, Rani-ji."

Well, his staff would have gotten him to the dowager's breakfast somehow, even if he had not asked that fatal question. Staffs managed such things and essential people turned up where they needed to be, on time, appropriately dressed.

But with that appointment in the morning, one more glass of wine tonight was not going to be a good idea.

"Beyond that matter," Narani said, "there seems nothing unexpected. Lord Topari is surely out of message cylinders: he has used five. Most people know you have not been in the capital. So does he, one is certain, but he keeps sending."

Topari, the mountain lord. The railroad matter Ilisidi was promoting. Lord Topari had a way of writing, sending, *then* thinking of an amendment. It was almost worth reading the letters in reverse order, if the letters themselves weren't as internally confusing as they tended to be, each referring to those preceding.

"No actual emergencies?"

"One thinks not, nandi."

The rest of the messages, then, were just ordinary business awaiting his return. And he trusted Narani's assessment. Message cylinders bore clan heraldry and personal seals. Narani would have done a good sorting of them. Narani would have notified him and read him a particular message by phone or couriered it to him at Najida had anything truly earthshaking come in.

Breakfast. At dawn. God.

He wondered if he should go to his office and try to put together the initial report for the dowager.

But he decided otherwise. Tomorrow before breakfast. Which meant getting up well before the crack of dawn.

More pizza appeared. Wine flowed. And gossip did, with every scrap of news from those letters out of Najida and Tirnamardi.

His valets entertained the company with accounts of the children's doings.

And there was, here in the Bujavid, a new rumor as of yesterday—that, while the lordship of the Kadagidi was still unfilled, Aseida, the former lord, had just taken a new appointment, as assistant manager in a spinning mill in Hasjuran—Lord Topari's holding—in the mountains, at the ragged edge of civilization.

No power. Definitely a chance to use his managerial skills on the independent-minded Hasjurani. A work schedule with very long hours. And no place to spend any graft if he could come by it.

That was fairly satisfying. It was the dowager's doing, he very strongly suspected, and very likely would find mention at breakfast.

He did need to warn Topari off that acquaintance, no matter how Aseida might try to leverage a meeting.

If Aseida himself had any sense, he could still redeem his mistakes. He was young. He had an education surpassing any in Hasjuran. By the time he had gray in his hair, he might have realized he had once had other choices, and should have taken them. He would have a life of should-have and could-have, and one had very little faith he would someday achieve awareness of should and could.

He might, however, develop useful skills at maintaining looms.

* * *

Bren meditated on his own should-haves, abed, in the dark, on that one glass of wine to the worse, that one last measure of self-indulgence before duty cut in.

He definitely should not have courted a hangover for the morning. He should have said no.

But he had gotten involved in conversation. It was so pleasant to be home.

He'd written reports that worried him.

But sometimes it was his job to keep secrets, to do the worrying. And think of solutions.

The door opened, admitting a sliver of light from the hall. And a shadow.

Welcome. Very welcome, too, that intrusion. He and Jago had been lovers for years. Being just down the hall from a number of youngsters with their own very alert junior security team had curtailed any getting together in the last month.

They were back home.

With no youngsters.

At long last.

6

Breakfast with the aiji-dowager was, even in warm weather, a chilly proposition, and nerves didn't help. Ilisidi's apartment not only had a row of windows, scarce luxury in the historic Bujavid—it had a balcony adjoining the breakfast room, and the dowager, an Easterner from the high mountains, always preferred to breakfast on that balcony in any conditions short of a blizzard.

It meant wearing a well-insulated coat, and one of the bulletproof vests, not for fear of incidents on this particular morning, but because the vest was another way of keeping one's core warm.

So Bren sat opposite the dowager, with the sun risen only halfway above the hills and the steam of hot tea tending to fly bannerlike from the cups. The ancient fortress that was the Bujavid loomed high on its hill above the busy streets of Shejidan, but there was none of the city visible from this side—only the foothills of the mountains to the south. And even in summer, those mountain heights and the small glaciers thereupon lent a slightly frosty edge to the breeze.

A servant ladled eggs in sauce onto the dowager's plate. The dowager used a toasted wafer to herd the eggs onto her spoon.

Bren preferred the grilled fish, and toast, sauces generally being the lethal aspect of alkaloid-laced atevi cuisine.

Much of the breakfast service passed in discussion of the weather in Malguri, and hunting in the highlands.

The dowager did discuss the new mill manager in Hasjuran. So far had Aseida fallen that he was *not* reckoned any longer as business, just as a tidy and satisfying bit of gossip.

One was properly appreciative.

Then the dowager asked, not quite casually, "So all our visitors are safely back in space."

"Indeed," he said.

"Did they enjoy Najida?"

"Very much so, aiji-ma."

"And you escorted them to the shuttle yourself?"

"Yes, aiji-ma."

"And what was my great-grandson's mood, so doing?"

There was the question.

"Sadness, aiji-ma. All the youngsters were sad. The young gentleman wished not to speak at all once they had gone. He slept most of the way to the city."

"He did not protest?"

"No, aiji-ma."

Ilisidi took a satisfied sip of tea that curled steam in the wind. "Excellent. Now that his guests have departed, he must show their visit to have had an extremely good influence. He must be cheerful, whatever the provocation, particularly with his mother. One trusts he observed our advice throughout."

The dowager favored a human connection for her great-grandson. That was not sentiment. It was purposeful, it was thought out, it was policy—and one didn't know precisely when she had taken that decision. But decision it clearly was, and would be.

He supposed he should be flattered. There had been a time the dowager would have been passionately against it.

"They were all exceedingly mannerly, aiji-ma. One believes indeed he observed your advice. And passed it to his guests."

"Well, well, he wants them back, does he not?"

A stiff gust challenged the weights on the tablecloth. They held.

And Bren thought, deeply troubled, of Irene's parting wish.

"He does want them, very much so, aiji-ma. And I believe *they* wish to come back."

"We shall support him," Ilisidi said, and immediately, irrevocably, shifted the topic elsewhere. "And how are things at Najida?"

"The windows you provided us, aiji-ma, are extravagantly beautiful. The first, the largest, is installed."

"Since they were my enemies who destroyed its predecessor, it seemed just."

"One hopes you may find some season to view it soon, aiji-ma. And the other windows, when they are installed. We have not yet roofed the new wing. But we shall have that done before the fall."

"Alas, my time away from the capital must be devoted to the East this year. And one hears you will be visiting the station. —Come, paidhi. You are shivering. Let us go inside."

Breakfast was entirely sufficient; and the wind was persistent, becoming a nuisance—he found it necessary to pin his napkin with a full water glass as he laid it by.

Inside, after hot, sweet tea with a touch of orangelle, plain business became allowable, even necessary, and the dowager had implied her central question—the thing she wanted to hear, and understand.

There *was* reason for question. She had laid out her agenda, things he had to do.

"A problem has arisen on the station, aiji-ma, and I fear I shall indeed need to go up there, at least briefly, to settle a human issue."

"Regarding."

"The Mospheiran stationmaster is uncooperative regarding the disposition of the Reunioners, and Sabin-aiji thinks I can be of service. Certainly I need to assess the situation." He saw the dowager arch a brow and his pulse kicked up. Did she know? Had she *possibly* gotten wind of Tillington's indiscretion? God, he hoped not.

The question, if it was a question, stayed unasked.

She asked, instead, "How long shall we miss your presence?"

"One shuttle rotation, one hopes. I do not wish it to be two. But I shall not leave on any other business until I have seen to every necessity now pending in your affairs, aiji-ma. I am determined on that, and I have told Jase-aiji so. I shall pursue everything as rapidly as possible here. I shall be meeting personally with Lord Topari on the routing matter. He seems to have found a new objection. Or a new request."

"That man!" the dowager said. "One hardly knows whether he is resolved to be difficult by stages, or whether he simply does not know how to organize his proposals."

"I have every hope it will be some very small matter. It usually is. There were five letters waiting for me. The fifth discovered his actual objection."

"What, were you at *correspondence* last night?"

"Early this morning aiji-ma."

"Earlier than I?" Again the arched brow.

"One had to know what was in the bowl. Curiosity overwhelmed me. And *his* letters were the reward of it."

"Well, well, I leave him to you, paidhi-ji, with gratitude. *We* shall deal with the Toparis of the East—of which I assure you there are several."

"Is it going well there, aiji-ma?"

"Oh, we have utterly amazed our neighbors. I have ordered the harbor channel dredged and a large pier built, where nothing larger than a trawler has ever docked, and this you may imagine provides great amusement about the region. These same neighbors will be pleading for access and jealous of every advantage once Machigi's ships arrive. —But in order to move Machigi to risk his ships on the southern passage, we need a demonstration from Lord Geigi of the accuracy of his weather forecasts. We have no doubt he will provide it, and we are working with the Messengers to assure the entire affair goes smoothly. But should there be a problem, and if you happen to be on the station, you will surely work out any difficulties of that sort. So your presence there may prove a convenience."

"I would certainly undertake to attend that, aiji-ma."

In the Southern Ocean, circumpolar storms ran unchecked and came round again increased in fury. The sea route between east and west coast had historically been impossible for shipping. There had once and very long ago been a diagonal traffic between the west and the Southern Island, at least from its northern shore, and that one approachable sea lane southward had been important—but cataclysm had overtaken that harbor and the civilization that had thrived there. A great wave had destroyed the port at the height of its prosperity, and made the survivors refugees in the Marid, that little nook of calm seas and rugged peninsulas on the southern edge of the mainland.

It had all happened more than a thousand years before humans ever had arrived in the skies, and sea trade now skirted the western coast, no more.

But the space station provided a hope that modern shipbuilding and space-based weather advice could make possible that southern passage by sea—at least during part of the year. That would link Lord Machigi, the dowager's new ally down in the Marid, to her own little fishing ports in the East.

So two of the poorest districts in the aishidi'tat looked to combine forces and improve their situations *outside* the thriving economy of Shejidan, which ruled in the center and west.

The East had mineral wealth and fisheries, and the Marid had textiles, leather, glass, ceramics and foodstuffs of more delicate sort—for starters. And though rail and air linked the capital at Shejidan and the mountainous heartland of the East, the rail and air network excluded the Marid—as it excluded the coastal areas of the East.

Joining the two orphans of the aishidi'tat by a wild and stormy sea was an ambitious plan. The Shejidani lords who understood it were betting most heavily on the new railroad linking the once-hostile Marid to the capital; and they were laying all their money there. They predicted that the sea venture would be all show, for the political effect, but that the real flow of goods would be the new rail line, and that it would be moderately profitable.

The dowager in fact had other plans, not that the Shejidani lords were going to *lose* money on their venture, but they would, in the dowager's intentions, not get all the gain. The dowager, champion of endangered species and threatened handcrafts, patroness of village systems and ancient traditions—had the very modern atevi stationmaster in space, Lord Geigi, for a close ally. She had, moreover, flown on *Phoenix* on the Reunion mission, and she understood what could be done from space. She understood it far better and with more imagination than most of the learned technical advisors who counseled her grandson Tabini-aiji.

Bet against her claim that a profitable sea route could link these two forgotten and marginalized districts?

Bren personally bet that she had *never* given up her decades-old plan to develop the south*west* coast of the mainland, and that the Marid trade link was only one step on a lifelong path—her design for the aishidi'tat, which she had maintained through three aijinates and her own regencies. Shejidan had long been the well into which all goods went, and what came out was, in the dowager's view, not quite equitable—in terms of districts and ethnicities.

"Notably," Ilisidi said, "we have just had a success in the Guild problem. The change of administration in the Assassins' Guild has helped us in more than one way. We may have brought back the old intransigent and inconvenient masters of that Guild, but these officers have returned to their posts with a new appreciation of our reasoning. They now admit themselves very glad that the East and the Marid have maintained their own Guild offices separate of Shejidan. They are now listening to Cenedi. They are respecting his advice, and this they would not do before."

Cenedi was the dowager's chief bodyguard, head of her security, and his absence right now, along with Banichi's, said that there was some intense conversation going on between the dowager's bodyguard and his own. The Eastern Guild out of which the dowager drew her over-sized bodyguard was differently organized than the Assassins' Guild in Shejidan. Most notably, it drew from local applicants without completely divorcing them from their local culture and their clans of birth.

When Ilisidi's marriage contract joined the Eastern and Western Associations the Shejidan Guild had been forced to acknowledge the authority of Cenedi's organization in the East, but that didn't mean they trusted it or even respected it. And now they applied to Cenedi for advice? They were considering the principle of local Guild as opposed to centralized Guild as something that might have advantages? The changes indeed represented a tectonic shift.

"One would hesitate to believe the leadership has *completely* abandoned their resentment of the regional Guilds," Ilisidi said, "but change is coming. We are privately assured the Assassins' Guild is drawing up a rule change to acknowledge our training center in Malguri Township, and once that principle is admitted, it will very readily extend to Lord Machigi's training center in the Taisigin Marid."

"Indeed!" He was beyond surprised.

"And where the Assassins' Guild goes, the Merchants, the Physicians, and others troubled by the matter of regional offices—will find their way. There may be a cost, however."

"There would have to be," he said. "What are the Assassins asking?"

"This, and in this consideration, your trip to the station may well prove a convenience. The Assassins wish to establish an office on the space station, as a condition to their recognizing the regional offices. So while you are preparing to deal with matters up there—*that* matter may well arise."

Deep breath. Half a year ago he would have been appalled, with a kneejerk no, absolutely not. *Never* let the Assassins' Guild up into Lord Geigi's domain—within reach of humans.

Now, in circumstances the dowager herself had created, with his help, it did not appear to be such a bad idea.

If the Guild sent the right people. The Assassins' Guild, effectively the justice structure of the aishidi'tat, needed direct access to accurate, unfiltered information—information which would help them guide opinions in Shejidan about situations the ground-based Guild could not readily imagine. Cenedi and Banichi—and Algini—had the ear of the Guild leadership. *They* might influence the choice of agents.

Having an informed opinion advising the Guild about Geigi's security up there could also be very helpful.

All this—granting what he never would have granted before: that the oldest of all Guilds was actually in a process of adapting and changing.

There *was* Tillington to explain to them. That underlying issue flickered like lightning on the horizon, illuminating a very scary landscape.

There was Tillington, there was Louis Baynes Braddock, and there were all the old quarrels that lay in human politics.

But those were the very matters the Guild needed to understand. The way humans dealt with their own and solved problems—they had to learn that, too, among very important considerations. High-level Guild were not fools.

And there was no better person on the atevi side to explain a situation to the Guild than Lord Geigi, who understood, for one principal difference, that human leaders were far more replaceable than atevi aijiin—and that a problematic opinion therefore tended to be an ephemeral condition that could change with a new appointment—short of the need for an assassination. And he hoped to illustrate that fact very quickly regarding the current human stationmaster.

"One does not foresee Lord Geigi objecting to that proposition, aiji-ma, though one is certain he will have some adjustments and observations."

"To say the least. And this human stationmaster. Tillington."

She knew the name. God, that was disturbing.

"Tillington," he said carefully. "Yes, aiji-ma."

"One hears he is inconvenient."

"Exceedingly. But a word from the Presidenta can remove him. He is an appointed official, not elected."

"Well, well," Ilisidi said, bypassing the entire situation with a wave of her hand, "one understands you will have various matters to deal with up there. The man seems singularly useless. I leave him to you."

God, *did* she know? He still couldn't tell. If she did know—she'd just posed a question. And he had to answer it.

"I shall deal with the matter of Tillington in the next few days, aiji-ma. I think he has become quite inconvenient. I shall begin, as I now intend, by asking the Presidenta to call him home for consultation, which may settle the entire problem with minimal fuss—at least as soon as we can secure a shuttle berth. When I do go up to the station, perhaps the Assassins should indeed send their mission with me and stay in close contact as I work—granted only they will agree to work with me and bring me their questions. Certainly they should develop a close association with Lord Geigi, and respect his good advice."

"It might indeed be wise," Ilisidi said, "to have the Guild receive an accurate interpretation regarding the human administration. And one wishes to be sure this new leadership in the Guild develops the proper sources of information regarding affairs in Geigi's lordship, as well. The Guild may seek information by clandestine means as a check, but they need guidance. Ah, well, well, one trusts you will find a satisfactory conclusion to all this business." Ilisidi waved the servants away. "We are relieved, paidhi. We shall see our great-grandson settled in peace and quiet in his household. Then we shall fly back to Malguri to enjoy the rest of the summer and threaten a few fools. Lord Tatiseigi may even join us there for a few days. We have absolutely no doubt Lord Topari will keep you entertained in our absence."

That was a joke. He was expected to take it as such. To hand it back.

"I shall conclude an agreement as quickly as I can, aiji-ma, and one trusts an escape to the space station will be far enough once I am done."

Ilisidi laughed quietly. She had said what she wanted to say, and the paidhi-aiji had received his priorities, one of them handling a *very* scary situation, where it regarded the Guild's arrival on the station. And another—on which he *still* had no idea what she knew.

In his immediate path, then, he had the groundbound problems, which the travel schedule made a priority. He might serve the aiji, but the aiji-dowager borrowed his services as often as she pleased. The railroad matter was the most urgent, in terms of the dowager's objectives. He was not *exactly* working on Tabini-aiji's orders in devoting so much time to the dowager's affairs. But between the railroad and Ilisidi's eastern port, they were about to conclude a peace that had eluded the mainland for two hundred years, a state of affairs *definitely* in Tabini's interests.

Tabini clearly thought that move convenient, too, or he would have put roadblocks in its path, including finding occasion to *send* the paidhi-aiji somewhere remote, and out of the aiji-dowager's reach.

The space station was about as remote as one could get. And he would have to work both situations up there with what diplomacy he could manage: human politics and the Assassins' Guild were *both* headed for Geigi's doorstep.

Maybe if Tillington were compelled to explain the human problems to the Guild it would make Tillington think twice about what he was stirring up.

If only that were likely.

He had a delicate letter to write to Mospheira, and best he get that entire business underway at the soonest. Along with that, he needed to phone Shawn and ask for a courier to be flown in on the next commercial flight. He wasn't willing to trust the Messengers' Guild with such a communication, even in Mosphei': they were the *other* problem among the guilds, one that no side ever trusted that far.

So he had to ask Mospheira for a courier to come pick up the letter, since despite all the improvements in relations, it still wasn't politic to send a unit of the Assassins' Guild to call on the Mospheiran President.

Dear Mr. President:

He didn't use *Dear Shawn* on official correspondence. And this was, above all else, official, designed to be quotable—useable as far as Shawn wanted to take it.

I hope my writing finds you well. I can assure you that the situation is vastly improved on the mainland. Tabini-aiji has very recently revised the leadership of the Assassins' Guild. This has corrected a long-standing problem.

He has invested Cajeiri as his official heir, which as you know must be approved by the legislature, but there will be no problem with that when the day comes, and there is general happiness to have that matter settled.

The young gentleman, on the occasion of his birthday, received a visit from three of the Reunioner children he met aboard the ship, as you are surely aware. A relationship has formed which may mature well.

The children also fared very well medically in their visit. There were no complaints of illness in the adjustment, and this is a situation that has acquired immense political implications, as you may imagine, considering the situation aboard the space station.

The presence of the Reunioners aboard the station, as you may have heard, is stressing station capacity. They are, I am informed, closely confined, have less than comfortable living arrangements, very few gain passes for special purposes, and fewer still have jobs. Mospheiran officials are reluctant to fill posts with Reunioner applicants.

This unhappy situation cannot continue indefinitely. I had a chance to speak frankly and at length with Captain Jason Graham, who accompanied the children in their visit, and I am now convinced that finding a solution for the Reunioner problem is beyond urgent.

Coupled with that, I received troubling news yesterday from Captain Graham regarding statements made by Stationmaster Tillington, who, as I am sure you know, favors the removal of the Reunioners to a new station at Maudit.

He has vehemently opposed the children's visit here as signaling a change in policy regarding the Reunioners.

As a statement of opinion and policy, this might have been tolerable, but it has now been joined to the explicit charge, as reported to me by Captain Graham, that Sabin engineered the original meeting of the aiji's son with these children aboard the ship, and that Sabin is pursuing a private agenda with the deposed Reunioner Stationmaster, Louis Baynes Braddock.

There is, first, no truth in this. I witnessed what happened on the voyage between the aiji's son and the Reunioner children. I also was in a position to observe the state of affairs aboard the ship and can attest there was no love lost between Sabin and Braddock.

Stationmaster Tillington's statement is a reckless attack on the integrity of two of the four captains, Graham and Sabin; it also touches me and my office, but far more seriously, it touches on the honor of the aiji-dowager, who was supervising the aiji's son. The repercussions of that must be dire, if this is ever known.

The implication of the statement translated into an atevi context is extremely serious and damaging—and while Tillington himself may not have understood how it would translate to atevi, it exists: he has said it. And while it has not been publicized as yet, I am extremely worried that the statement will find a way to the atevi side of the station before some action can be taken on the human side absolutely to disown it.

I have not relayed the statement in question to the aiji-dowager or to the aiji and I hope it will not be repeated on the station. I hope to settle this quietly and quickly and head off any consequences, but I have some reason to fear the dowager may privately be aware of it. If this is the case, her patience is extremely limited—and must be. Should such charges reach other ears—a situation very likely, given that Stationmaster Geigi understands more Mosphei' than he speaks; and so do some of his staff—there must be severe repercussions, including the bringing of capital charges against Tillington. The dignity and integrity of the aijinate is at issue.

I have no choice now but to urge that Stationmaster Tillington be relieved of duty and replaced with all possible speed and that his successor be strongly cautioned against any statement which, whether intentionally or otherwise, could be interpreted to question the integrity of the aijinate or the ship's officers.

Should the current statement become public with Tillington still in office, the aijinate would be forced to demand the delivery of Tillington and his aides to the mainland, with no likelihood of their return. The damage to relations and agreements between Mospheira and the aishidi'tat at that point would be extreme.

There can be no remedy by apology. The atevi administration cannot excuse such a reckless charge.

As a second point, in the official view of the aishidi'tat, the disposition of the Reunioners is not solely a station issue, but an international issue, to be settled at Presidential level and at the level of the aijinate, in consultation with the Ship, and in no way at the level of the Stationmaster.

We now know, as a result of the recent visit, and thanks to a medication easily available to the ship-folk, that this space-born population can adjust to life on the planet. This adds a new choice. In my own view, the best solution for the Reunioners is movement toward permanent residency on Mospheira. These are skilled workers whose technical expertise can easily be applied on the planet. The Mospheirans on the station may be joined one at a time by Reunioners who have cleared the same screening they passed, but for the majority, including families with children, the planet offers the best answer.

I hope in all good will for your quick assistance in these matters. I cannot stress enough the urgency involved.

Damn, he didn't want to send that letter cold. He wanted it to sit for at least four hours for several reviews of the wording.

Shawn Tyers, multiple times President, past head of the Department of State, and, in the early years, his direct boss—had been his friend and sometime sounding board in years since.

But for various reasons—his own mother's death, Toby's role as go-between during the years he'd been gone—he hadn't talked with Shawn all that often since he'd landed amid the troubles of the aishidi'tat. *So glad you're safe. Very glad to hear from you.*

He hadn't communicated officially with the Mospheiran government even to ascertain whether he currently held any official position within it. No one had ever withdrawn his appointment, true. But no one but Shawn in this entire last year had so much as asked him a direct question—and he had never asked in what *capacity* Shawn had asked him.

So now, out of the blue, he asked Shawn to use Presidential power to fire a very high level appointee, one who probably had political clout that could come back to haunt Shawn's party.

Then he had to urge Shawn to take in the Reunioners, against strong objection likely from various interests inside Mospheira—and that led to the knotty question of where Reunioners might be settled with least problem. He wished he'd kept the contact with Shawn a little more current—though he didn't know when in the last frantic year he'd have found the time.

Well, a personal phone call to precede that unpleasant letter was at least a start on patching the relationship and figuring out what his position officially was, these days.

He called for the phone, and for a line to the Presidential residency across the channel.

Narani brought the phone—and at least a connection to the residency. Beyond that point, it became a problem in Mosphei', and Narani never attempted to translate.

"This is a member of the Presidenta's staff, nandi," Narani said. "At least one surmises him to be such."

It was, as turned out, indeed, the President's staff—but a secretary to the head of staff.

"This is Bren Cameron," he said, "in Shejidan. I need to talk to the President. Personally."

That took a bit. Three separate senior secretaries were sure they needed to talk to him instead.

"This is classified and this is urgent," he said. "Advise the President."

He definitely needed to have called Shawn before now. He didn't know any of these people.

The President was at breakfast. Fine. The President could take five of his minutes away from the table and get on the phone. Urgently.

The President had been told he was calling. The President was coming to his office. Please wait.

He waited.

In the old days there was no likelihood of anybody successfully eavesdropping on the call. Nowadays it was a certainty there would be such people all along the physical route of the call. The Assassins' Guild had a few members who could get the gist of a conversation, he was near certain. The Messengers' Guild he was sure cultivated the same talents, and those people were likely working very hard to improve their linguistic skills.

The longer the call waited, the more likely eavesdroppers could get into position.

Fifteen minutes. He took a few notes on other matters, with the handset braced against his shoulder.

"Bren?" Shawn asked.

"Shawn. Good to hear your voice."

"Problem?"

"There is. I need you to get a courier to Shejidan on the afternoon flight. I'll have one of my bodyguard run the document out to the airport, deliver it straight into your courier's hands, and stay there 'til the plane takes off again."

"Understood." Shawn didn't ask the subject or the urgency that demanded such precautions. The last completely couriered exchange had been his report to Shawn on the voyage, and on Tabini's return to power, a report which had massed more than five hundred pages. Back had come Shawn's answer, also in writing, and classified, and in four words. *Thank God. Stay well.*

Beyond that—he'd sent a few reports over by courier, usually to relieve worry. The recent assassinations in the north—that had required a routine advisory note from the aiji's office to the President's, to assure Mospheira that everything was under control and that the young visitors were safe—should the station ask corroboration.

But the most recent and critical situation—the profound change in the Guild—he hadn't had a clear enough picture to deliver a final report to Shawn.

Now events got ahead of him.

"How are you doing?" Shawn asked.

"Really very well. Had a great visit with Jase Graham and the kids." Dead certainty that Shawn knew whatever details of the visit the human side of the space station knew, but with what slant in Tillington's report was uncertain. "They did marvelously. Nobody was sick. The kids were outdoors, running all over the place, no problems. They had a great time, I'm glad to report."

"Glad to hear it. I hear the aiji's named an heir and now has a new daughter."

"He has, both. Everybody's happy, the baby's doing fine—the aishidi'tat is very happy with the situation. I'm glad to report everything over here is in great shape."

That slid rapidly across two topics in the letter the courier had to pick up, and the kids' visit and the new daughter might have Shawn thinking down other problematic paths as the possible subject of the letter—the changes in Tabini's family, the appointment of an heir, and all the upheaval and assassination inside the aishidi'tat.

All those matters—and that Jase had paid a visit.

One of those items was certainly dead on. And if anybody in the information chain was going to leak information up to Tillington, he didn't want to explain it was Jase's visit that now occasioned a couriered message. Tillington might well add two and two.

"How are you getting along?" Bren asked.

Code for: is there a circumstance I should know that's going to complicate the situation on your side?

"Pretty well," Shawn said—freighted with the current situation in the Mospheiran legislature, Bren was sure, applying to Shawn's health, the prevailing weather, and the stability of current politics. It began to feel like their conversations before the voyage, the polite inquiries, the subtexts they both knew, the fact that the courier that came to the mainland to carry back the letter *he* was sending was very likely to bring an answering letter from Shawn. *"Typical weather for the season. Fairly pleasant in the capital, however."*

"Same here," Bren said. "I'm very delighted to report. Wife and kids?"

"All fine."

"That's great."

"Congratulations to the aiji and the consort. I trust that's appropriate."

"Entirely appropriate. I'll relay the good wishes."

"Really good to talk to you."

That was a sign-off. And it was time to get off the phone, before they stumbled into the wrong territory. Specific topics could trip over things the courier ought to carry. Shawn would get the letter. Then they'd talk again.

"Same," he said. "Really good. Thanks."

Shawn broke the connection from his end. Bren hung up and re-read what he had written.

It still said what needed saying and implied everything that needed implying. He put a salutation on it. He put a wax seal on the paper, his own, which made it official. He separately added his notes on the Assassins' Guild situation—*I have no concrete reason to use the word 'optimistic' in this case, but I am cautiously inclined to hope—*

He finished it. And he called Banichi.

"I've asked Shawn for a courier to fly in this afternoon," he said, and Banichi gave a single nod.

The words Tillington had let fly, if spoken on the mainland, would engage the Guild, no question. There was no way to insert that awareness past the barriers that existed in Mospheiran thinking: right and wrong and personal rights and personal entitlements were in the way.

He wasn't entirely sure Shawn himself was going to feel in his gut what Tillington's statement would do, if it ever reached the atevi public. But Tillington had just, no question, made a career-ending mistake.

And for what?

Resentment for the crowding and the rationing and the discomfort? Maybe. But being Mospheiran—one didn't think another Mospheiran population would have met that kind of anger. No. One could sacrifice comforts. Mospheirans had a tradition of helping their own, doing without, making do. Historically, they'd had hard times, and had always found a way of getting through to a better life.

Besides, granted there had been rationing, it hadn't been rationing of everything. There were comforts. Atevi and humans alike had done everything possible from the ground to ease the strain, especially regarding foodstuffs.

How that relief had been administered aloft, he was no longer sure.

Disquieting thought.

Tillington distrusted Braddock. That was a given. They had all distrusted Braddock. Unfortunately the move onto the station had not isolated him from the rest of the Reunioners.

But Tillington had, from the outset, not let the Mospheiran and Reunioner populations mix. Security concerns. Rules. Regulations. The Reunioners had never passed screening, had no security clearance. Records were supposedly in the ship's storage—at least they had been. But either they hadn't been released to Tillington's administration—for reasons that might lie in ship politics—or Tillington had them and it didn't matter. Tillington still would not let the Reunioners merge into the station: they lived in special sections. Didn't have clearance to enter operational areas . . . and how the station defined operational areas was nebulous. A few Reunioners found employment, but most, he had learned during the children's visit—waited.

Waited for a general solution to their status. Which was tangled up in a general solution for the entire refugee population.

And Tillington backed moving the Reunioners out to build at the lifeless ball of rock that was Maudit, with all the delays and costs and risks involved.

He himself had thought of setting up a new colony at Maudit as a slow process, a first-in team, a habitat to build a structure, to set things up, a process taking years, while the Reunioners found employment on the original station manufacturing elements of the new station and running their own operation. He hadn't, he thought with some disquiet, *liked* the notion of Braddock's involvement, but it had seemed to be what the Reunioners themselves were pushing . . . a process too preliminary as yet even to talk about the need for the Reunioners coming under the Mospheiran treaty with the aishidi'tat . . . which he was firmly determined they *would,* for very solid policy reasons.

Not so, apparently, not in the way Tillington was pushing to have all the Reunioners sent out there right now—which was apt to lead to more hardship.

He didn't readily dislike people. Dislike was not useful in his job, wherein he occasionally had to deal with the difficult, the problematic, and the entirely objectionable. Jase himself had felt out the matter to the last—felt his way through a cultural interface last night that, indeed, did make Mospheirans and ship-folk two different questions: he detected that.

But he did trust Jase to tell him the truth, even if Jase had to go against Sabin. And the awareness that had flickered into Jase's eyes when he'd expressed the dowager's position in Ragi: *that* sealed it. That was truth.

And the sudden recklessness, the fact that Tillington was playing into a known rift in the Captains' Council . . .

Tillington's interpretation of the kids' visit, as all part of a plot . . .

All that came into focus, a complete unwillingness to shade anything in gray, that roused an emotional response of his own regarding Mospheiran politics, and the suspicion of an old, old division. He had detected the reaction in himself when he had to deal with Braddock, even at distance. He'd smothered it. Applied cold logic. Or tried to.

Both Braddock and Tillington were pushing Maudit—with haste. Emotionally.

And ironically they were doing so, in high emotion, with exactly the same aim.

Division. Separating the populations into us and them.

No, he wasn't feeling charitable toward Tillington.

They'd been through the Heritage Party's brief accession to power on Mospheira, when people had gotten on television to talk about human entitlements, and ownership of the station, and how nobody should trust the atevi, either. The Heritage Party's view had been that war was inevitable. And that they should arm themselves, and get to space, and rain fire down on atevi civilization.

Shawn's administration, succeeding that period of madness, had tried to keep that attitude off the station, when they'd populated it. They'd screened applicants. They'd tried.

But nobody could police thoughts and attitudes if the holder never stood up and said it, never threatened anybody—until a highly pressured situation changed a man in power.

Had Tillington possibly been a Heritage supporter before he'd arrived in office up there? Or had he turned under pressure? There'd been no skilled translator: no paidhi to interpret or explain what Tillington would have found strange and frustrating, and a robotic numbers transaction couldn't explain intent or reasons. Had things gone that bad between Tillington and Geigi that Tillington's thinking had just clicked over into old Mospheiran attitudes, focused now on resentment from a human event two centuries in the past, dead, gone, and buried—

Or was it just a habit of being in absolute power over Mospheiran affairs up there, and a frustration at having all the years of work suddenly down to rationing?

It was a good bet Tillington, if he was tending to the Heritage mindset, was not going to favor settling the Reunioners on Mospheira.

Braddock, on the other side, wouldn't want his constituency divided and removed to earthly cities, either.

Those two were likely allies for completely opposite reasons.

Granted his own thinking wasn't purely, abstractly altruistic, either. A planet changed things. Changed people. Changed politics. Not always for the good. But changed them. But five thousand people? Mospheira could swallow that with barely a blip in the polls. No question.

Communication, first and foremost. He and Jase had to have a long talk once he got up there—something they'd started that last night, and he wished they'd had the time and privacy to do earlier, without the kids who had a way of turning up unexpectedly.

Definitely, when he got up there, he would find that time. And not just with Jase. He needed to build trust—with Sabin, among others. With Ogun—if he could.

He needed to find out how serious the division among the Captains was. Ogun's new appointment to a captaincy—Riggins—would be a fourth, inauspicious and paralyzing fourth, vote in the divided Captain's Council. Atevi would *never* have set up a system that could go to stalemate in a crisis. Humans did it regularly to achieve balance.

Balance wasn't quite working up there, was it? And in his preference, and by Jase's recommendation, Tillington did *not* get to break the stalemate.

Did he believe in Jase's motives?

Absolutely. Trust him?

With his life.

It didn't mean, however, that the paidhi-aiji was through gathering information, either—just in case there was more to be learned. *He* had a side in this, too, and it wasn't, at the moment, Mospheiran.

He sent an encrypted message up to Geigi.

Bren, paidhi-aiji, Lord of Najida

To Geigi, Station-aiji, Lord of Kajiminda.

One urges you ask Jase-aiji to your table, if you have not yet done so. He will bring you the seasonal reports from Kajiminda among other matters.

One regrets that I was not able to visit your estate during my recent visit to Najida, but the estate reports are encouraging of a good harvest this fall, and I have made it urgently his concern to convey those to you.

He will also, if he has not designated it to go to you already, send you baggage which the young gentleman's guests cannot contain within their quarters. As a favor deserving the young gentleman's gratitude, please store those things against a future visit.

I have included siai tea in the shipment which is for your use only. Please use it in good health.

The tea was a code word, which between them meant: read between the lines and act.

Geigi quietly detested that tea.

Please care for your health, and please enjoy your visit with Jase.

Could he say it any plainer?

Likewise assure him that I accept his very good advice.

I shall be coming up to the station on business soon, and look forward to the pleasure of your society.

As regards Jase-aiji, please tell him—

Now came a deliberate security test. The news could break now—or later—and *if* it leaked immediately, at any level—they would find that out through Jase, if no other way.

I shall be escorting elements of a regional Assassins' Guild office to be set up within the atevi section, to operate under your authority. Its central function will be liaison and information-gathering for the Guild.

It is my task to interpret this new presence to the humans on the station, who may have questions about the nature of the office, and who, while they will not deal with that office directly under any ordinary circumstances, will need to understand and accept its function. It will be useful to have another atevi presence in direct communication with Shejidan, and the Guild will benefit from their skilled observation of situations. One hopes they may resort to you for guidance and assistance.

This should be a benign and beneficial presence, reflecting beneficial changes in Guild organization in the aishidi'tat. Its man'chi is now strongly toward Tabini-aiji.

I shall escort them to the station and explain to the ship-

aijiin. Jase-aiji will be a useful contact preceding this process. And as always, I rely on your good will and your wisdom.

One understands there is some stress regarding the human situation. Please be aware, but let me deal with Tillington-aiji on my arrival.

Which was to say, talk to Jase, fast. We've got the Guild asking questions, launching a fact-finding mission, and there are things you desperately need to know before they get there.

Leave Tillington to me.

Very good to talk to you, the message came back from Shawn early that afternoon, not a response to his couriered letter, which had left on the plane that delivered Shawn's letter, but Shawn's own state of the state message, in a letter crossing his.

And then the part that mattered.

The visit of the Reunioner children to the mainland has stirred controversy here. It was generally assumed that they—and a significant number of Reunioners in general—would not be able to live on Earth even a few days without difficulties. The extension of their visit and reports of their inclusion in official events have raised questions.

Stationmaster Tillington reports that the children were given a drug to enable this, and unfortunately this report has become public this week, elaborated into unrealistic reports that this new drug enables the Reunioners to land en masse. This frightens some people.

Good God. How do they land, in the shuttles we have?

Five thousand ordinary citizens, including old people and kids, a threat to a planet?

The petal sails all over again?

I am assuming your letter crossing this one may involve the Reunioner issue, and whether or not this is the case, an exchange of information will be useful.

Sanity. He drew an easier breath.

Tillington has reported that the Reunioners themselves have followed this visit with some speculation that the children will be taken from their parents and that all children will be taken away before the Maudit expedition.

God.

Tillington reports he has made statements strongly denying this, and he urges the legislature make a decision in favor of the Maudit venture, as the integration of Reunioners into the station population poses significant security risks. We have received Tillington's very detailed proposal to send a small exploratory team to Maudit, to establish an orbiting station—for which Lord Geigi may be solicited for materials support. The proposal, in effect, establishes the Reunion colony at a remote distance.

I am not fully in support of this idea, and it is meeting opposition, again on grounds of security.

The pro argument is that the need for supplies to move to such a new orbiting station by Mospheiran supply ships will foster a necessary cooperation between the populations.

The counter-argument is that atevi will likely demand the treaty be extended to mandate equal atevi presence on that station and this is argued to lead to a separate arrangement between Reunioners and atevi if Mospheira does not send more personnel to balance them, and this would make an impractically large station at Maudit, far larger than the one now orbiting Earth. If atevi would count both stations together for the purpose of parity that might be workable. But even so, it poses difficulties.

We are now at the anniversary of the restoration of the atevi government and we understand that the aishidi'tat is now resuming programs once suspended. We hope that atevi attention to the Reunioner matter should become a priority, and we hope to work cooperatively to resolve these issues.

Tillington's put a strong push on his own program, while the children have been down here. Interesting.

I have been hearing nothing but the Maudit proposal for the last year, as I think you have likely heard the details. I have advised Tillington previously not to press Lord Geigi for materials until there is a decision. We have no wish to stir up argument on an issue not yet decided.

Bet on it. Geigi is not going to say a thing officially until Tabini gets involved.

I say in confidence I am not convinced that moving the Reunioners farther from our centuries of experience onworld is the right answer. It is a solution attractive to some who believe their existence threatens us. But in my view our security is far more threatened by keeping this population unified by frontier hardship while we live in comforts they do not enjoy.

Bravo, Shawn.

If this new drug can let these people adapt to Earth I would favor it. I had rather see the Reunioners distributed across Mospheira, but there is no means to provide security for these people as scattered immigrants, which I regret to say could lead to difficulties in some areas.

He knew the areas—pockets of regional discontent that still spawned problems, where remnants of the Heritage Party had taken stubborn root.

I have a specific solution in mind. But there is a set of tech-based industries on Crescent Island, in which they could be valuable.

Space industry.

The environment is a little trying.

Humidity and torrential rain.

But there is employment, and a space-oriented population, which may better understand the environment from which they come.

The tech unions were going to have a fit.

I solicit your advice in these matters. I understand that you have shaped your position in the aishidi'tat and that you now serve unique functions in the atevi world. I do not urge your return to Mospheira in this context or at this moment; once we have settled the problem the Reunioners pose, that may be a good time.

Translation: you're not that popular here, Bren, and if you should become tangled in the Reunioner issue, you could become less so.

I hope that your message, which necessarily crosses this one, does not present difficulties with what I have set out above.

Sorry to say, Shawn, it does.

I hope to renew our previous frequency of communication.

I remain hopeful that we can resolve whatever matters divide the people we guide.

I'm with you on that one, Shawn. God, I am *with* you.

But Tillington has to go. Next shuttle. Call him home. Find a reason. Any reason.

Next shuttle. Next *Mospheiran* shuttle. Two week rotation. And if it kept schedule, it had already gone up. The Mospheiran shuttle had never reconfigured its cargo bay in orbit. It could. Theoretically.

They either had to withdraw Tillington before he had a replacement, or get a replacement up on the next rotation. Neither was a good option.

Granted Shawn could get one.

A phone call came at dusk. Bren took it, barefoot and in his shirtsleeves, interrupting his dressing for dinner.

"I have it," Shawn said, first off. *"God, what a mess. I understand. I'll keep you posted."*

It was all they could say on the central matter, where the connection might be compromised.

"Good," he said. And understood, by the careful tone of Shawn's statement, it wasn't something Shawn could do quickly or without political danger.

Heritage Party. The source of simple answers that always looped back to the same proposition. Humans first. And *us* first of all.

He and Shawn talked for a few minutes, then wished each other a pleasant evening and broke off.

God, Bren thought, laying the receiver in its cradle.

Three years of not dealing with human problems . . .

And there it all was again, same old theme, different verse. *Them.* And *us.*

It was a quiet dinner. He invited his aishid to join him, and to take brandy after, contrary to their habit. What he had to explain was convoluted, and needed interpretation.

And there were questions. But mostly they listened.

"Tillington worries you considerably," Jago observed later, in bed.

"Immensely," he said. "I grew distracted, Jago-ji. I let myself fall out of close communication with the Presidenta. That was my first mistake."

"You could not have visited Mospheira without comment—and not without speculation on this side of the strait, either. *Messages* that go back and forth occasion comment. There is no diplomatic bag that goes that the guilds fail to know it. Your staying here, throughout the restoration of the aiji, was important."

Every breath he took, this close to the aiji, and involved as he was in politics with the Marid, politics with the dowager, politics with the northern clans, politics with the Tribal Peoples—everything was parsed by a dozen agencies for clues about his mood, and clues as to his consultations and his associations.

Message Shawn at every turn? There'd been no great emergency involving Mospheiran affairs.

But after a year putting out fires on the mainland, the fact that the heir had had a birthday and invited human children down from the station—Reunioner children—had hit the rumor mill over on Mospheira with a force *he* hadn't foreseen, in a context *he* hadn't been tracking as closely as he should. He'd had his mind on security, on the assassination of Cajeiri's grandfather, and several attempted assassinations aimed in what turned out to be the youngster's vicinity—not to mention questions about the integrity of the guilds. He'd been preoccupied. He'd been staying alive and keeping the kids safe and happy.

But he couldn't drop stitches like that. He couldn't rest confident that people outside the mainland were going to think to advise him of their crises.

Hell, he'd *deliberately* disconnected himself from Mospheiran politics, because he'd been working closely with Tabini, working closely with the dowager, and constant communication with Mospheira during that period of recovery would, as Jago said, have said something he didn't want said. It would have undermined trust, thrown his loyalty into question.

But Shawn had said it: it was not a good time for him to return to Mospheira. He couldn't help anybody if he became tangled in political issues on Mospheira, or, for that matter, aloft. He'd kept out of the Mospheiran upset over the Reunioners' arrival, trusting Shawn to calm things down. The fact was that Mospheira and the station had been maintaining calm and keeping their treaty agreements as they should—one reason they'd been able to do that, he'd thought, was because he'd not roiled the political waters around them, and because the ship's independent authority up there had kept the lid on things.

Well, he got Shawn's signal loud and clear now. The Heritage Party hadn't been a problem so long as the Reunioners were out of sight and removed from daily consideration. It was going to be a problem if they started landing. Tillington, likewise grounded, was going to find backers for his position, and he had to be careful with the situation. Use extreme finesse.

Finesse in the Guild's terms—*was* one answer that leapt to mind, removing a man who wanted to play politics with kids' lives, who wanted to create a situation that stirred up the worst in Mospheiran society. But it wasn't a route he wanted to take. It wasn't a route he ever could take, not remotely, and maintain any semblance of a link to Mospheiran society.

No, let Shawn arrange some sort of soft landing for Tillington, get him out of the way without creating wreckage in the system—or damaging his administration. That needed thought. It needed calm. And it needed, most of all, a little time.

Well-fed and content to retire was the best disposition for a man who'd served tolerably well—until the arrival of the Reunioners had triggered something in him that wasn't at all pleasant.

Maybe a University sinecure—

No. The man should not teach. If he entertained Heritage ideology—he should not have students in his hands.

Ilisidi, with the Assassins' Guild entirely at her disposal, had managed to find a spot for the former lord of the Kadagidi, supervising a textile mill. Well-paid. Quiet. Not political.

And under another lord's thumb.

Solutions like that, unfortunately, weren't readily to be had on Mospheira.

Not as secure, not as quiet, and not with that kind of well-watched certainty.

Unfortunately, sending Tillington *himself* to non-existent Maudit wasn't an option.

7

"And was it a regretful parting?" Lord Tatiseigi asked, regarding the young gentleman's guests.

"It was, nandi," Bren said. The two of them occupied opposing green-upholstered chairs across a low table in the legislative sitting room, two days on from the exchange of messages with Shawn.

On the wall, a wooden scoreboard reported a slowly progressing tally of votes on the forestry bill—a certainty to pass. Half the people who should be voting were in the lounge at the moment having a cup of tea, but that didn't include the representatives of the Edi and the Gan peoples, who were exercising their very first votes as members, and who were early on the floor to cast them in favor of something that would benefit the Edi district.

It was an auspicious beginning to the tribal peoples' admission to the aishidi'tat. The bill established and funded a new open game reserve, land donated by the Taisigin Marid, the tract to be reforested on the western side, with game corridors that would improve three other hunting ranges in the direction of the Edi lands *and* the Marid.

The bill included restoration of species drawn from the other shore of the Marid, moreover, which was another popular new notion in various quarters—bringing certain trees and shrubs back to regions where they had once flourished.

Free land, a new spirit of cooperation from the Taisigin Marid, and a wide-reaching ecological repair. Those were attractive notions to party leaders on both sides of politics—especially when the more suspicious conservatives, in favor of all lordly prerogatives across the board, had had the aiji-dowager pushing them to approve the measure. Well, as Tatiseigi expressed the conservative sentiment, the entire forestry program would probably not be *too* high a financial cost to run, and, key provision, it improved the hunting, which improved the economy, which improved local chances of peace. Atevi might farm grain and vegetables, might have orchards, might run a business like egg-gathering, and fishing—but everything was seasonal. Wild game was how districts put autumn meat on the table—huge tracts given over to nature, and hunting.

Bren had cast his vote already; so had Lord Tatiseigi, both favorable to the measure. Not infrequently their votes cancelled each other out; but today they happily agreed.

And they had tea together.

"Did the youngsters seem sad to leave?" Tatiseigi asked.

"Indeed, nandi. They will miss the young gentleman."

"One observed that they seemed sad to leave Tirnamardi."

The old man was justifiably proud of his estate, his collection, his stables.

"They were delighted by Tirnamardi, nandi. They were entirely delighted, and there could be no better place in the world to show them so much of history and art. They will certainly never forget that first experience of your collection, so long as they live."

Tatiseigi cleared his throat. "Well, well, perhaps we shall find time to host them next year."

Now, that was the most unlikely thing in the world, that Tatiseigi should not only tolerate the youngsters, but miss them and court their return. The childless lord had demonstrated an unexpected soft spot for children—even, it turned out, human ones.

"Nothing would please them more," Bren said. One suspected it was as much Tirnamardi's lawns and open spaces the children regretted, as the baroque and gilt of the Bujavid's great halls, or the collections of antiques and pottery—but so had Tatiseigi delighted them, personally. "They will miss you, too, nandi, one strongly suspects. They greatly enjoyed your stories."

A second clearing of the throat. "Well, well, the staff certainly was charmed. They have inquired repeatedly after the children's well-being."

Not Lord Tatiseigi, himself, oh, no, not possibly would Lord Tatiseigi personally miss a handful of human kids.

He had messaged Tabini, spoken to him once since his return—a pleasant conversation in Tabini's downstairs office, and the topic had, beyond the Tillington matter, mostly been on operational matters and the legislative session.

But in his *second* such session with Tabini, after the vote on the forestry bill, and in Tabini's sitting room, Tabini asked a more direct question:

"You just have exchanged letters and messages with the Presidenta." Tabini's information-gathering was markedly improved, since he had taken the dowager's men as his security. "Does it regard the administrative matter you mentioned?"

One never knew, sitting down with Tabini, where a conversation might go.

"It does, aiji-ma. Tillington, and the Presidenta's search for a resolution of the Reunioner situation, which is at the heart of the problems aloft. I have expressed quite firmly that the Reunioners must be counted toward the treaty balance, whether at this station or any yet unbuilt. The Presidenta is inclining to oppose the creation of a Maudit colony at all, and may be leaning toward bringing them down to Mospheira. But that solution would have to involve a very few at a time: there just is not room in the shuttle schedule, even with the Mospheirans increasing their fleet. It cannot be any faster."

"These children? Their families?"

"One would not press for them to take priority without your direction, aiji-ma, and the matter is only theoretical. Should you wish them brought down first, however—the Presidenta would, I am sure, agree—even as a case separate from a general resolution. But politics—as usual, aiji-ma, politics will complicate any actual decision." A deep breath, a decision. "The *Heritage Party* is not entirely dead, aiji-ma, and the Presidenta has no wish to see them find a foothold in this case."

"And you will entangle yourself in these affairs?" The pleasant casualness faded. Became a frown. "For whom are you paidhi—when you go up to the station?"

He was caught unawares by that question. It was a fair one. "For you, aiji-ma," he said. "One begins to feel one does not know all one should know, aiji-ma, to give good advice. I have become uneasy in my understanding of politics aloft. And I cannot advise to any good advantage without better information. If I can, in the process, *solve* a problem—"

How much dare he say? How much *should* he say?

"Clearly you are troubled, paidhi."

"I cannot advise without knowledge. And that is my office. I ask your patience, aiji-ma, while I try to understand the politics which may be forming around the Reunioner issue. One does not wish to be caught unaware, and far less—to be advising you amiss."

"Or advising the Guild amiss."

"That, as well, aiji-ma. One would wish them to be informed—in the best way. If I and my aishid can help, understanding that the Guild advisors will be going up, I would wish, for one thing, your appointment to go with them, and mediate for them, and advise them."

"Did you mention the new Guild office to the Presidenta?"

"No, aiji-ma. I did not. I shall, however, bring it up at an appropriate moment—with your permission."

"Tillington," Tabini said.

"*Yes,* aiji-ma. I have advised the Presidenta. I have urged action."

"You believe the Presidenta *will* replace Tillington. He has the power to do this."

"Aiji-ma, he has the power to call him home, and to send a representative to fill the office until there can be a legislative approval. And I have urged him to do it rapidly, before the aishidi'tat need take any notice of Tillington's existence. I have not had his answer yet. But I hope you and he can work to relieve this situation in a good way."

Tabini gave him that flat, expressionless stare that could unnerve councilors and make lords reconsider.

"Will such provocations cease if you bring these people down to Mospheira?"

"One cannot promise that, aiji-ma, but one expects cooperation from Tillington's replacement to improve matters."

Tabini nodded. "Do not believe my grandmother lacks resources. It would be well to deal with this in utmost urgency. And do not waste your talents in lengthy politics with this man. I have other uses for you."

God. He knows.

"Aiji-ma. One is grateful for your patience."

"Depose this troublesome human, paidhi. Observe the situation up there. Report to us."

"With all my energy, aiji-ma."

"If you are going up there," Tabini said, "one does foresee my son asking to go."

One did, indeed, foresee that, with no trouble at all. "I would discourage it," he said. "I cannot predict events up there. And I shall need all my resources, and all my attention, centered on dealing with this man. I do not expect resistance, but there will be tension. I would urge against it, aiji-ma."

"So would I, for reasons *here,*" Tabini said. "My son's first actions after his Investiture are under close scrutiny. It satisfied public curiosity for his young guests to attend him here, as applicants for *his* favor. For him to go to the station to visit at this stage—is quite the opposite implication. He should never be seen to attend *them.*"

"One entirely understands the difference," he said. "And I think, aiji-ma, that if you explain to the young gentleman in that way, *he* will understand."

"You have great confidence in my son."

"I think, without any flattery, aiji-ma, that your son has deserved my confidence. He will not be happy at being left behind. But he will understand, if you explain it to him."

"He will not be happy," Tabini agreed, "but this is likely the best decision. *Of course* my son could not possibly choose three young associates from Mospheira itself. Preserve these young people, paidhi. Keep them out of politics. That is a policy matter. I have signed it, I have set my seal on it. I trust that document is being conveyed to the ship-aijiin. That is absolute."

"Am I to encourage your son in his hope for another visit here?"

A moment's silence. "Oh, I think we are ultimately doomed to that event, paidhi. Not only do we have my son on his best behavior—we have my grandmother and Lord Tatiseigi on theirs. Together." Tabini drew a deep breath. "One finds it frightening. Where do you look to settle these children—if they are agreed someday to land?"

He had in no wise gotten to that question, in his thinking. Or he had, but only in the vaguest way. "As to where—I have no idea. I cannot think it would be good to have them settle on this side of the strait. They cannot be separated from their parents."

"No," Tabini said. "It would not be good at this stage. But we have a decision to make. We must either take these three away from him soon, and permanently assign them residency on the station—or allow them and all their influences from now on, such as those influences may eventually be. If these children descend to live across the straits—shall we foster this association freely? Their connections may endanger them there. That is foreseeable."

"It is, aiji-ma. One confesses it."

"We shall have to protect them, on whatever side of the strait they settle. We shall have to see to their protection, lifelong."

"One foresees that, aiji-ma."

"Thus far their influence has seen my son become compliant and polite and *patient.* We have to wonder whether the mental strain of obedience is warping his character."

Levity again. But quite serious, couching a world-affecting question.

"Do *they* wish this association, paidhi? Do these children remotely see what association with my son will cost them?"

"I do not know. I think they have some notion. And I cannot predict what pressure human politics may put on them or on their parents. Nor can I predict how strong this association may remain over time. They have a great deal of growing to do."

"We cannot predict either, paidhi. My son has yet to reach that stage when he believes he understands all philosophy and reason. Baji-naji, my grandmother has set some sense into him. But, baji-naji, we shall not be in charge of him forever, either. We can only set the course."

"I would agree, aiji-ma."

"So," Tabini said, "go up there. Shake this tree and see what falls out of its branches. Investigate the children as well. But I charge you—report, paidhi! No more of this secrecy. The Guild is approved to go up there. I could have stalled that. I might yet, if you do not wish to take the time."

"If they can observe the several matters at hand, aiji-ma, if they can observe, and learn how things are done, and *why* things are done as they are regarding humans, it may be a better education than any explanation can provide. I by no means ask to know their secrets, but if they will hear why things are done as well as what is done—it would become an asset up there."

"I shall have that understanding with them," Tabini said, "and I shall receive their reports and compare them to yours. Be sure, when I do so, it is the *Guild* I shall be testing."

8

A solitary lunch was rare. Bren's aishid was about their own business. Banichi and Algini were downstairs in the Bujavid, in conference with representatives from the Guild on matters which no longer—thank God—involved the paidhi-aiji. Decisions ricocheted from Guild Headquarters to the aiji's office, but *not* to the paidhi's personal attention. The Guild was in the process of choosing its on-station observation team—and while the paidhi-aiji was interested in the outcome, it was not his choice.

The Guild *was* consulting the few Guild members who had experience in space, both about the physical demands of the flight up, and the nature of life on the station. That was why they asked Banichi and Cenedi—who would also tell them that *mental* flexibility would be an asset; and that assassination was *not* an option outside the atevi section, and would be dimly viewed within it. The Guild served as peacemakers as well as peacekeepers and security, and *that* would be their desired function, as well as information-gathering and communication.

Tano and Jago were likewise absent from the apartment, off conferring with the dowager's staff just down the hall. Cenedi was busy with the Guild selection, but Cenedi's second-in-command Nawari had scheduled time for a conference, a last information exchange prior to the dowager's twice-delayed flight to the East.

There had just been, in Bren's schedule, and in the dowager's, two days of conferences with the Taisigi Trade Mission regarding the depth of dredging in the harbor the dowager was arranging in her district.

That issue was now settled, and there had been conferences with Geigi's team aloft, interpreting data from orbital survey. They had the details nailed down. So the aiji-dowager could now escape the city.

The paidhi-aiji had no such escape.

Shawn delayed about his answer. There was, one could imagine, difficulty.

Politics. And shuttle schedules.

If Shawn had *any* encouraging word to send him—would Shawn not have sent a courier from his side?

Was it that damned hard to pull Tillington?

What kind of political allies did the man have?

What was being argued over there, across that narrow span of water?

Or was it simply down to shuttle schedules? God knew Tillington had gone *up* on an atevi-built shuttle, though from a Mospheiran port.

Politics would likely forbid he come down that way. No, Mospheira ran its own program now. Was fiercely proud of it.

He went back to his little office, unexpectedly snagged his coat sleeve on his fingers, of all things, and settled to sand down his fingers for the second time since he had been home. Even this many days after his vacation, they were rough—from handling harness, making fires, hauling on rope, and working with canvas—and, he recalled with pleasure, uncrating the paired stained glass windows for the new dining room, then crating them back up again to await their installation.

Not that he lacked help to do that sort of work, but he greatly enjoyed working with his hands. He had used to do far more of that. Much more.

And it was amazing how quickly callus, however long ago gained, came back at the least excuse.

Alas, no need of hauling rope here or splitting wood in the Bujavid. Here, within walls, in baroque luxury, his routine required wax-smooth fingers and the fluid use of a quill pen—a quill pen, for a script highly directional, depending on the flex and edge of the natural material for its thick and thin lines.

Atevi maintained a respect for calligraphy which the advent of humans and technology had never changed. The traditional system of written correspondence remained obstinately handwritten, wax-sealed, and formal. Even casual messages generally did *not* go by computer link.

Some messages, however, *must* speed along by modern means. The Messengers' Guild, no fools, had been quick to adopt the convenience and speed of telecommunications, once such became available, so that most computer correspondence, such as letters from the space station, arrived in traditional little steel cylinders, in computer print, and under the Messengers' own seal, since a seal there must surely be!

And one such message had arrived today, at dawn, from at least one party in a position to give answers.

From Lord Geigi.

And after the usual salutation:

Regarding the Guild observers, they will be welcome. I have an excellent office in mind for them, a residency near my own. I shall be pleased to establish an official communication with whatever persons the Guild selects.

Read between the lines, paidhi. I shall want to know where they are and what they are doing, and I shall be very glad to provide them reliable staff for clerical work.

Politics and policy as usual. There would assuredly be spying.

On the matter of children's baggage, I am certainly able to provide wardrobe storage for the young people and also for Jase-aiji, who informs me that, as you say, their personal circumstances provide no space for such.

So what have you told Jase, Geigi-ji? What did you discuss?

I had a very pleasant dinner with Jase-aiji some days past and again last evening, but not yet with the children, whose parents have claimed them, quite properly jealous of their time.

Understandable.

But it's a little worrisome, all the same.

Jase-aiji assures me that in the orders issued by Captain Sabin, and in response to the aiji's official request, these three children will always have free access to reach me. I have ordered our security to admit them or any persons with them on any request, urgent or casual, and to notify me immediately, at any hour, of their arrival.

I shall issue invitations to the children and their parents for some future evening of their choosing, and look forward to hosting them, but Jase-aiji will surely advise me when will be a good time to make that gesture. He advises caution at the moment.

Jase and I had a lengthy exchange over brandy, and this renewal of association has been very enlightening.

Jase advises caution.

Caution in dealing with humans, was the likely interpretation. Caution in pushing anything. Or pushing back, if Geigi had gotten a whiff of what was going on.

Certainly Jase would have told Geigi that Tillington was coming under official displeasure. Would Jase have told Geigi all of it, told an ateva with an ateva's emotional wiring, trusting Geigi not to react in an emotional way?

Geigi might also, given a good grasp of the situation, have decided not to write to Tabini and Ilisidi on that topic, but only to him, who had sent Jase to speak to him. Logical. But, God, how convoluted could it possibly get?

Well, he should assume what needed to be said had been said aloft. But he could not reach Ilisidi at the moment and he had every suspicion both Ilisidi and Tabini knew what there was to know, in a deafening silence.

What he did reasonably need to advise Geigi of, in the workaday world, was the details of the Guild office being sent up into his territory—a significant change for Geigi, about which Jase knew nothing and could not have forewarned him. Adding two and two and two more, an action as natural as breathing for an ateva, Geigi was doubtless putting together Jase's information on massive changes in the Guild, information on the Tillington matter—and his sudden presentation of a Guild office on the station. Geigi *had* to be coming up with some very pointed questions he hesitated to ask. But unfortunately it might add up to a mistaken conclusion.

That was the downside of perpetually reading between the lines.

He didn't know Geigi's thinking. He could only try to signal that the decision to send the Guild office was due to local changes.

Ultimately he had to talk to Geigi directly. He had to signal him, however, that it was not forewarning of the assassination of the Mospheiran stationmaster.

Operationally, on his arrival up there *with* the Guild observers, there was going to be some head-butting, one could foresee it, with Geigi's bodyguard, who were *not* suddenly going to regard the new office as *their* superiors, and who, being from the southwest coast, would not have quite the seniority and political clout of the Guild observers—in the minds of the Guild observers, at least.

He had to hope for the best in that.

He also had to figure how to break a new fact of life to the human side of the station, Mospheiran *and* Reunioner, before they drew their own conclusions about the Guild presence.

The short answer for the humans would be—never deal with the Guild directly. Go to Geigi. That was the way it should theoretically work, and that was all anybody on the human side ever needed to know. How complicated that office *really* was, under that layer—just wasn't human business at this point.

And it would not, if he had anything to do with it, entail an assassination.

He wrote a short note to Geigi.

I have nothing of substance, nandi, about names, but I assure you that the Guild is attempting to become better-informed and more forward-looking than in the past, and they will greatly value any instruction you can give them.

This is an atevi matter which I have not yet explained to our partners in station operation.

Geigi would also know that once the Assassins gained an office on the station, other guilds would clamor to get a foothold in what amounted to a new atevi province in the heavens. He saw it coming, and certainly Geigi would. He could all but hear the swell of debate among the Guilds over who was to have what priority, since it would depend on space available.

Precedence by antiquity was the only criterion that would not provoke debate; and the Assassins, first up to the station, were in fact the oldest of all guilds, so at least that worked. Transportation and the Scholars were the most directly involved with the station. The Messengers—*there* was going to be a lively discussion, in a community intimately linked to computer communications. If they went by seniority, the Messengers would take a place in line behind Transportation and the Builders. But they would argue. Passionately.

Geigi could well figure that a riotous tide was coming in and details were going to have to be worked out.

Tabini was the one to moderate the Guilds—including the requests to go to space. The paidhi-aiji did not have that thankless job, though Banichi and Algini were discussing things downstairs with officers of the Assassins' Guild at the moment. They likely *would* consult Tabini next—which was the way it ought to be.

Major changes are occurring and regional offices are being recognized in many guilds. This will place this office under your able supervision over procedures and associational boundaries. I have every confidence you will be pleased.

I look forward to our meeting with great anticipation.

That should relieve Geigi's apprehensions.

He was watching the atevi shuttle schedule, with the notion that Shawn was likely watching it, too, watching both shuttle schedules, not wanting news to arrive ahead of a replacement, not wanting to advertise their intentions, not wanting to stir up debate in what, at least on an emergency basis, could be done by decree.

And where it came to *his* schedule, there was one final problem before he could insert himself and his aishid into the shuttle schedule.

That problem's name was, as the dowager had said, Topari.

With deep resolution, he leaned forward, shook back his lace cuffs, and uncapped the inkpot. He positioned a new piece of paper on his desk and set the bridge on which the hand rested.

A Ragi document, this time.

Bren Cameron, paidhi-aiji, Lord of the Heavens, Lord of Najida

To Topari, Lord of Hasjuran, of Halrun in the Southern Mountains

Salutations.

From correspondence with Geigi, to a very formal letter to the lord of a weather-worn little train station, a highly diffuse population of less than seven thousand, and a ruling clan of about thirty-five people, whose land just happened to sit astride the only sizeable flat spot in the southern mountains.

We would be pleased if you would share our dinner table two days hence.

We shall be inviting your brother lords of the district as well—

He wrote it in the most florid calligraphy he could muster, and added the proper titles for the lords of the little mountain association, in absolute exactitude, before he gave it a ribbon and seal.

Two days' grace would let Lord Topari and his neighbors hold whatever conference in advance they needed, let these rustic lords find the right wardrobe for formal dinner with the paidhi-aiji, and let them actually *get* to Shejidan if they had chanced to be at home in the mountains when they received their invitations, as could well be the case. He tried to impose sufficient burden of formality on them that would let them feel the weight of his office, impress on them the importance of his good opinion, leave them limited time to get an agenda together—and still manage to have them in a good mood when they arrived.

He wanted to deal with the railroad problems all in one group. He wanted to ply them all with food and wine and lay them out a fair and attractive proposal as a group before he dealt with Lord Topari in private—and, God! he so fervently wished he and his aishid had gone with the aiji-dowager to Malguri, instead.

She sat in her mountain fastness clear at the other end of the continent, where even a phone was a rarity—though it was not the case with her security office. *She* didn't have a shuttle schedule to think about.

Lord Tatiseigi was headed for his estate at Tirnamardi tomorrow, having finished his work.

They were both leaving him to mop up. The essential major bills had sped through the legislature and they were off to deal with their own local problems.

He had his dinner party with the mountain lords.

And a railroad deal of great importance to the dowager's trade proposal with the Marid hanging in the balance.

9

The dinner party small talk was, alas, and as Bren had feared, an indelicate series of business questions insinuated at table, and the affair extended into completely blunt questions during brandy afterward.

But one could consider it a moderate success.

Far too much brandy proved to be the answer. When voices rose and the objections of private interest became wildly unreasonable, Bren signaled and staff kept pouring until the conversation descended to incoherency, and sober bodyguards—two apiece—took the befuddled guests safely down to the Bujavid train station and back to their hotel, probably confused as to whether a deal had been made.

Lord Topari's enthusiasm for the project had, however, only increased. *He* was the one who had begun a heated argument with his neighbors and—in Lord Topari's evident opinion—subordinates, and he had seemed to be winning his points. That the argument might continue back at the hotel seemed very likely.

Twice in the days following the dinner party, Lord Topari positioned himself beside the only door of the Transportation Committee conference room, to pounce when Bren exited the committee meeting, wanting this and that addition to the agreement.

Two four-man bodyguards stood at right angles to such encounters, one Guild-trained, the other composed of leather-clad high country hunters armed with pieces of, Banichi said dryly, a caliber hard to come by in Shejidan's shops.

"Have you heard from the aiji-dowager?" was the daily refrain, referring to Lord Topari's new requests: he wanted to extend roads from *his* domain into those of his neighbors, making the rail station in *his* district the center of a hitherto primitive transportation network.

It was not an unreasonable notion. It was even desirable—but a road was still a lower priority, a matter to be dealt with once the station itself was approved and underway. It was, however, a moment at which Topari had gotten the agreement of his neighbors—and Topari wanted the matter included and attached to railroad finance in the original proposal.

Topari might act the country novice, but he wisely wanted an agreement set in stone, sealed, filed in the national archive, and the agreement removed from his local politics, so that his neighbors could not change their minds.

"I have something for you, indeed," Bren was able to say, finally. He had anticipated the encounter, and had a member of his secretarial office in attendance *with* a set of papers. He smiled, showed Topari into the now-vacant conference room, and beckoned the young man with the briefcase.

The young man set it on the table, opened it, and drew out five, fortunate five packets, laying them in a fan on the table.

"For each district affected," Bren said with some satisfaction in his handiwork, "indeed, nandi, anticipating that we *might* meet today, I have prepared a plan, *with* the requested road work, and there will be an adequate warehouse, *and* a Transportation Guild establishment in the station. You recall—"

"Foreigners are not acceptable!" was Topari's immediate and negative response.

"Ah, but the Transportation Guild, in agreement with other changes going on within *all* the guilds, *will* recognize your local offices. Representatives of that guild will induct five local residents, one from each of your districts, train them, and then assist them to train other candidates for their guild, setting up a model establishment for others—completely local—to be set up in other districts across the Southern Mountains and southward into the Marid. The original representatives will return to Shejidan when training is complete, leaving your own people in absolute authority over operations at your station. And this office is budgeted in *with* the road-building, to be sure of that standard you ask."

Local authority would be indoctrinated, trained, educated, and bound by Transportation Guild standards, regulations, and procedures—including road width. It was a training process that might take years, but he neglected to mention that. He pointed out for the lord, who was not adept with legal language, the salient points of the agreement.

"Local control," he said, pointing to a paragraph of fine calligraphy. "Local authority—in your office, which will be the first and senior Transportation Guild office in the district, supervising all offices that later exist. You will have complete local control, and there will be no running to Shejidan for approval for matters involving the rail in your district. Your rail center will communicate decisions to subordinate stations, which *you* may decide to set up, or not. Your rail center will become, in fact, a central office."

"Central of what?"

"Of whatever you instruct them to be, nandi. As the foremost clan of your local association, and as lord of the territory where the rail office is located, you may choose to negotiate a Transportation office in each of your member districts, but one assumes you will choose to keep the *regional* Guild office in your rail center, bound together by the several roads."

He could see the glitter in Lord Topari's eyes.

"They will be in direct communication with Transportation Guild Headquarters here in Shejidan, so you can be confident any matters *you* deem important enough to report will go straight to the highest level of the Transportation Guild in Shejidan, at the speed of modern communications—that is to say, instantly. And your report will go from them to the aiji, should there be any problem they cannot resolve. Any of your neighbors' difficulties will be routed to your *local* office before being relayed to Shejidan."

Topari listened to that, and his eyes began to sparkle. "Direct from Halrun to Shejidan."

"At a simple phone call," Bren said. "As will be the case, of course, with any other guilds you yourself deem useful to your district. Establish a local office in your district, and establish minor offices reporting to it from other members of your association, and you will be the center of such operations. One would recommend that the Builders' Guild be among the first to operate on that level. Likewise the Trade Guild might be useful to you. I see that you are amply defended by your bodyguard. But perhaps the Treasurers would be useful, to be sure every report and record is proper and to the established standard. Many districts have found the Treasurers a great convenience, eliminating any confusion about accounts."

"We are not on the gold standard!"

"Absolutely," he said. Topari's folk, poor in that resource, dealt in a mishmash of equivalencies and direct barter of everything from furs to foodstuffs. "Which is all the more reason to have *your own local people* in the Treasurers' Guild, trained to deal with exchanges, knowledgeable enough to agree on fair values locally—and to be certain your standards are being observed when the value of items is translated to Shejidani currency."

A worried and calculating look. "*One* of my associates will not favor that."

"Each may have whatever offices he wishes to admit, under your authority—though of course if they want the full advantage of the system—ultimately—they all *must* deal with the offices in your district, nandi. It will be an advantage to them to have their offices directly connected to the rail office, and to the warehouses we shall build there; and to have them on site where the goods meet the rail in Halrun. So perhaps your lone objector will find the system to his advantage after all, as the operation progresses and profits flow. One is certain he will not want to be left out of your road system—and when he finds that your commerce is proceeding without delays and inquiries, he may wish to participate. Meanwhile your station will gain from rapid processing of exchanges, and if Halrun makes it most convenient for traders, Halrun will get the most benefits. Fortune and geography have settled a great benefit on your home district, nandi, and, as a coastal lord, I can add that with the improvement of the Najida spur, as the dowager and Lord Machigi intend, you will find those warehouses full of goods going not only north-south, but also coming up from the west coast. And of course your local products will always have direct shipment to the Marid and the west coast, rather than going down to Shejidan for packaging and shipping. Your district will derive a fee from goods in storage in those warehouses—fees which have hitherto gone to Shejidan. An efficient operation in your district, perhaps with additional warehouses, as lords become aware of the advantage of a central distribution point, can be very, very profitable."

"*Excellent* creature!" Lord Topari exclaimed. "*Excellently* done!"

And Topari was out the door and off down the hall with his guard.

Bren drew a deep breath, aware of his own aishid around him, doubtless suppressing the strong desire to open fire.

"Nadiin-ji," he said, choosing amusement, and experiencing a certain satisfaction, "your restraint is admirable."

"You have inserted an Assassins' Guild office into that territory," Banichi said, in that dry tonc of on-duty humor. "Manners must soon follow."

"*Creature!*" Jago repeated.

"Views will change," Bren said, "slowly. The man may even realize his slip—and worry about it later. Or his guard may."

"It is important his guard know the problem, however," Algini said, and Banichi nodded.

"Indeed," Banichi said. "Tano."

Tano left their company on his own mission, to pass a word to Topari's bodyguard, namely that the paidhi had magnanimously forgiven the small slip in protocol, but that the paidhi's guard strongly suggested that a reconsideration of vocabulary in private might prevent future incidents in public—lest he make that reference in the hearing of the aiji-dowager, or with some of the more conservative lords.

"A good lunch at home," Bren said quietly, and started the three walking toward the main hall and the lifts.

The dispersing committee had long since moved on, thank God.

And attitudes toward humans *had* shifted to the positive during his tenure. Attitudes were still shifting, penetrating areas they had never reached. And change was now reaching the mountains, or Topari would not be dealing with him in the first place. Attitudes would change. A moderation of the language would follow. *Excellent creature* was already relatively benign as a description.

"I have concluded," he remarked to his aishid in the privacy of the lift, "that Topari is, whatever his faults, an *honest* fellow."

"But he is still a fool," Banichi said, which was, unfortunately, true. And because he was a fool, unfortunate things would continue to happen in Lord Topari's dealings with the great and powerful of the aishidi'tat.

The best they could do for Topari as a political ally was to insulate him, keep him safe in his mountains, between small experiences of the larger world, and keep him happy to *be* in his mountains. Of all the several mountain lords who could rise to head that association—Topari, who had the exploitable advantage of that tiny wide spot in the mountains, was also the most adventurous, the most willing to brave the modern world and its ways, and equally likely, Bren surmised, he was the one lord the others agreed couldn't tell them a lie.

It was a time of opportunity in the aishidi'tat, a time of opportunity that a brave few were beginning to recognize. The shakeup in the Assassins' Guild was proliferating scarily fast through other guilds, which had felt the pressure regarding regional guilds for decades and staved it off, saying there was no way to change the system. Things were suddenly possible that had not been possible since the foundation of the aishidi'tat.

Which was all the more reason to couple the Assassins' move to space with his trip up to the station, and give that ancient guild a little peaceful time to settle in and learn the environment, so they could advise and temper the guilds that would come up behind them.

The new Guild office on the space station—which would quickly have to understand an array of technical issues and precautions—was part of a very large picture indeed.

Change was coming, and if they could just achieve internal peace long enough to see it all work, they were going to knit the Marid, the East, and the southern coast into the Western Association—and now the station—in a way that Tabini's predecessors had only dreamed of doing.

Boundaries had always been vague in the atevi world. A common language across the continent, local trade and intermarriages and leaders based on that biological determiner, man'chi, worked against such absolutes. The formation of the aishidi'tat had fundamentally shifted that balance with a vast number of independent clans recognizing a central authority, the aiji. Man'chi, yes, was involved, but laws and the new guild systems reinforced that union, providing regularized commerce, communication—and peacekeeping based on efficiency and surgical precision, not numbers and brute force.

The aishidi'tat became a thing apart . . . until the marriage contract between Tabini's grandfather and Ilisidi brought the Eastern Association into an uneasy alliance, and the boundaries began to blur once more. Thanks to recent efforts, those boundaries might soon all but disappear, as the political leaders of these four highly independent regions recognized the benefits of cooperation, and sought a compromise of Guild structure that would enhance their strengths and minimize their vulnerabilities.

The real change wrought since Tabini's return to power was not in boundaries. It was in the lines of *control* that had, from the outset of the Western Association, centered so rigidly in the capital, in the form of the Assassin's Guild. In the earliest days of the aishidi'tat, clan loyalty had made unity impossible. But arising from, of all things, the building of a railroad, guilds arose that transcended clan interests, that demanded man'chi to themselves, to the aishidi'tat, and ultimately to the aijinate. The Assassins were the first, the oldest of guilds—taking in applicants from any clan, but insisting on man'chi to itself and renunciation of any other loyalty. The Assassins assigned bodyguards to various leaders they wanted to protect . . . and removed those they wanted out. And the aiji in Shejidan, by one move and another, sheltered them, used them, bestowed their services on those *he* wanted to survive.

It had, in effect, *built* the aishidi'tat. But it could only build it so far—among clans of the midlands culture, the Ragi, who spread their power as far as the mountains and the sea.

Beyond that, in the generations since, other associations created their own such forces, and other guilds, paying allegiance, for reasons of politics, to the Shejidani guilds, but always excluded from the highest offices, and from power.

But the oldest of guilds, the Assassins' Guild, retained the notion that it had created the aijinate and the aishidi'tat—and held that it could re-create it, should an aiji lose the Assassins' man'chi.

And when Tabini had allied himself with humans, and began

to site industry in some provinces and not in others, when he pressed ambitious building programs, some elements within the Assassins' Guild began to move assets on their own, bent on setting another aiji in power, one who would take their orders, follow their programs, and purge anyone who opposed them.

When it was clear that Tabini-aiji had positioned his heir and the aiji-dowager out of their reach, the shadow elements within the Assassins' Guild moved to kill him and set their own man in office.

Several things saved the aishidi'tat: the move Tabini had made, getting important people out of reach; the loyalty of senior Guild who quickly retired or disappeared, who began to work with the Mospheirans *and* with Geigi, up on the station; and the independence of the stepchild guilds, the regional guilds, whose attachment to clan and region, hitherto viewed as unfitness—held them steady in their opposition to the coup and their refusal to accept the new aiji.

The scattered edges of power had fought to get control of the Guild back into their hands, and to restore Tabini to office.

And now the Guild, restored, looked far more kindly on the regional branches—which served both Geigi *and* Ilisidi, which had just rescued the government. Now a third region asserted itself, the Marid, whose principle reason for rebelling from the aishidi'tat was the matter of regional guilds.

The rules changes the Assassins' Guild were working on would beget a hierarchy of subordinate field offices, still controlled from the capital, but each with a certain local latitude for the unique issues the local office understood.

And they were going, according to Ilisidi, to Cenedi for advice.

Cenedi, notoriously regional, and backing, in the aiji-dowager, the second greatest power in the aishidi'tat.

And the Shadow Guild, that rogue splinter group off the Assassins, which had directed the coup against Tabini, was, one hoped, no longer able to have its way in anything.

If it had leaders still alive.

As for the issue of too much modernity and the space program, the new Guild leadership was, Jago said, computerizing Assignments and records-keeping, so that one clerk could not control a system his superiors could not access. That was a revolution in itself.

Other guilds were making similar changes.

The very air in the capital began to feel freer and safer for the changes underway. The revised Guild systems would be less centered in the capital, but paradoxically, the regional lords—the truly powerful lords of the aishidi'tat, who had maintained these somewhat illegal splinters of the traditional guilds under *their* close supervision, would be drawn *closer to* the aijinate.

It all was proceeding apace, disturbing some guilds and some lords, pleasing others.

Oddest result of that tangled Guild housekeeping, the paidhi's bodyguard, all western, all trained in the Shejidani Guild, ranked next to the dowager's. Banichi's and Jago's assignment to the household of the paidhi-aiji had started back when Tabini had been keeping a suspicious eye on him—and one of the first things Banichi had done was to hand him a very illegal gun.

At whose order? To this day, he had no idea.

Then Tano and Algini had arrived. Bren had no idea what Algini's rank actually was, but he had a definite knowledge of the inner workings of the Shejidani Guild—and Bren held more than a slight suspicion that the Guild had assigned Algini to Tabini originally to keep an eye on Tabini's doings. But Tabini had promptly shunted Algini and his partner Tano over to Banichi's unit, possibly as a way of rebuking the Guild—or even of giving the Guild close access to the paidhi-aiji's doings, and answering questions before they were asked.

Now Guild leadership realized it was in their interests to work directly with Lord Geigi—who had yet another regional-guild situation in his establishment, in a Guild unit that had ended up directing atevi operations on the space station.

And they were asking the paidhi-aiji's aishid for advice on who to send up there.

Oh, yes, things in the aishidi'tat were changing.

Changing too fast for stability? He hoped not.

Now he had to make a decision of his own. He had upcoming committee meetings he was scheduled to attend. He had Lord Tatiseigi coming back to the capital for one of them. He had asked Shawn to fire the current Mospheiran stationmaster. He had to pick an upcoming shuttle launch and make arrangements.

Days had passed, and he had *not* gotten a response from Shawn, not found out whether Shawn was arranging to put the brakes on Tillington, or whether there was something preventing it. He'd hoped for a quick answer. The fact it had not been quick—said there might well be problems.

And he had to decide whether to involve himself in Mospheiran politics, or leave it totally to Shawn. There were sources he could tap . . . but he hesitated to do it and possibly stir things up that might further complicate the situation.

God, he wished he knew. If getting Shawn to move against Tillington was asking too much of Shawn or if it put Shawn in political danger—that worried him almost as much as the situation on the station. And he might need to hasten his own trip up there, to start the matter into motion.

There was a shuttle preparing to launch in a few days. The Guild team wasn't altogether ready to go up on this one; he wasn't ready, either. He only now had time to clear the decks and make plans.

But he did need to send to the Port Director and advise her they would be asking for the smallest of the passenger compartments on the next shuttle after this one. That let the Port Director shift cargo priorities about, to make sure that bulky cargo had room and that critical cargo still moved. There was still time to make adjustments, but he had to make his mind up and set a date.

That meant of all people he had not yet notified—the Port Director was definitely coming into need-to-know. Theoretically he could even launch from Mospheira under extreme emergency, the Mospheiran launch usually coming five days after this particular shuttle's launch, with their single shuttle—but with the politics involved— no, he didn't want to consider that option. He *hoped* Shawn had plans for somebody to be on that shuttle. But maybe the best thing to do was to get up there.

Time to call the Port Director.

Today.

But that was—

They stepped off the lift to a boom so loud he stopped in alarm, instantly thinking of an explosion of some sort in the building.

"Thunder," Banichi said, amused at him.

He was amazed. Then he laughed and felt foolish They lived sealed so deep inside the Bujavid he could lose all notion of sunrise and sunset. And he'd been buried so deep in work, he'd paid no attention. "One takes it we are having weather out in the world?"

"A strong front," Jago said cheerfully. "And fast-moving. We had an advisement from Najida last night. They are secure and battened down, and they were able to get the gable end closed and the tiles in place."

"Excellent, that." A second thump from the heavens sounded much more like thunder—but loud. It was unusual to hear it inside the Bujavid's central halls, let alone feel it.

"Storms have spread all the way to Tirnamardi," Jago said, "and reached as far south as Separti Township. The front has blown past the coast now, but the midlands are due a soaking."

Weather that came across the straits and up from the southwest often came in with truly major force, and the thunder said this was one of those storms. He wished his apartment owned windows to fling open—to smell the rain, watch the lightning, feel the wind.

But he owned no windows to fling open, and it was a quiet afternoon of office work he had planned, letter-writing, mostly.

Cajeiri, he imagined, would have darted for his own apartment's windows, drinking it all in.

Thunder.

Cajeiri's aishid was off having lessons. Boji had been misbehaving all morning, bouncing about his cage, knocking his water askew and making a puddle. Eisi had been putting the water bottle to rights, when the boom hit, and with that boom, Boji—

Boji had flown out past Eisi's arm, up a hanging and up atop the rod of a tapestry.

Now he was perched up there on the rod, above everything but the chandelier, screaming his disapproval of the storm.

"Boji," Cajeiri said sternly. "Come." He held out his arm, patted it.

He could get Boji to come to that summons—sometimes.

Second big boom.

Boji flew across the room, wild-eyed, scrambling atop the buffet, his nails endangering the ancient wood.

And the sitting room door opened.

"No!" Cajeiri shouted. *"Shut the door!"*

He could hear his sister screaming in the distance. Boji shrieked and leapt from the buffet to the cage roof.

Eisi caught Boji by the leg, and Boji bit him.

Eisi yelled and Boji escaped, this time running in huge leaps back to the bedroom.

Eisi was bleeding, Boji was still screaming, the door was still open, and *Mother* was standing in the doorway. She stepped into the room and shut the door at her back.

"Honored Mother," Cajeiri said, appalled. He sketched a little bow. So did Eisi.

A furious shriek sounded from inside the bedroom. Liedi came out, holding Boji by the nape of his neck. Boji struggled, waving his arms and kicking, showing white substantial fangs and the whites of his eyes and hissing like a teakettle.

Eisi held the cage door open. Liedi put Boji in and shut it, fast.

"Your servant is bleeding," Mother said.

Eisi's hand was dripping and Eisi was trying to contain the drip to keep it off the carpet. "Please go to the kitchen, nadiin-ji," he said, and Eisi and Liedi quietly bowed and went back into the bedroom, where a servant's passage offered a route to bandages that did not lead past Mother.

Boji went on rattling his cage and bouncing and screeching.

"One regrets the noise, honored Mother."

"Is this the *normal* operation of your household, son of mine?"

"No, honored Mother."

Thunder continued to rumble.

"Lighting has hit the Bujavid roof. One thought you might be alarmed."

He made a very deep bow, trying to be a little touched that his mother had thought of him—but suspecting there was a hostile reason in her visit, likely involving his sister. There was always a reason, usually involving his sister. And if the roof were afire from that lightning strike, he was sure he would not be his mother's first concern.

There was one sure distraction for her. He had found that out. "Is Seimiro safe?" he asked.

"Indeed. Beha is with her. And there is no danger. There may have been a little damage to the roof, but nothing that need concern us."

"One is glad," he said, ducking his head, still mistrusting the visit. "Thank you, honored Mother, and one regrets the commotion. Boji is not usually like this. He had overset his water when the big boom came. We were working with that, his door was open, and the thunder came again—"

"What are you hiding, son of mine? Did he bite you?"

He had his hands behind his back. He had not even been conscious of it. But he brought them forward reluctantly, showing his right cuff lace sadly ink-stained, and wrapped in a handkerchief, and, he suddenly feared hiding the fact that he had just distributed still-wet ink to the back of his coat.

"The thunder," he said. "I was doing my lessons, honored Mother. The ink spilled."

"Commendable, regarding the lessons. But what else was ruined? Let me see your coat. Turn."

He turned, obediently, and turning full about, saw the answer in his mother's frown.

"That will never come out."

"One deeply regrets, honored Mother. One thought—"

"One thought?"

He had thought better of saying it, but found nowhere to go from there. "One thought for an instant it was artillery, honored Mother."

His mother gave him that flat, unexpressive stare that might be disapproval. Or not. "We know," she said. "Your father and I know. Such times these are, that my son thinks of such a thing! Did any get on the carpet?"

"No. No, honored Mother. It was a puddle on the desk. I mopped it and blocked it off with my handkerchief, but it reached the cuff. Nothing dripped, however." He carefully unfolded his balled-up handkerchief, showing the limit of the damage, which was not much—except to his cuff lace and his coat.

"And why are your valets not seeing to your shirt?"

"Because my aishid is off at training, honored Mother, and my valets were catching Boji."

"Such a household!"

"If my aishid were here, indeed they would have helped, honored Mother! But Boji was loose and we had to catch him."

There was a moment of silence, and slowly, silently, his mother nodded, with just a hint of amusement.

"*There* is my son," she said. "I have not seen him in some time."

She confused him—except that her jealousy of Great-grandmother was extreme, and constant, and colored everything between them. He took a chance, and answered back, just a little shaken, but what Great-grandmother would call *pert.* "And I also see my mother," he said with another bow. "One is very glad of it."

"*Her* manners."

"No, honored Mother. *My* manners. One is very glad you came. *Thank* you for coming to be sure I was all right." He piled another pertness atop it all, but he meant it. "I would be happy if you would sit and take tea. Eisi will be back in a moment."

"Oh, you keep glorious state here, do you? We should not repair to the sitting room, safe from wild creatures and ink?"

"The sitting room is my father's sitting room. This is mine. *My* apartment."

"Your suite of rooms."

"Yes," he said, maintaining a level stare. It was not his intention to argue with her. "It is just a suite. But my staff is good. And if you would like tea, I can make it myself."

"With such hands?"

He wiped his hands with the better side of the stained handkerchief. "I can."

"Then I would, indeed," Mother said with a faint smile, "take a cup of tea." That somewhat surprised him. He went to arrange the chairs—and remembering his dirty hands and still-damp cuff, he refrained from touching the fabric, and wiped the wood with his elbow where he touched it. He carefully arranged two cups, opened the tea canister and added tea to the ceramic strainer, then filled the pot from the spigot of the antique samovar, trying not to fingerprint it. His mother adjusted the chairs herself and took a seat—having inspected the chairs for ink. He set the pot and cups on the tray and added the sugar caddy. His mother preferred sweet tea.

He took the tray to the side table, and carefully served her cup, just as Liedi came hurrying back from the rear of the suite to take over.

"Thank you, Liedi-ji," he said quietly. "Is Eisi all right?"

"He is very well, nandi," Liedi said quietly, and offered the first cup to Mother, who took it with a careful smile. Cajeiri took the second, and Liedi slipped out of the way. Boji began to set up another fuss, but Liedi had wisely brought an egg from the kitchen.

"That is the *hungriest* creature I have ever seen," his mother said.

"He will always behave for an egg," he said. "He really will do no real damage when he gets loose. He only bites if you take hold of him by surprise. And he will come to me, most times."

"He has an aroma."

"He bathes every day. We bring water, and put down towels, and he washes himself."

"Well, that is a good habit," Mother said, with a sip of tea. Thunder rumbled again, and Boji, in his cage, looked up nervously toward the ceiling. "Such a storm. Your father is in a meeting downstairs. One believes his guard will have told him we have been struck by lightning."

"But we are safe," he said. It was a question.

"Oh, one is very sure," Mother said, and then, pensively: "You were away on the ship for two years. While we were in hiding, there was a storm, a very bad one. Your father and I were sleeping in a storage shed. And the roof leaked. Then half the roof fell in on us, midway through the night."

He was not sure he should laugh. His mother and his father had had Shadow Guild hunting them during that time and it had been very grim. "What did you do?"

"There was nothing we *could* do," Mother said with remarkable cheerfulness. "We sat there. We could see the clouds and the lightning through the hole. But we doubted we would catch fire if we were hit. We were too wet."

He still wasn't sure whether he was supposed to laugh. Mother was like that.

"We had no breakfast either," his mother said more somberly, taking a bit more tea. "I shall always remember that morning. I have never been more miserable than that night. But we were very glad to see the sun."

It was the first story he had heard from his mother or his father about the days when he had been away on the ship and his mother and father had been hiding in hedgerows. Everybody in the Bujavid apartment *except* his mother and father had eventually been killed.

From those years forward he had attached man'chi very strongly to his great-grandmother, and also to his father, but not so keenly. His mother—

He had lost her, he thought distressedly. He had lost her when he had left the world. And she had been with his father, while both of them were being hunted through the north.

But he had missed all that.

Why *did* you come this morning? he wanted to know. But he was afraid to ask. It was too close to a challenge, and he did not challenge his mother.

There was a smaller peal of thunder.

Why are you here instead of with my sister? he wanted to ask. What do you want?

But that was a challenge, too. He found nothing he dared ask. Thunder boomed, distant and retreating. And he saw a brushy hill in his memory. And Najida's lower hall.

"The thunder makes a noise and Seimiro frets and goes back to sleep," his mother said. "She has no understanding of it. My son sees fire and smoke. And feels shells landing."

He looked at her, disturbed. "It does sound a little like that."

"Is that so?" she asked him. "Is that what you hear in the thunder?"

"Yes," he admitted, disturbed, and tried not to let the inky cuff-lace touch the cup. "Yes, honored Mother."

"One thought so," his mother said, and took a sip of tea.

She was *different* than Great-grandmother. A great deal different. He had no idea what she wanted.

"An attack would sound like that," his mother said. "Is that what you thought?"

"One did," he said, "For an instant."

"So," his mother said. "So did I. For an instant. We have that in common, son of mine. We have both heard guns in the distance. We have both seen things we wish not to have seen. And your father is in a meeting and your bodyguard is at training. So I thought, My son might find a visit just now—comfortable."

He was not comfortable. He had had Boji loose, he had ruined a shirt *and* a coat. He had put inky fingerprints on the tea-caddy, and the teapot, and might have inked his trousers as well—not to mention the chair arm, where he was doggedly remembering not to set his hand down.

"One greatly regrets the accident, honored Mother." Boji would not stay quiet. Boji had finished his egg, and was now becoming a nuisance, rattling his cage.

"Thunder," Mother said. "Just thunder. The coat is not your best one. The ink missed the carpet, did it not?"

"It did, honored Mother." It was the second time Mother had asked that, and she didn't make that sort of mistake. He wondered if there *was* a spot. "It never got to the edge."

"So," Mother said, and set down her teacup. "The storm seems to have gone over us. I shall go back to your sister—so long as you are well."

She rose. He set aside his teacup, stood up and gave a little bow.

She went to the door. He hurried, before Liedi, to open it for her.

"Visit me," she said. She only lived down the hall in the same apartment. They saw each other, and Father, at breakfast and lunch and supper, every mealtime since he had gotten home. It was strange to say, *Visit me.* But he felt it as a very solemn invitation.

"I shall," he said. She left, and he shut the door.

His fingers had smudged the white paint near the door latch. He thought about rubbing the mark off, but that cuff was what had done it. He used the other elbow, the coat being beyond salvage anyway, then walked back to his room to change clothes.

A second thunderstorm came rolling in half an hour after the first, with thumps that Bren swore all but made ripples in his teacup, even within the thick walls of the Bujavid.

Lightning had hit a pole and dislodged some tiles from the Bujavid roof, which rather well accounted for the initial boom. A work crew was up there assessing the damage from the inside. He thought they could have rather well waited in case of another strike—and he hoped they had run for cover as the second wave rolled in.

A report from Jeladi said that there was a handspan of water on the rails near the Guild District, by the old canal.

Power had been out for a bit in the east end of Shejidan, again due to a lightning strike.

Najida had gotten its share of rain from this system, Bren was sure. And the assurance the workmen had gotten the new wing roof sealed was good. He just hoped *Jaishan* was safe at dock and not in transit with the peninsula and its rocks alee.

The winds of an ordinary spring met summer and did ritual battle. It was a rhythm old as the hills—literally. And it was a warm and comfortable thing to have the city's most solid walls between him and the storm.

He'd had lunch. Now he had those letters to write, and when the storm passed, a courier could go out to the spaceport by train, quietly, and without publicity of any kind, bearing his request for passenger space on the next shuttle after this one. He could surely manage to wrap up his business sufficiently in the next couple of weeks, and he rather hoped a quiet message had already gone up to Tillington from Shawn saying, simply, Make no statements whatever on the Reunioner matter, so that at least nothing worse would happen up there.

On his agenda, too, was a matter which achieved more significance with the Tillington matter afoot. Cajeiri had written to him this morning, a formal letter with only a few childish calligraphic shortcuts, reporting that everything was very well next door and would he *please* invite him to a dinner party soon.

But there was a second issue, and a more troubling one. Cajeiri added that he had written to his associates up on the station—and he had somewhat expected letters from his associates to come down on this current shuttle. He was worried, but he did not want to ask his father, and he felt that asking Lord Geigi would attract his father's attention.

It would. It attracted the paidhi's attention and made him ask why, a second time, was there possibly a problem with correspondence being delayed, and who was at fault?

Perhaps the children had just not written in time to get their letters included in the physical mail. But—all of them?

He was a little concerned. He had put off his answer to the young gentleman's letter this morning only because he had had the committee meeting. But he intended a serious inquiry into the possibility of missing mail, and he sincerely hoped that the answer was a simple case of the kids missing the deadline.

But—missing mail had been a problem before this. And the fact that Tillington's office was on a rampage about the children's visit and the children's ties to Cajeiri did occur to him in the question. If Tillington had taken it on himself to stop the children's letters, a call to Jase was in order, and there was one more point in his problems with Tillington, depending on whether he wanted to go up quietly—or with forewarning of official displeasure. He had to decide on that matter.

But before he made that call, he wanted details from Cajeiri, to start with facts.

That was one issue on his mind, that, the letter to the port director, and the fact that, perhaps at breakfast tomorrow, he had to break the news to the boy that *he* was going up to the station and Cajeiri wasn't. At least he could promise Cajeiri he would find the letters, if they'd been sent.

He hadn't seen the boy since he'd been back, hadn't communicated with him as he'd intended to do. He'd met with Tabini more than once, had been *in* the apartment, but the boy had evidently been told it was business and he should stay out of the way. He'd managed to talk with Ilisidi twice before she left. He'd managed to exchange a few words with Tatiseigi in the legislature before *Tatiseigi* left for his estate. He'd even exchanged a few words with Damiri.

But Cajeiri—no. Cajeiri hadn't been accessible. He'd been telling himself for days he needed to make time to check on the boy—but problems kept coming up and the schedule kept pressing on him. Now the boy had had to write a letter to tell him something he should have known about, and beg him for a breakfast invitation, poor lad, now that all his other prospects had left town.

He'd had far, far better intentions than that.

A knock came at the office door. Narani entered, bearing the message bowl with a single cylinder.

"This just arrived, nandi."

Not Shawn, which was the letter he had been waiting for. *That* would have been under Presidential seal, and in a diplomatic pouch, not a plain steel cylinder that meant the Messengers' Guild had transmitted it.

That left few possibilities. Jase. Geigi.

He reached for it and opened it, extracted and flattened the message while Narani waited for a possible response.

It was from Toby. His brother, who lived aboard his boat.

Storms in the strait, he thought instantly.

God, are he and Barb all right?

Hi there, the typescript letter began. *We're fine, that first. We took a little bit of a beating two days ago, lost the antenna and a railing, not to mention both bilge pumps, which was the greater concern. We've just limped into Najida on the manual pump and they've offered help putting things to rights. We could make it back to Port Jackson now, I'm pretty sure, now that I've located a new bilge pump—I'm going to owe a local fisherman. The front's moving past, but we're real tired, and Najida was our safest choice. We got in an hour ago, still having quite a bit of wind here. Ramaso says we should stay as long as we want, but I think officially I should ask.*

We're fine. Barb was with him. They were both all right. They'd gotten to Najida.

He just hoped the boat wasn't too badly damaged.

With your permission, we're going to be here a few days. We're likely going to do a little more repair, either locally purchased or shipped over. Ramaso says not to worry, that he'll order anything we need and put it on your tab. But I'm going to arrange a transfer of funds to cover it; we'll feel better. I don't know how to convey that to Ramaso in a way he'll understand.

You can't, brother, and it's not a language problem. Ramaso knows what I'd say about your paying anything. I'll get the fisherman a new pump.

I'd love to see you in the meanwhile. Any chance you could take the train over to Najida for a couple of days?

Oh, damn, he so wanted to do that. Did he have time? He might—if he flew, and worked on the flight to and from.

"The storm damaged nand' Toby's boat," he said to Narani, who was standing by for a reply. "Toby has put in to Najida for repairs and he asks whether I can come out there. One is very strongly tempted, Rani-ji. The trip up to the station—I have to arrange. But two days—if nothing else blows up—I could possibly spare that."

"Indeed, nandi. There are a few meetings on your schedule, but those might be rearranged. You could fly, or even take the train, and the bus could have you at Najida tonight."

"Meeting with the young gentleman. Answering his query. The committee meetings in three days. Lord Tatiseigi is coming back tomorrow. *He* could deal with the Transportation committee. He intends to be there, regardless. We absolutely agree on the issues."

"Indeed he might chair them quite ably, nandi."

God, he rarely did things on the spur of the moment, these days—or he did, but those generally regarded politics or the need for firearms. Doing something this self-interested was an entirely different prospect. He should, he thought, feel guilty for even considering going out there.

But, hell, Tatiseigi *could* deal with the meetings. And whatever Jase answered about the kids' maybe-missing letters probably should wait for him to get up to the station. He wanted to talk to Tillington, get the measure of the man, personally, maybe impart a quiet understanding as to *why* Tillington needed to go home on the next shuttle and seek a nice job in the space industry, with no damaging fuss about it. That was by far the most constructive solution.

That left the Transportation Committee and that series of meetings—which he could come in on toward the last, if Tatiseigi was there to handle the initial phase.

Narani had his orders. He personally had just a few things to mop up, now. He needed to message the Port Director, confirm that he *was* indeed taking next rotation up. He had to meet with the Guild observers, everything as previously arranged.

And if anything critical came up in the committee meetings, he could be back in Shejidan by plane in a couple of hours.

He could do it. Fly out, fly back. No need of formality or any great furor, or any fuss with the wardrobe, not for informal Najida and working on his brother's boat.

"Let me compose an official permission for his landing, Rani-ji. I shall send that before all else, just to have the legalities in order."

"Will you indeed go there, nandi?"

"I think I shall. Tomorrow. I have a letter from the young gentleman, asking for a breakfast tomorrow morning." God.

"And *he* will be entirely put out if I go to Najida without him. I shall ask his father. It might salve the matter of the *other* trip, which he cannot take. And there are phones, after all. I can call Lord Geigi and inquire about his problem from there."

"Indeed, nandi." Narani let the bowl stand on the little table by the door and quietly left.

Bren spread out a new sheet and dipped his pen in the inkwell, in rising good cheer.

I hope the damage is by no means extensive. You are of course welcome at Najida as long as you need and I shall make every effort to free my schedule. I am sending off the necessary permissions for your landing, with notice to Tabini-aiji, and the Assassins' Guild. If your schedule is flexible, too, we may be able to gain a day or so together.

If you need greater assistance of any sort, absolutely rely on me. I can locate supplies and repair items with no great difficulty at all and have them in your hands within a day or so.

Please take advantage of every resource Najida can offer for your safety and comfort meanwhile.

He hesitated at the last line. Always, always, there was politics, even within the family.

I hope that Barb is well. Give her my regards.

The letter would be physically delivered. He *could* pick up a phone and ask for direct contact, but if Toby and Barb were busy trying to bail out the yacht, he had no wish to call them up the steep hill to the phone. He simply spindled it, shoved it into one of his own official white cylinders, and rang for Narani to come back and take it. He could phone Toby tonight, perhaps, after everybody had finished for the day and had a good supper. Ramaso would see to that.

But express mail, couriered to the train, should make it by suppertime. And with luck—he could follow it after breakfast tomorrow and surprise Toby.

"To my brother," he said simply, "on the regular train."

"Nandi." Narani took it, to be carried by one of the staff, who would pack an overnight bag and make it to the main train station from the Bujavid transport stop.

Thunder boomed and crashed, the storm had done with Najida, perhaps, but it had not yet quite done with Shejidan.

And if Cajeiri was to go out to Najida with him he needed clearance from Tabini. If they flew, on a charter, it would be quick, it would be secure, and if the plane waited, he could easily get himself and the boy back to the capital within an hour of any phone call.

He pulled down another sheet of paper, deciding that, hell, yes, he *would* clear his schedule, and he would go next door and see if he could liberate the young gentleman into the bargain, perhaps for dinner this evening, and have their breakfast on the plane at the crack of dawn.

Bren, paidhi-aiji

To Tabini, aiji of the aishidi'tat

A request has arrived, aiji-ma, from Toby my brother, who has had an emergency at sea. His boat took damage from the storm, and by my prior permission, he has put in at Najida for repairs. One begs you grant him an extended stay, of whatever length repairs require.

He also requests me to come visit him there, if this is possible. I am delighted to do this and believe I can do so without adversely affecting my schedule.

It also occurs to me that the young aiji would greatly enjoy a very brief—

A knock came at the door. Narani came in, bowed, and, without the bowl, handed him a *second* steel message cylinder.

This one did not have the Mospheiran color. It was plain.

Toby being in worse trouble was his first fear—but a message from his estate manager, Ramaso, should have the blue Najida band. He opened the cylinder, extracted the message, again one of those coded prints.

And not in Ragi.

Jason Graham, Captain, starship Phoenix.

Bren Cameron, paidhi-aiji, the Bujavid.

Unicorn sighted. ETA fifteen days. Operation here as discussed.

Reply requested.

His thought—if it was so coherent as a thought—was, Oh—my—*God.*

He read it twice. Looked up at Narani and didn't trouble to keep the distress off his face.

"Rani-ji, the *kyo* are here—fifteen days out from the space station. All plans—my entire schedule—everything has to be suspended."

It was more than a question of operations *suspended.*

All manner of operations had to be gotten *underway*—many of them not confined to the Earth.

And a very dangerous set of strangers they had met at Reunion was arriving to be entangled with the problems he and Jase had been negotiating.

Tillington. And the Reunioners.

The Reunioners were going to panic when they heard. The Mospheirans might well.

He couldn't *wait* for another shuttle rotation. If he and his aishid had to ride up in the cockpit with the crew, he had to get up there.

He glanced at the calendar, in its nook on his desk. The current shuttle was launching day after tomorrow.

Narani was still waiting.

"I need to phone the Port Director, immediately, Rani-ji. I have to delay the shuttle launch, if at all possible. Call her, and let me tell her as much as she must know personally. I also need my aishid to report in, whoever is on the premises."

"Nandi." Narani left, and almost immediately after he had closed the door, footsteps went both directions down the hall. Narani was bound for his office to look up the spaceport code, likely—it was not one they routinely used; and Jeladi was likely headed deeper into the apartment, to advise his bodyguard they had a serious problem.

Fifteen days.

No trip to Najida. That was out.

Silly thought. The whole world was in danger. And he spared a thought for his brother, in dock at Najida, waiting for him, with no idea what had just shown up in the heavens.

The dowager needed to get back to Shejidan. *She* was involved in this.

He and Ilisidi likewise had a codeword for the kyo—but passing *through* Assassins' Guild communications what was clearly a codeword that the Guild was not permitted to understand, at a time when they were trying to establish trust—

He had to play *those* politics carefully. Everything involving the guilds was new and no little touchy.

He had intended the Guild observers to go up to the station with him. He had to take them now, or have them arrive later, uninformed, in the middle of a situation, to try to figure out what they had done. That, or put them off indefinitely.

Tabini needed to know what was going on, immediately.

It was a nightmare. A damned nightmare, unplanned, unstoppable.

Jase and Sabin would have to handle everything on the station until he got there. Ogun, the senior captain, had no experience with the kyo. He might be in charge of the station, he might be senior captain and giving orders—but he was an unknown quantity to the kyo, and he fairly well was an unknown where it came to working with the atevi.

Sabin and the kyo had parted amicably at the last, if one dared use the word *amicable*. At least the kyo had agreed to let them evacuate the station before they removed the human construction from space they claimed.

In that meeting, the kyo had warned them they'd come calling, eventually, since, as best one could understand abstract thought across the language barrier—the kyo held that all things once joined *were* joined, or however that philosophy worked out in the minds of a species who didn't share a planet or a history with them, had never dealt peaceably with another intelligent species—and didn't want any strangers in their space.

Forever-joined could mean alliance.

It could mean some other type of relationship—not all of them happy thoughts.

But *arguing* abstract philosophy in a language where they lacked definite vocabulary posed dangers. Big ones.

So they'd promised a further contact. He'd known the time *could* be short—and everything he'd started to do since he'd come home was to try to fix what had broken while he was gone and set things in order. He'd worked, hoping the contact would come later. Even a lot later. That perhaps the kyo would have to digest what *they'd* learned, and maybe postpone it for decades, after a lot of scientific wrangling and debate.

Not—this soon.

He flexed his fingers, his hands gone cold with uncommon chill.

They had to be damned careful how they responded to these visitors, when they had so very little language to help them.

They had to hope, first of all, that it really was the kyo, and the same kyo that they expected, and that these kyo were in a peaceful frame of mind—because *Phoenix* had very little in the way of armament, while the kyo ship they had dealt with had at least enough firepower to blow Reunion into scrap metal.

They really hadn't wanted to let the kyo know that their entire presence in space was one unarmed ship, posing no threat and having no defense. They hadn't been able to protest the notion of the kyo coming to visit them—they'd had no finesse of communication to make discussion possible, or safe.

The kyo knew that humans knew where *they* lived. It was fairly reasonable, in human terms, that they wanted humans to know they knew where *humans* lived, and that they *could* get here.

Tit for tat.

But then it got complicated. Kyo had seemed to be amazed by the concept that humans and atevi, though different, got along. They'd seemed both interested and strangely upset by the notion. That was what he picked up—or what he thought he understood.

But understanding *anything* in an interspecies contact was like wandering around a strange building with one's eyes shut, trying to imagine what was *in* the building and what its purpose could possibly be.

Interspecies contact was what the paidhiin were trained to do, however. It was the way he had been trained to think, the judgments he had been trained to make. He personally had the accumulated notes and observations of every paidhi since Romano. Studying that body of information, learning to decipher concepts that might run totally counter to all human expectation—that was how he'd begun. His original job had been a matter of a word at a time, making the dictionary larger, step by tiny step—assisting two very different peoples to understand each other and to keep their hands away from weapons, until—on his watch—the knowledge base had reached critical mass and events from the heavens had poured down on them.

Phoenix had come home, and he'd concentrated all his efforts on putting out the fires that had broken out in their absence. He'd gotten humans to understand atevi and vice versa. Moderately.

The kyo were completely off the chart. And dealing with them out at Reunion, on two ships strange to each other, and far removed from both their homes—that had been one thing.

Doing it here, with everything humans and atevi owned at immediate risk should he make a wrong move—that sent cold fear through him.

But in terms of negotiating—he *was* what the world had, for good or ill. He, and Jase. And Yolande Mercheson, and that small cadre of translators in the university over on Mospheira, who'd never spoken directly to atevi. Language was a field very few went into, one that *no* kyo had ever remotely conceived of going into, by all he knew. It must be a non-existent skill, where there was, for whatever reason, no surviving Other, no rivals, no memory of foreign contact.

Except there was another out there, by what they had learned, one *other* species who'd taken exception to the kyo, far to the other side of kyo space.

Enemies. Armed and space-faring enemies. The kyo had hinted such was the case.

That meant the kyo themselves were not the *only* visitors who could come calling on them. The kyo were the most likely. But *not* the only possibility.

He could not, however, afford scattered thinking. Wide thinking, yes. He was obliged to that.

But if there was one individual on earth who could *not* afford to panic right now—he was that one. Ahead of Tabini, ahead of Shawn, and all the ship captains, *he* had to think what to do, and how best to do it, because calm, accurate communication with that inbound ship was critical.

First things. Essentials had to be gotten up there. The dowager. Himself.

And—Cajeiri.

They were the three the kyo had met personally. They were the ones the kyo knew and expected. Somehow the dowager's age and Cajeiri's youth both mattered in the kyo view, calming apprehensions, perhaps, perhaps evoking something symbolic—they were far from analyzing such things in their exchanges; but the kyo had attached some significance to their presence.

So he needed them now.

A jet might not be available at Malguri's airport to get the dowager here. He might have to dispatch one.

Cajeiri, however—

Steps hurried back *up* the inner hall. He swung his chair toward the door.

A knock, an immediate entry: Jago and Banichi turned up, silent, competent for anything. Tano and Algini came in behind them, and the little office became smaller.

"Nadiin-ji," he said calmly. "The kyo—logically one believes it is the kyo—are fifteen days from the station. They are here."

Immediate understanding—no consternation, no alarm, just—an understanding that things had to be done, plans had to be changed, priorities had to be adjusted. God, he loved these people.

"One assumes we shall go up there," Banichi said.

"Yes. We have to alert the dowager. One hopes the Guild's communications might be more secure than the Messengers."

"Yes," Banichi said, covering an immense territory in one word.

"The Guild observers probably should still go, if they are to understand this event from the beginning. But they must go now, whether we can use the shuttle at the port or whether we have to beg transport from Mospheira. And I do not know whether I can get seats for them."

"We shall make that clear to the Guild," Algini said.

The Guild's internal communications turning reliable did make things much, much easier; and accurately informed observers directly connected to that guild's administration could become an asset. One hoped—*hoped* things would never require their assistance up there.

"I have very minimal information at this point," he said, "beyond a message from Jase-aiji, giving the code for an unknown in the solar system and putting it at fifteen days away at its current speed—which may change. At this point one hopes it is the kyo, and not their troublesome neighbors. But we shall have to go up there, we shall have to take charge of the encounter—and very unfortunately—we may have to do so with Tillington still in charge of Mospheiran operations, if the Presidenta cannot move fast enough to replace him. Assuming we *are* dealing with the kyo, I hope to take up that discussion with them where we left off. I am about to request the shuttle change its plans, offload all its cargo, install the largest passenger module—assuming the dowager will not come with a small staff—and fuel for an express run. And somehow we shall have to do this quietly. I do not wish to make the kyo presence public knowledge until we have a response in place."

"Yes," Banichi said. "Should *staff* know?"

About his own staff's man'chi and the intent of their honest hearts, he had no doubts at all. His staff would have to arrange transportation and pack their baggage, creating some disturbance in routine, and they would likely need to deal with outside agencies that might ask interested questions.

Bet that somebody might not make an innocent mistake, trying to cover things—

"Nand' Toby's boat," he said on inspiration, and with only a twinge of conscience, "has just arrived in Najida with storm damage. I was intending to go there to assist him. Let that be the story, for all outside agencies that have to know anything about my movements. Staff may be told the truth, but tell them that all any outsider should know is that I am taking the train to Najida to meet my brother, that I shall be taking the young gentleman with me, and that the dowager might join us for a holiday."

He hated to use Toby's presence that way and he hated to lie to the public. But it was cover they needed, to give them time to get some answers, and not to have a public furor interfering with their needful movements to the spaceport—which lay in the same direction as Najida.

But that also meant somewhere amid the confusion he had to get an honest word to Toby about what was happening.

That needed more couriers.

"I am about to talk to the Port Director," he said. "Advise the aiji's aishid I need to speak to him immediately, but do not tell them why. The rule is—anyone inside these walls may know the whole truth. Outsiders are not to be given any of the truth unless I personally and specifically give clearance."

"We shall advise them," Banichi said.

"Tell the Guild what you must, and use your own judgment. I shall try to reserve seats for the observers. One unit?"

"Four, yes."

"Once they get to the station, they should understand they will be entirely dependent on Lord Geigi for briefings. I shall be occupied, to what extent I cannot predict; and you will be, likewise. We shall brief them whenever possible, but if we cannot spare the time, we cannot. Protocol with humans or atevi cannot be my primary concern on this trip. Make sure they understand that."

"Bren-ji," Banichi said, without batting an eye. "We shall make very sure they understand that."

They left. It lifted an immense burden, just knowing they were engaged with the problem—and that a certain part of it would not be in his hands.

But before the door had quite swung shut at Tano's back, Narani swung it open again, quietly plugged in a phone and set it on his desk. "The Port Director, nandi," Narani said quietly, "is waiting on the line. I have told her nothing."

Different mental track. Logistics. Estimates.

And a need for immediate action.

He picked up the receiver. "Nand' Director? This is Bren-paidhi."

"Nand' paidhi?"

"There is, nandi, a sudden and very critical need to get a large number of personnel to the station, and one now profoundly apologizes for what one must request. Can you possibly make a massive change in the launch preparation? We need the largest passenger module and we need an express flight—the day after tomorrow would not be too soon—but we cannot in any way compromise safety with this passenger load. Can you make an accommodation faster with this shuttle rather than by waiting for the next, or applying to Mospheira for their space? I beg you, tell me this can be done."

A space of silence. One could hardly blame the woman. It had to have come like a meteor strike, amid a routine and orderly process that was within a day of completion.

But lading was the final process.

"We have not loaded but two carrels of cargo, as of this hour, nandi. That can be reversed. As to whether it is better to rely on the next shuttle landing—one can never guarantee that there will not be a mechanical delay with a launch preparation. Regarding Shai-shan, *we have already* had *our inspection, so in that,* Shai-shan *is ready. To install the passenger module you request and deal with fueling, however, is a lengthy process."*

"One understands, nand' Director."

"Let me consult with staff, nandi. I shall make inquiries about time required."

"Indeed, nand' Director. Let me stress that time is extremely critical; so also is safety. We might, at need, manage with the mid-sized module and a greatly reduced passenger list. Or if absolutely desperate, one person, riding with the crew. But that would be our very last choice." He could go up, alone, with only hand baggage, relying on his household aloft and Lord Geigi—but he hoped—he hoped desperately for more resources. "Please see what can be done. I cannot stress enough: safety is definitely an issue; budget is not. The shuttle schedule *can* be adjusted up and down the line."

"Yes, nandi. One understands. One will do one's best."

"Thank you. Thank you very much, nandi." He hung up. And propped his head on his hands and did rapid mental math, conscious of a headache gathering at his temples—pressure; fear; and a dearth of information.

The dowager's minimal complement of servants and security, plus herself, would be about twenty-one persons, counting she maintained an ample establishment on station—a caretaker staff that managed her apartment. Many of her servants he knew were plain-clothes Guild.

But figure thirty-one for the dowager's company. If they could get the larger module, they had room enough. Even for the observers.

The young gentleman's company would be seven, if he brought his servants; five if he brought only his bodyguard, and it would be a good idea to have the bodyguards—but the young gentleman could easily do without his servants.

Himself—even with staff aloft, he ideally wanted Narani and Jeladi with him—he wanted their experience and cool competency, among other things. They'd been in space before and they knew the staff up there.

His aishid, like the dowager's, was absolutely essential to the situation. Seven.

He wanted Asicho, who'd also been there. Bindanda. God, yes, Bindanda. He could not forget Bindanda.

So he and his staff were nine.

That was a number of outstanding felicity. But all together—it was a large number of seats. And they had the Guild observers.

Thirty-one, five, and nine. Forty-five. And the four Guild observers. Forty-nine.

Plus Guild equipment; and court wardrobe for three persons.

He started figuring baggage, a hopeless enterprise—they simply had to give priority to security and wardrobe and trust their bodyguards. He gave that up, opened his computer and started identifying files and codes he had to have.

The Port Director called back. He didn't wait for Narani to take the call.

"Five days, nandi," the Director said. *"We can launch early on the fifth day from this. Can you give us that much time, nandi? I am looking at the weather. It should be favorable."*

"With no compromise of safety."

"No compromise of safety, nandi. Be assured. The shuttle itself is completely checked out and ready. We have loaded only two carrels. We assume using the regular baggage module—that the passengers will observe regulation for baggage,

regulation weights. We allot four carrels. That is the module's regular configuration."

"We *will* be within that limit."

"We shall ask to have all carrel baggage in our hands on the third night, nandi. Launch before dawn on the fifth."

"Excellent. Please express my gratitude to staff, and my hope, my trust and confidence that everything will be in good order. Please assure everyone that there will be both recognition and recompense for their efforts."

"I shall, nandi. May we request a written order for this, specific paper for the records?"

"I shall deliver a signed order in person, on my arrival, with all appropriate seals, but I shall provide an interim order from the aiji. Please trust me on this until these arrive."

"Yes." The answer came, from a woman balancing her career on that choice. *"Yes, nandi."*

"Carrel baggage will arrive the third evening or before, ready to go, sealed and attended by the Guild."

"That will be extremely helpful."

"There will be hand baggage within regulations. Needless to say, this is all highest security. Crews may know only that it is a station security emergency and that very high-level personnel are going up to deal with it. The less information you give out beyond that, the better."

"I shall give those orders, nandi."

Thank God.

Thank that woman.

"The aiji's seal will be on this entire operation to confirm my orders, nand' Director. Thank you. Thank you very much. My own staff will contact the Transportation Guild at executive levels on that day. They will be informed that it is a security emergency, and that a high-ranking team is going. If possible, use a technical malfunction on the station as cover."

"One understands, nand' paidhi."

He ended the call.

Drew a breath. Stared at a blank wall and saw the deep of space, blackness, and somewhere out there, a blip.

A presence in the dark.

They had expected the kyo, yes. Sometime. In the future.

Considering what they'd come home to, thank God they'd had a year.

But then—what was the kyo intention? Was the timing, a year, the passage of a reasonably temperate Earthlike planet around a reasonably temperate star, significant somehow?

Other things the kyo had done weren't what humans or atevi were likely to have done. Kyo had two legs, two arms, they breathed the same air and could eat the same food—with some sensible cautions. But there the similarities stopped. Their expressions were hard to read, their body language was obscure. They'd said they would come. Nothing more. Abstracts like *why* and *what for* were far too obscure for communication such as they had established.

And if the kyo were going to show up, he supposed a year was a reasonable time to wait. He *might* have thought so, if he had had time to think about the kyo in any great detail.

But he could quite easily think other things and draw other conclusions. The kyo might have used that time to go home, with some new information *they* had to talk over with their authorities.

Presumably the powers that governed the kyo had thought it over, discussed it—assuming there was a reason to discuss it—and likewise reached a conclusion that they should come visit.

If they were lucky, the kyo had sent the *same* ship. And *only* the same ship.

Assuming the blip out there actually *was* kyo, and not the kyo's unknown enemy—which had indeed crossed his limited conversation with them.

God. Now *there* was a black hole of consideration.

But he couldn't waste time thinking down indefinite branches of the problem. Five days to launch: that was his time frame. Three days to have all the bulky baggage at the port.

With the dowager still in Malguri and Tabini still unaware of the situation.

He had things to do. People to notify. Personally. It was nothing a note could convey—pardon me for bothering you today, aiji-ma, but I have just commandeered the shuttle, tossed the cargo off, ordered more fuel, and I need your son and your grandmother to go with me to meet aliens of indefinite purpose and disposition—

No.

No note was possibly going to cover *that* situation.

He went out into the hall and found Jeladi in the foyer. "Have we heard from the aiji, Ladi-ji?"

"Yes, nandi. The aiji will see you at your earliest convenience."

"Then I shall go."

"Nandi." Jeladi went immediately to the foyer closet, took out his third-best coat, adequate for the job, and gave curt orders to a passing maidservant, who broke into a run for the back halls and the security station.

Bren slipped off the day coat, and Jeladi deftly whisked it over an arm and held up the other. Bren slipped his arms in, cleared his imperiled queue and ribbon himself, and adjusted the cuff lace with Jeladi's help.

He turned, in the process, saw Narani in his own little office, on the phone with someone—very likely someone involved in the logistics, and as he turned about again, he saw Tano and Algini coming down the hall, still buckling on their hardware.

He wasn't alone. He never was alone.

Thank God.

10

There was no drawing room reception in Tabini's apartment, no waiting for tea. Emergencies made exceptions to custom. There was just a meeting in Tabini's residential office, quiet, quick, with Algini in the room, Tano outside, and none of Tabini's own staff present. Algini was there to hear and pass on to his teammates and others what was done and said, and Tano, as a guard on the door at Tabini's own insistence, would not let any staff come near enough to overhear.

"This regards a matter of utmost urgency on the station," Tabini said, leaning back in his office chair. "This much we are given to understand. Sit, paidhi."

"Aiji-ma." Bren took one of the two small chairs near Tabini's working desk. "A foreign ship has arrived in our solar system."

It was surely not the sort of emergency Tabini had envisioned. He drew in a slow breath and frowned. "So. Is this the anticipated visitor, paidhi?"

"We hope it is nothing *other* than the anticipated visitor, aiji-ma. We have every reason to think it is indeed kyo, and that it *is* the visit we were advised to expect, but I have only the barest coded message from Jase-aiji, and I doubt he knows the nature of these visitors yet. He gave none of the codes we reserve for its positive identification. One believes that *Phoenix* has just now detected the ship. The station may not yet know. Likewise the visitors on that incoming ship may not yet realize they have been seen. We have no idea what their normal procedures might be. If they are who we believe, if they are coming to see how we conduct our affairs—they may observe for a while before contacting us. We have fifteen days before it arrives, if it stays at the same speed. At a certain point we hope they will break their silence and contact us. We have a set of responses that should be given to that move. And one does advise—with trepidation, aiji-ma—that we need to meet them up there and talk with them precisely where we left off, with exactly the original persons, the persons who last spoke to them."

"Yourself, Sabin-aiji, Jase-aiji—my grandmother—and my son."

"Indeed, aiji-ma."

"Do you apprehend danger in this meeting?"

"Not personal danger in the meeting itself, aiji-ma. Potentially great danger to everyone on the station and on Earth if we and that ship fail to understand each other. But we parted last in agreement and we were able peacefully to collect the Reunioners and leave. I do not foresee personal danger to the delegation, no, aiji-ma, nor would I hide it from you if I did."

"Tillington," Tabini said.

There was no ready answer for that one.

"The Presidenta has made no definite move as yet to replace him?" Tabini asked.

"I do not know, aiji-ma. I have come to you immediately after hearing the news. I have called the spaceport and made some arrangements to secure passage. I have asked my aishid to inform the aiji-dowager. But regarding the Tillington matter, and the Presidenta, I have not informed him of this new emergency, and I do not have any word that he has taken action on Tillington's replacement. I still do expect it. But our time has suddenly become much shorter, and we are both constrained by the shuttle schedules."

"The Guild observers?"

"One believes it might be best if they *could* observe the entire situation, aiji-ma; and their presence would give us several more skilled personnel up there—should there be any difficulty, their views might be of use. I am most concerned about the Reunioners' reaction when they hear the kyo are coming. They may panic. I am likewise concerned for Tillington's reaction, and for his leadership. But I count on firm support from two of the ship-aijiin, and I expect cooperation from the other two. They have more sense of who the kyo are than Tillington does, and more sense than the Reunioners will have of what our options are."

"You believe you can deal with these people."

"Our communication with the kyo is adequate for objects we can point to or demonstrate, things common to folk who work in space and deal in numbers—but abstract concepts, like *why*—we have not yet refined. The kyo received us at Reunion with courtesy and respectful ceremony. And your son exerted considerable influence over one of their number. How that forecasts their actions here—one cannot say."

"Geigi's residency is secure up there?"

"Indeed. Physically secure, with barriers as sound as any on the station."

"And you and your company will be residing within Lord Geigi's security?"

"Absolutely, in a section of several apartments and a common hallway, which is fairly close to the command center, and independent. Neither Tillington nor the ship-folk can control anything within the atevi sections: they are independent and secure even regarding the air and water and security functions. We shall reside in the atevi area, we shall speak from there, we shall contact the kyo from that vantage, and we shall generally use that insulation to keep all human quarrels out of view of these visitors. It was not human officials the kyo dealt with at Reunion: It was the aiji-dowager and your son—and myself, as your representative. I take the position this visit is to atevi authority, *not* to the ship-aijiin, not to Mospheirans or Reunioners."

Tabini heard that, and thoughts passed through his eyes. Then he said: "I shall make it clear to the Guild what your authority is, and it will be, save my grandmother's presence, as if you bore my ring a second time."

That was a powerful statement. An affecting statement. Bren gave a little bow of the head. "Aiji-ma, one will consult. *Whenever* possible."

"Considering rank of these visitors—who do you think they are? What do they want?"

"I have asked myself that. I have wondered whether their statement they would come was ever more than a courtesy. I have asked myself what they *would* want if they did come. Sending even one ship such a long distance is a massive investment of resources. My thinking, one regrets to say, was only guesswork then, and it is no better now. But our last encounter left them with two questions which, in their place, I would wish to know. First—were we truthful in our representations to them that our two species really live at peace here? And second—do we pose any threat to them and have we deceived them to hide that? One does not know how to read their nature. We do know they used weapons against an unarmed station, but it seems, by all I can learn, that they were provoked by the ship's intrusion into their space. We know that they crippled the station instead of destroying it. They then sat and waited for a response. I think they wanted to find out what we would do."

"A very dark supposition indeed."

"I put nothing off the chart where they are concerned, aiji-ma. And I do not conceal my worry. Understand that they could track the ship going and coming as clearly as a trail through meadow grass. There was no pretending our course to reach Reunion had been other than it was. Ship-folk knew there was a risk of being tracked, but their determination to remove records and find out what had happened there overrode their fear. I do not think they remotely expected a kyo presence after such a passage of time, nor did they detect it . . . and one suspects they were looking for it and taking precautions. One has learned from this, at least, to believe the kyo have abilities the ship-folk did not expect—but that places their actions beyond predictability. I cannot even say that the ship we now detect has not *been* there for this entire last year. The kyo lay hidden at Reunion for more than ten years. Is it curiosity and inquiry? Or is it a hunter's patience? I do not understand the technology. I cannot swear to understand the character of those I met. They *seemed* reasonable individuals and they *seemed* to acknowledge personal indebtedness, in terms of the one we rescued from captivity on Reunion Station. On that very scant foundation, aiji-ma, I have laid everything. Certainly we did not invite them to come. We were presented the proposition they *would* visit us. Asking them not to come seemed more dangerous than agreeing."

Tabini nodded somberly. "We do not encourage landing. *One ship* brought us humans, and changed the world. We scarcely manage with that association. We do not want another."

"One understands. One entirely understands, aiji-ma, and I shall discourage that, but I think their physical discomfort in our environment is also a discouragement to any landing. If one can venture a guess about their purpose and their actions, I think they will look to see how we live down here, how advanced we are, how warlike we are, how we build and what we do. They have seen only one human ship. They have not seen its weaponry—which is more the use of tools the ship has for other purposes, tools which can be formidable as weapons. The kyo may have no sure knowledge that *Phoenix* is our *only* ship, and for various reasons I do not wish even now to make that clear to them. They may also wonder if we have any contact or association with their enemies."

"We certainly do not wish to join their wars."

"I shall make that clear, too."

"And I forbid foolish risks up there—to my son, to my grandmother, *or to you.* If we lose you, paidhi, we lose our principle means of dealing with these strangers. *Trust your aishid.*"

"My aishid reminds me sternly of that requirement, aiji-ma."

"If you can restrain my grandmother, it will be a wonder. My son, however, will follow orders this time. He *must.*"

"He *will,* aiji-ma."

"I have the duty to inform my wife."

That was not going to be a happy task.

"Assure her, aiji-ma, that we shall do everything to protect him and bring him home safely."

"We shall support you. Whatever permissions or orders you need, we shall give."

"I do need a document for the Port Director, nandi, giving me the power to order what I have already ordered. Dated an hour ago, if you would."

Tabini nodded. "That you shall certainly have. Supplies, transport, any manner of thing."

"Thank you, aiji-ma."

"Do not stand on protocols hereafter. We have spoken. We have agreed. You have told me what you know and what hereafter you must guess. Leave informing me to your subordinates and concentrate on the details. We approve whatever things you need. Go bring us a solution, paidhi-ji."

Four days to do everything. Launch on the fifth.

"The word has gone to the dowager?" he asked Tano and Algini on the way next door, back to his own apartment.

"Yes," Algini said. "We have it confirmed from Cenedi."

Rare, in strictly normal operations, that he should get that sure a knowledge of how that information ran. But knowing Cenedi was on the case helped his stomach. If Cenedi was now engaged, the dowager was, and he was no longer running the operation solo.

The apartment doors opened. Narani and his valets waited to exchange his coat a second time, a ritual undertaken almost non-stop in his course across the foyer, and with no delay at all for courtesies or questions.

He went immediately to his office, and left the door open for emergencies. Tano and Algini lingered in that doorway, silent query. Narani arrived just behind them, present, but not intruding.

"Nadiin-ji," Bren said to Tano and Algini, "we are settled in for a while. Do what you need to do. —Rani-ji," he said to Narani. "Come in, please. I need to consult with you."

There were staff decisions to make. For three and more years, he had had very good people stranded on the station, maintaining his residence there. They had Geigi's staff and the dowager's similarly stranded caretaker household for company. There was a large community of atevi workers.

But until recently there had been no room at all on the shuttle for any exchange of personnel even on an emergency basis, let alone small staff furloughs down to the world to visit their relatives. He had used personal privilege, gotten a few people down to the planet in answer to emergency situations, sent a few up, and he understood—Narani had reassured him of it—that the fifteen now left up there constituted a very tight association, a sort of family who did not want to be broken—nor should he reward their service by bringing staff in to take over their jobs.

Up there, he would be relying a great deal on those good people. He was sure he *could* rely on them. But there were a handful of personnel he was used to working with, and who were used to reading him—notably the ones who had been with them on the ship, the ones he had brought back down to the world as soon as it had become possible—and now needed back up there with him.

He sat down at his desk, and angled his chair toward Narani.

"Nandi." Narani bowed. An old man, showing his age: Narani lately dyed his hair black—a little point of vanity—but his face had experience written deep on it, gained in some very hard places.

"Rani-ji. You may know the kyo are arriving, and I have to go up to the station."

A little hesitation in the space he left—but not even the lift of an eyebrow. "One has understood so, nandi. And one also understands that there is a political difficulty among humans on the station."

"You never fail me, Rani-ji. We hope the meeting with the kyo will be a peaceful discussion, that it will not take us away from the world for long, and that human problems on the station will not intrude on the kyo matter, but I shall be inventing my responses as I go. I have no good map of either situation. I am composing a list of those staff going with me. I shall be very glad to rely on the household on the station. I have every confidence in them. But I ask, Rani-ji, have you any desire to make the trip up—not necessarily to resume your post there, but to stand by me personally and handle small emergencies? Seating is limited. Very few staff can go. I can swear at least, a solemn promise, that I will bring you down with me and back to this apartment as soon as the emergency is over, but I cannot say when the emergency will end."

Narani bowed. "If I do not go, nandi, I shall worry about you every hour."

"We would have communication from here to there. You could advise me from here."

"And one is certain there will be very tight security, nandi, that cuts us off from knowing what we most want to know at the moment we would most wish to know it. One earnestly wishes to go."

"Jeladi would wish to go, too, do you think?"

"He will, nandi. I am very sure of it."

"Who else would go?"

"Asicho. Asicho would say so instantly, nandi. And Bindanda, one believes."

Asicho had tended Jago's wardrobe needs on the ship, a point of modesty which in no wise bothered Jago, he suspected, but it was a convenience.

And Bindanda was already on the list.

"Tell them individually, Rani-ji, that I need to speak to them."

"Indeed, nandi."

"One considers, perhaps, Supani and Koharu might fill your post and Jeladi's, until you return."

"An excellent choice, nandi. Jeladi and I, rather than displacing any of the household up there, might fill *their* posts quite comfortably, if you will."

That was exactly what he had thought. He nodded. "Absolutely. And as to the content of my wardrobe, I leave it entirely to you, Rani-ji. Utmost court dress, for some meetings. You know my needs, you know the customs restrictions, you know the environment and the requirements, which already relieves my mind of a list of burdens. Do everything discreetly as touches the outside world: the fewer staff that know any details of timing, the less chance someone will slip. For public distribution, I shall maintain the same story: that I am traveling to Najida to see my brother and help him repair his boat from storm damage."

"Entirely understood, nandi."

"*Thank* you, Rani-ji."

"Nandi." With a composed little bow, Narani left on his business.

And with Narani fully informed and on a mission, *he* could stop worrying about household details.

Now it came down to a letter that had to be very carefully phrased—and transmitted in highest security.

He was accustomed to compose on paper, with a quill and inkpot. But this one was going by different means. He set his computer up onto the desk, and opened it.

Bren, Paidhi-aiji,

To Geigi, Lord of Kajiminda, Station-aiji—

There were half a dozen other titles. He keystroked them in, and wrote:

The porcelain with the fishing boats has been located, nandi, and will be returned to your collection in fifteen days.

Translation: the kyo are here: we have fifteen days.

Might you find time, nandi, to invite Jase-aiji and the heir's recent guests for a very extensive debriefing on their recent visit? I hope you will be able to extend your hospitality to them over several days. It would delight them.

Translation: get the kids into your section and hold them there, because of circumstances you can imagine.

You may reliably use Jase-aiji as an intermediary. He will know how to observe human custom in the invitation. Please add him to your guest list.

Translation: work with Jase. Don't do anything to upset the parents. Get as many to safety as you can.

The kyo visit was going to upset everybody, human and atevi—and Louis Baynes Braddock wouldn't hesitate to use that fact.

Braddock and Tillington would take extreme positions, and the result might be outright violence. Arresting Braddock in advance might be a good idea, but they had to get Tillington out first.

The ship could take the children and their parents aboard if push came to shove. The captains might be reluctant to take that step and create an issue with the Reunioners—but so might the youngsters' association with Cajeiri create an issue with Tabini-aiji should Braddock or Tillington attempt to use them politically. Delaying too long in protecting those kids, who now had an official relationship to the atevi court, could blow a minor difficulty up into a major and distracting problem.

The ship had territory it could seal off unto itself. Geigi held territory that was fairly well sealed.

And Geigi could always claim convenient ignorance of human custom.

That was one vital letter done, waiting to be sent.

The next letter—

Toby. Frozen Dessert, as his code name was, when he was an agent for the Mospheiran government. Toby's service to Mospheira being much more current than his own, Toby very likely had codes and accesses he didn't have, these days, with no need to rely on couriered messages. He hoped so. He fervently hoped so.

Brother, our aunt Margaret's headed for a visit, and I'm trying to arrange things. Didn't know about this in advance. I'm sorry.

Translation: the kyo are here, brother. We've been surprised and I've got to deal with it.

So sorry about the damage to the boat. Please ask Ramaso for anything you need and enjoy the hospitality of the estate, so repairs can get underway. I'm sending you one of my personal staff who speaks Mosphei'.

I hope you can extend your stay. I've got your official permission. And as soon as I clear up Aunt Margaret's problem I'll be on my way to Najida myself.

Translation: you're fine where you are. I've got to deal with the kyo. The aiji knows you're there and it's all right for you to stay a prolonged time.

Toby was his backup, of humans who knew enough Ragi to put two sentences together. There were people at the University who could manage, but nobody who'd actually dealt with the language in the field. Toby had. Toby could do it. Toby docked on the coast of the mainland and ready to assist Tabini and Shawn with direct communication was the best situation he could ask for.

Love you, brother. Love to Barb.

That last line didn't need interpretation.

He printed out and put that letter into a plain steel Messengers' cylinder. *That* was going out via numerical transliteration, as an ordinary telegram. *That* was the cover story, and if spies intercepted parts of it, that was what they could have. It was all the word Toby would have until a courier could get there with a physical message.

Toby would be keeping all options open until he got further

instructions—and he'd be expecting that couriered letter, no question.

Quill and paper, then, and a second letter to Toby.

And this letter—this further request of Toby required a change of plans, a request he didn't want to make—but he couldn't do two jobs, couldn't handle a fight with Tillington and Braddock *and* prepare a mission to meet the kyo. The Reunioners weren't going to be calmer or easier to reason with when the news got out the kyo were coming in. And they couldn't have two leaders up there pouring fuel on the fire.

Obviously I can't make it to Najida. I'm headed upstairs in five days, and I need you to get a message to Shawn, speed of the essence, but not outweighing security. He doesn't know what's happened.

He's already working on a problem for me. Stationmaster Tillington stated that Captain Sabin was behind Cajeiri's meeting the human children, and that she made a private deal with the Reunioners. It implies an attempt at overthrowing Captain Ogun and overthrowing Mospheiran authority on the station with, by implication, atevi standing by idle. This accusation has implications involving my integrity, Sabin's, and considerably beyond. I leave it to you to imagine. Whether or not Tillington has any concept what he has set in motion, he has to be replaced, and I've contacted Shawn with that request. But with this new event his replacement and repair of the damage has just become urgent.

I suspect Shawn's silence after my request means he's encountering some political resistance regarding the Tillington situation. You may know that better than I do. But now there's no leeway left in the situation and Tillington's presence is a problem. We can't have him and Braddock going to war in the middle of this situation, not to mention the atevi reaction if those provocative statements get out—and we have, with luck, fifteen days to settle this.

Tillington needs to be removed immediately and replaced

with someone who can take definitive charge of Mospheiran operations without an argument. Once the Mospheirans settle, then the captains can do something about Braddock, on the other side of the line.

If you can call Shawn securely from where you are, tell him. Jaishan's *equipment is at your disposal. If that's not possible, take* Jaishan *and courier that message over there yourself. But if you can do it otherwise, stay put so you can serve as paidhi-aiji in my absence. Love you, brother. Wish we could have had that holiday.*

Wish us luck.

Second piece of paper.

He wrote, furiously, also in Mosphei':

Mr. President, this information is critical beyond any communication I have ever sent you. An unidentified ship is now in the solar system. We believe it is kyo. This arrival is known only to a few as yet: myself, my brother, the ship captains, Lord Geigi, the aiji-dowager, and Tabini-aiji. We hope Tillington does not know. We will delay releasing the information to the public below and aloft until we organize a response, and we hope to delay release of that information until Tillington's replacement is in charge.

I have delayed our next shuttle launch. Five days from now I shall be going up to the station with the aiji-dowager and the aiji's heir to take charge of contact with these visitors. We are the persons the kyo dealt with last time, and we wish to take up our dealing with them exactly where we left it in the hope of achieving a peaceful dialogue.

This event has made the Tillington situation extremely delicate. If the dowager officially hears about his statement regarding the young gentleman, the political consequences will be dire, and if the information reaches the atevi community aloft it will be politically necessary for the dowager to take measures.

In the strongest possible terms, I again request his immedi-

ate removal as Stationmaster, and his replacement by someone carrying Presidential authority during this critical meeting. I strongly suggest Kate Shugart for that role. She has high credibility with the Mospheiran workers. She knows the technicalities, she knows the systems, and she would be an asset to my mission.

The kyo ETA is fifteen days at their current rate of approach, which could change considerably in either direction. Again, I cannot stress strongly enough, the kyo must not see evidence of conflict among us.

If your shuttle launch can configure for passengers and go on your original schedule you will arrive right behind us.

The Mospheiran shuttle launch usually followed an atevi launch by a margin that gave the atevi shuttle ample time to offload, clear the small docking area, and move over into the service dock. That meant that his delaying the atevi shuttle five days would automatically delay the Mospheiran launch by an equal time—unless Shawn gave orders to the contrary.

I will try to avoid confrontation with Tillington until his replacement arrives. Once Tillington's agitation is removed, the ship-folk can then deal with Braddock and I will be urging them to do so. A human quarrel in front of the kyo could be disastrous, casting doubt on what we assured them was a firm alliance.

Toby took storm damage at sea. He's at my estate at the moment. His antenna is gone, but Jaishan*'s is fine. He has lines open at Najida that can reach the aiji. Please use them at need. I have gained him permission to stay in place as long as he wishes, and respectfully suggest he could be valuable there.*

I will attempt to hasten the departure of the atevi shuttle to clear the bay for your early arrival.

Be assured I shall do my best to communicate with our visitors and to secure a peaceful and productive meeting.

It might not be the most coherent letter he had ever written, and it intruded into business which, since he was no longer operating under presidential orders himself, was no longer *his* business. But it was critical he make it clear: they had to get Tillington out. Fast.

The exchange of couriers necessitated one more phone call to Mospheira, one more phone call to Shawn's office.

Shawn, it developed, was at a committee meeting.

"I have to talk to him," he said to the aide who took the call. "It's fast." And gratifyingly quickly, he had Shawn on the line.

"Bren?"

"Shawn, more than the previous matter. It's critical. Courier. Charter jet. Please."

"Done," Shawn said.

"That's it," he said. "All I can say."

"Understood," Shawn said, and Bren hung up the phone—then carefully put the two letters to be couriered into distinctive cylinders, sealed them with wax and his imprint, then reached for the bell-pull and called Narani.

"This one," he said of the unsealed message, "must go right now to the Messengers, in an initial answer to my brother's letter, telling him to await a courier. The other," he said, handing Narani the second, more ornate cylinder, under his personal seal, and bearing flowers carved in sea-ivory, "staff must physically courier to Najida, this hour, by charter. It explains everything to nand' Toby in plain words and sets him to stay in position to keep the Presidenta in communication with the aiji. I need a courier who will not delay, attract attention, or make any mistakes. That person must get this cylinder into nand' Toby's hands personally. That person may then relax and stay a few days at his leisure. Ramaso can send one of his staff back here with any reply. Speed, Rani-ji, and extreme secrecy, is of the essence. The courier will also be carrying orders for Ramaso and an emergency permission for my brother's presencc on the mainland. Please put those together for me. That will be the cover story when we engage the Red Train for the spaceport. Use completely ordinary procedures on the steel cylinder. It goes to the Messengers' Guild, to transmit to Toby within the hour. It will lead him to expect our couriered message to follow."

"Nandi. One understands."

"*This* one," he said, regarding the second sealed cylinder, a distinctive one with sea-creatures, "goes to the Presidenta. A charter jet is probably leaving within the half hour, bringing the Presidenta's courier to us, and two of my aishid should meet that plane to hand on this cylinder, so that there are no delays whatsoever."

Narani did understand him, he had every confidence. The letters went. Things were out of his hands. The best people he knew were on the job, and Toby was hereafter going to be in place to link the Presidenta to Tabini, where it was useful to pass messages.

Sorry, brother.

He hadn't written that part in his letter to Toby.

I'm scared as hell.

He hadn't written that part either.

And he didn't envy Shawn *his* job, or the political consequences of removing a powerful appointee. But the nature of the matter, the fact that it was reasonable to *need* a total change of management to handle the unprecedented visit imminent, might provide salve enough for political sensitivities and let Shawn bring Tillington home for that favorite euphemism for executive displeasure—*consultation.*

He had local staff moves to make, too. He was going to rotate a small number of household staff home to Najida once he left. They could go on furlough by turns during his absence, partly to relieve the pressure on Koharu and Supani, in their first stint at managing the household from the executive post, partly because they deserved some time at home, and partly because people arriving from his Bujavid staff could answer Toby's more detailed questions, just for Toby's comfort—assuring Toby that he had left the world in good order and in confidence.

Bren found himself staring at that spot on the office wall that was always his recourse, catty-angled opposite his desk—that spot that his aishid and his staff occupied, when there was something they could do about a situation.

When that spot was vacant, because his staff was already doing everything they could do—the worry was all his.

Communicate with aliens who'd seemingly been surprised by the very notion that there *could be* peaceful cooperation between species?

It certainly didn't paint a sunny picture of the history of the kyo homeworld. Species didn't, to his knowledge, grow up in isolation. Humans had had antecedents, as a species. So had the atevi.

Yet the kyo were astonished by cooperation with another species.

What else he knew about the kyo—was that they had also made an enemy in a neighboring region of space, one potent enough to worry them.

He knew that *Phoenix*, before it had returned to the Earth of the atevi, had accidentally attracted kyo attention, and the ship's actions had angered or scared the kyo. *That* had apparently led the kyo to hit Reunion . . . possibly because they thought their enemies were involved. Or possibly because it was kyo policy.

The kyo had fired, destroying part of the station, and *then* sent an investigatory team in— or they had fired once a team they had sent in reported trouble. That sequence of events had never been sufficiently clear. Station records said the former. But that was the word of Louis Baynes Braddock that the kyo had fired without provocation.

Did he believe it?

Braddock could tell him the sun was shining and he'd look to be sure.

Then came the natural question. Having blown a third of Reunion Station to hell—why had they then failed to finish the job?

Because the team they had sent in could still be alive in there? Did they care about their own people?

Maybe.

Or had they waited because they wanted to give whatever ships belonged to that station an incentive to show up? *Phoenix* had indeed come in to remove the colonists. But it had taken them ten or so years to do it.

The kyo had turned up immediately.

And either the kyo mode of communication and transport was quick beyond anything they could conceive, or that ship had indeed been sitting out there, watching, waiting, for all those years.

The kyo had had one of their own, Prakuyo an Tep, detained in human hands all that time, as well. They hadn't gone in to get him out.

Why hadn't they, in ten long years—if they were just sitting out there?

Why not, if they had weapons enough to blow the station apart?

Ethics?

Timidity?

Curiosity?

They'd waited for something to happen. For a ship to come in, as it had?

Why?

To find out its origin.

That was the likely answer.

Nor had Reunioners during all those years ever gotten Prakuyo an Tep to talk to them.

On that thought—uncomfortable as it was—he had to stop staring at the wall.

I've got Braddock to deal with.

I've got Tillington.

And the new Guild office going up there, along with everything else.

God. I do not *intend to explain Tillington to them.*

But maybe I should. Let them know that, in this environment, at close quarters, we cannot afford to react as we might in an atevi dispute.

He leaned back in the chair, eyes shut.

Of all guilds—the Assassins' Guild understood politics. The Assassins' Guild had had the vision to turn around and work with Mospheira when Tabini was overthrown. It had abhorred humans, before that.

But during that emergency, in very short order, they'd become far more respectful of ideas they'd once considered foreign.

He could not let himself be led too far by an analogy.

One species was not another.

But after two hundred years of opposition, the Guild had shifted its attitude toward humans in two years.

Why?

Because the Assassins' Guild *and* humans had found a common interest in preserving Tabini-aiji. Not for who he was—but because Tabini's flexible governance benefitted them both. And once humans and the Guild had seen that—things changed.

Of what possible benefit were humans and atevi to the kyo? What common interest?

He pulled down yet one more clean sheet of parchment, dipped his pen, and started a brief note to Lord Tatiseigi—certainly not the political ally he would have envisioned for himself a few years ago, but the old lord was the best ally he had now, where it came to dealing with the touchier, more traditional parts of the legislature.

He and Tatiseigi had worked out a system: he represented the aiji, who swayed the liberal side of the legislature. He himself had a certain cachet with the liberals and the outliers, frayed as it occasionally seemed to be. Tatiseigi had the old-line conservatives on his side.

And between them, if they two could agree, they could often

work out some common-sense give-and-take to make both sides happy, and make both Ilisidi and Tabini happy—which once had been a mutually exclusive proposition.

The current effort added up to the dowager's long-held plan, a smoothly developing strategy to stabilize mainland politics by linking the troublesome Marid with the highly independent East—and the key parts of it were happening at a time convenient for Tabini's own aims.

In this case—Tatiseigi *was* his backup with the legislature, while he, along with Ilisidi, were so to speak, *called out of town.*

That meant Tatiseigi was going to have to work with Tabini during his absence—and vice versa. There had been a time when *that* would not have worked.

There was the specific legislative agenda to handle—coupled with public pressure, once the public knew what was going on.

But politics would not cease. The Liberals and the new tribal peoples' representatives were going to have to do some trading and hammer out practical agreements while events were going on in the heavens.

Domestically, the worst disagreement was past and the tribal peoples were in the legislature.

Now they had to find associations compatible with their interests.

And, a complication in those dealings—there remained the issues raised by the railroad to the south, God help them, which paid off Machigi of the Taisigin Marid, which was *how* they had connected the Marid to the East and gotten the young southern warlord Machigi and the staunchly conservative Lord Tatiseigi *and* the very liberal Lord of Dur all to back passage of the tribal peoples bill.

Tatiseigi could shamelessly raise regional and conservative interests as a negotiating position, but the man was better than that, cleverer than that—more of a statesman than that.

He wrote, to Tatiseigi: *I have very lately reached certain understandings with Lord Topari in the railroad issue, under-*

standings about which he seems very enthusiastic, and I believe we can get the building of this line underway, except for one serious difficulty. I am unexpectedly called out of the capital. If you would take the matter under your management—

No, that wouldn't do. There was *no* way to explain the kyo situation adequately on paper—and he dared not scant formalities with the old man, who was a stickler for proper form. He had to steer Tatiseigi, among other things, toward a social contact with the younger lord of Dur.

Young Reijiri, the rebel pilot whose yellow plane had once thrown the skies above Shejidan into chaos—had never been a close associate of the Conservatives, even in his more mature years. That partnership needed careful introduction, on a matter of common interest.

He wadded up that paper and took another.

It joined the first.

He pulled down another sheet and simply wrote: *Nandi, I must speak to you at the earliest on a matter of great importance. May one call on you this afternoon?*

It was going to take time. Everything with Lord Tatiseigi took an extraordinary amount of time, and usually a face to face meeting.

There might be arrivals in the heavens at any moment the kyo decided to apply some speed.

But on Earth, proper form was absolutely mandatory.

Antaro and Jegari slipped quietly into Cajeiri's sitting room, and Cajeiri looked up from his lessons. He was waiting for an answer from nand' Bren. But it was nothing of the kind.

"Your father wishes to see you, Jeri-ji," Antaro said—they were formal in private only when something was absolutely dire, so it was likely nothing much, probably something about some important old person coming to dinner. He could not recall anything he had really done wrong in the last several days. So it was probably that.

He knew his father and mother had been in conference for a long time. And it *could* be about him. He gave a sigh and got up. "Where are Veijico and Lucasi?"

"Waiting at your father's office," Jegari said.

Well, that was not unusual either. He went out and down the hall, where Veijico and Lucasi waited; and he did *not* get the warning signal that meant *your mother is present.*

So he let his unified aishid take up their largely decorative positions at his father's door—they did not habitually go into the office with him—and walked in, far from sure what the problem was.

His father was alone, sitting at his writing desk. His father finished a sentence, laid the pen in its holder, capped the inkwell, and turned his chair toward him, a degree of attention he did not always get.

"Honored Father," Cajeiri said, with a little bow.

"Son of mine. Sit down."

Sitting was unusual, too. It was apparently *not* about a dinner or anything ordinary. That was not necessarily good. He pulled one of the chairs closer, and sat down.

"Bren-paidhi," Father said, "has had a message from Jase-aiji today. There is a strange ship in the heavens. They think it is a kyo ship."

He forgot to breathe for a second. Things unrolled fast and far. He very vividly remembered Prakuyo an Tep, massive, wrinkled, gray, in a white room, sitting across a bare white table enjoying teacakes.

He remembered the inside of the kyo ship, dim, dark, with draperies and screens, so one could not tell how the room or even the corridors were shaped.

He remembered great-grandmother, and nand' Bren, and their bodyguards and the kyo in that place, and the voices, that rumbled like distant thunder.

The smell of the place had been different than anywhere else: it was age, and damp, and smoke and spices and something else.

"You are requested to go up to the space station with nand' Bren and your great-grandmother," his father said, "to deal with this visit."

He was requested. He was just barely fortunate nine years old.

But he understood instantly why he was one of the ones to go. Nand' Bren and mani herself had warned him someday the kyo might come and he might have to deal with them, and he had taken it seriously, as something to be proud of.

He had talked with Prakuyo an Tep. He had helped nand' Bren learn to talk to him in the first place.

And he had taken it as a very serious responsibility to keep all his own notes on the kyo and to remember what he had learned. He had even taught his aishid. They used kyo words when they wanted to say something truly secret.

Prakuyo an Tep had promised them they would come visit.

So now he had.

It was definitely scary. The kyo themselves were scary. But they—he and mani and nand' Bren—had shared water and fruit with more than one of them.

Nand' Bren and Prakuyo an Tep had worked hard to make a dictionary in the few days they had stayed after that. Nand' Bren had not only let him see the dictionary, he had given him a copy of his own, and he had added words he knew, and copied into his own study notebook all the words that were new to him.

Words—a few of which he knew were bigger ideas than just one word in Ragi. The kyo language was like that.

"Are you afraid?" his father asked him.

"No," he said, which was at least halfway true. He decided the whole truth was due. "One is a little afraid, honored Father. But still may I go? Nand' Bren needs me."

His father looked a little taken aback, then seemed to approve. "Yes," his father said. "You will be going."

"Are we taking the ship?" He thought they might go out

among the planets to meet the kyo. He saw, in his head, the ship tunnels, where he had met Gene and the rest.

And he remembered the upstairs of the ship, the middle levels, and, very vividly, Prakuyo an Tep.

He remembered Jase-aiji and Sabin-aiji and a dinner party.

And where he and mani had lived, and the wonderful corridor where he and Banichi had made toy cars race. That was the best place. That area of the ship had been home. Mani's apartment, modern, but very much mani's; and nand' Bren's apartment, with all the curtain of plants that he had had. The plants had grown enormously, whenever the ship had traveled through space. That condition favored them, nand' Bren had said, even if one felt strange and disconnected and not really quite well—

All of that came back to him, more real than where he was at the moment, the way it sometimes did in dreams.

Gene's face, and Irene's, and Artur's, and Bjorn's, too—in the dark and cold of the tunnels. Those would forever be a safe, secret place for him.

"To my knowledge," his father said, "you are going only as far as the station and these visitors will come there. Mind, you are not up there to spend time in another visit with your young associates. One hardly knows whether you will get to see them. Nor are you to ask nand' Bren to seek them out. Do you understand, son of mine? All this is too important for personal concerns. There may be political problems. Understand that."

"Yes," he said. One always had to say *yes* to Father. But he did understand. Business was business when things got scary, and things could get really scary with the kyo. He was older, now, and he knew that in ways he had never understood when he was meeting the kyo the first time. It was amazing how much older he had gotten, in just two years. He *did* know what could go wrong, and it was terribly scary.

But he was going to be with mani, and nand' Bren, and they would settle things.

And then maybe he *would* get to see Gene and Artur and Irene.

"You also know," Father added, "that your *mother* is not happy about your going up there."

"Yes," he said. "I know. But I was *there,* honored Father. I can *talk* to the kyo. I was the first one who really did."

"So one understands. One does not easily imagine it, but it seems nand' Bren believes you have a useful and pacifying influence, and he advised us a year ago that should this day come, he would call on you, and on your great-grandmother. Your association with this foreign person may put you in some danger, and as much experience as I have had of negotiations with difficult people, I cannot imagine what these people want that will agree with us. Please do exactly as nand' Bren instructs you to do. Do not draw nand' Bren or your great-grandmother from their jobs. Do not distract them with requests for personal favors. Smile, bow, be pleasant to this individual you know, assuming he will be aboard. But do not be pert with this stranger. Do not assume you know anything at all without talking to nand' Bren. And do not under *any* circumstances leave the area of the station or the ship where you are supposed to be."

He had gotten in trouble on that score. More than once. "I am older, honored Father. I shall be very careful. And I shall obey mani and obey nand' Bren. Absolutely, I shall."

"These visitors overwhelmed and destroyed Reunion Station. The humans there could not stop them."

"I know, honored Father. But nand' Bren can talk to them. And I can. And if it is dangerous, so are places I have been, and I *learn,* honored Father. I have learned from *everything* since we came back. Even nand' Bren's bodyguard trusts me."

His father nodded slowly. After a moment he said: "You have indeed learned. I am *proud* of my son."

Cajeiri drew in a breath. A deep one, and bowed his head, not knowing what to say, except, "Thank you, honored Father."

"You must not tell anyone what is going on. Not even your

servants. Your aishid may know about the kyo and about going up there but they are to tell *no one* else, even on my staff. The very fact that these foreigners have arrived is secret. Your leaving will be secret. Nand' Bren has called your great-grandmother back to Shejidan, but the reason is secret. He is arranging transport, but only the people who are involved in the planning are being told at this point. Do you understand all this? Can you keep it secret?"

"Yes, honored Father. I can."

"Just so. You will naturally take your aishid with you. The seating on the shuttle is very limited and your great-grandmother and nand' Bren will necessarily have a large bodyguard and staff all of whom have bearing on this matter. I only insist you take your aishid. If you *can* take your valets, that might relieve the duties of other staff who will be attending your great-grandmother and nand' Bren. But that may not be possible: you will have to ask nand' Bren how many seats you are allowed and with whom you will be staying once you are up there. Understand, you must make yourself and your comfort the very *last* consideration, where it comes to staff."

"Yes, honored Father," he said.

He suddenly thought of Boji. Boji was a silly creature. But Boji depended on him for everything. He had no trouble at all figuring how much trouble Boji could be with no gravity in the shuttle, and with all that racket, and goings-on—and getting loose on the station—

No. Boji had no place up there. Certainly not on the station. It would smell strange. Boji would not be happy.

"Eisi and Liedi could stay here and take care of Boji," he said. "I know how to take care of myself, mostly. Except the laundry. And my aishid can help."

"I assure you—Boji will be safe and cared for here. And we shall not let him escape or annoy your mother."

He felt embarrassed. "He is such a silly creature," he said. "And he wants his eggs, and he misbehaves if he has to wait, and *that* is when he bothers Mother. So he is very much better if someone can talk to him during the day and brush him and see he has his eggs."

"Indeed," his father said solemnly. Father was such an important man, and Boji was so small and silly he was embarrassed to be talking about Boji as any consideration at all in his father's business. But Father was also far more patient with silly things than Mother was. "Rely on us," Father said. "Boji will have his eggs on a silver plate if he needs them. Free your mind of him."

"Yes, honored Father," he said quietly.

"Good. I already have broken the news of this trip to your mother. You may understand she is upset. One would recommend you go see her. You may choose your time. But let me tell you something you may not have observed: your mother is as touchy about her prerogatives as your great-grandmother is. Do *not* just agree with her. And do not delay telling her. Understand and pay attention. She finds herself in a difficult situation in your going."

"She is jealous of great-grandmother."

"She is *rightfully* jealous."

It is *not* rightful, he thought. He held himself from saying that, but he realized he had let his expression slip.

"Son of mine, you left *her.* It was not your fault and it was not your great-grandmother's, but it certainly was not hers. *I* sent you away."

"You had to," he said.

"Indeed. You were in danger. You were inquisitive, you were elusive even at that age, and you were a vulnerability someone could exploit. I could have sent you to Malguri—indeed, I considered it. But your great-grandmother chose to go up to the station. She could keep you safe. And as it turned out—none too soon."

"One has thought, honored Father, if you had been taking care of me, you and Mother might not have gotten away."

His father had a grim look, a very grim look—and nodded. "Very likely not. And during the years we were in hiding, it was often enough worse. We were in places, your mother and I, where a small boy could not have kept up, or climbed, or fared well in the cold. Understand, son of mine, at times your mother feared the ship was lost and you were dead. And at the worst times, she still held out hope that if we both were lost, *you* would grow up and come back and set things right. But all of it was hard. Every day was hard. She never let you go. And of course once you did come back, you had attached to your great-grandmother. You were that age. Your mind was waking. And neither you nor we can reach back and change that. No more can your great-grandmother mend you by unraveling what that time caused to happen. Nor—likely—*would* she. Man'chi goes both ways, son of mine. So nothing can change what happened, and your mother and I are not children. We understood what we were doing when we sent you, and when your great-grandmother made the decision to go out on the human ship—we knew what she was doing. But things were less and less stable on the Earth. I felt—and this is difficult, son of mine. I felt that the world was changing. That I had let something loose that was changing the world, and I knew no better answer—for you—than to put you into the tutelage of the woman who taught me, the woman who twice ruled the aishidi'tat—and who remembers more of how things came to be than most still alive. I knew that you would see foreign things your mother and I would never understand. I knew you would not be ours when you came back, I knew, and I gave you to her. But give your mother what honor you can, son of mine."

"I always try!"

Father nodded. "I know you try. But understand what I have just told you. Your great-grandmother calls you clever. *Find a way,* son of mine. Your mother knows what I did and why I did it. She has had a very difficult several years since. Today I have had to tell her you are leaving us again. At least—try to talk to her."

"Yes," he said. He did not want to. In some ways his mother had been behaving strangely since the new baby had come. Her coming to his room—having tea—

That had just been uncomfortable. Though they both had tried, it had been uncomfortable. Threatening, in a way. Challenging him.

And now this happened.

Maybe he should have gone directly to have tea in his mother's room and not invited her to take tea with *him*, as if he were aiji. Maybe that was what she had wanted him to do.

Except it was his sister's bedroom and his sister was always sleeping, always not to be disturbed.

"You know what your mother went through having your sister," Father said. "You saw the pain and inconvenience of bringing a child into being. Always remember she did the same for you. And then lost you. She forgives me for it. Or tries to. But I ask you bear a little discomfort yourself, son of mine. Try. Even if she will not hear it. That you tried will matter sooner or later."

He understood. He understood scary things, some of which mani had told him, some of which he had guessed. But he also knew his mother was going to be furious with him about going—for leaving in the first place, which was not his fault; and for leaving with mani, which was not his fault, either. And angry for everything that had happened in the past. There was current trouble, too: grandfather had been assassinated, Ajuri clan had no lord, and Father would not let Mother take the lordship, and certainly would not let *him* take it—so Ajuri was not in good favor right now. And there might not ever be a new lord, which would break Ajuri apart and make it dependent on two or three other clans for everything administrative.

His mother was mad about that, among other things.

But Mother could also give orders that would make trouble for Boji while he was gone, and he knew his father would protect Boji for him, but he just did not want to create that situation or get his father into an argument with his mother on that, when there was so much else wrong.

His father wanted him to go in there. His father said now was better than later—when his mind wanted to argue he could deal with the kyo and come back with everybody's man'chi and then his mother would see he was right and not be as angry.

But that was building a house from the roof down, that was what Lord Geigi said. That was starting from *after.* They already had more *after* than they could deal with.

So, leaving his father's office, he paused with his aishid outside his father's door and drew a deep, deep breath, still not having the least idea how he was going to do what his father asked. "The kyo have come, nadiin-ji, and I have to go up to the station, and it is all secret from the rest of the staff. I am going to talk to my mother now. Wait for me."

They heard it, they listened. And it was nothing they could possibly save him from. He walked on down the hall with his throat gone tight, and knocked at his mother's door.

Mother's chief maid answered, and without a word, let him into the first room, that with the beautiful windows, all in white filmy curtains.

The most beautiful room in all the apartment was Seimiro's nursery. And Seimiro spent her time asleep in her crib, oblivious to the weather outside, which he supposed was typical of babies. He walked over and stood looking down at her small frowning face.

Her mouth twitched. Maybe she was having a dream. He had no idea.

But she was improving. From nobody—before she was born—she was becoming a small mystery. He wondered what she thought, *if* she thought—whether she noticed things or enjoyed things.

Like the wonderful windows he so wanted.

His mother came in, a frowning, ominous presence—frowning, he instantly thought, because he was standing over his sister.

He moved back and gave a deeper than needed bow. "Honored Mother. I know Father has told you—"

"Yes," she said coldly, not acknowledging his bow in the least.

"One is obliged to go up to the station, honored Mother," he said. "One has no choice."

Mother said nothing at all. And he simply said the next thing in his head:

"It *is* dangerous. The kyo blew up the station at Reunion. But we can talk to them. Nand' Bren can. And I can. Myself. I know one of them and he was very polite to me and he will remember me. So I have to be there to help nand' Bren."

"Who was the person who thought a *child* should be brought near one of these people in the first place?"

"Honored Mother, we were *all* near these people. Their weapons could blow up the whole station. So we were all in danger of being blown up, wherever we were. We are all in danger, this time, even here on Earth. You. Father. My sister. The whole *world* could be in danger from these people if we make them our enemies. So we *have* to do this."

"And who put my son in charge?"

"I happened to meet this one kyo, honored Mother, and we got along. And I know he will want to see me."

"You know."

"I do know, honored Mother. I am not afraid of him. And I know how to speak to him."

"Oh, certainly! You should reason with these people!"

"Nand' Bren will talk to them. We will manage, Mother. Nand' Bren will talk to them, and we will make an agreement and then we shall come home, honored Mother. This will not be a long time!"

A small silence. "You will have your aishid with you."

"Yes, honored Mother."

His aishid would be absolutely no help to him if the kyo blew up the station, but it did not seem helpful to say that.

"Well, good that *someone* will have your welfare foremost. Clearly you must do as your father thinks best. I do not approve, little good it does."

"I have to be there, honored Mother."

"Because *humans* went out where nobody should go and went pressing and pressing until they ran into these people, and now here they are, threatening everybody, as if it were our fault!"

That was more or less true. "They have not threatened anybody. We promised them when we left, that if they came we would meet them. And now we have to do that. Nand' Bren will make an association with them. They really live very far away, so they probably will not come here—"

"It certainly *seems* as if they have no trouble coming here!"

"—but not at all often, honored Mother. Not at all often, at least."

"Is this the paidhi's estimation?"

It was impossible to argue with his mother. He started to say, "I have—"*—met them and you have not* was the next part, but it was not smart to say, so he kept it quiet.

"Bren-paidhi and your great-grandmother have gotten us into this ill-advised meeting, which was originally *only* the humans' business, and now here we are, afraid the world is to be blown up, for no fault of ours!"

"Nand' Bren stopped them blowing up the human station with all those people on it. Now—"

"Now he has to persuade them not to blow up our space station with my son on it! One cannot think this is a great accomplishment!"

His mother could unnerve him, and make him forget everything he had to say, but right now, he was in the right, he knew he was, and the whole argument was going off into what was and was not the humans' fault, instead of what he had come here to say.

So he said it, right in the middle of her argument. "I know

why you had to send me away in the first place, honored Mother. I am sorry. I am sorry I feel man'chi toward great-grandmother, but I was on the ship while I was growing up and I cannot help that. When we got home I wanted to come back and find you. I want to find man'chi here, too. I know I have it for my father. And I *think* I really have it for you, too, if you would just be happy."

"I have reason not to be happy about this, do you not think?"

"Honored Mother." He thought he should just bow at this point, and leave, but his feet refused to move and he stood there staring back at her, hurt, as he had expected to be hurt when he had come in here, and not knowing what to say or do, except, finally, to set his feet and give her his real expression. *"No.* No, I do *not* think you have reason, honored Mother. I do not think I deserve it."

"I have never directed my anger at you!"

"You do not approve what I say. You do not approve what I think. You do not approve my associations. And you say you are not angry at me?"

Seimiro began to cry.

"Hush!" Mother said. "You are frightening your sister."

It was time to bow and leave. But it was not just leaving the room. It was leaving to go far, far away, into something really dangerous, and he did not deserve to be ignored. So he stood fast, angry, jaw set, while Seimiro cried, and stared at Mother staring at him.

"I am *right,*" he said. "I respect you, honored Mother. And I think I do have man'chi toward you. I think *you* have none toward me."

"That is outrageous! I have done *nothing* but want you back!"

"Then why have you never *taken* me back? Why do you keep telling me to leave?"

Seimiro let out a yell, and Mother's maid darted in to pick her up and quiet her. Still he just stood there, getting mad, and madder. And his mother was mad. Seimiro was mad, loudly so. He *expected* his mother to take Seimiro and leave the room with her. That was what she did any time Seimiro cried—his mother dropped everything and coddled Seimiro.

This time his mother stood there facing him with an expression like stone. And it was the maid who took Seimiro out of the room.

His mother gave him no expression, none, and he could all but feel mani thwacking his ear hard and saying "Face!" because he had let down control of his own, but his mother would not give him her face. That was how much his mother had won.

"You are right," his mother said then, very controlled. Then suddenly there was expression on her face. Pain. "You are right."

He did not want to be *right*. He just wanted his mother to be polite to him, and not make his leaving again difficult and hurtful. He wanted to escape. But that required bowing and then turning his back and having his mother say something to upset him further on his way to the door.

"Man'chi was broken," his mother said quietly. "There was a point I let you die to me, son of mine. I told myself you were dead, so I could think about your father. And when you did come back, with *her*—I found no way to light that fire again. Nothing that could mend what had happened. I knew by then I would have another child. I turned my thoughts to that. It was not your fault."

He felt cold, cold through. And felt his great-grandmother's absent hand give him a little shove, a light little thwack on the ear. "Pay attention," mani would say. "These are grown-up things, but understand that you *are not* the world. You will *never* be the world. Other people will do as *they* will do and you will have to determine what *you* will do about that. That is your business. The rest is theirs."

"One does not believe it was your fault, either," he said, and meant it. "I wish I could have helped."

"I am *still* glad," she said, "that you were *not* there that night at Taiben. We all could all have died."

"That would not have helped anything," he agreed, which was what mani would say about it.

"No," Mother said, "that could not have helped anyone. Come." She held out her hands. "Come to me."

He did not trust the gesture. His instincts said bow, and leave, and shut the door between them, get away. She was not acting like the mother he knew.

But it might be the only chance he ever got. He came closer, and when she opened her hands, he reached. Her fingers closed on his, chill, and hard, and she looked at him—she still could look down at him; but not by much. He was growing. Every season he was growing. And he was a long way now from a baby.

"Nothing can mend what was," she said. "I cannot get that time back. What I shall have is what I have right now. And I want you to come back safely, son of mine. You are so, *so* like your father. I very much want to see the man you will become."

"Honored Mother." It was hard to talk. He squeezed her fingers. "I shall do my very best up there."

"You are far too big to hold again," she said, and let go his hands. "*Protect* yourself, son of mine. Do *that* for your mother. Obey instructions. Be wise."

"Yes," he said. It was a dismissal. Mani had used to thwack his ear so it hurt for days, but that was because mani was taking care of him and wanted him to be safe amid the dangers of the ship. He was going away again. This time *she* sent him, herself, and things she had said hurt worse than a thwack on the ear. But her face had changed. She was trying her best to make peace. For the first time in memory, he believed it. "Thank you," he said, and bowed, twice. "Thank you, honored Mother."

She said nothing. She gave him a little nod, a courtesy. He left, and shut the door himself.

His aishid was waiting for him outside. They never asked

questions about the situation between him and his mother. They just expected him to be upset and tried to ignore that situation. But this time they gave him a worried look, far from official. So he was not in control of his face.

"Things are better," he said to them. He thought they really might be better. His mother wanted them to be and he wanted them to be, both at the same time.

That was a start, was it not? She had said he was like his father.

But now he could feel his great-grandmother staring at the back of his neck, saying, grim-faced and frowning: "Concentrate, boy. Concentrate. You have only one task now. Think on that."

11

Supper. All the messages had long since gone. The courier Narani had sent out to meet with Toby was one of the chambermaids, who was both happy to have a few days at Najida and of course glad to carry an important message to nand' Toby.

So that had gone by plane, hours ago—and Toby should have absorbed the message by now.

The other message, also by plane, would have gotten to Shawn. There was no way he and Shawn could discuss the problem securely. The Messengers collected data and they used it, and no aiji had ever been able to control that guild. And now the Messengers' problem posed a serious, serious threat to the world.

Bindanda turned up after supper, when Bren was leaving the dining room, in a moment when no other staff were near—a stout man, their very excellent cook, and possessed of a number of less evident skills.

"One hears you are going up to the station, nandi. That you may need me to go with you. One would be honored if that were the case."

"The kyo have come calling, Danda-ji. They will be here, shortly. *That* is the matter at hand."

"Indeed," Bindanda said with the lift of a brow and a very sober nod. "Then one is doubly resolved to go with you, nandi."

"We are leaving in as much secrecy as we can manage."

"I shall bring everything I need."

He had to smile. "Your teacakes are an irreplaceable asset, Danda-ji. Official word remains that I am going to Najida to meet my brother, who has come into Najida's harbor to repair his boat. That is the story for everyone outside this apartment."

"Yes," Bindanda said. Rock solid in every good sense, Bindanda was. In point of fact, he was covert Guild—not an uncommon double role in those heading the kitchens of great houses. Bindanda had been in Tatiseigi's house, serving Tabini, and now served in his—surely a spy from Tatiseigi—or Tabini keeping an eye on Tatiseigi before Tatiseigi had lent Bindanda to him; but Bren had never been so indelicate as to ask anyone which, and if his aishid knew, *they* had never said.

The mission was shaping up to be for his household, himself, and four plain-clothes Guild in addition to his aishid, covert Guild who might not be up to date on weapons-practice, but who weren't going to have the naïveté of Najida-born servants, either. The arrangement would protect his household in a major way.

But he hoped that problems up there never escalated to that point.

"We have a conclusive selection from the Guild," Jago said that night, in the dark, when she came late to bed, "of the persons they will send up to the station."

One feared the news he was about to receive might not be conducive to sleep. Bren waited as Jago settled into bed and laid her head on the pillow.

"The Guild has designated a unit of four. Guild-senior is Ruheso. Her partner is Deno. They are senior, long service in many difficult areas. Their partners are Hanidi and Sisui, two brothers-of-different-mothers, from the west coast, a little younger but they have been together for many years. They have no man'chi outside the Guild. They served well in great hardship during the Troubles, and Banichi knows Deno personally.

His word is that the Guild is not sending fools up there. We can rely on them."

"Then one is glad to hear. Reasonable people. I can sleep, then."

"Do you want to sleep?" Jago asked, winding a strand of his hair around her finger.

"Not yet," he said.

They did sleep, after a time, in each other's arms.

The house didn't rest. From time to time, the noise of someone awake somewhere intruded into the bedroom—waked Jago first, certainly, since she was awake whenever a sound waked Bren.

Night staff. Usually there were only the laundry staff awake—but laundry had been going on all day, and now packing was in progress. Staff had nearly emptied the closets this evening.

If there was anything he was going to need on the station that Narani might not think to pack, that would be his problem to think of—because earth to orbit was not like running downtown. They took everything they could possibly need: uncompressed clothing, unlike some of the loads the shuttles carried, was low mass. They brought foodstuffs, and a few gifts for staff; but those were no problem.

So there he was, lying beside Jago, staring at the dark ceiling of the bedroom in the stillness after a small sound from the foyer, thinking and thinking and worrying over details—like needing to advise Geigi about the team from Headquarters, which he had hoped not to be doing in the small hours of the morning. But if he wanted to talk to Geigi before Geigi went to bed, he had to get up early.

Then he heard the front door of the apartment open, and Jago stirred just slightly, enough for him to know she had heard it.

"It may be a courier," he said.

Jago reached for something, and did not get up. He began to, and found his robe as Jago, in the dark, talked to someone in numbers.

"It is a courier," she said. "From Najida."

He belted the robe and heard Jago slide out of bed on the other side. He had no desire for sleep now. He felt the slight raw edge of nerves from an already restless night and he sincerely hoped nothing involving his brother or the mainland had gone wrong. He waited a moment for Jago to find her own robe; and before they could go out, he heard a gentle rap at the door.

Jago turned on the lights just as Jeladi opened the door. Lights were dimmed out in the hall, ordinary for nighttime. But the offering of a message bowl was certainly not ordinary, in the bedroom, and at this hour. It held one cylinder, which proved to have Najida's blue band.

"Ramaso-nadi sent Sindi and Tocari with the message, nandi," Jeladi said. "Ramaso told them nothing, except not to delay about it, and not to respect the hour."

"Indeed. Hospitality of the house for them, Ladi-ji." He was anxious to read the letter, too anxious to go to the office for its useful tools. He uncapped the cylinder, sat down on the edge of the bed in his nightrobe, and with a practiced snap of his wrist and a little tug, extracted the letter.

It was in Mosphei', in Toby's casual hand, which, they had joked, only a brother could read. There was no extensive message—just a few lines.

Called home about Aunt Margaret. Explained everything about Uncle T's behavior. Papa says he absolutely agrees. He and I talked. He's working on the problem.

Bravo, Toby. *Bravo.* And thank God.

So word had gotten to the Presidenta. To Shawn Tyers. And Shawn now knew what was going on up on the station and understood that getting rid of Tillington was now beyond urgent. It was a sudden flood of good news.

But could he go back to sleep after that?

Not likely.

"The message went through," he translated for Jago. "The Presidenta has gotten my message about the kyo. He is either going to send someone to manage Tillington, or outright replace him, and I hope for the latter." He felt superstitious even about saying it. "All good news, so far."

It was, a check of his watch proved, an hour before dawn. So, perched on a counter edge in the security station, he had tea and cakes with his aishid, where no protocols held and business was always allowable.

His aishid, having their own breakfasts, sat at their various consoles, chairs more or less facing him.

"I am confident," he told them, "that we will be rid of Tillington as a problem as soon as a shuttle can get there. A few days with him, we can manage. One hopes."

"The Presidenta will deal with him," Algini said. "And will this effort weaken the Presidenta?"

Leave it to Algini to think *that* thought. "Possibly. The Presidenta has been keeping very quiet about the situation, but one does not believe *Tillington* will be silent once he gets back to Earth. He *will* find those to listen to his complaints. But we hope they will be few in number."

"Heritage Party," Banichi said. Human words rarely passed Banichi's lips. But these two words they all knew.

"Indeed. I fear the Heritage Party will seek Tillington's acquaintance very quickly once he does set foot on Mospheira. But I think the Presidenta can deal with them."

There were still frowns. Man'chi was an emotional word. It ran in many directions, and there was a chemistry about it, the same as in humans' associations: at times that word translated. But some human actions remained a complete mystery to them. He doubted even his closest associates really understood Mospheirans' continuing anger toward the old colonial management. Despite everything the aishidi'tat had been through with the Assassins' Guild, there had never been a time at which atevi had even conceptualized class warfare. It was all clan advantage.

Atevi, too, would logically appoint one of Shawn Tyers' relatives or in-laws to direct the station—precisely because a relative would logically want Shawn to succeed in a job that would benefit the whole aishidi'tat. Mospheirans chose appointees with heritage and interests as separate from Shawn's as possible. Both were absolutely sure they were assuring a stable, balanced government.

"Mospheirans," he said, "do not see benefit in supporting the Heritage Party nowadays. In recent memory, the economy suffered from its activities. The fact that Mospheiran enterprise is now deeply entwined with atevi companies means Mospheirans now see their prosperity and atevi prosperity as linked, and they now assume atevi will be as quick as they are to support what they support. They're as dangerously mistaken as they ever were, but at least they're mistaken in a more peaceful direction."

"So far," Algini said.

"So far," he said. "Indeed, so far. And while the interface between humans and atevi becomes more and more mistaken, it becomes less and less feared—and that is dangerous for exactly the same reasons it once was. One has no idea what Tillington thinks the situation with atevi is. I doubt he thinks about it much at all. He simply runs his half of the station as if the atevi half were not there at all. Computers do the translation for supply, now. The translation programs we developed during the shuttle-building went on expanding while we were off at Reunion. There is still is no paidhi up there. Effectively, there is not. Mercheson-paidhi has resigned, as we know. Tillington disdains Jase as an ally of Sabin-aiji. So Tillington relies entirely on the computers, and Tillington and Geigi do not speak.

"When we were absent, they managed the station. They secured their food supply, independent of the world. Geigi built his landers and refused to release the remaining shuttle. Mospheira began to build its own shuttle program. And perhaps

Tillington began to settle his hopes on that. Geigi built landers to recover the aishidi'tat, and Tillington occupied his own workforce in building room to receive a small number of refugees, if any did return, and by building comforts and resources, as I have understood it, should the station have a long isolation. When we came back, bringing five thousand refugees, outnumbering the Mospheiran population on the station—whatever Tillington envisioned turned inside out. Sabin's order put them off the ship and onto the station, and this greatly upset Tillington. It was an invasion of his authority, a collapse of all his efforts. All his building had to be turned to housing. His comfortable sufficiency instantly became shortage. And the refugees sharing the Mospheiran side of the station, crowding them, but not atevi—are not Mospheirans. They are descended from people who used to be lords of the station and give orders to the ship. I do find understanding for Tillington's situation and his emotional state, if not for his actions. One does not well judge whether he has held this anger from the beginning of his service, but it seems now to have slipped all sensible restraint. He is trying to turn one ship-aiji against another. He has made accusations which atevi cannot tolerate. He is isolating the Reunioners, so that the Reunioners have only Braddock to turn to. In the present situation—he is a danger that has to be removed."

"Are we to remove him?" Jago asked outright, and to his own disquiet, he found himself thinking it would be so simple.

But the consequences would not.

"Politically, for the Presidenta, for the Treaty, no, Jago-ji. I cannot do it. But there is a human finesse that we can apply. I had begun to apply it—and now there is no time for intricate maneuvering. The Presidenta will act. He has powers he can use in emergency; I have informed him, and it will very soon be clear to everybody—this is an emergency."

"The kyo have not announced themselves," Banichi said. "But can we be sure Ogun-aiji has not confided the information to this man?"

Bren drew in a breath. "We cannot be sure. But indications are still that no one up there knows except the ship-aijiin, and certain ship's crew, but not necessarily all of them. I suspect that *Phoenix*' technicians have been closely monitoring our backtrail over this last year, in exactly this concern, and while they may have become aware of that ship, one does not believe the station has anything like the ship's capabilities in that regard."

Tano asked: "Can the kyo have followed us? Could they have been there all this last year, nandi, silent—as it was at Reunion?"

"That is *entirely* possible. If it has been there, we have no idea what prompted it to move. But for whatever reason, I gather it is moving toward us on the same side of the sun, which the kyo know will lead to discovery. So one does assume the kyo will at some point announce themselves." Bren took a sip of tea, as thought proceeded down that track to the inevitable conclusion. "Once it does, one may assume the station as well as the ship will hear it. And when that happens, there may be panic on the human side."

"How much shall we tell the Guild observers?" Algini asked.

"At this point, tell them all we know, and caution them not to spread the news beyond Council, and to urge Council to keep it secret, as the aiji's business. If the Guild still has leaks—best we find out now where those channels run."

"One agrees," Banichi said.

"The dowager's plane is now in the air," Tano reported. He had been watching that situation, minute by minute.

"Good," Bren said. "One hopes her return will be taken as typical of her sudden decisions. And once we do make the public statement to the people, we shall simply report that what is impending up there is a state visit on the part of the kyo, to which we are responding at a high level—certainly historic, but nothing worthy of general panic. People will need some image of what is happening. Best we shape it in a peaceful way." Last sip of tea. "But one must also expect the dowager will do as she pleases about releasing information."

"Cenedi indicates," Tano said, "that her public reason is a visit to Najida, the matter of the new windows."

Leave it to Ilisidi, who cloaked her reasons inside reasons inside reasons, and let everyone guess.

Bren nodded. "Once she lands, and from then until we stand in the presence of the kyo, *she* will be in charge. But Cenedi will need to have advice from us about travel arrangements."

"We are in contact," Banichi said. "We will keep him advised."

Mani's plane was landing. And mani would be arriving in the Bujavid very soon, but Cajeiri had no real hope of seeing her when she did. His father would say mani had no need to be bothered, and he could not go to mani's apartment unasked.

So he simply continued quietly making his lists of things to pack, thinking of all the things he might need, what he would want to bring, because—nand' Bren's aishid had warned his today—warned his aishid directly, as if he were grown-up and important—that the public thought he was going with nand' Bren to Najida for a few days, with mani.

About the new windows.

Which was only an excuse.

But it would explain to anybody why he needed court dress despite it being the country.

Nand' Bren's aishid had also warned his bodyguard that he should not attempt to send letters or messages to his associates on the station, either before or after they arrived. Everything had to be kept quiet, secret, and with as little fuss as possible, because there were troubles on the station between the Reunioners and the Mospheirans, and nand' Bren did not want him or his associates up there to be involved.

Nand' Bren's aishid had relayed the question, too, how many seats he needed for his party, and he had thought hard and fast, then answered definitely that he was coming only with his aishid.

He very much wished he could take Eisi and Liedi. They should learn about space. And if he had them he could possibly be more on his own, and not depending on mani's staff—but he also knew—he had heard from his associates—how very crowded people were, and how scarce things were, and he thought maybe an emergency was not the time to try to be independent of mani. His aishid knew nothing at all about living up there. And he did know.

But the station was different than the ship—so he had things to learn, too: he was sure of it.

He wished most of all that he could tell his associates he was coming—and most of all tell them that everything would be all right despite the kyo coming—

But they would not even know about the kyo yet.

And he could not promise them anything about grown-ups and politics. That, he could not control.

So he reviewed his little dictionary and remembered words.

And he so hoped Lord Geigi would have taken his associates into his section and protected them. Grown-ups sometimes forgot things like that when emergencies happened.

He had to trust that, this time, grown-ups were paying full attention.

12

"We trust all is well here," was the dowager's opening statement during breakfast service, on the windy balcony.

And, toward the end of table-talk, one single question that verged on business: "Have you taken Lord Tatiseigi into full confidence, nandi?"

Bren swallowed a bite of spicy toast. "We have talked, aiji-ma, but little about the nature of the emergency."

"He will join us after breakfast," Ilisidi said. She laid down her napkin, a signal that they could come in from the cold.

In fact, there was a to-do at the outer door just as the two of them were taking chairs in the warm sitting room, and in short order Lord Tatiseigi did enter the room, which entailed rising and bowing—not on the dowager's part—and a new pot of tea.

It came down—past polite inquiries after business in the East, and the dowager's inquiries on the legislation—to dismissing the servants for more serious talk. Cenedi and Nawari, the dowager's two senior bodyguards, held the door. Banichi and Jago were with them, and now Tatiseigi's guard, Easterners from Ilisidi's own Malguri, were in the hall to conduct their own briefing on affairs in the north.

Lord Tatiseigi had to take over the legislative effort in their absence, and also had to stand ready to deal with any situation that spilled over from orbit, or any detail Tabini-aiji needed attended in the meanwhile.

But regarding the kyo themselves, Tatiseigi was informed with only the broadest details.

"Have these strangers spoken yet?" was Tatiseigi's first question.

"Nand' paidhi?" Ilisidi deferred the question to Bren.

"No, nandi," Bren said, "they have not as yet, and we are not absolutely certain they know we have seen them. One thing we do know, nand' Tatiseigi: *we* have experience of meeting strangers, and these visitors do not. In *understanding* strangers at close range—the kyo have only their brief experience of *us.* So what they will do and why they will do it we cannot predict."

"Are these the people you dealt with?"

"We are not entirely certain. Another set of foreigners seems to live on the other side of their territory, remote from them, and seem currently to be at war with them, for what cause we have no information. If these other people are warlike and hostile, the kyo are, on the one hand, valuable as allies; but on the other—if the kyo have provoked a peaceful people, the kyo pose a problem. I cannot guess at this point which is the case, nandi. We are so very different from the kyo we do not know *why* they declared they would visit us. Likeliest in my own opinion, they have come to see whether we have told them the truth."

"Perhaps they have come to see our defenses," Tatiseigi said.

"Indeed I would not deny it, nandi. They would surely be interested to see how advanced we are, how strong we are—"

"And did we invite these people?" Tatiseigi asked disapprovingly, as if these were unbidden visitors at a dinner party.

"Precise exchange of intentions or purposes is likewise difficult, nandi," Bren said.

"They had," Ilisidi remarked dryly, "blown up part of Reunion Station."

"Well, and now they come to *ours?*"

One hesitated to argue motivations with Lord Tatiseigi. It was rarely productive. But Ilisidi answered quietly, "As the paidhi-aiji notes, it is difficult to know their thoughts, their fears, or their customs. It is quite certain also they do not know ours, and if they are wise, they will be as cautious as we shall be. They stated, in the limited way we can understand their speech, that they would come one day. And now they have appeared."

"One does propose," Bren said, "that we withdraw *Phoenix* somewhat from the station. It might be provocative to do it just as they arrive. One thing we should by no means tell them, aiji-ma: that *Phoenix* is the only ship we have. The ship under construction indicates our ability to build. A hundred more ships could be out and about the heavens, for all they know. Ships do apparently leave a trail, and I do not know how long it persists, but surely there could be other ships or stations in our control, and we shall not tell them otherwise."

"Which is to say," Ilisidi remarked, "that we are in fact quite defenseless, but that we must behave as if we are not—since what they do *not* see cannot be demonstrated not to exist. So we shall let them deceive themselves, if they need to be deceived. The humans, Tati-ji, feared their library would fall into enemy hands, betraying our location and situation. Unfortunately, as one understands, the arrival of our ship to recover it blazoned our origin and our path through the heavens quite, quite adequately, which was the chief piece of information we wished to keep secret in the first place. Kyo territory is not, one understands, a deep mystery to the ship-folk or the Reunioners. Humans intruded where they ought not, apparently provoking and alarming the kyo, which may have occasioned their appearance at Reunion Station. The kyo, having received our assurances we shall respect their territory, are here now, surely, to look and see for themselves what we are—or perhaps simply to balance the human intrusion into their territory with an intrusion into ours. We do not know."

"So how shall we deal with these people?" Tatiseigi asked. "What shall we expect?"

"We are not close neighbors," Bren said. "We scarcely

threaten one another in terms of territory. There is no pressing need for conflict, which could prove expensive in every sense. Atevi understand that numbers rule the universe and readily accept that people may belong to many associations at once. The kyo seem to believe—and this is murky—that associations once made must be permanent."

"Permanent," Tatiseigi echoed, frowning.

"We do not understand what kyo mean by associations, or if the word is correct at all. This is one of many things we have yet to understand. The dictionary, such as we have developed it, has fewer than three hundred words."

"Which is certainly better than we began," the dowager said, "and a great deal to the credit of the paidhi and my great-grandson, who gathered words and wrote them down."

"And the young gentleman and yourself, aiji-ma, who engaged them and calmed them."

"Pish," Ilisidi said. "We need more words, paidhi. We need precise words and more of them, aptly used, so we may be *better* able to deal with them."

It was, indeed, what they had for resources.

Given that *Phoenix* was all but unarmed, words were *all* they had.

Time was running. Next day was the fourth, their last whole day in Shejidan, the last day before they would take the train to the port, and the port crew understandably wanted their baggage early. Crates stood in the hall now, about to go downstairs to the train station. Staff hurried back and forth. A grocery order arrived, with a large supply of orangelle concentrate that didn't so much as visit the kitchen before it went straight into a crate with other non-wardrobe items, including real flour, fine cooking oil, and granulated sugar.

Even during the meeting with the dowager, two crates had arrived in Bren's apartment from next door: Cajeiri's wardrobe crate and a smaller one belonging to his bodyguard. Staff had simply stacked them on baggage trucks and they stood there overshadowing the foyer.

"We are ready," Narani said by late afternoon. "The baggage is ready to go, at your word, nandi. One believes the dowager's staff is likewise ready."

"We shall send ours the moment hers has cleared," Bren said, "at your discretion, Rani-ji."

So the crates began to disappear then, as many as they could fit in the lift at once, until the foyer stood empty. Exhausted staff ate sandwiches, and slept—finally, slept.

Bren's own supper was a very informal affair—the junior cook, a lad from Najida, had presided over the kitchen amid Bindanda's raids on the spice supplies. And brandy afterward was an uncharacteristically solitary affair. His aishid joined him for a conference, but, being on duty, would not take a drop.

"Go to bed, Bren-ji," was Banichi's advice. "You, above all, cannot become over-tired."

It was good advice. His bodyguard would continue to work, in shifts. He took his bath and put himself to bed early.

He had talked to staff, and made final assignments. Supani and Koharu were distressed to know they were *not* going aloft. They protested their willingness to go on a later flight, if they turned out to be needed, and he had assured them both that would be a consideration.

But to be set in charge of a large household staff—next to the aiji's own, that was no minor thing, either.

Their distress concerned him, however, at a time when he could not distract himself with worries or second-guess his decisions. The baggage had left for the train station. Staff was still moving about, excited and distressed at once.

To shut off distractions, he took the kyo dictionary to bed and thought and thought, recalling the circumstances and the locale and the expression behind the words he had written down himself, trying to get a clear focus on the syntax, difficult as it was. The language held nothing like the numerical content of the atevi language, and, like Mosphei', was more than a little confusing regarding what was a noun versus what was a verb.

Verbs combined, and seemed hell to figure, in forms and nuance. They were dicey things, like nouns or states of being embedding outcomes, and a few infixes giving clues to desirable and undesirable values.

If they were even verbs. Or if that ancient concept was not misleading him.

Could one negotiate a treaty with only nouns?

Easier said than done.

Did the kyo even have a concept like *treaty?*

It was a state of being. So there was a possibility.

His eyes were tired. He was asking himself about abstract nouns while attempting to decide whether there was any internal clue to tell *chair* from *sit*—that was how basic it was. The phonics in which he had written words down were his own system, and he had had to invent symbols along the way. Consonants and vowels were similarly difficult to define. The language boomed and resonated. He had tried to note distinctions. A human throat could hardly manage some sounds. And what he might have missed—or said by accident—

He found his eyes closing repeatedly while he was trying to read, and he finally got up, went to the wall and turned the lights out, then crawled back into bed and burrowed into the covers.

There was an uncommon chill in the air, tonight. Or he was that tired, and Banichi was right: he was trying to do too much himself, wearing himself down before he was really needed.

Time was running. That was the scary thing. He dreamed about girders, and vast cold spaces, where one needed a coat. That was the station docking facility.

He dreamed about a white room, and knew he needed to meet someone there, and could not remember—

Thump.

No. Hollow thump. Rap on the door. He opened his eyes, alarmed, saw a seam of light, a figure entering the room.

"Nandi." Jeladi's voice. "One apologizes. There is a phone call from nand' Jase."

He came awake fast, slid off the bed, hardly stopped to snatch up his nightrobe from the end of the bed. Shejidan's night was Jase's watch, the period in which he was in charge of the ship's functions, aboard or on the station. And staff was under orders not to delay any message from the station at any hour.

The office offered the closest plug for the phone. "Tea, please, Ladi-ji," he told Jeladi, on his way out his bedroom door, and indeed, the office door was open, the light was on, and the phone already sat on his desk. He was shivering as he picked up the receiver.

"Jase?" he said, heart thumping. The floor was like ice. "Bren, here."

"Bren. They're talking. Signal is exactly the same as two years ago, simple beep and pulse of light, repeating every fifteen point three five eight minutes. Station picked it up right at the last of the Mospheiran shift and Tillington kept them on duty. Discretion in the Mospheiran section is now completely blown and it won't be long before everybody knows. News leaked onto B deck inside five minutes, at least that there was a signal out there."

He'd had about two heartbeats to think, first, that Jase was breaching security, calling him and discussing the kyo directly, and another heartbeat to think, *Thank God,* regarding the nature of the signal, and a third heartbeat to realize what time it was.

Damn the unlucky chance that it had come in Tillington's watch.

They were now in an entirely different game.

The robe was not enough. And his feet were approaching frozen. He sat down at his desk, shivering. "Immense relief, here, really, at least that it's the visitors we expect. But we've got to tell Lord Geigi officially and we've got to tell the Reunioners and reassure them. What's the reaction up there right now?"

"Communications are buzzing all over, but Ogun called up second- and third-shift ship techs to duty—that's the ones that were at Reunion with us. He's shut down the station com system except for official announcements. Tillington's also shut the section doors in all human sections to prevent section-to-section movement, but he can't hold that condition forever."

"Is Geigi aware?"

"Yes. Expect a call from him, when he can get it out."

"When he can get it out?"

"Ogun's locked down com. We're not transmitting at all, except this one call, pending your clarification."

Good. "Echo. Precisely what we did in the past. Observe their timing. Otherwise normal traffic. Just keep me posted."

"Relaying that," Jase said, and a moment later: *"Also advising Geigi."*

"What's his status?"

"It's calm, over there. No lockdown. Up in ship-sector, the captains are all awake. Ogun's ordered me to advise Geigi delay his going on-shift until we can get the humans calmed down. I did relay that. Sabin's order was to call you. I told Geigi I'd report back, and that Sabin's watching the situation with the Reunioners. As of five minutes ago Tillington was headed up to ship-sector for conference with Ogun. Sabin's making an official announcement to the Reunioners just about now, what's happened, the reason for the doors shutting, requesting calm, and everybody staying where they are."

Understandable. Not optimum, but the situation up there wasn't optimum.

"Atevi won't riot. They *will* want to get information fairly soon, so stay in close communication with Geigi. They *will* expect the captains to have a plan and tell them about it. You can break the news to all concerned that we're headed up there.

You know the kyo pattern. We're likely to have time. Calm and communication are the best route."

"I'll relay that to all concerned. I hear we are gaining some time. The kyo shed a little V at the same time as they started transmitting. They're going to be arriving at least a day later. Maybe a lot more if they repeat the decel."

That was another relief. The knowledge that Ogun had called the second and third shift *Phoenix* technicians on duty was a relief. *They* understood what had worked before. And the senior captains had authorized Jase to bring him into the loop. As had to be.

"With the kyo, we have to do everything the same as before. That's official, from me. *Phoenix* has the records. But if anything happens that isn't in the prior pattern, consult me before any response. Just repeat your prior response and stall with that."

"Understood. I'll relay that. I'll be in touch when I know something more."

"Right." *Damn* it. "Tell Geigi call me if he needs me."

"I will." Contact clicked out.

The time? He had no idea. He had no clock in his office: a reminder of time was a nuisance when he was working.

Call Geigi? He needed to do that.

Call Ogun? Tell the senior captain what to do in his command?

He didn't want to get into an argument with Ogun. Mistrust and infighting inside the Captains' Council dated back at least to Ramirez—and likely from long before anyone now holding a captaincy.

Every Captain had his allies. Sabin and Jase had the paidhi-aiji, and Ogun, Ramirez' closest ally, had—unfortunately—Tillington.

This was not going to be a happy divorce, upcoming, Ogun from Tillington. He'd known that before the kyo had entered the picture. Before Tillington had slammed doors shut as if the station were under attack.

Now that the kyo were involved, administrative changes that had had time to work out were coming on like snowballs rolling downhill. He couldn't wait any longer to open discussions with Ogun. *He* had to deal with the man and tell him what was going on and about to go on, without letting the situation between Ogun and Sabin blow up.

And Tillington was in Ogun's office for conference right now.

He feared he might have waited too long.

Jeladi arrived with a fresh pot of tea, quietly set it down and poured it. Jago arrived right behind Jeladi, in uniform, awake and on duty, and bearing his bath slippers.

He slipped his feet into them. They were numb. He accepted the cup of tea, and cradled it for warmth, while Jago and Jeladi waited for information his brain was rapidly sorting.

"Jase-aiji just called. The ship is signaling, nadiin-ji, transmitting as they did at Reunion, so it *is* the kyo; and the news is out, on the station. Ogun has taken command, and is conferencing with Tillington. Ogun has shut down all communication; I have asked it be opened, and authorized a response. Meanwhile the atevi section seems in good order, but Tillington has shut all the section doors, confining both the Reunioners and the Mospheirans wherever they happen to have been at the time. Sabin is advising the Reunioners what has happened. Tillington has likely made an announcement in the Mospheiran sections. I have authorized Jase to release information that we are coming up there. I cannot complain of the orders Ogun has given, though I am uneasy about Tillington. Advise the dowager's staff, Ladi-ji, of all this. Jago-ji, advise the aiji's bodyguard. There is no reason to wake him, but that will be at his staff's discretion. It was well I caught a little sleep. Our day is starting early."

There were solemn nods and, as quietly, both left.

He sat staring at nothing in particular, and the tea failed to warm him. Staff was already moving about the halls in greater numbers. Day staff was waking, not necessarily fully informed, but understanding the day was starting, and likely getting information from night staff.

The contact with their visitors was not going that badly. There had been *far* worse possibilities.

Now there was a manageable event, but it was acquiring a texture of small, troublesome details—one of which was that he had, pursuing the Tillington matter, been preferentially working with Sabin and Jase, who were *not* in the best relationship with Ogun.

Bet on it, bet on it, Ogun was getting Tillington's opinions now. And Ogun wouldn't be talking to the Reunioners, who had experienced this twice before. Or to Geigi, whose section was the only one not in turmoil. The Reunioners and Geigi were not Ogun's usual contacts. The information flowed as it was accustomed to flow, and in this case, not from the best source.

He wrote a quick note to Tabini:

Aiji-ma, the incoming ship has signaled identically to the ship we dealt with at Reunion. This is very good news.

The signal has just been picked up by the humans on the space station and the news has spread unrestrained to all human sections of the station. I have asked Jase-aiji to relay information to Lord Geigi. Geigi and I discussed this scenario, among others, during his visit here. We have already laid out what to do and in what stages to do it. I have every confidence he is doing exactly that now, and if he encounters difficulty he will contact me with certain coded words. If anything disrupts communication with him, Jase-aiji will contact me. That, also, we have arranged. So I am confident in our arrangements.

Therefore one recommends that the lords of the aishidi'tat should now be given the news to let them prepare their own statements. One recommends this be announced as an impending state visit. We sincerely hope this is the truth.

To Ilisidi:

Aiji-ma, a signal from the foreign ship indicates these are the kyo, and one now has some reason to hope that the individuals we know are part of this mission.

Humans and atevi on the station are being informed of the situation. Transmission from the station has ceased, but I trust will resume soon. Humans on Mospheira will likely get the news as the sun rises if not before. Lord Geigi is implementing plans long since laid. I have advised the aiji your grandson that the lords of the aishidi'tat should be informed at this point. We are not officially releasing the information here on Earth that we are going up to the station, but the station is releasing that information.

The ship is also slowing slightly, giving us a day or two more, but our launch is firmly set and on schedule.

To his staff at Najida: to go by the Messengers' Guild: *Nadiin-ji, an urgent message is arriving simultaneously for my brother. Please wake Ramaso and nand' Toby to receive it.*

To Toby himself:

Toby, phone Mospheira immediately. At this point news will be breaking on the station and it will be making its way through channels by dawn, if it has not already arrived from station operations to Mospheira.

The kyo are signaling. We recognize the signal and it is optimistic. We regard this visit as a diplomatic contact. By all signs, it is the kyo we were dealing with.

Tell Shawn all other things apply.

Urgently.

God. One more day. One more day, and they would be on the shuttle headed up there. But now that the news was getting out, public disturbance might make it difficult to get safe transport to the port.

Call Ogun at this point— or keep operating through Jase, whose immediate superior was Sabin?

He didn't personally trust Ogun. There was too much cloudy history there—too much of the very history the Heritage Party pointed up as reasons not to trust the administrators, too many things Ogun had done high-handedly, without consultation with Sabin, since Ramirez' death.

And perhaps because of that clouded history—Ogun's having been a part of former senior command—in his heart of hearts he didn't personally rule out *Ogun* as the origin of Tillington's unfortunate remark.

Sabin and Ogun didn't agree on a wealth of matters—spectacularly, they didn't agree. Sabin had organized the mission to Reunion without Ogun's full agreement. Sabin had hoped to prevent exactly what had happened: another species getting their location.

It was no fault of Sabin's that the mission had given the kyo their point of origin. The other species had very likely been sitting there when they arrived, thanks to moves Ramirez had made, as he suspected, leading the kyo to Reunion in the first place, when their decoy effort failed.

But tell that to a man who had had issues with Sabin for a long, long history of a divided Council. Ogun very possibly had been in command along with Ramirez when *Phoenix* had intruded directly into kyo space—

No way to know that now. Only Ogun knew what Ramirez had done. The other people closest to Ramirez were dead. The surviving crew that had been on duty, with a fragmentary picture of what had happened, might have loyalties to one captain or the other—but they had no whole understanding of what had happened or what decisions had been made and why.

At a certain point, in this current situation, the hell with it. So much unhappy history *should* be cut loose and let go, if they could just let go the distrust and the recriminations along with it.

And if he kept talking only to Sabin—at this critical juncture—he made himself part of the pattern. He could back Sabin all the way to marginalizing Ogun—or splitting the crew.

With Ogun—rested so much information.

And with Ogun—stood a good number of the ship's crew

and the Mospheirans on station, who trusted him—for one thing, as the man who'd kept the station functioning when the coup in the aishidi'tat had cut off supply and left them suddenly on their own.

No, the man had been on the wrong side of one historical situation. But on the right side of the other. Sooner or later he had to deal with Ogun, and with Ogun in charge of communications and with the risk of the station sending some wrong signal back to the kyo—*later* did not seem a good idea.

He picked up the phone, began the process to get another station contact, and hoped Jase had been able to get communications cleared.

He had.

And the voice was Mospheiran. *"This is Station Central."*

"This is Bren Cameron, in the name of Tabini, aiji of the aishidi'tat. Get me Captain Jules Ogun. Not his office. Captain Ogun, personally, by whatever channels it takes. As long as it takes."

"He's in a—"

"I understand that. Unfortunately no one he can contact down here speaks Mosphei' if he tries to call me back. And there's an extreme emergency in progress. Can you give me a time at which he will be *out* of his meeting? *Your physical safety* is at stake."

"Just a moment, sir. Please wait."

Communications up there, in whatever Central was active at the hour, was accustomed to his contacts with Geigi, and occasionally with Jase. Probably somebody had to get somebody to authorize a contact that didn't have a precedent, and very likely Ogun had given direct orders not to be disturbed during a series of meetings of his own choosing.

Communications took far more than a moment. Bren began sorting papers on his desk, and thinking. Hard. He had to engage Ogun fast and turn the conversation to the positive. Had to. He didn't want to start with an argument.

Click.

The man *did* have curiosity, from past observation. And he was a bit touchy about criticism.

"This is Ogun."

"Bren Cameron here, Captain. I know what you've done and so far everything you've done has been absolutely correct, to the letter. I've been following the situation. I have information. Have you a moment?"

"Go ahead."

"You are now receiving a signal identical to previous communications with these people. This is a *good sign.* This is exactly the pattern of the last contact, which ended peacefully. You should be echoing their message back exactly at their interval."

"Appreciated." The tone was not appreciative. *"And* then *what do we expect, Mr. Cameron?"*

Not a happy man today, no.

"Keep repeating the initial message and interval identically, sir, no matter what they send, and notify me if they change it. I'm heading up there tomorrow with the same team that handled the last interaction with the kyo. We'll be traveling express."

There was dead silence from Ogun's side, no encouragement at all.

"We are bringing up linguistic records from the meeting at Reunion and we will back you, sir. Speaking for the aiji, we place human safety, including yours, on an equal priority with our own. I would also respectfully suggest, sir, that you detach *Phoenix* from the station now and move out very, very slowly to a convenient distance. Doing it later might send the wrong signal."

"Captains know where and when to position the ship, *Mr. Cameron."*

"Your translator, Captain, in your service, knows what may be misinterpreted as a hostile move at a later stage of these negotiations. With all due respect, *please* separate *Phoenix* from dock now, to preserve all future options. The kyo do not know how many ships we have. They do not know where they might be."

"No thanks to your efforts at Reunion!"

"*We* know the kyo are definitely armed sufficiently to take out the station. I do not serve any *side* in this, sir, except Tabini-aiji. The aiji has every interest in assisting you, and I am personally assigned to be a resource at your disposal, sir. I am willing to support you at any hour, at any time. If that signal changes in any detail before I get there, *please* keep me advised before you alter your own response."

Still a lingering silence. But the contact persisted. Then:

"How are you at taking orders, Mr. Cameron?"

"I am excellent at it, sir, and I am equally excellent at my job. I have met these people—"

"People, *is it?*"

"*People,* sir. The gentleman I dealt with at Reunion is an imposing fellow named Prakuyo an Tep, very smart—a thinker, a very tough individual, and very civilized, who endured ten years of captivity without hating humans indiscriminately. I *hope* he is aboard that ship. I very much *hope* he is in a position of authority on that ship. Whatever the situation, sir, I am deeply devoted to the survival of our side of this encounter, and *our* side includes, as a very high priority, the safety of the ship. I am calling now to offer you my respects, sir, and I hope to work closely with you."

Again a silence, which extended beyond time-lag.

"Mr. Cameron, you say you will take orders."

"I assure you, sir, I take orders very well, but my job is to keep the opinions of various sides from intersecting badly. That is *my* expertise, and I will be as zealous in communicating your point of view or Prakuyo an Tep's as I am in representing the aiji's view: that *is* the job I have, sir. I am charged with bringing *all* these views to the table and finding some way for them to be compatible."

"I'll tell you what I want, right now, Mr. Cameron. I want these strangers out of here, and while you're at it, I want some lasting solution to five thousand people who don't like your people, and who happen to be led by the single damned bastard who created this mess."

Interesting classification—regarding Braddock.

"I understand and agree in all points, sir. I suspect the kyo ship is here on a fact-finding mission, and I hope we can satisfy them and send them on their way. A year's voyage to reach us is hardly the sort of thing that defines close neighbors."

"I have things to discuss with you, Mr. Cameron."

"I would be very glad to have that discussion, sir."

"Going up with the shuttle tomorrow, is it? You *were the delay."*

"Yes, sir. Tomorrow is as quickly as I could get the shuttle reconfigured. In the meantime, sir, the *pattern* of our communication with the kyo has previously been an opening of reciprocation. *Phoenix* has all the records of the last exchange, and it also has the personnel who handled the communications. I am extremely glad you have them for a resource. If you start receiving anything different than you are now receiving, I cannot stress enough, send it to me and don't respond to their signal until I've seen it and we've had a chance to confer. The kyo will take a continual repetition of the identical pattern quite patiently. I would *not* like to enter an escalating series of reciprocal actions with them that could be misinterpreted. Their timescale does not seem to be ours."

Small silence. *"I follow your logic, Mr. Cameron."*

That was a relief. "I will be up there as soon as possible. Express, sir."

"I'll see you in my office when you get here."

"Thank you, sir. I'll be there."

Click.

Connection broke.

He looked across the room, aware now that Jago had come in.

"One could not follow enough of it," Jago said, which was some encouragement to hope the Messengers' spies couldn't, either.

"I have now told Ogun-aiji we are coming. I neglected to mention the aiji-dowager or the young gentleman. Ogun-aiji and I at least reached a civilized understanding this time. But I am not confident I understand Ogun that much more than I understand Prakuyo an Tep. And I do *not* know his history. I wish I did."

"How so?" Jago asked.

"Very possibly Ogun has *seen* the kyo world—or at least knows where it is. I have no access to the ship's records. And I am not certain the information Ramirez-aiji concealed from everyone is extant or accessible in those records. There may be areas of the ship's records that Sabin and Jase cannot reach. Ogun may know where the first meeting with the kyo was, and under what circumstances. He may not. And despite Tillington's charge that this entire situation is Sabin's fault—by all I can gather, *Ramirez* was the captain on duty when the ship entered into the kyo solar system. The ship was spotted by the kyo, and it left quickly, leaving, of course, a trail to say where it had come *from*, exactly the thing Tillington charged Sabin with doing at Reunion, in coming here. The ship took a circuitous course getting back to Reunion, presumably under Ramirez' orders. When the ship did arrive back at Reunion, it found Reunion had already been hit, and that they were consequently without a secure base—with Braddock in charge, trying to invoke command over the ship. There were two ways to go, then: rebuild Reunion, with the constant threat of another strike—or come back here. Ramirez apparently wanted to abandon Reunion and bring the population here, but Reunion being under Braddock's orders—Braddock refused to evacuate, and the ship just left, possibly by another indirect route. Ogun was second-in-command. He may have known what Ramirez knew regarding survivors on Reunion, and Ogun's dealing with Braddock may go back to that time."

"But would not Sabin know this?"

"If she was off-shift, decisions might have been taken that she had no idea were taken. Allegedly Ramirez gave Braddock the order to evacuate his people from Reunion, and Braddock refused him. *Did* he refuse? I think it likely is the truth. If the ship had come back here and found no human survivors, they would have lacked laborers and technicians to create any new human settlement. That argues that the ship really did urge Braddock to evacuate—that Braddock in fact did refuse, and that Ramirez-aiji left them stranded because his priority was to protect the ship and re-establish a base here. What he had done troubled him deeply. He revealed the truth about Reunion only when he was dying—but was it to force Ogun by popular sentiment, or was Ogun as surprised by the truth as everybody else? I am convinced that Sabin was indeed surprised by Ramirez' confession. I do not know what she was doing while Ramirez was making some of these decisions, but I strongly suspect that she may have been barred from the bridge—and that her feud with Ogun and the division in command goes that far back. I have very many questions about Ogun, what he did, who his allies were—but most urgently I need to know what his state of mind is now, and how much the past affects his relationship with Sabin."

He turned his chair, leaned back—looked directly at a face more familiar than his own. And not human. And beloved.

Strange how a few moments of using the language and thinking human thoughts shifted his whole world.

Jago shifted it all back into the order he much preferred.

"Tillington became Ogun's ally during our voyage to Reunion, and Ogun will *not* be pleased," he said, "when he learns I am requesting Tillington be replaced. But he will accept it, one hopes, before the kyo arrive."

"Will he be reliable?"

Instantly: where is his man'chi? That was the math Jago lived with.

"One is not sure how Ogun regards me, despite his promise to hear my advice. But if he will hear me for a few moments I think he will realize I can be of far more help to him than Tillington can. Certainly I can be more help than Braddock can."

Jago gave a silent, grim laugh. One knew what *Jago* thought logical, regarding Braddock's fate, and the math made sense. Humans were, in Jago's estimation, endangering everyone and everything in the world, all to avoid one quiet, well-deserved disposal.

"We Mospheirans are," he said, "a little crazy. And I *wish* I knew for certain whether Ogun *was* complicit in what Ramirez did. It bears on how he makes his decisions now, and what he might want to hide from discovery—as if it could matter now, at least to me. I think, in simple terms, his man'chi is most of all to the ship. And at this crisis, I care very little what Ogun has done or not done in the past. Our problem is immediate, and my concern is a peaceful, constructive talk with that arriving ship and a negotiation that disengages us from all the kyo's concerns."

"Yet," Jago said, "did the kyo not indicate that an association can never be broken?"

"They did," he said. It was not a comforting thought. "But it can have a happier interpretation. And perhaps a closer association can be postponed."

"One certainly hopes so," Jago said.

13

It was ungodly early to be up and about. But lights were on, staff turned out, and the kitchen had swung into action this morning under Bindanda's assistant, while Bindanda was going over his checklists.

Acknowledgements came in.

From Ilisidi: *We shall keep the agreed schedule.*

From Tabini: *We have confirmed all orders you have issued. Our son will join you at the appointed time tomorrow.*

And from the Guild, through Tano: *The Guild unit will join us at the train station. They are advised about baggage and security requirements. They will carry only hand baggage. They will rely on Lord Geigi for supply, and he is preparing a residence for them near his own.*

Matters he hadn't personally overseen were being handled. Baggage had gone out last night. The Red Train was undergoing preparation to take them to the port before tomorrow dawn, and that preparation would be guarded, and closely supervised.

Now the nerves started. Breakfast sat uneasily on the stomach. And Bren found himself looking at familiar faces, familiar things in the apartment, telling himself he *would* be back, and all these people would be safe if he could just quit the dark train of thought that kept intruding and concentrate on business at hand. Staff knew what to do. His bodyguard did. They were in close communication now with Cenedi, Ilisidi's Guild-senior; and with Tabini's. They were giving orders to Cajeiri's young bodyguard, and that unit was being overseen by Tabini's bodyguard. Everything was happening as it ought to.

He sat down in his office to have one more cup of tea, review the dictionary one more time, seeking insights, and think through everything he had on his own list.

A very illicit little Guild communications unit was going with him. They were not telling the Guild observers about that item. His handgun, however, was staying on Earth. If he turned out to need a weapon, his bodyguard would provide it. *They* were amply armed, and understood far better than the unit from Headquarters what they could and couldn't do in that fragile environment, and where they could and couldn't do it.

Trust that the unit from Headquarters was going to be a quick study on such points, and that they would grasp the problems of using weapons on the station. It left them a wide array of things they could do—and shouldn't have to.

And they would also be dealing with ship security, whose personal armament could blow the side off an earthly building.

He sat. He studied.

"The news is now broadcast to the public," Jago arrived to inform him. "There is, on the part of some, alarm; and of course the rumor has begun to circulate that the kyo will land as humans did, though the report directly denied this will happen. Lord Machigi has sent an inquiry through staff to his Trade Ministry asking whether there is more to know on that matter. The dowager has responded that we had no means to predict the timing of this visit, but that there is no such landing contemplated, that the kyo are most probably here to confirm what we told them, and that we are going up there to conduct a diplomatic meeting."

"Indeed," he said.

So their close allies were asking reasonable questions and getting one small piece of truth more than the public was yet getting. The world was in acceptable order.

"I shall draft a similar letter to Dur and the Atageini."

It was something to do. It was a function he normally had. It avoided thinking of more troublesome details.

And when he had done it, he wrote an advisement for his secretarial office: he customarily received direct communications from citizens, even atevi children, asking for explanations, and his secretarial office needed a list of prepared statements that could answer those questions.

It was now down to pure time-filling. He had done everything he could do. The baggage was out of their hands, the shuttle was loading and fueling, and everything was starting to roll downhill with a dreadful inevitability. All that was left was asking himself over and over if there was possibly anything he had forgotten, any item he was going to need, any instruction he had failed to give, or any letter he ought to have sent.

Topari. God. *Topari.*

He wrote, briefly: *Please be assured, nandi, that everything we have discussed will go forward without interruption. The heavens have other residents, and one of these, as you will have heard, has come on a courtesy call which must be addressed in due form and with proper ceremony. We believe this will be a brief visit concluded with the departure of these visitors. But I have arranged for business to be conducted as usual in my brief absence.*

I am confident of a good outcome. It should not in any wise delay the fulfillment of agreements between yourself and the aiji-dowager.

God, one earnestly hoped it worked out that way.

14

Morning.

Mother was upset, and trying not to show it. One was very grateful for that. Father was being official, and expected his son to stand straight and show well in front of staff and family. Most of all, Father expected his son to be brave.

Cajeiri kept his face calm, though indeed he found himself scared—just a *little* scared. He had a fluttery feeling in the stomach, as the whole staff and everybody turned out to bid him good-bye. Only his sister was missing from the event, and she had slept through all the coming and going in the halls this morning in perfect serenity.

Was it an omen?

He was no longer a little child. He did not hold with omens. Omens were the number-counters' way of scaring clients into hiring them, that was what his father said. Aijiin had to be smart enough to know what superstitious people believed—and never scare people by seeming to disregard it—but they should never *be* scared by the numbers.

Still—

There was one courtesy not done.

"Please wait," Cajeiri said, and dived past his mother and father back through the servants and the bodyguards, all the way back to his mother's apartment, and opened the unlocked door without a knock.

His sister was asleep in her crib. He thought he might have

his mother on his track at any moment. His mother's maid came in, from the archway, but it was no surprise *she* should be here. He went to his sister, looked down at her, reached out and shook her tiny shoulder. "Sei-ji," he said. "I shall be back before very long. Be good."

He was making everybody wait.

But he felt as if now he had tied off all the loose ends. For superstitious luck. He went out into the hall, gathered up Jegari and Antaro, who had followed him, and hurried back through the crowd in the foyer.

He reached his parents, bowed for his father and again for his mother.

"Are you all right?" his father asked. Probably his parents thought he had had to go to the accommodation. Probably everybody thought it.

"I am quite well, honored Father," he said. "I shall follow instructions. I shall be very sensible, and I shall try to send a message back, if there is a way."

"Salute Lord Geigi," his father said.

"I shall, honored Father. And I shall be safe. I really shall be."

"Behave," his mother said, which was all she had said. He knew she was upset, and that it was not anger, this time: it was her worry about him.

"I shall, Mother. I truly shall."

"See you do." She gave him a little bow, and that was a dismissal. So he drew a deep breath and turned. The major d' opened the door for them, and Eisi and Liedi were standing right by the side of it, sad to be left behind, and wishing him and his aishid a good trip and a good return.

It was real. He was really going. And he *was* scared, as he walked out the door with just his bodyguard.

He was more scared, hearing that door shut behind him, the lonely echo ringing up and down the hall.

It was just himself and his bodyguard, now. He was fortunate nine, he stood nearly as tall as nand' Bren, he was nearly as strong as nand' Bren, and he was going to go help nand' Bren and mani do something no one else could do. He had his dictionary: Antaro was carrying it for him, in a shoulder bag. He had memorized it all. But he had it with him, in case; and he had it to write down new words.

He was sure Prakuyo an Tep would remember him. He certainly had never forgotten Prakuyo an Tep.

He had, he thought, been far braver when he was younger.

But two years or so ago, he had had far less understanding of what could go wrong.

The foyer was already crowded when the young gentleman signaled his arrival, and there was no more room there, now. So Bren gave the order. Koharu and Supani, acting in their new capacity, simply opened the door, and the foyer emptied into the hall for their good-byes: Bren, and his bodyguard, Narani and Jeladi, Bindanda and Asicho, and now Cajeiri and his four young bodyguards. There were good-byes and well-wishes, courtesies from those staying.

At the very last moment, Narani remembered the vacation schedules in his desk drawer. "Use those if we are delayed, nadiin-ji," Narani said to Koharu and Supani.

"You shall not be, nadi!" Koharu said fervently. Koharu and Supani were not ordinarily superstitious. But they were quick to reverse the omen. "It will not be that long!"

"Nandi," Bren said to Cajeiri, then; and to the rest—"Nadiin-ji. We shall go now."

So they started off, fourteen in all, down the ornate hallway to the lifts.

"Your great-grandmother is already downstairs," Bren said to Cajeiri. "Did you have a good breakfast?"

"I had toast," Cajeiri confessed. "I brought fruit drops."

"Well, well, there will be something on the train, too, one is certain."

They barely fit into one car. Tano keyed them through as

express, they packed themselves in, and the car started down and down the levels, familiar trip—familiar destination, if one thought of it only in bits.

Cajeiri gave a palpable shiver against Bren's arm. It *was* chill in the car. And the boy was in light dress, for traveling, and comfort—wise of his valets and his parents, but just a little thin for this hour of the morning.

"All of us are anxious," Bren said quietly. "Except your great-grandmother, of course. She never is."

Cajeiri flashed a grin. "Of course not," he said, and laughed.

Reassuring to the soul, that grin. He didn't have an ordinary child in tow. He had a boy who'd absorbed his great-grandmother's training *and* his father's, and who had an increasingly Tabini-like head on his shoulders. The boy was old enough to be nervous. He had reason to be nervous.

But he was not likely to panic, either.

"You know the Guild is sending a new office up," Bren said, by way of distraction. "Four observers are going with us, to make the arrangements."

"A new Guild office, nandi?" Cajeiri asked. No, apparently he had not heard. And Bren explained.

"It has been agreed. The Guild has chosen four observers to understand the station. Banichi says they are good. And they will have a great deal to learn."

The car dropped rapidly through the levels, then slowed to a stop, and let them out into the echoing vastness of the train station.

Beyond the concrete block of lifts, the Red Train waited. The passenger car door was open, a bright rectangle of gold light. Two of the dowager's men, armed, waited at the foot of those steps.

They crossed the intervening space, met the dowager's guards, and climbed up the steps of the Red Car.

Strangers were in the aisle, indeed, Guild, four of them, conversing with one man they knew very well, graying, Guild-uniformed, lean and tall: the dowager's chief bodyguard, Cenedi.

"Nandiin," Cenedi said with a little bow, and proceeded to introduce the four newcomers, themselves a bit grayed; two men, two women, and one of the women, Bren noted, lacking her right arm, the jacket sleeve folded and tucked.

"Ruheso, Deno, Hanidi, and Sisui, nandiin," Cenedi said. "The Guild Council's representatives."

Nods defined them, and the order of introduction gave seniority. The one-armed woman was Ruheso, Guild-senior. Deno was her partner. Guild-second was Hanidi, younger, maybe, but not by much. Sisui was missing half an ear. Field work. A lot of it, Banichi had indicated, in some very hard places.

Cajeiri, without prompting, gave a little bow. "Nadiin."

"Young aiji," the immediate response was, from all four. Bren gave a bow of his own.

"Nadiin. We had not planned to have you arrive in a state of crisis, but we shall keep you briefed at all points, and answer questions where we can, in whatever detail we can. You are very welcome with us."

"Nand' paidhi."

Another exchange of bows, and the appropriate title for the aiji's representative in the field. It was his first meeting with the team, and he was relieved to detect no reserve of expressions, nothing but intense attention to his position, not his humanity.

That spoke volumes. Smart. Sensible, able to absorb new things and take advice.

"Please assume inclusion to all conferences, nadiin," he said to the four, and escorted the young gentleman toward the back of the car, to that long red velvet bench seat under golden lamplight where Ilisidi sat waiting for them.

"Aiji-ma."

"Paidhi." Ilisidi held out a hand sparkling with ruby and topaz rings. "Great-grandson. Sit."

They sat. Everyone had risen in respect, staff having distributed themselves in seats along the way. Now everyone settled, bodyguards taking the seats reserved near their lords.

The door thumped shut. The train began to move out at its usual sedate rate.

And the dowager's staff, alone rising to tend the small galley, provided tea in fine porcelain cups, steaming and welcome for jangled nerves. Tea went from there to the bodyguards, to the observers, to all the staff, followed by small sweet cakes.

And the Red Train chuffed down the long winding track that would exit the Bujavid hill and take them across the city.

They were on their way.

15

It was strange, Cajeiri thought. Up in the Bujavid hallway, and going down in the lift, he had been so scared his teeth were almost chattering. Now he felt strangely eager to go. The train, headed for the spaceport, was a place he'd been very recently, and when he thought of that, and the parting from his associates, all the fear left him. His three associates had gone where he was going now, and they had made the trip safely. So would he.

And even if he had business to do up there, and very important business, being what he was, he would surely get a chance to see them before he came back down again.

Even if they were holding meetings on into the evenings, there had to be suppers and some hours of rest.

And there had to be a little time for them to pay courtesies before they came back to Earth. It seemed only fair.

His arriving there would likely surprise them, unless nand' Geigi had already told them he was coming. He envisioned a fine dinner, with crystal and porcelain, and flowers—well, probably not flowers—but a proper dinner, with everyone in court clothes.

Well, except probably the parents, supposing Lord Geigi had invited them.

But that would be a problem. Lord Gcigi might trust his three associates, on his word, to tell them what was going on—but not the parents.

No, Lord Geigi would leave that to Jase to explain.

And Jase-aiji probably would not tell them. Jase-aiji would not trust the parents either. He rather well had that feeling.

He hoped his associates had gotten a chance to come visit Lord Geigi. Even if the mail had had a problem.

But a lot had been going on. Tillington had messed everything up. And very probably *Tillington* was the problem with the mail.

He was personally upset with Tillington-aiji, in that suspicion. But there were far more important reasons nand' Bren and Jase-aiji were upset with Tillington, and that forecast there was going to be trouble, at least for a while.

He could not imagine Tillington clearly, who he was, how he looked. He kept imagining an atevi lord, specifically Lord Aseida, who had made all sorts of trouble, but Tillington would not look like that, would not dress like that, and probably—a good thing—would not have a bodyguard to make trouble.

He hoped nand' Bren would just tell Tillington to be quiet and go pack, that was what.

Then they could meet with Prakuyo an Tep, and find out why the kyo were here, and then he could get to have the dinner party he imagined, well, maybe without any parents. Maybe with mani and nand' Bren and Lord Geigi and Jase-aiji.

And maybe he could even get a few days, just to walk around the station with his associates and see what there was to see.

His last trip through the station, they had been running. Literally, in places, which was remarkable, with mani. It had all been a jumble of halls and the docking area and the yellow tubes and then the shuttle, and with everybody hurrying so that somehow their enemies on the ground would not expect them.

He remembered flying in the shuttle just over a year ago, and landing on Earth—he knew for a fact that he had ridden the shuttle up to the station in the first place, but all the memory he had of that was a vague recollection of things floating about the cabin, and mani telling him to get back into his seat.

He had been a *lot* younger then.

Now, while the joints in the track clicked past, nand' Bren and mani and he all sat having tea, and the four strangers from the Guild stood back by the rear door talking with Nawari and Banichi and Algini. And despite the kyo arriving and all the troubles with Tillington, it was just *business,* back there. None of them were afraid. They were sharing details of where they were going and how things stood. Occasionally they even laughed.

But for once he was sure he knew a lot more about their problem than the four who had joined them—because *he* knew where he was going, and what he was going to do, and who he was going to meet, and why it was dangerous.

"You have not asked where you will stay when we are on the station," mani said, distracting him onto a very different track.

"No, mani." He remembered how it had been on the ship. In his head, he had confused his memory of the ship with the station, himself with one little room behind mani's several rooms connected together, with all the odd doors. He realized now he could hardly *remember* the station apartment.

"One thought—one expects one will stay with you, mani."

"Indeed. And there have been changes in the apartment. There is now a real guest quarters, which is, one is informed, simply an adjacent set of rooms with a door connecting. It lacks a sitting room, but has an arrangement for your aishid and servants. One understands you did not bring your valets, in favor of the Guild delegation."

"Indeed, mani. But Jeladi and Lucasi can keep my clothes in order."

"They may pass items for attention to my staff," mani said, in that tone that said that was how things would be. "Ask my staff for anything you need. Your aishid has no experience up there. They must ask Cenedi for a thorough briefing. Regarding this outside door, it is to remain locked, and all callers should go through *our* main door. Do we adequately agree that this is no place for misbehaviors and rule-breaking?"

"Mani, yes. One understands."

"You will *promise* us. Station politics is highly unstable at the moment, and there is danger. I shall expect you to keep that in mind."

"Mani, I do promise."

"Excellent," mani said, in that tone that made it law.

So that was where he would stay. It was all right. He would stay where he was told. He would do everything right. He would deserve favors. That was his plan, to get things *he* wanted. And he watched the tea service go around again. There was no convenient way to go sit with his bodyguard. One did not fidget in great-grandmother's presence.

And present company was not just people they knew. The Guild observers were observing, one supposed, things to report to the Guild and his father—such as how his father's heir behaved.

He sat and sipped tea while nand' Bren and mani invited the Guild representatives over, and told them things about the kyo and about station politics—which was worth hearing. Nand' Bren warned the representatives about things that were no surprise at all: that extreme options were not open to the ship-aijiin, and that Lord Geigi could not use them without authorization, and authorization could only come from Father.

Nand' Bren also warned them about Stationmaster Tillington and said that once Tillington was replaced, then the ship-aijiin could get rid of Braddock. That was an interesting plan.

If they could get rid of Braddock, then maybe there was much less likelihood of shipping the Reunioners out to Maudit. He was definitely in favor of getting rid of Braddock.

Things he had heard only in bits and pieces began to make sense. He sat there saying nothing, not moving a muscle except to drink his tea, and to accept another cup.

He had brought his kyo dictionary. He had brought his Mosphei' dictionary. And he had brought his Ragi dictionary, because he had thought that was going to be useful, too.

He was right. He was not even at the spaceport yet and he was gathering a basketful just of Ragi words to look up.

The Guild observers made complete sense: a senior unit who had been in the field, serving in the southwest, in a Tajidi Township clan, until Ruheso's injury. They had served in and out of Guild Headquarters between Ruheso's injury and the coup, as investigators—a variety of police work unique to the Guild, where a Filing of Intent and a counter-Filing both involved charges of illegal activity, or where an appeal to Tabini-aiji for justice raised issues that needed sorting out in a certain district.

A number of years ago, Bren thought, he might not have quite appreciated what this unit was, and what their job was, but they were indeed no fools. They asked questions, they sifted statements, and asked other questions. They were *far* more outgoing than most Guild, and, battle-scarred as they were, they smiled a great deal—which was, one was sure, part of their skill. They encouraged trust, and confidences, and probably read very well between the lines.

Interesting, Bren thought. His aishid and the dowager's had both urged a little caution with them. Yet on one level he *did* know exactly what they were doing: he knew the techniques himself.

Banichi said quietly, when they were close to the spaceport, and when everybody was moving about collecting luggage, "They are hearing, Bren-ji. They are impressed."

That was good to hear. But this battle-scarred unit had only met one human in their lives and never had to cope with them en masse. Where they were going was a very different place than they had ever planned.

The same bus waited at the station, with the same security personnel, and a similar exchange of codes—but this time there was no baggage truck. All that had already gone aboard. There was just the hand luggage. Bren allowed Jago to take the computer as they walked across the platform to the bus, and she would stow it—the one thing he would keep by him. His bodyguard had their single bag apiece, and Narani and the others had each a very small personal kit. Cajeiri's four—had a bit more, but they would manage.

There was the long dusty drive up to the gate, and through, then the smooth, slow movement up to the yellow hazard line. Their shuttle waited out on the runway, in a cluster of service vehicles.

This time *they* walked between the painted lines and boarded by the personnel lift, which raised up and let them out into a pale modern interior. The baji-naji symbol of the space program was blazoned on every seat back and on the bulkhead door. The flight deck lay just beyond that thick bulkhead connection.

It might have been any modern airliner, except for the complete lack of windows, except for that unusual bulkhead door.

There were active screens at every seat, and what they showed as they settled in was the preparation going on around the shuttle, the movement of trucks and personnel.

They secured their luggage, such as it was. Ilisidi beckoned Cajeiri to sit by her, with Cenedi and the rest of the bodyguard and staff directly behind.

Bren and company took seats opposite, and the Guild observers sat behind them. Behind them, domestic staff settled in, most of them veterans of previous flights, able to instruct the novices.

The seat backs had a written admonition to use the provided tethers and clip to the rails when moving fore or aft. The interior was far more refined these days, the rules more defined, polished by experience over the years, and he knew the incidents where some of the rules had originated. Moving workers up to the station, the problems had echoed to his desk in the early years.

A different set of priorities was on their horizon. A different set of worries and problems. There was no longer a need for security from assassination, not here, not now, not until the shuttle let them out in what was definitely another world—and even then, the problems Tillington posed were of a different sort.

So just as well to shut the door on Earth for a while. The rest of the planet, in learning that they had visitors coming, would get a further bit of news—that the dowager, the heir, and the paidhi-aiji were all going up to deal with these expected visitors, further developments to follow. And that meant that the station necessarily would find it out. They'd advised Geigi the news was going to break on Earth. Tillington, where the news had already broken, would be aware an atevi shuttle was coming express. Presumably he would learn the Mospheiran shuttle was launching uncommonly close behind it, which in Tillington's mind would immediately suggest both were related to the emergency, and that there was going to be a conflict of scheduling at the station's single personnel dock . . . among other complications.

The orderly conduct of the Mospheiran side, and coordinating the unprecedented situation of an atevi shuttle and a Mospheiran shuttle en route that close together was the last reliance they hoped to place on Tillington.

Tillington should naturally conclude under the circumstances that the Mospheiran shuttle was bringing some sort of Presidential response, to which he would have to answer.

Maybe Tillington would conclude in his own head that he should get things in good administrative order and not roil the waters.

They settled in, disposed items where they had to be for safety as well as convenience. The special routing would shave a good twelve hours off their flight—but there would still be a very long time spent in these seats, a long time under acceleration and an equally long and generally uncomfortable braking at the end, after the body had been some time in weightlessness. He didn't sleep on the shuttle, excepting catnaps, and he was particularly concerned for the dowager.

Cajeiri was out of his seat: that was predictable. But he was leaning on the seat back, constructively pointing out things in the safety instructions for his young aishid—it being their first trip into space—and being very restrained. Cajeiri and his bodyguard had all been very quiet, very by-the-book from the time they'd left the Bujavid.

Exemplary level of attention in the youngsters, all through the train ride. The shuttle was preparing for launch and they were still being very quiet.

It was more than an excess of good behavior. Distractingly more. The dowager's presence could account for it. But Bren thought not. Likely the dowager herself thought not.

This extremely adult behavior? This complete lack of fidgeting?

There's something he wants more than he wants anything on Earth, something recently given to him, and taken away, and now threatened by the kyo, up there.

This is Tabini's son. The dowager's great-grandson. With the stubborn will of both.

He's more than a kid. But he is *a kid.*

He won't disobey his great-grandmother. He probably won't disobey me.

But if something untoward happens—

I know which way he'll want *to jump.*

But man'chi overrides.

He is *atevi. He's definitely become that, since he was last off the planet.*

The speaker came live.

"This is an express flight," word came from the captain. "We will enter prolonged acceleration once we reach switchover, so it will be some time until we become weightless, but you will experience a gradual feeling that the shuttle is becoming vertical, and the center aisle will become a long fall for the duration. Keep your seatbelts fastened, and for the safety of others, do not attempt to retrieve items from storage. A period of free fall will follow when you can safely move about. I shall advise you again before our prolonged braking and maneuvering to dock. Whenever you are in your seat, it is a good idea to have the seatbelt fastened. Remember that the aisle will be, for anyone above the last three rows of seats, a very serious fall, endangering others below. Whenever you are moving about in free fall, please clip to the line that runs fore and aft on what is now the ceiling. Please use the clip at your seat to secure any object that you are actively using and please put such objects away securely when not in use.

"Please attend any personal needs before takeoff, or wait for the inertial portion of our flight. If you have any emergency during acceleration, please push the button at your seat to advise us."

Bren read the information card. Even last year, they'd upgraded the flight protocols to include the express routing, and, to his slight surprise at the time, they hadn't needed him to do it.

The thought of instructions written by computer was a little scary. But they read fairly well, considering.

Computers likewise laid out their course—but one trusted the course plot was a little better than their grammar.

Warning sounded.

Deep breath. He watched the screen as the service vehicles pulled away.

They began to roll a startlingly short time later, gathered speed as the view began to be sky and a very low horizon. Airborne.

No weather, no obstacles now. They went on climbing, and Bren sat and watched the display as the power began to press them back in their seats and changed the orientation of *down.*

The engine-switchover when it came was sleek and smooth, and they went on climbing. The view in the screens had been blue, then more than night—deeper, and colder, because they weren't on Earth any longer.

No phone calls were likely. Nobody would come knocking on the door with a problem.

And there was nothing to do but sit and imagine what was out there in that darkness, and wonder what they wanted, and to try to rehearse, in his own head, what he could say to Tillington to get the man to take dismissal quietly.

What could develop next.

What he could do about Braddock.

He had a recorder with him, a wonderfully tiny device, that stored all the records they had made of kyo speech, of their conversational sessions, such as they were. He put the earpiece in, started it going, put his mind to work, tired as he was, hoping that it might calm his nerves enough. He *didn't* want to rely on the pills for sleep. He needed mental acuity.

The kyo voice—a human couldn't reach that pitch. Possibly atevi couldn't. There were distinctions hard to hear.

And it wasn't calming. It was a case of trying to resurrect the thoughts he'd had then, the tissue of supposition and guesswork that he'd framed around the language. Long hours on the voyage after, he'd made his records, tried to construct the grammar, the logic, get sense of a language unlike any he'd worked with. He had his computer, up in storage. There was that.

There was so damned much to do that he hadn't even been able to touch, with the need to handle logistics, trying to think of every little thing they might need.

He had had no time to handle the most essential thing—which was in the recording, in the notes he'd taken. He could reconstruct it in his head, but he wanted confidence the reconstruction was accurate. He counted on the time the flight would take, to peel away the two years between himself and that time.

God, there were so damned few words. How did he turn a vocabulary of nouns into an exchange about reasons, necessities, *safety* for everybody involved?

Jago, in the seat next to him, touched his arm.

He blinked, drew his mind back from the place he'd been.

Jago said, "Bren-ji. Crew advises there is a transmission from Mospheira, wishing your attention. They believe it may be the Presidenta, or some message from him."

They were no longer in the purview of the Messengers' Guild, now: station shuttle ops and Mospheiran ground services would be handling communications. But given the hour . . .

Tillington's staff would be handling Central at this hour, and while they didn't control ops, which for an atevi shuttle would all be Geigi's people, they were on duty and able to eavesdrop on any communication that flowed in Mosphei'.

He took the handset with some trepidation, hoping Shawn's office was aware of that fact.

"This is Bren Cameron. Advising you this is not a secure transmission."

"Bren. Shawn. Looking for an official word from your office, in your old capacity, if you will, no need for secrecy at this point. News of the ship has been released here on the island. Understand the same on the mainland. There's some general distress about this arrival here, and some confusion. Is there anything we haven't heard?"

Shawn wasn't informing him about Tillington. The call was purely a call for the record, now that, as Shawn said, the news had broken. The public needed information.

But *in your old capacity?* Shawn hadn't invoked him as a Mospheiran government official since he'd come back from Reunion. And he hadn't *served* as a Mospheiran official in the last three years.

Maybe it was a comfort to Mospheira to think they had him on duty on their behalf. It was all right with him if that was the case.

And they needed a speech. All right. He could do that, ex temp. He had his wits in good enough order for that.

"As far as I know, Mr. President, there's nothing much to tell beyond the early reports. We've gotten a patterned signal, identical to what we had at Reunion, and we're responding the same.

"We think it's a very good bet, given that exact signal, that that incoming ship carries the individuals we dealt with in deep space. We parted on good terms.

"These people come from a very, very great distance, at considerable effort. It seems to be only one ship, very likely a combination of diplomatic mission and scientific inquiry.

"We're going up as the original contact team, the persons who last dealt with these people. The mission includes the aiji-dowager, myself, and the aiji's nine-year-old son, so you can see the aiji has considerable confidence that this will be a peaceful meeting.

"We expect to start the conversation with them exactly where we left off.

"We have the help and support of the *Phoenix* captains and we're quite confident that this will go as amicably as the last meeting did.

"And should anyone ask the obvious question, there's no reason at all to expect that these people will want to land on our planet. Their normal gravity is a little off from ours: it's not likely they'd be at all comfortable on Earth for an hour, let alone a longer stay."

God, he so wanted to ask Shawn where things stood with the Tillington situation. But he wasn't going to trade that information in this conversation.

"That's my answer, Mr. President. My best estimate. I hope everything is going well there. We're having a good flight, preparing for our mission. I'm reviewing our language study on the way. We expect them to come to the station, possibly to wish to meet ship to ship. In either case, we can manage."

"All's well here," Shawn said. *"We're keeping our regular launch schedule, right down your track, so we hope you will be able to clear dock for us up there."*

Right down your track. Express. And only two days behind them. Shawn hadn't said Presidential envoy, but pressing the shuttle dock facilities that tight—that was no freight run, either. He understood. Anybody who understood space operations would understand.

Tillington, whether he was listening now, or whether he got the word from ops, would understand it, very clearly, that the President was sending something.

"The technical lads are muttering about sequencing and docking room up there, but they'll cope. No problems that we foresee."

"Thank you, Mr. President. We'll urge that our shuttle be moved out of the way as soon as possible. We don't have that much to unload."

He *hoped* for Kate Shugart. God, he hoped for Kate Shugart to be Shawn's appointee.

But he still couldn't ask that question and Shawn wasn't advising him before advising Tillington—*if* Shawn decided to advise Tillington.

That gave them two days on the station deck with the kyo incoming, both halves of the station aware of the kyo, Tillington in charge and the china all balanced in tall stacks, as the atevi proverb had it.

"Have a safe trip," Shawn said.

"Thank you, Mr. President," he said, and the contact shut down, leaving him with the unsettling realization he had just gotten his official Mospheiran title back.

His connection to the University and the State Department apparently was renewed along with it.

So he was going to have to speak for Shawn, too, without quite speaking for Shawn, until the Mospheiran shuttle got there with whatever news it brought.

Springing a replacement as a total surprise, two days after their arrival—that was going to be a dicey moment.

But a hell of a lot worse if Tillington decided to resist removal.

Have a safe trip.

Good luck, was what Shawn could well have wished him.

His brain had been full of surmises about kyo grammar and sentence structure.

Now he had to map a meeting with Tillington. In case.

And a meeting with Ogun, to explain it all.

Jago, sitting beside him, gave him a questioning look. The exchange with Shawn had been via the earpiece. Atevi hearing could pick up the voice despite the ambient noise of the shuttle under power, and Jago understood more of the language than the University on Mospheira would like. But Jago would not pick up all the verbal code behind the words.

She queried him in the mere arch of a brow.

"The Presidenta asked me official questions, only so he can relay my answer to the news services, regarding the visitors. The real news is that the shuttle from Mospheira is running only two days behind us. I believe he *is* sending someone to replace Tillington. He also addressed me as paidhi representing Mospheira."

"Has there ever been another paidhi?"

"No." One couldn't count Yolanda Mercheson. "None in the last three years."

Jago gave a tip of her head, less surprised than he was, he was sure.

And a lot more confident.

"I hope for Kate Shugart," he said. "I hope there has not been politics in the appointment, but likely there was. The ability of Mospheirans to imagine conspiracies is exceeded only in the Transportation Committee of the aishidi'tat. And I have no time to become involved in a discussion. *Being* paidhi for the humans—means I am charged with securing cooperation."

"From Ogun-aiji."

"From Ogun-aiji to start with. I think it will be politic to meet with him directly on arriving—before meeting Sabin-aiji, unless she comes to meet us first, and I do not believe she will. Ogun being seniormost of the captains, he is due respect."

Jago listened: one saw the analysis flicker through her eyes. "One assumes that Jase-aiji has an association with Sabin—and with you. Which is stronger? Will approach to Ogun weaken Jase-nandi, regarding Sabin?"

"One does not think so. One hopes not. For any repercussions—I have to trust Jase." The route past Ogun's expectations of treachery was forming in his brain as he talked—where Ogun's loyalties lay now, and where they had been when Ramirez had been alive, and the mess Ogun had had to deal with when Sabin and Jase had taken the ship out to Reunion.

Why had Ogun let her take the ship?

Possibly because he couldn't stop her without armed force.

Perhaps because Sabin had threatened to take the truth to the crew.

She never had. But there might be facts known among the Reunioners, kept vivid by their resentments for being left—when *Phoenix*, under Ramirez in those days, had run, and left them to face the kyo.

That information, coming out from the Reunioners and apt to reach the Mospheirans *and* the ship's crew, might be one reason Ogun was upset.

Grant that Ogun hadn't been the one to make the decision to leave Reunion. He'd been second to Ramirez. Ogun might have compromised his conscience to make what he had thought at the time was the only choice.

He'd been rather well forced, also, so long as Ramirez was alive, to oppose Sabin, who was *not* well in accord with Ramirez. Where had Sabin been during the kyo encounter? He had no idea, nor did, apparently, Jase, which said something.

But all that was old history. That was something interior to the ship and maybe something he would never know.

But what *was* steering the current problem was Ogun's support for Tillington. It was understandable. When Sabin had set out to settle what had become of Reunion, Ogun had had to work with the man, half-fearing, perhaps, that Sabin might not come back, and half-fearing that she would come back with information that would ruin him.

He'd had Tillington, with whom he could communicate. But no paidhi to communicate with Geigi—they'd had to route matters through the University linguistics department, through translators who read the language, but could not speak it. They'd done their best. He'd supported Geigi, so far as *requesting* supplies for atevi projects—not demanding them; and Geigi had responded positively, for the most part. They'd limped through a very bad time, while the Mospheirans were trying to build their own shuttle, and Shawn had been quietly supporting Geigi and backing atevi trying to bring down Murini's regime.

Then Sabin *had* come back, bringing a man Ogun held accountable for the whole situation. Louis Baynes Braddock, Chief of the ancient Pilots' Guild—who had wanted *Phoenix* to take on the kyo. Braddock, stationmaster over Reunion, had arrived with five thousand survivors, and no supplies.

More, Jase Graham arrived home with Sabin, perfectly fluent in communication with Lord Geigi, and when Tabini-aiji took back the aishidi'tat, and everything began flowing that hadn't flowed during the hard years of their absence, effortless. Shuttles flew. Supply arrived. If it had all been good change, Sabin might have won the Mospheirans' good will despite the gift she'd brought.

But all the new construction, all the gains the station had made in the Mospheiran section, had to be diced up to house the Reunioners—lifelong stationers, who had skills, and wanted jobs, which the Mospheirans weren't going to surrender.

He'd known it was difficult. He'd not known how difficult.

And insofar as Tillington had made himself the champion of Mospheirans seeking to hold on to their station—Tillington would have support. Insofar as Tillington supported Ogun and made Ogun feel he had allies—Tillington would have Ogun's support.

Insofar as Tillington wanted to play on the old, old resentments of the colonials against the governors, claiming conspiracy—Tillington could wake something deep in Mospheiran roots that had not slept that long, that had waked now and again in Mospheiran relations with the aishidi'tat, that was certainly *ready* to wake, when Mospheirans identified modern Reunioners with the hated colonial administrators and the ancient Pilots' Guild.

He had to move in ahead of that situation, get Ogun to listen, create a *place* for Ogun in the arrangement they had to have with the human side of things, and *not* let a war break out between the Mospheirans and the Reunioners.

Or have a mutiny within the ship's crew.

With the kyo inbound.

Represent Mospheira?

God.

He had to think.

16

Debarkation was what the crew called it. It was a new word in Cajeiri's notebook—or it would be when he had a pen.

Debarkation involved a lot of preparation he never remembered before.

But the last trip he had made to the station, he had had no idea what the shuttle was doing, except when it behaved like a plane. He had had no idea what was up in the front of the shuttle except a lot of dials and lights, and he had not paid a great deal of attention.

Now he did understand. He was much more grown up on this trip. He was a *person* and not a baby. He had spent hours and hours with his notebook, in the seat next to nand' Bren, and they had compared their notes, and spoken back and forth in kyo. Bren had asked him his opinion on meanings, and he had answered and nand' Bren had taken him seriously and even made notes. He was very proud of that. And mani had given him a nod, after, as if she approved. He held that in his mind and worked it over and over when he read his notes.

An ap wo su pargha. Please sit down. An ap wo hi ga sha. Please open the door . . .

He remembered words he had written down but had no idea what they meant, but nand' Bren had guesses.

That was how they had spent their time. And Veijico and Lucasi had told them stories about mountain winters. And Antaro and Jegari had told them about hunting in Taiben. He told them about crossing the straits on nand' Toby's boat, when he had first seen that much water. And how he and mani and nand' Bren had ridden in a train car with fish.

Then he and his bodyguard had gotten to hook up and go forward into the crew compartment, with all the readouts and computers, and the copilot had explained how they would dock with the station when they got there, and even demonstrated some of the interesting-looking instruments.

That had been yesterday. He wished he could be up there during the whole last hour, just to watch, but he had things to gather up and mani's orders to listen to, and they did have the television to show them what was going on, slow as it was.

Most of all he was beginning to be very ready just to be out of the cramped space of the shuttle seat, where one had to stay, once they started braking, and that was sitting still for a long, long time.

Braking had stopped, they were floating again, and he had hoped they would be allowed to get up, at least at their places, but the crew came on the address system and warned them all they had to keep the safety belts on and that there could be bumps.

It was an awfully long time.

And they had not been able to see anything but a wall for quite a while, on the displays. There was one blinking light. Just one.

Suddenly there was word from the crew to take hold.

He took hold of the seat arms. He already had his seatbelt fastened.

There were a lot of bangs and thumps as the shuttle made connections, and he expected those. He even thought he knew what they were, because the crew had told him.

The view in all the screens still just looked blank, but that, he understood, was because the cameras were aimed at the surface of the mast where they docked, and they had just latched on—at a relative stop. The crew had explained *relative stop,* too: meaning they were still going faster than anything on Earth, but they and the station were going very fast together.

And now the station's docking machinery had them, and hugged them close. The thumping and whining going on was the connections being made for air and power.

Finally came a very big noise, which he had been warned would be the passenger debarkation tunnel locking on.

The most exciting thing in their arrival so far was seeing *Phoenix* from the outside. He had never seen the ship, even after traveling inside. And now he could show his aishid what he had been talking about forever. The ship was as beautiful as he imagined, complicated, huge, all white where it was white and absolute dark where there was any shadow.

Crew said that *Phoenix* ordinarily stayed up at the top of the mast, so people could come and go from it. Quite a few of the crew lived aboard, but now, they said, the ship had moved off a little—to give the kyo room, when they came in.

So the crew said.

But something his aishid had heard from the seniors said the ship moved out because it was just smart to have options when the kyo came in; and that sounded a lot more like the truth.

Debarkation was the next step, meaning to get up and leave. And the signal came.

They unbuckled and clipped on their safety lines, and put on their heavy clothes and gloves and masks for the actual crossing. In free fall and with the safety lines, it was not easy, and mani just wrapped herself in an immense velvet cloak that she had brought from Malguri.

Then it was time to leave. Two of the crew came back to guide them.

Mani went first, well, except for Cenedi.

"Thank you, nadiin," mani said, in leaving, and gave the crew a little packet, which Cajciri knew was a bundle of event cards, already signed and ribboned with red and black; and Cenedi gave them another set with a white ribbon, which came from nand' Bren. Families collected those, generation to generation; and in their comings and goings on the shuttle, they had not had the chance to give cards before this, but they took care to do it now, and the crew, all in masks and gloves and heavy coats, too, bowed in the odd way one had to bow in free fall.

The strange thought came to him that the really unique card to have would be from the kyo themselves: that was one *he* would like to have—but the kyo would not be passing out any such when they came in, he was quite sure.

Still if he did get any keepsake, he would be sure to give it to his father. He decided that would be a good idea.

Maybe one for his mother.

Maybe one for Sei. That would be politic.

The hatch opened. The air that leaked in from the opening of that door was colder than anything one could even remember. It was so cold the outgoing gust from their shuttle made a sparkle of crystals against the ceiling lights. They had to move quickly now because of that cold, clip onto the safety line that was in the ceiling of the tube, go for a little ways, and then once they were entering the exit, transfer to another rail, all of which one had to do calmly and quietly, with one's hands freezing, because getting in a hurry and dropping the line could make matters worse.

He was the one of his little group who knew how to do it: *he* was the one who had no hesitation about this part. He was very proud of that. In the lead except for Banichi and Jago, and the two crewmen going out ahead of all of them, he clipped onto the little unit on the line that went out to the tube, and pushed the button himself, the way crew had told him he should do. It yanked him immediately out the door.

And at that point the station swallowed them up, a ribbed yellow gullet with cold that bit deep and fast, between the heaters that operated at intervals. Cajeiri ducked his chin to keep the warmth inside his coat and hurried along, already panting a little, because it was so cold. Mani and Cenedi and Nawari went right behind him, and nand' Bren and everybody else came right behind that, he was sure. Frost crystals sparkled in on the yellow ribs between the lights and the heaters.

At the end of the tube was the big dark cave of the mast itself, which was so big that lights could not touch the other side of it—and everybody had to stop, unhook from the first unit to another clip on another line, which snatched them along into a blue tube, and then just nothing—nothing, no tube, just the line. The crewmen ahead all whirled away into the gloom, and all one could see was the small light on each clip where it attached to the line, like lonely little stars.

Then they vanished. The mask limited his vision, and for a moment he saw was no light but the glow from the connection that was pulling them along. But it was all right. He was moving too.

Then there was a bright light, and shadows of people in suits: the lift shone bright in all that darkness—whether they were up or down or sideways he had no sense at all. He just wanted the machine to hurry, hurry, get them all where there was something but darkness.

That light came at a steady pace, surrounded them, drew them in, and people waited there, station crew, he thought, in bulky suits, who unclipped them and steered them like so many floating balloons into the lift car, which now, yes, he did remember. He was sure it was Nawari who gathered him in next to him and kept him from floating away; and near Nawari he saw mani, bundled tightly in her cloak, and Cenedi, who never left her. More and more of mani's young men arrived in the lift.

Then he saw nand' Bren, the other person smaller than his aishid, and once they were in, last of all, the crewman pushed buttons and extended safety bars. Those rods separated them into sections and sorted out where down was going to be—he remembered that part, too, all in a flash, that one would not want to be facing wrong when the lift moved.

The big lift car was filled shoulder to shoulder.

The door shut.

And, thump! the car began to move.

The floor came up to meet his feet. And there was a *down* again. Tall bodies in front of him cut off the view. The frost was melting fast around the heating outlets. Some people started taking their masks off, which made him think it was probably all right. He pulled his off, and breathed in air still icy cold and so dry it made him cough. He was by no means encouraged to take off his heavy coat. But a hot wind was blowing hard from the vent, and the lift went on clanking and moving, pressing their feet hard to the floor.

"Keep the gloves on," he heard someone say, and he did. He could see Cenedi from here. He saw Banichi, who was taller than most everybody, up near the doors, and that was where nand' Bren would be standing.

He began to shiver, and he kept blinking fast because of the cold, but the hot air kept flooding in, and eased breathing. They were all heavier: it was like taking off in a jet standing up: the lift was moving that fast.

But that feeling let up so they almost floated, and then a warning began to sound and a loud voice said hold on to the bar, just before the whole lift thumped, and jolted awfully, sideways.

Cajeiri could see nothing on eye level except the back of a Guild jacket, which he thought was Algini's.

But their weight was just what it ought to be.

Then the motion had slowed so it just felt like any lift anywhere, well, mostly, except the walls were still cold, even where the hot air blasted out and melted the frost so fast it evaporated. The air became less dry. Breathing was easier.

Then they slowed, stopped, so he had to take hold of the bar. He was a little worried about mani. But Cenedi was there. Nawari was. They would hold her.

He remembered. But some things were different. They had changed the lifts. It had used to be much scarier. Or he was that much bigger.

He definitely remembered getting *to* the shuttle by the lifts.

But not getting *from* it the first time, before the voyage.

He had been very little. And someone had held him close.

He began to remember the corridors inside the station. He remembered the texture of the decking, and the way the walls curved. All sorts of details came back to him. Human faces, all of them together in the dark.

And the apartment and his room there.

But that had been on the ship. Textures and smells and sights that had gotten away from him. He remembered. He went on remembering, pieces sliding into place.

Tunnels. And mani's pretty draperies. And nand' Bren's plants. There had been one plant. In space, it had just kept growing. And making more stems, that made more plants, all white and green, Great-uncle's colors. It was like a dream. But it had really done that. He had not imagined it.

Everything jumbled up in his mind. Memories exploded through his head, so fast. Where things were—routes they had taken—but those were on the ship.

The halls they had run through, to get down to Earth before their enemies knew.

The places he had been before they had gone on the ship. Everything was confused.

He was *never* lost.

Except now.

He had been young. Now he was fortunate nine, and remembered three worlds—four, if one counted the kyo ship. Memory. Dreams. Sometime nightmares, on the world and up in space.

He was back where most of his real memories began. And he felt an unaccustomed fear, because before his memories, before his first flight, where his parents had been—so much of it was just blank.

He had never known there was so much gap. But the gap had happened here. In this place. Here was where he had forgotten things.

Where he had forgotten his parents, and most of all, his mother.

The readout panel had said *aishidi'tat* at the beginning, in Ragi characters—which, Bren thought, should warn any human he'd stepped into the wrong lift if he didn't want to go to the atevi section . . . where he was extremely relieved to be headed, given the troubling fact Central direction had been in Mosphei' for the rest of the flight. Central had picked up the kyo signal, Central had gotten word from the ship—and Central had not budged since, no ordinary switchover to atevi control, no communication to speak of, except the steady direction from operations, which *was* under atevi control while an atevi shuttle was inbound.

Operations—and, early on, and again before they committed to dock—he had talked to Jase.

Who periodically assured them, in Ragi, that there was no change in the kyo situation, and that they should proceed as planned. It *was* Jase, definitely. They had exchanged their code words, and Jase hadn't given him the one that meant trouble.

What is going on with the station communications? he had asked Jase in the second of those two conversations, and Jase's answer had been simply, The man refuses to leave.

Well, they had a problem. And they were about to have another, since the Mospheiran shuttle was entering the picture, with a need for their spot at the mast much sooner than they had ever asked of the technical crews.

But viewing that they had Tillington sitting in Central, he left that communication to ground control and Tillington.

"Everything is prepared," had been the end of Jase's communication just before dock. *"You can skip customs. Your lift will be routed to station nearest the residency. Lord Geigi will meet you."*

One hoped. He had quietly advised Ilisidi.

"We have the option to remain at the mast, docked," he had

said, regarding whether they should board the station or wait for atevi direction, "but this will become increasingly uncomfortable for us. We shall do better, one thinks, to go ahead."

"Of course we shall go ahead," was the dowager's answer. "Shall we be inconvenienced? We shall expect Lord Geigi has things in better order."

So.

They had, among the few things they did carry, the black bags that remained in Guild hands. They had the atevi crew's communications with atevi ops should they have to call on any outside assistance—and they had the crew riding with them in the lift, inputting their destination.

Not to mention half the station in atevi hands and half the ship captains disposed to their side of an argument, if it came to that.

There were only Mospheiran numbers at the first of their journey, during the long trip up to the horizontal shift. At that point the lift moved sideways, like a train, and there began to be Ragi numbers, then Ragi names on the board: the Fortunate, the Auspicious, the Happy, the Healthy, the Wise and Creditable, and within them, East and West, North and South—such things flickered past in mad succession. Those were sections. They were in Ragi territory.

Until, amid the Celestial, in the North, the lift slowed and stopped, sanely, as tamely as a train coming into the station.

The separating bars retreated smoothly. The door opened.

And Lord Geigi himself, with his bodyguard and several station staff, was there to meet them—a very welcome sight, that round, smiling face, a vast relief.

Jase, however, was *not* there.

Bren took off his mask as others did, slipped the fastenings on the insulated coat and let it slide, stiff as it was with cold, glistening with melted frost. Beside him Ilisidi emerged from the insulated cloak looking as if she made this sort of trip daily. She leaned on her cane, not a hair out of place, and Cenedi took the thick garment over his arm. Tano took Bren's coat, and, as they exited, dropped it on the floor.

The sign on the wall said, in Ragi: *Please deposit your cold suits and masks carefully so as not to obstruct the doors. Station staff will return them.*

"Welcome, twice welcome," Geigi said, with a little bow, with open arms. "Aiji-ma, young aiji, nand' Bren. Welcome."

"Our Geigi," Ilisidi said, "is always a pleasant sight." Thump went her cane on the decking. "We trust all is in reasonable order."

"In reasonable order indeed, aiji-ma. Your staff is ready to welcome you. Our people are ready to welcome you."

"And others?" Ilisidi asked sharply.

Geigi bowed slightly. "One regrets to say—there has been some little alarm on the Mospheiran side, which has caused Tillington-aiji to set himself in place, and to refuse to turn Central to us on schedule. We trust this can be remedied."

"What alarm?" Ilisidi asked. "Have we frightened them?"

"News of the kyo, aiji-ma. There has been some continued concern."

"Well, well, they are behaving irrationally." Second thump of the cane, dismissing the matter. "Shall we go, then?"

"Have we heard from Jase?" Bren asked his aishid under his breath.

"No," Jago said, close by him.

"Indeed," Geigi said, answering the dowager. "And are these the Guild observers, aiji-ma?"

"Nandi," Ruheso said, in the sorting-out. The car had since closed and left, but there were still people to arrive, more of the dowager's young men, and the staff, who would have taken shelter in the baggage discharge area, to supervise and identify baggage and bring up the contents of the carrels.

"We have an apartment ready," Geigi said. "Near my own. Be welcome!" Geigi, with a gesture, indicated a door beyond, where they should all move.

"Geigi-ji," Bren said quietly. "I have promised to talk to Ogun. What is going on?"

Geigi dropped the official mask on the instant, and lowered his voice as staff opened the door. "Tillington-aiji, Bren-ji. Jase-aiji intended to be here, but neither he nor Sabin has left Central since the news broke. Tillington will not permit the handoff to us, and Jase and Sabin will not leave him unattended while he maintains his hold on Central."

Ilisidi had stopped to hear, and her brow quirked, the dangerous one. "What is this problem?"

"Aiji-ma," Geigi said. "The station is calm. There is no disorder. The ship imposed restrictions on all movement in the first hour after the signal arrived. But—"

"But," Ilisidi said, impatient, while noise in the system forecast another car en route.

"Tillington-aiji is now overtired and refusing to reason. I have asked Jase-aiji to relay my request to stand aside, and my assurances I would keep him informed, but he will not hear either captain, and Ogun-aiji has issued no order."

"Indeed," Ilisidi said frostily.

"One is aware this cannot continue. I have ordered our technicians and our security to stand ready to assume posts, in our own center, but without the active station switching control over to our boards, we are in a difficult situation, and it seems of no profit to overtire our personnel by having them stay. Since your arrival was imminent, aiji-ma, one decided to wait. So, we believe, Ogun-aiji is also waiting. He has made no official statement to us. We believe he is at odds with Jase-aiji, and will not speak through him; and Mercheson-paidhi does not speak to us."

"So," Ilisidi said. "Force and threats sit in the heart of operations, with Ogun-aiji's tacit approval."

"I urgently need to talk to Ogun, aiji-ma," Bren said. "Before anything else. I promised this. I have some hope I can deal with him."

"You should know, paidhi," Geigi said, "that Tillington

locked all the great doors in the first hour. He opened them again for the Mospheiran areas, but not the Reunioner sections. Ogun-aiji has ordered ship security to the great doors and order is preserved there, but," Geigi drew a breath. "The supposition seems to be that the Reunioners will be in a state of panic, because of the kyo presence, and will take violent action."

"I shall talk to Ogun," Bren said. "I shall try at least to get Central control passed."

Ilisidi set her jaw and gave him a direct, cold stare, or what might have passed for one. There was one muscle, one little angle of the eyelid that said, Yes.

"Go," she said.

He'd wanted to change coats, contact his staff—wait for his staffers who were still in transit. He was chilled through, still shivering, but whether from the residual chill or the news from Geigi, he was no longer certain.

They had the Mospheiran shuttle on the way. An upset, irrational director in charge of Mospheiran Central was one thing—they might wait and let Shawn's representative sort it out. But the doors still shut? Guards?

Jase and Sabin, keeping uninterrupted watch in human Central, with the kyo approaching?

Damn. No. The standoff couldn't go on. Endurance was going to play out. Emotions were going to come more and more to the fore.

He didn't get to change coats.

He didn't get to stop to consult with Jase and Sabin, in Mospheiran Central, or try to reason with Tillington.

No. Ogun was the one who had to do something.

Clearly there was trouble, and Cajeiri had *not* guessed it on the way. Everybody had been tense back on the shuttle, but that was, he had thought, because they had procedures to remember, and business, and scary cold to confront. And in the lift everybody had been bundled up, showing nothing.

But when they had met Lord Geigi, *then* he had begun to read something else, and then he heard about the doors, and Tillington.

Then, with hardly a word, nand' Bren collected half of Lord Geigi's bodyguard, and his own, and two of mani's, and called another lift.

Nand' Bren had made three trips to the cockpit, in the hours before they docked, and the grown-ups had been talking quietly, and frowning a lot, but that was not unusual, and one had supposed it all regarded their docking and their meeting people, and maybe some things about Tillington.

The car arrived. Nand' Bren headed off to talk to Ogun-aiji, and Cajeiri watched the door shut, feeling his stomach upset.

Are my associates safe? he wanted to ask. But he had promised not to ask about them.

Are we safe? He wanted to ask that, too. But that lift door had hardly shut before the lift beside it opened. Mani's staff, mostly, and a few of nand' Bren's came out, shedding cold suits as they had to do, happy at first, delighted to be arriving—they all had been at first.

But they caught that something serious had happened—they caught it very quickly. Nand' Bren's staff looked about, a little worried, a little confused.

Mani herself told them that nand' Bren had gone off to settle a small emergency. That was what she called it. But mani always understated when she was mad.

And she was. Cajeiri had no doubt of that. Lord Geigi was all seriousness now, and the arriving staff went about shedding their coats into the pile on the floor, looking worried and attentive to business.

If nand' Bren needed help, they would hear it. He was sure of that.

And over to the side, more confused than anybody, even staff, he saw the four Guild observers, not expressive at all, just watching, full of questions they had no way to answer, and with no one specially telling them.

Those were dangerous people, he thought, if there should be trouble. They might be older, and one with only one arm, but they were dangerous people. In those black bags the Guild carried were weapons. They had not taken them out, and nand' Bren's escort had just taken their sidearms and left the Guild baggage to mani's bodyguard, but Cajeiri began to be just a little scared Cenedi might open up those bags, and so might the Observers. If the Guild decided they were under threat, if mani were in danger, the Guild could very quickly become its own law.

They had only just arrived. And the kyo had not even shown up. And already grown-ups in charge were being fools.

"The paidhi-aiji will do his job," mani said then, with a sharp thump of her cane. "We are all here. We are all secure. Our remaining baggage will arrive in due order. We could well do now with tea in a proper cup, and a chair that does not insist upon safety belts."

"Indeed, aiji-ma," Lord Geigi said, and guided them away from the lift, and toward a set of doors, which opened at a touch of his hand. A hallway with four doors was beyond, a short hall, and another door.

So mani wanted them to go on as if nothing had happened.

Ship security had their own terrible weapons, if it came to shooting. Cajeiri had never seen the white guns fired, but he had stood on the driveway of Lord Tatiseigi's estate and seen ash coming down from fires they had created.

"Remember the way, Taro-ji," he muttered to Antaro the moment the doors closed at their backs. "Map the corridors we use getting to the apartment, in case we have to get back here on our own."

He was good at mapping places, himself. He had learned to remember his way in the dark and cold of the ship-tunnels; and if things went very badly, they could very well need to know their way back to the lifts.

But if that happened—there was still no place for them to go without a shuttle, was there? And none of them could operate a shuttle—even if it had gone through all the refueling and sat ready to move.

They could not get off the station without the pilots, who would be finding their way up to a special residency, too.

They had no way off. And he urgently wanted to understand what was going on.

Another door opened, and the place beyond was huge, upcurving as long hallways had to be, with people going and coming. It was a corridor of offices and even what looked like shops and restaurants, wide as a city street. There were hundreds of people. A scary lot of people. But all atevi.

Their people. Who stopped still, and moved to the sides of the corridor and bowed politely.

Word evidently spread; suddenly there were even more people coming out into the corridor, emerging from places that were, he thought, *shops,* just like a street in Shejidan, except for the ridged decking instead of paving.

Regular people, he thought. People who ran the station, who lived here.

Not dangerous people.

People such as he saw from his father's balcony. People who moved, very small and far below, in the street at the foot of the Bujavid hill. One of his earliest, strangest memories of all was his father holding him on the rail of that balcony, with all the city at his feet, and the streets and the city below the hill.

And he had stood at that rail again this year, years older, wondering, just wondering what it would be like to go down there and walk on a public street.

Geigi had surely had a private way to take them to their residence.

But Geigi had taken them out where people were, where people lived, people who seemed respectful, if excited, and *glad* to see mani and Lord Geigi.

And maybe, he thought, glad to see *him*. Because he was,

like mani, official. Things had been scary, and still were, and Lord Geigi was doing a demonstration, letting people *see* that they were here, taking care of them. He saw mani glancing from side to side as she walked, nodding politely to people who bowed, just as if it were a court appearance, and these were lords invited to the festivity.

So he did what mani did, and put on a pleasant face, no matter that strange people were very close to him. His aishid stayed right next to him, absolutely on alert; he felt it. But it was scary and exciting at once—and he *felt* these people's attention, felt it as if their anxiousness were propping him up and weighing him down at the same time.

All these people trusted *they* were going to fix things. That was what he was feeling. Their being here was like a promise they were making.

And for the first time the people on the station were not just numbers he heard about. They were *these* people. They became real to him. And he and mani became real to them.

He only hoped he looked more confident than he felt at the moment.

Consternation spread, the moment they got off the lift, one human in sensible brown atevi traveling dress and a dark tidal wave of Guild headed straight down the middle of a station corridor. But ship's crew, who owned this area, clearly knew exactly who they were. At least half the ship's crew had seen such sights before, and security at various points evidently had a standing Don't Interfere order. Doors opened for them, passing the traveling disturbance from one area's concern and letting it into another.

Bren walked at top speed, not out of breath, but keeping pace, moving along the up-horizoned corridor with all the strange perspective that played tricks with earthborn eyes. Lord Geigi's two men were in the lead to guide them, but in point of fact Bren himself recognized a hall he had walked before, the administrative section, where *Phoenix* captains held absolute sway, apart from the other occupants of the space station—and apart from the ship itself.

He didn't personally remember the guards on duty at the end of the executive corridor, but then, the one part of the ship's crew he didn't know by sight—was Ogun's.

"Sir," the response was, at those doors, before he said a thing. And as the door opened. "The guns—"

"We won't use them," Bren said, and walked past.

"Sir!" he heard behind him, and he raised his voice without looking back. "Appointment with the captain! Don't delay us! My guards don't speak *ship!"*

It was the last short office-lined corridor to the number one office at the end. A secretary had a desk to the left of those double doors, a young man talking to someone on com as they approached.

The word came back, apparently, before they arrived. The doors opened. But—

"They stay here, sir."

"Two with me," Bren said curtly, and walked on in, Banichi and Jago accompanying him.

Ogun pushed back from his desk and scowled as Bren stopped midway from the door, and as Banichi and Jago took up a position behind him and to either corner of the room.

Dead stop, then. One didn't breathe hard. One didn't give any indication of disturbance.

Ogun, a middle-aged man with intense dark eyes and a complete lack of hair—even the eyebrows—took his own position, leaning back in his chair, hands clasped on his middle, giving no sign of disturbance either. And none of welcome.

"Captain Ogun," Bren said. *"Thank* you. I'm glad to say the aiji-dowager and the heir-designate are here with me, all in good order. We've brought you what resources we have. Tabini-aiji and the President of Mospheira will wish me to convey their offer of cooperation as well."

"Sit down," Ogun said.

No bow was due that reception, just an unhurried nod of acquiescence. Bren took one of the two chairs, arranging his coat and cuffs, with all courtly grace. *I'll sit. Let's talk. But I'm not your subordinate. Sir.*

If it were a Ragi lord, there would have been a good quarter hour of tea. Ogun just stared, grim-faced, for a moment. "You've talked with Geigi."

"I have, sir. I understand Stationmaster Tillington is upset and there is a small situation in progress. I hope we can get past that."

"You come up here high and wide, apparently with a program and your own intentions. Let me make something clear, Mr. Cameron, if there's been any doubt at all. I don't give a damn for your groundbound politics. And you don't decide things up here."

"Let me make clear my position, also, Senior Captain. There's a problem approaching this station, probably intending to dock. I'm the best resource you've got, I've met the kyo before, I'm here to arrange a peaceful contact with this incoming ship, and I assure you, I equally don't give a damn about issues that divide you on this station. I don't *have* a side, except insofar as I want everybody to come out of this alive and happy. If we can get past our internal problems and arrange tight control over what signals we send out to that ship, we'll all be safer."

"You say you don't give a damn. Unfortunately you *are* terrestrial politics, *personified.*"

"The Central schedule is disrupted. I take it the issue is Stationmaster Tillington."

"The *issue* is five thousand unscheduled problems you dumped on my deck, Mr. Cameron! The issue is potential riot and sabotage, which has now gone critical, thanks to the kyo you stirred up. You're here to damp it down? *Fine.* Now explain how you're going to deal with that ship."

"First off, Senior Captain, I strongly suspect the kyo are here to reconnoiter. I think they want to know what we are, how extensive our holdings are, and how many ships we have. But I don't think I want to tell them that."

Ogun let go a slow breath.

"So?"

"We know there's another species out there besides kyo. The kyo may be looking for evidence of our dealing with their enemies. They may also want to verify that we haven't been lying in what we have communicated to them. We have very little in common, physically. We don't share the same comfort zone. Trade is certainly inconvenient over such a distance. Maintaining a presence here—I hope is equally inconvenient for them. I think they're here just to look."

"You're betting on it. You're betting a lot, Mr. Cameron."

"The extent to which I bet will change as I get information, Senior Captain, and I will be reporting to you as I get it. I'll be hoping for all the help I can get."

"You brought the aiji's kid up here."

"The contact we made was through that kid. And through the dowager."

"As a woman?"

"As an elder. We think. As we think the boy's youth was also a positive. We honestly don't know the age or gender of anyone we dealt with. We guess. But we don't know. It's that basic. We want to re-create what understanding we had, take up the conversation where we left it, with the very same persons we were talking to, granted the person we met is on that ship. We hope he is. We were trying to gain an understanding of each other—despite the fact most of the kyo words we know are things like tables and chairs, food and drink. But that's my skill, sir. That's what I do. That's what I'm trained to do. You on this ship have never made close contact with another species. Neither, as I gather, have the kyo. Atevi and Mosphcirans have. *Our relationship* is the equation I think that ship is here to solve. It puzzles them. It seemed to interest them. And we *don't* want to present them the spectacle of quarrels in our midst."

He left a small silence, then, and Ogun sat staring at him, but with an occasional redirection in the stare, a thought hurtling meteor-like through a mind itself quite, quite foreign to atevi or Mospheirans.

"They're transmitting," Ogun said, tight-jawed. "They're repeating a series of beeps. Whatever that means. We answer the same. They haven't changed. What's your opinion?"

"That they have no desire to startle us, perhaps. That they're inviting a changed response from us. Or intending to give one themselves as they get closer. In short, I don't know. We've had no experience to tell us, except that this was exactly what they did the last time, and we're doing what *we* did the last time."

"You think you can talk to them, in some meaningful degree."

"I'm certainly prepared to try, sir. We were able to meet face to face with what may have been significant higher-ups aboard their ship. The presence of persons of older and younger age among us, notably the aiji-dowager and the aiji's son, did seem to impress them. They may have taken it as proof of a peaceful intent." He wasn't sure he was getting through to Ogun in the least. The jaw stayed set. He tried something less conservative, involving more guesswork. "They blew hell out of Reunion, but they didn't destroy it. I think they sat there silent and at distance and waited. They appear to have watched *Phoenix* come in when Ramirez was Senior Captain, then watched it leave without removing the population. They then went on sitting there, evidently, for ten more years, knowing what direction you'd gone and probably which star was your likeliest destination."

Ogun's jaw clenched and a muscle jumped. That was all.

"Possibly they've also been sitting out in the fringes of this solar system for some time," Bren said, "watching us the way they watched at Reunion. I understand we *could* miss that sort of presence, if they weren't actively transmitting." And right into the heart of the old feud. "And regarding that, I have a question, sir, that could be important to know. When the kyo spooked *Phoenix* out of their space, back under Ramirez' command, did you come into their space directly *from* Reunion, and did you go directly *to* Reunion after you were spotted?"

The jaw worked a moment. Ogun knew *exactly* what he was asking. And it was extremely sensitive territory. "Not directly. We tried misleading them on our exit, which is how they got to Reunion ahead of us. Unfortunately our back-trail hadn't faded. The back-trail was, yes, what they followed instead of us."

"So they're *not* communicating faster than they can fly."

"Nobody can do that," Ogun said.

"Did you pick up any attempt to communicate the first time you met?"

"No. They showed, and it was Ramirez' decision to move. Fast."

That mattered. *Phoenix* popped up in kyo space, didn't talk, ran without trying to talk. Just spooked out.

"It helps to know, sir. So we don't know what sort of ship they took you for. We have no knowledge what sort of species they're at war with, either. Or whether they've ever talked to *them*."

"Meaning?"

"They crippled Reunion. They went straight there instead of following you, and crippled it. And waited. Whether another ship followed you wherever you went in your retreat—whether there's always been just one kyo ship—there's no indication. That ship attacked Reunion, and it's my suspicion they sat just watching Reunion try to recover, waiting for a ship to show up. And when you did come in to Reunion, you found it damaged, you found survivors, and, apparently after an exchange with Stationmaster Braddock, Braddock refused to abandon the station and Ramirez left them in their situation. Am I right? Ramirez kept that communication secret, had *only* his aide in on it, and didn't tell the captains who were off-duty. Did he spot that watcher? Did he spook out and run because of it?"

Silence for a moment. A muscle jumped in Ogun's jaw.

"That's a damned interesting theory, Mr. Cameron. Not correct in all points, but interesting."

Ogun. The man who'd posed heated objection to *Sabin* taking a mission back to Reunion to recover the human library—objecting that Reunion would have no living survivors.

Sabin had gone back after the library. And Ogun's reason for anger at her was, according to reports, her coming straight back here to Earth once she'd encountered the kyo.

But was it the real reason?

Was there *guilt* involved in that anger? A secret that had eaten Ogun alive and poisoned relations among the captains for more than a decade, now?

"The kyo sat there for ten years, sir, just waiting for that situation to play out. But at some point they went inside the station, perhaps to explore the architecture, perhaps to capture someone for interrogation. The Reunioners snatched a member of their investigating team, and the kyo immediately backed off. Still with no communication. No further interference. And *finally* we came back. When we did, they signaled us. We responded. They let us contact the Reunioners. They let *us* remove them. We retrieved their crew member, we talked with him, we returned him to his people, and through him, we were able to meet and talk with them. We may have talked with kyo fairly high up in authority. But the point is—they *tested* the situation. They waited. They have patience in ten-year packages. So, no, I don't want to rush the communications. And if you *do* know anything bearing on what I've just outlined, sir, without prejudice, without judgment, without any opinion of the rightness or wrongness of what happened—I just want to know. I need information. Correct information."

Small silence. "Was *Sabin* part of this meeting with the kyo?"

"The participants in the conference with the kyo, sir, were

myself, the aiji-dowager, and the young aiji—both of whom have come with me to reprise the contact we had going."

Ogun's jaw worked. He said nothing.

"We *have* a moderately good record with them, sir: we respected their territorial claim, we retrieved their crewman, returned him to them. We were allowed to take the Reunioners off, we left the area, and there were no shots exchanged. I suspect they *may* have some key concepts in common with atevi—maybe more so than they have with humans. And I will *use* that, if applicable."

Eyebrows lifted, carefully. A question.

"Association, sir. *Aishi.* For one thing, since it was the *atevi* the kyo contacted, it's become the atevi language that gives us our bridge to understanding kyo. For another, the word *association* is one abstract concept they seemed to reach for. I think it *is* an emotional word with them. If I can assign emotion to people who can wait ten years. I don't know."

"People." That concept seemed itself challenging—to Ogun's thinking. And not in a welcome way.

"Whatever they are, they seem to be motivated to ask questions instead of shooting at us. I have no clue what their concepts are of nations or politics, I don't know how their decisions are made. But as long as we *are* talking instead of resorting to weapons or laying claim to each other's property, we can figure how to maneuver with them."

"Where do you propose to meet them?"

"Likely they'll come much closer. I'm personally prepared to meet them on their deck or on the station, and the aiji-dowager and the boy will be with me—hoping we do know who we're dealing with. It's far more dangerous to let our fear feed theirs or to hang back and let their imaginations and ours work. We need your support, on all fronts."

Long silence.

"You come in here to take over from Tillington. You're prepared to do that."

That explained a bit.

"Is that his official assessment of my mission?"

"That's his concern. He says you've gone atevi."

"In point of fact, a paidhi works both sides of a situation. My job is to 'go atevi'—or human—alternately. And completely. My last conversation with Tabini-aiji was the day before launch and my last conversation with the President was a call en route, so I'm up to date with their wishes, which are to do what I can to communicate with the kyo and prevent any misunderstanding. But as regards Stationmaster Tillington's fears about me—that's not my mission. *The President* is sending a special envoy to assume command during the emergency, to manage the Mospheiran workforce, and likewise to assure that *Mr. Braddock* doesn't cause problems, now or in the future."

"So we get one more side in this mess? One more finger on the buttons up here is no damned help, Mr. Cameron."

"The Presidential envoy will consult with *you*, sir, and your approval will rule all matters with the ship and weigh heavily with the envoy. Presidential authority, however, *will* end the discussion between Mr. Tillington and Mr. Braddock."

"And if the Reunioners don't give a damn about your President?"

"The President is seeking to cooperate with you personally, sir, in finding a resolution to the Reunioner problem *after* the kyo have departed the system. So will Tabini-aiji. The President does *not* back Tillington's proposal. Mospheira doesn't need a separate human population with separate interests. Atevi object to that, and to their presence here. The composition of the station population is half *Mospheiran* and half atevi, by treaty, in cooperation with the ship. Creating a separate station under *Mr. Braddock's* authority? No, sir. That's definitely not acceptable."

Ogun shoved his chair further back and canted it. "So we're completely reversing position."

"The President never approved the plan. If Stationmaster Tillington represented that it had the President's approval, this is not the case. The President is *also* distancing himself from a statement Stationmaster Tillington made, and which, if the aiji-dowager needs to become aware of it, will bring extremely unpleasant consequences with the aijinate."

"Is that a threat, Mr. Cameron?"

"No, sir, a warning. You may not be aware, sir—I assume you are not. Mr. Tillington suggested, before witnesses, that the meeting of the aiji's son with the human children was politically motivated, and Captain Sabin's doing. I assure you that does *not* translate into the atevi language in any fashion which could exempt the aiji-dowager from his accusation. She would be within her rights to File Intent on the man."

"Is that this mass of security arriving with you?"

"This is the aiji-dowager's usual escort. I haven't officially informed her about the statement, but there is no guarantee she is not privately aware of the incident. If she *should* choose to be informed—there would have to be diplomatic consequences, and this is the worst possible time to have that happen. The President *does* know about it. And for this and other matters of policy and failure to consult, his envoy *will* replace Stationmaster Tillington, I hope gracefully and privately, without any reference to the aiji's son, so we can get on with the business at hand and never mention it happened."

He saw Ogun draw a breath to retort, scowling, and he kept going. "You will have, on those terms, sir, the *full* support of the President, and the envoy will stay on the station until a permanent appointment can be made. I can say with fair assurance that it will be someone you can work with."

Silence. Again. Ogun wasn't pleased to be challenged. He wasn't pleased to be handed a solution to *his* mess. He wasn't pleased at being handed anything he hadn't chosen . . . including, clearly, the presence of a Presidential envoy.

He had a card.

And maybe it was time to play it.

"You also have, Captain, at the direction of Tabini-aiji *and* President Tyers, *my* support, which I am glad to give. I voyaged with Captain Sabin and Captain Graham, so I do communicate well with them, but that is *nowhere* comparable to my obligation to a populated planet which is my *home,* sir, as the ship is yours. I have every interest in keeping this station *and* the ship and all its options safe, and to do that, I need to do what I'm damned *good* at, sir. But to do that, I need humans on this station not to be conducting a civil war at my back. You *are* the authority above other authorities up here, so I'm backing you, as I hope you will back me."

"*You* are an arrogant bastard, Mr. Cameron."

"One *entirely* at your service, sir, and in that interest, let's create an understanding—and I *have* discussed this with President Tyers. You want the Reunioners taken out of your way. You wish they, and their politics, had never exited Reunion. And you wish Braddock would take a walk in space. We're not far apart in that opinion. There's no way to deal with that situation until we handle the kyo, and we can't let Braddock use the kyo's presence as a launch of his second career. If we manage things right, the kyo will come in, they'll dock, we'll speak to them, and with the Presidential envoy in charge of the Mospheiran half of the station, things there will stay perfectly quiet while we do it. If we *don't* manage to talk to the kyo, the very best outcome we may get is a permanent kyo observation station sitting out there destabilizing our politics and limiting our options for a very long time to come. The President doesn't want that, the aiji doesn't want that, and I don't think you want that. Tillington is making himself an obstacle to our dealing. His replacement will not. And we will *move* the Reunioner population down to the planet, where it will not be a further issue."

Ogun blinked. Just that. "Whose word backs *that,* Mr. Cameron? And how do they get down there? Parachute, like your ancestors?"

"The Mospheiran shuttle program is getting into production,

sir. And they will have help from the aiji, who is equally in favor of seeing this issue resolved. It is a viable option. It's the *only* viable option, which *became* an option thanks to your medical folk. One could assume you had some such in mind, when the young aiji's visitors were able to thrive down there."

Ogun's notion? Or was it Sabin who had pushed the meds? Or Jase himself? *Someone* had, whether for practical hope—or politics.

Ogun stared at him, mouth just a little less clamped. "So who *is* this envoy, Mr. Cameron?"

"At this point, sir, I haven't been informed. Communication has been severely limited, so long as Mr. Tillington has been sitting in a position to intercept messages between myself and the President, and so long as communications on the planet are subject to eavesdropping by various agencies. The President may have considered alternatives I know nothing about, but I have a strong hope the appointment will be somebody who's been here before, who knows the station and its systems."

That was a very short list.

And Ogun drew in a deep breath. "Mr. Cameron, I hear both good and bad about you. I hear you do get results. So let me give you one very clear warning about dealing with us. Don't *you* try to play politics with the captains, even if you think it might benefit you."

"I have no such intentions. If I can do anything to prevent any problem among the captains, or if you feel I'm not seeing something I should see, inform me, and I'll do all I can to work with the Council as a whole, because it's in all our interests."

"So are *you* going to break the news to Tillington?"

"Would you prefer to, sir?"

"Not my job," Ogun said with a wave of his hand. "Your Presidential envoy comes up here—fine. He keeps order and follows regulations. You say you can deal with the kyo. All right. I've got no other offers on my desk. You say you can fix the *Reunioner* situation so we never see it again. Good. I'll *remember* that. Right now—go settle in, and don't disturb what's not rattling. No changes in orders as they stand. Understood?"

He supposed that was a victory of sorts. Ogun pushed him. He could say, You don't order me. Or even: Be damned to you: you're not irreplaceable, either. It was very possible that Ogun had partnered with Ramirez in his decisions. Possibly Ogun had helped bring about the situation they had now, and possibly he'd deliberately kept Sabin in the dark.

But this was also the man who'd managed the station during two years of hell and continued to hold it during the last troubled year of unplanned residents and short supply.

So he contented himself with a quiet, respectful nod. "Absolutely. I'll work with you, sir. In all respects. Right now I'll be going to my apartment, dealing with my staff. If any problems come up, if you need a translator—at any hour—you know where to find me."

The residential area was restricted, beyond a guarded door, with, on the other side, all that area of shops and apartments, tiers of them, balconies and shops above the shops, Lord Geigi said.

But past that door and up a level, they had come to this short hall, less wide, far less high, just a little nook above all that huge space.

And suddenly Cajeiri had remembered this specific place. The rest had changed. But not here. Not that much. There was nand' Bren's apartment, just as he recalled. There was nand' Geigi's. And there was mani's, in that short hall, and farther down, three other doors that could be storage or passage accesses or most anything. He remembered.

Three years ago he had thought this hall was huge. It was not quite as big as the halls of the Bujavid. And the hall was not as wide nor its ceiling nearly as high as the big area with shops. But it was, more than anything they had seen below, atevi, kabiu, and had a feeling of comfort.

They had hardly been there a moment before the area door opened, and the second part of their company caught up, having come a different way, just ahead of a mass of baggage on carts. Everything was confusion for a moment. Mani's apartment opened up, pouring out staff excited to welcome them. People he did not at all remember said he had grown so much—

That was true. But it was still strange.

But, sadly, when nand' Bren's door opened and the staff came out, they had no one to welcome, except Narani-nadi and Bindanda and Asicho, who stood by giving orders and helping them identify and move the luggage. "They will come," Narani-nadi said. "They will be here soon."

But that only made him think all too vividly about the trouble they could be in, and the necessity to keep a calm face and to pretend, like mani, like Lord Geigi and everybody else, that there was absolutely nothing wrong, and that there was no trouble anywhere.

"We shall have tea," mani said now, after formalities, and invited Lord Geigi, who had just been introducing the Guild observers to the four of his staff who would show them to their apartment, down the hall.

It was certain mani and Lord Geigi would get down to serious talk, after tea. There were so many questions, so very many scary ones—and he was not sure whether he would be invited to hear the news, or whether he would be shut out. He was not even sure whether he wanted to hear—but in his heart, he wanted to.

And once the outer door had shut, and they were in mani's apartment, he found he was indeed included in that invitation to tea, and very quickly then sitting in a chair in a triangular arrangement, mani, and him, and Lord Geigi. He was served his cup of tea, much nicer than what they had had on the shuttle, where the air made their noses sore, and dulled tastes. He sipped his cup carefully, at mani's pace, wondering all the while how nand' Bren was doing, and what information Cenedi was getting from the man who had gone with nand' Bren, and if they were going to hear anything at all.

But if information from nand' Bren had not been coming, Cajeiri told himself, Cenedi would not be standing so quietly at mani's shoulder.

So he hoped nand' Bren was safe and that everything was all right. And he hoped the same for his associates, off across the station, with the locked doors that still made him mad even to think about.

He wondered if they had heard he was here, and wondered whether, just possibly, once everything calmed down and nand' Bren came back safely, Lord Geigi might answer a private question and tell him what might have happened to his mail.

There was nothing but idle talk, with tea. Talk about production schedules, about weather on the coast. He sat and sipped tea while baggage carts rumbled in the depths of the hall and staff back there began to sort things out. Clothes would be going into closets and belongings would be set where they should be. They were settling in—and it was still uncertain what was going on over on the human side of things, or up where nand' Bren was.

Jase-aiji was watching Tillington. That was a good thing. Jase-aiji and Sabin-aiji, who was almost as fierce as Great-grandmother. Tillington would feel her staring at his back, whatever he did.

And his aishid, standing with the senior Guild outside the door, would be asking questions he could not ask. They would be talking to Lord Geigi's bodyguard, right along with mani's young men, and mani's men would be asking questions his aishid did not know enough to ask, finding out things, so his aishid could tell him what was happening without his breaking promises.

Clearly some people, including Tillington-aiji, were not being smart. People were acting as if only their way mattered, while people as dangerous as the kyo were arriving.

Reunioners knew firsthand what the kyo could do. And he knew. And all the fuss among themselves was just stupid. But no one was interested in hearing a boy say so.

The kyo will come someday, he had said to his associates two years ago, when he was much younger, when they were all sitting together in the dark of the ship-tunnels, and he had told them about meeting the kyo face to face. *But we will know what to do when that happens.*

Nand' Bren will know what to do.

He still believed that. He truly did.

Cenedi went out to the foyer and came in again, gave a little nod to mani and another to Lord Geigi, and a little one to him, too.

"Nand' Bren is returning," Cenedi said. "He has gained Ogun-aiji's agreement on some matters of import, but they have not yet resolved the situation in Central."

"At least there is progress," mani said.

But it was not agreement on everything that was going on, and people were still being stupid.

Maybe tomorrow nand' Bren would work the rest of it out.

But Cenedi said, too, "Nand' Bren pleads he is quite tired, and wishes leave to deal with his staff."

That was a disappointment. He wished he could go across the hall.

But likely nand' Bren said that because he wanted to think.

"As he should," mani said with a wave of her hand. "Advise him so."

17

There was at least, Bren thought, the hope of a quiet transition—granted Ogun didn't, the moment the door was shut, call Tillington in for conference and create a worse mess.

Bren personally hoped for better from Ogun. He hoped they had made headway on more than one front. And a double-cross didn't make sense, given what was truly in Ogun's own best interests—unless there was an emotional side to the question, and there *was* certainly emotion in Ogun's dislike of Sabin.

But one didn't get to be Senior Captain by being a fool. And in playing the one piece of advantage he'd had, the disposition of the Reunioners, he'd given Ogun a path that led in a better direction for everybody, Ogun included. If Ogun saw it.

Or believed it. There'd been a long history of deception, all along the ship's course.

He couldn't undo that. He had to keep on Ogun's good side. He also had to stick by his own allies, including Sabin, and he had to do it without making trouble for Jase in the process. Sabin was all the fallback they had, if Ogun turned unreliable.

He'd been unspeakably glad to put the ship-folk's stationside administrative section behind him.

He was gladder still to be in the lift headed back to atevi territory, and when he and his escort passed the door into the aishidi'tat's executive residency, it was as if he'd finally found breathable air.

The corridor was quiet and deserted as he and his escort entered. His own door was across the hall from the dowager's apartment doors, down the hall from Geigi's. Cenedi's man, with a parting courtesy, went across to Ilisidi's door, and the fact that Geigi's men, also leaving him, likewise went over to the dowager's door, said that there must be a meeting still going on.

But he had too much going on at the moment, and to his advisory message, the dowager had relayed a gracious encouragement to go settle in and rest.

Which was a great relief. Right now he wanted no more input, nothing that would require a defense or even an explanation of what he had just done—because there *was* no answer until Ogun did whatever he decided to do, and he had so many pieces and particles suspended in his head. He needed to take notes. He needed to remember just how the argument had flowed, and everything, every nuance, every hint of Ogun's guarded expression.

He reached his own door with only his aishid, and without them so much as pushing the button, it opened.

The spicy smell of pizza wafted out. Narani and Jeladi were there to meet him, with Kandana and Sabiso, with Asicho and Maruno, and people he had not seen in far too long. It was celebration. It was his staff. His people.

"Nandi! Nand' Bren!"

Faces beamed with happiness. There were more people in the hall, Bindanda, the whole staff turned out.

He found a smile, an expansive gesture of thanks, least he could do. There had been conspiracy about this welcome, one was quite certain: pizza could not have happened on station commons. There were a few faces sensibly a little worried—seeking some hint of the situation in his demeanor, but he could not spread fear in his own staff, either. He gathered up his energy and broadened the smile, and found their happiness pouring strength into him. Granted one did *not* seize on Kandana and Sabiso and the rest and hug them bodily, his gesture won smiles all around, happiness from one side of the little foyer to the other, and back into the hall.

"Nandi!" Kandana said. "Welcome! Three times welcome! Are things well?"

"They are indeed improved," he said, shedding the traveling coat, itself a vast relief. He was offered another, a soft, favorite coat he had not seen literally in years, and such was the stress of recent weeks, the coat still fit. That was a surprise. All around him, familiar faces beamed warmth and welcome. He found himself energized, surrounded by people who, far from ordinary atevi reserve, touched his arm or his shoulder as family might, in sheer happiness to see him.

Pizza meant informality. People snatched a little piece and a glass of something compatible, and milled about in, for a courtly atevi party, a riotous good time.

"Welcome, nandi!" Sabiso bade him, handing him a glass. "Welcome! We are so relieved!"

"We were worried there might be a problem," another voice declared. "But now we can deal with these strangers!"

"Our lord will bring the human folk to sense!"

Their lord sincerely hoped so—and didn't miss the fact the human situation found mention right along with the oncoming kyo ship.

He had no answer to give them. Not yet. He wished he could be in two places, here *and* across the hall, hearing what Geigi and Ilisidi were saying. But his aishid was in contact. Likely Ilisidi was getting more information than she gave, and if what she was getting from Lord Geigi was the atevi situation, that seemed in fair order. If what she was getting was Tillington's history—please God without Tillington's statement—he knew enough.

Best course, he decided, was right where he was, meet staff, draw breath, have a little supper, and honestly get some sleep in a proper bed, not the situation aboard the shuttle. He couldn't ignore these people now. He'd had to leave them when he'd come down to the world. He still couldn't help them get home, with shuttle space restricted as it was.

"So many welcome faces!" he said so everyone could hear, and weary as he was, felt a sudden dampness about the eyes, hoping it would not get worse. "And such a welcome! Nadiin-ji, thank you, thank you all! You have been so patient, so much more than I could have reasonably asked, under every circumstance."

"Bren-nandi!" came the response, all of them crowded close. And from Kandana: "Welcome, nandi! Indeed, we *know* you will bring order out of this!"

There was, of course, tea. The household was a little short of wine and brandy, supplied from the world below, but there were certainly spirits to be had—vodka distilled from what, one dared not ask. He hesitated at taking any alcohol, still fearing a summons.

But none came.

And there were, aromatic as the pizza, fresh teacakes. The orangelle flavoring was a special treat up here, and they had brought a lot of it.

There was news, the new windows at Najida, the children's visit—he met and talked with every individual of his little staff. He answered questions about relatives, and the Bujavid staff, name by name, where they were, how they were.

But tea and sugar could only carry him so far, with, finally, a small glass of vodka. Exhaustion was setting in, and he went to what served as his sitting room and simply collapsed into a chair for a moment of peace and silence.

Strange how one conversation with Ogun could have sapped that much energy. But it had. And he was very glad the dowager had spared him a formal report tonight, because nothing he had tried to do was concluded, and nothing was certain.

Finish the vodka. Have one more cup of herbal tea. Go to bed. That was his plan.

"Go off duty," he told his aishid, who had come in with him, standing, after all this. "I hope things will be quiet for at least a few hours, but they will assuredly not stay that way. The shuttle from Mospheira is coming in two days behind us, and I am hopeful now we shall at least have Ogun's silence while we manage a transition with Tillington. I shall talk with the man tomorrow and see if I can persuade him to stand down. Well done. Rest. Please."

"Bren-ji," Banichi said with a nod; and here in the heart of a loyal staff, they left for their own quarters—likely not to sleep yet, but to trade condensed information with Cenedi and with Geigi's staff, and then, he sincerely hoped, they would take their own overdue rest.

He picked up the requested cup of tea, and was about, with two extra sips, to go get some sleep himself.

The door opened. Jago came back in, having hardly had time to go all the way down the hall, and with a look like business.

"Bren-ji. *Jase-aiji* is on the phone."

Phone meant another sort of instrument, on the station. This one arrived in Jago's hand, a device like one of the Guild units, and a glance told him what button to push, not needing to leave his chair or plug anything in. "This is Bren," he said, while Jago waited.

"Hear you just talked with the senior captain."

He'd come home, exhausted. Gotten distracted. No, he hadn't called Jase. Or talked to Sabin. Or even thought about it.

Never take your allies for granted. Big mistake. Especially with Sabin.

"*Good* conversation, actually," he said. "I think we agreed on most points. I hope you haven't heard anything to the contrary."

"No. Actually not. Everything is quiet here. I was thinking about dropping by your place on my way off-shift."

God, he couldn't. The minute he'd met the glass of spirits, his brain had started turning to homogenized mush, the more so now that he'd sat down alone in quiet. He'd not reported to

Sabin. She probably wanted information, and asked Jase to get it.

But running from Ogun right back to Sabin . . .

No, he *shouldn't* have done that. He was dropping stitches even thinking he should have gone to her. He'd done the right thing going straight to Ogun. Sabin would know that. Absolutely she would. And he'd done right, to come straight home.

Jase, on the other hand, could be signaling him about another problem. They could cover the visit with the party winding down in the dining room.

"Sure," he found himself saying. "We're sort of settling down for the night here. But you're very welcome. Hope things have gone all right."

"Peaceful regarding the visitors. No change in the signal. They're signaling us, probably automated, at a fixed interval. We repeat it at that interval. We're not changing anything until—"

Jase broke off. *Something* was happening where he was.

"Just a minute," Jase said. *"Stay with me."*

Adrenaline kicked up. Bren waited. It was all he could do.

Maybe it wasn't an emergency. Maybe it was somebody just trying to ask Jase a simple question. Casual interruption.

If only it was that.

The silence went on. And on.

Maybe Jase had completely forgotten about him. Maybe Sabin was saying something.

Maybe some technical thing had developed a problem.

Maybe he should just end the call. Let Jase call him back when he had time.

He kept hearing voices. Strange sounds. Jase was carrying the com unit with him as he dealt with several people. He heard bits and pieces of instruction and query. Then:

"Bren."

"I'm here."

"Transmission just changed. Velocity hasn't. Course hasn't.

The transmission has gone to audio, but I think it's a recording. I'll patch you in."

Pop. Static. He heard then a rumbling sort of voice he hadn't heard in two years—and the world below them *never* had.

"Bren. Ilisidi. Cajeiri. Bren. Ilisidi. Cajeiri. Bren. Ilisidi. Cajeiri." And silence.

Three repeats. Like the pattern signal.

Click. *"What do we answer?"* Jase asked.

There was some sort of disturbance near Jase. He heard a voice. An angry one. Then Jase again:

"Stationmaster Tillington is demanding I get off the com. Captain Sabin is telling him to stand by for your answer and do nothing himself. The stationmaster wants their signal echoed as is."

"No. In point of fact, we need to answer this one."

"Go ahead. I'll capture. We'll play it as you direct."

Call Prakuyo's name? They had no guarantee Prakuyo was on that ship, and no guarantee what Prakuyo's status was, whether currently in good favor or not.

"Bren. Ilisidi. Cajeiri. Sit. Talk."

He had said it in kyo.

"Got it," Jase said to someone. *"Recorded. Transmit that three times in close sequence, on same interval as their transmission."*

He heard an immediate loud argument from someone near the com.

"You have the order," he heard Jase say then, angrily. *"Transmit that in the pattern as ordered."*

"Damn you." He heard that, too, and guessed it was Tillington.

"I'll talk to Tillington," he said.

"He's all yours," Jase said, and evidently passed the com. He heard a click. Then:

"Cameron, damn your arrogance, you come on board here and start giving orders—"

"Mr. Tillington?" he asked, dead calm. An adrenaline surge did *wonders* for exhaustion.

"Mr. Cameron, you do not countermand an order from Central."

"Mr. Tillington—"

"That's Stationmaster *Tillington."*

"Stationmaster Tillington, I have dealt with these people. I established the protocols in the first—"

"You have no authority here!"

"I'm here at the request of the President and the State Department."

"You don't represent a damned thing, Cameron! You have no authority! Your commission expired when you left your job unfilled and the continent in a mess."

"Mr. Tillington, it would be in your best interest at this point to come to my office."

"You don't have an office!"

"Effectively, I do, but I was about to say, despite the hour, I would also come to yours. The kyo may be responding to the shuttle arrival. Very likely they are observing—"

"You're not in command of this station and you do not give orders in Central!"

"Stationmaster Tillington, we need to hold a discreet and private conversation. We can do it in the morning, but in the meanwhile, that transmission needs to go out."

"You have no authority to be anywhere, and you damned sure don't have it to give orders to my staff!"

"You may say that, Mr. Tillington, but I do have the authority, I hold a commission from two governments as well as the approval of the Senior Captain, and I sincerely hope you are the only one hearing this. For your personal good, Mr. Tillington, and in the interest of handling the question of my authority quietly and with dignity, please come and discuss the situation with me in private."

"I don't go to that side of the line."

"Mr. Tillington, *Stationmaster* Tillington, contact with the kyo is a matter requiring experience and expertise. I have dealt with these people before. I have every confidence I can bring this meeting to a safe conclusion, given—"

"They're here because of the Reunioners, because Sabin, *here, failed to take out the damn Reunioner records, and she's standing here trying to run my staff! Call* her *to your damned office!"*

"Mr. Tillington, you are wrong. And there's no sense carrying on this discussion long-distance. Return the com to Captain Graham, and I strongly urge you take his suggestions at this point. I've given you a response that should hold the status quo with the visitors for the next few hours, granted they follow pattern, and I am extremely tired. I would ask we let tempers cool and take up the technicalities of my status here tomorrow. Can we set a time and place to meet, sir?"

"You hide over on the atevi side. Fine! You operate from there. You keep the hell off the human side of the station! You don't belong here, you're not wanted, and you're not needed here! The hell with you!"

There was some little disturbance in Tillington's background. Bren didn't break the contact—figuring that Tillington's shouting would have informed Jase they were getting nowhere. He hoped that Jase would take over the com.

But the connection broke. Possibly Tillington had indeed thumbed it off.

He clicked off, from his end. He waited.

And waited, figuring that whatever had happened, Jase would manage it better without him calling into the middle of it. He laid the com on the table to wait, and took a sip of cooling tea, noting that Jago had come back into the room during the final exchange, and that she was standing attendance by the tea service, beside the servant.

Jago gave him a lifted brow. Likely her hearing had picked up the louder bits.

The com vibrated, and he picked it up and pressed the button. "Bren here."

"Thank you, Mr. Cameron."

Not Jase. Sabin herself. *Second*-senior captain.

"Captain Sabin. A pleasure. I regret the circumstances. I fear I didn't do well with Mr. Tillington."

"His choice. Your transmission is going out as requested. Tillington's left Central. Senior Captain is aware."

Ogun knew Tillington had left. Tillington had held on to the station controls very possibly as Ogun's ally. And now he left in high temper. Gone to Ogun? Maybe.

"I'm a little concerned that he's upset." Understatement, but everything they said was passing through the system, accessible by techs in that room. He *could* order Tillington's arrest if he thought it necessary. He had every confidence Shawn would back him if he did that.

But at possible political cost to Shawn, and maybe exacerbating the situation Tillington had stirred up on the Mospheiran side of the station.

So Ogun had pulled the rug from under Tillington.

And Ogun had been in contact with Sabin. Had at least gotten her advisement.

Sabin was probably running on high adrenaline herself, and there was some chance she was a little upset that her supposed ally in the aishidi'tat had put a conference with Ogun at the top of his agenda. But he didn't think so. She was canny and practical, in a major way.

"I'm relieved," he said. "I just had a very productive discussion with Captain Ogun on the kyo situation. I think we can work this problem out very quickly with Mr. Tillington. I'd like to meet with you directly at your convenience; and I need to talk to Mr. Tillington in a calmer frame of mind. Has the kyo ship had time to respond?"

"They're about three hours lagged. Just had a repeat of their new transmission, identical to the last. Interval identical. They

won't have gotten our transmission yet. We'll be keeping the same schedule, with your message."

"Possible their message is related to the shuttle docking?"

"Not timed to it, but very possibly they observed the shuttle approach."

"Well, we're here, we're available to you at any hour. It's my sense they're going to continue their own speed for a while. And that they're going to repeat that statement of theirs at the same interval for a while."

"It's my sense that they're observing, mapping, and taking notes as they come." Sabin's voice was grim. *"It would be odd if not. But we don't know how long they've been out there."*

"I agree with you, Captain. I'm going to go off call for a few hours and get some necessary sleep to get my head clear. But I remain available for any other change in that transmission, any trouble or change from any source. Are communications to Central secure?"

"Not that secure, unfortunately."

"I understand." From whom it was *not that secure* remained a question—whether it was one of Tillington's techs still on duty, or Ogun himself that Sabin was worried about. "I'm going to ask Lord Geigi to bring his shift on now and possibly stay on extended watch, the Mospheiran crew having been on, I understand, a very extended session. Let them get some sleep. Will that be acceptable, to give you and the human staff some rest?"

"Acceptable and very welcome at this point, Mr. Cameron. We will order a shift of control to the atevi stationmaster as soon as we have his signal, and the head of staff will *implement that shift, or we'll work down the list until someone will. We only ask to be notified of any change in the kyo transmission."*

"Absolutely, Captain."

"Sabin out."

The contact clicked out.

Geigi would be in control of operations from now on until Tillington was replaced.

That was an immense relief.

But had he done an entirely good job? He didn't think so. He'd just sent a very upset Tillington off to his Mospheiran allies to complain, granted that was *all* Tillington did. He entertained a somewhat uncharitable wish that Tillington would call down to Shawn's office tonight to lodge a complaint. Or protest to Sabin.

Neither, however, would lead to a good solution. It would be far better to have Tillington accept the change that was coming, and he hadn't set that up at all smoothly. One could only hope that Tillington and Jase had been inside the office with the door shut, and not out on the floor when Tillington had lost his temper.

Maybe the stress had just piled up. Maybe Tillington was reaching a point where he would welcome being relieved of duty, maybe given at least a sideways promotion on Earth—

But he was beginning to believe he shouldn't recommend the man for any such consideration. An official who saw an alien warship bearing down on his station, locked his fellow stationmaster out of controls shift after shift—

Tillington wasn't the first to wish him in hell, but he had certainly been passionate about it. Maybe Tillington had been following Ogun's orders—or guiding them. Walking out like this—Tillington had been camping out in Central shift after shift after shift, sleep-deprived and not at his most rational in the first place. He might have reached his physical limit. He *might* have gotten an order from Ogun.

Morning might bring more sober reflection. He hoped so.

But at the moment—that shuttle bringing Tillington's replacement couldn't get here fast enough.

And whatever was done at Tillington's orders or by Tillington's people right now—he wanted someone keeping an eye on station systems.

The original dual setup of Central had been a remote redundancy in case of disaster, two Centrals each on a different power unit, and at a considerable remove. They'd used that, finding it a way to share control between atevi and humans.

And mad as it had seemed during negotiations for the initial setup, the system had not only worked, it had continued working during the coup, when the station had had to fend for itself—when the station had had no functional translator. In the system as it had developed, as he understood it, humans and atevi "talked" personally through the input keyboards and the displays. Nearing shift change, human Central would begin passing off working situations to atevi Central: the automations all went over at the flip of a digital switch, but the transfer of active problems required an atevi worker who didn't speak the human worker's language first to shadow what was going on and understand what had been done—or vice versa—

Those procedures Geigi said worked amazingly well.

And sharing the same job, seeing the same problems over and over, workers who had never met, and who could not speak to each other outside their keyboards, worked together day after day on a kind of interlingual shorthand that had spread somewhat uniformly through both sets of techs, tagging familiar problems with their own set of descriptive icons. Neither side would understand the other's discussion of the problem—but both sides always knew exactly what was going on.

Not infrequently, though illicitly, so Geigi had explained, pairs of techs shared pictures of family and spouses. The relationships weren't the same, across that line; but sets of techs had become people to each other, across that barrier.

And would those techs, right now, running on nerves and with their chief officer in an emotional state—be *glad* to make the turnover to their atevi partners and go home to rest? They were divided into two shifts, so they had some relief, but even so, it was sleep and work, sleep and work, with no break, under a man undergoing a meltdown . . . a man whose insistence was that atevi were siding with the Reunioners, in a plot with the two captains who were standing watch in Central, with the kyo bearing down on them. The techs had to be at their own breaking point.

"Jago-ji, advise Geigi to be ready to make the shift in Central just as soon as he can get his team there, and treat the other side very gently. Workers there are exhausted. Tillington has just walked out and left his staff upset and without direction. Tell Geigi that the kyo have begun transmitting our names now—that part is good news—I have responded, in a repeating transmission, at an identical interval, and he must wake me and also report to the Captains if there is any change in what I have left in operation. One cannot assume it is definitely Prakuyo an Tep we are dealing with, but the kyo are asking to see me, the dowager, and the young gentleman. Tell Geigi workers may be advised that this message from the kyo is a favorable change."

"Yes," Jago said, and left. Every detail he had enumerated would be handled, and handled quickly. He could rely on that.

But the problem inside Mospheiran Central remained far from resolved.

The servant still stood by. Bren sat there a moment, still holding the com: tired or not, there was no way he was going to sleep until he had word things were on an even keel and the switchover was complete. He looked at the servant, made a slight move of his hand, and in very short order another cup of tea arrived on the side table.

"Thank you, nadi-ji," he said to the servant.

"Nandi," the servant said, all earnestness. Staff knew. Staff knew enough to make *them* worry right along with him.

And he was supposed to solve it.

He felt that expectant look. He felt it and asked himself what in *hell* he could do.

The com in his hand buzzed.

"Bren?"

It was Jase.

"I'm here."

"Just reporting in. Sabin's finally going off-shift. I'm going to stay here in Central to supervise the handoff to Geigi's crew and to officially dismiss the shift. I want to talk to Geigi for a moment after we hand over. By the time I get through here, I imagine you'll be wanting to be in bed, too, right?"

"I do think I'll make a lot more sense in the morning, but if you want to drop by tonight, I can manage."

"No sense wearing yourself out. Things are under control. I'll see you in the morning. If anything goes amiss, I'll call you."

"I'm going to need to talk to Tillington tomorrow, after he's had a chance to calm down. I'll try to resolve that situation. At least calm it down."

"Good luck with that operation. —And thanks, Bren. Thanks. *Good night. Get some rest."*

"You too," he said.

The com clicked off. He laid it down on the side table, beside the teacup.

What he was going to say to Tillington tomorrow to calm things down he wasn't sure—and it probably wasn't going to improve with *you're being replaced.* Tillington already wished he'd take a walk in space. Maybe Ogun wished the same, though he thought he might have made a dent in that attitude.

One could hope the technician pairs in the two halves of Central would communicate a calm switchover despite the outbursts and tension from Tillington.

And that Jase, physically standing in Mospheiran Central, would advise the human techs exactly what Geigi would tell his own workers, that they were making progress with the kyo and that they all needed to keep things low and quiet.

Could he read anything at all into the timing of the change of communication from the kyo?

It did suggest the kyo ship might be aware that a shuttle had docked.

Meanwhile the kyo ship would also be reading space itself, looking for trails of ships departing or arriving. The kyo would be seeing only two local ships, *Phoenix,* that they had seen before, and the other ship under construction, with its hull not quite complete. Everything they owned was laid out, impossible to conceal.

Were there other stations? That was the one thing the kyo might not be able to know by observation. Unless they had been there a while.

It was among those things he was determined not to tell them—just in case.

Baggage in Great-grandmother's apartment had given up all the things they had brought from home. There had been soft bumps and thumps, doors opening and closing, all the while they had tea and cakes in mani's sitting room, but now Lord Geigi had gone home, and had an apartment ready for the strangers from the Guild, too, so they were settling in, and would not be staying in mani's residence.

And nand' Bren had come back, and Guild had told Guild certain things were settled with Ogun-aiji. So at least everything was settling into place.

Cajeiri was glad of that, and glad to be able to go to his own room, his own little suite, and shed his coat again and sit in a soft chair. He was feeling frayed at the edges—that was nand' Bren's expression, and it fit.

Maybe, he thought, everything would settle now and everybody would use good sense.

And he was very willing to rest. So was his aishid, who were all stripping down and taking advantage of the shower in the servants' hall behind their quarters. That was very well. There was a large bath, too, and the idea sounded very pleasant but he was just too tired. He thought he would take a turn in the shower, too. He had not really had one of this sort since the ship: it was all fog, and strange, and pleasant to breathe.

The bedroom in mani's apartment was strange to him, half-remembered, but still strange: they had made the rooms connect the way they did in atevi houses, so it felt more normal than on the ship, but it made things feel odd, homelike, and very definitely not at all home. Behind the hangings the walls were metal and plastics, and over by the door, trying to look like a small carved cabinet, was a whole console to control all the things the lighting and fans did. The hall doors were pressure doors and massive—there was no disguising that. The inside doors slid rather than swinging.

It was both remembered and strange-feeling, like a dream he had had more than once.

And if he could have been with his associates in a visit here, he would have found it all exciting.

But things were not ordinary. They had had tea and cakes and staff had all been delighted to welcome them. They had had an informal tea and mani and Lord Geigi talked about things that he was sure he had not heard the half of.

Then Lord Geigi had gotten a sudden call from nand' Bren and excused himself, saying he had to go bring atevi Central on duty and that the kyo were now talking, which was both scary and encouraging.

It meant everything they had planned on was starting to happen, that was what. And that could bring good or bad.

So nobody right now had time to have a boy in the way, especially a boy who mostly kept thinking about the fact they had locked the big section doors on the Reunioners, and nobody was even mentioning that as one of the problems.

So now he was here, tucked in a bed, with no Eisi, no Liedi, no Boji in the premises, but his bodyguard was with him—little that they could do if things went very badly with the kyo.

Lucasi and Jegari would sleep on fold-up beds over across the room, and Antaro and Veijico had fold-up beds in his little sitting room, because mani's was a very proper house, wherever she was.

He stared at the ceiling in the very dim light and thought about the kyo. But that was a little scary.

He thought about his life on the ship, and that led him to think about his associates, and whether they knew he was here, so close. He hoped so.

Lord Geigi had said something troubling tonight to mani. That Tillington-aiji had separated off the Reunioners behind locked doors when they got the news about the ship. And people could be stuck wherever they had been when that had happened.

That was going to affect a lot of people, he thought. He thought of Bjorn, who had a ship-folk tutor, with other students, who might even be caught somewhere on the wrong side of the doors.

He thought of Bjorn's parents, who were technical people who were lucky enough to have jobs of some sort that they had to go to. Had they gotten home?

Artur's father worked somewhere, too. He had no idea whether that would be affected.

Gene's mother had no job. He had never heard Irene say whether her mother had one.

But stupid Tillington had ordered the big doors shut with practically no warning, and while he had opened them again for atevi and Mospheirans after an hour or so, he had just kept them shut for Reunioners, and people had panicked, so they had had to call out ship-folk guards. Nobody could get through those doors, in either direction.

Lord Geigi was not arguing too much about the Reunioner doors, because, Lord Geigi said, he wanted Tillington-aiji not to take the notion to seal the whole Mospheiran section off from his, and separate them from the ship-folk.

We would not tolerate that, mani had said.

He would not tolerate what had *already* happened, or those doors still being shut—but nobody asked a nine-year-old boy.

Section doors were supposed to be a protection in case of fire, or an asteroid, or something. A particular section could lose all its air and heat, if its door was sealed, and nobody else would be affected.

That was scary. That was just really scary. That was how so many people had died at Reunion, when half the sections had blown out, but also how so many had lived.

He had seen how the station looked, with wrecked sections with no lights, just torn up and dead.

The kyo had done that.

But the instant they realized the kyo ship was out there, Geigi had said, Tillington-aiji had ordered the doors shut, claiming it was a ship order. Geigi said he was not sure that was true at all. Tillington had gone on public address, said it was an emergency, and doors were closing in a quarter hour. And people had started running.

What did one do if one's residence was too far away? The station was a huge place. People were assigned where to eat. Where to live. Where to work if they were lucky and had a job.

But what if they *were* caught away from where they were supposed to be?

And before the doors had shut, the news about the kyo ship had gotten out on public address, because someone in Central had pushed a wrong button. That was what Geigi said. Since Geigi's people were not in charge of Central when it happened, Geigi could not tell who had done it, and supposedly it was an accident, but Geigi was not sure.

There had been a panic, and Reunioners had tried to get the section doors open, which was really dangerous. Ship security had tried to keep order and that was when the ship-aijiin finally put guards inside to keep people back from the doors.

And all the doors were open now *but* the Reunioner doors,

because, Geigi had said, they were the ones who had attacked the doors.

So it was quiet now. And the ship-folk guards were still at the Reunioner doors, while everybody else could walk about as they pleased. Reunioners caught out had been arrested and put back into the Reunioner sections . . . as if they had done something wrong.

It was *stupid.*

He had sat through Geigi's report and not said anything.

But now he was so worried about his associates he was not likely to sleep.

He was not supposed to ask about his associates, but he *had* asked tonight about his mail, since that was not forbidden.

And Geigi had said he had sent it across to the other Central. And nothing had come back.

So *that* upset him, too.

And then Geigi had said—without being asked, so he had not broken his promise—that Jase had visited him twice since he had gotten back to the station, and Lord Geigi *had* taken the baggage and put the clothing in storage for everybody. And then Geigi had asked Gene and Artur and Irene to dinner, with nand' Jase, and with their parents, an invitation which Jase had translated and he had sent in ship-speak, but Geigi had never gotten an answer to the first invitation, and before he had sent it again, the kyo ship had shown up.

Then Tillington had done what *he* had done.

And things were in a mess.

He hoped his associates knew he was here and that he would do everything he could to get them out.

He wanted so much to ask favors. He wanted it so much he had bit his lip sore. He had looked at mani and looked at Lord Geigi and he knew *they* knew what he wanted, but nobody suggested what to do, or said there was anything they *could* do.

He pounded his pillow into a lump and whatever it was made of just would not stay where he wanted it.

Meanwhile Lord Geigi was taking over Central, now, which was a good thing. *So can you get a phone call to Artur, nandi, or to any of them?* That was what he had wanted to ask Lord Geigi. *Can you at least find out how they are?*

But he had kept his promise and said nothing.

He hoped his aishid was able to sleep. He was not doing well at it.

"Bren-ji."

Waking. Light overhead. Jago in uniform. Himself lying face-down with his arms around an unfamiliar pillow.

On the space station. That was where.

Tillington was in a snit, the dowager was across the hall, Geigi had gotten control shifted to atevi Central, and the kyo were on a course toward the inner solar system.

He shoved himself up and swung his feet off the bed, hands rubbing his face and partly shutting out the light. "Jago-ji. Is there a problem?"

"It is 0500 by the local reckoning. Tillington has just returned to Mospheiran Central and called technicians to come in. Lord Geigi remains in atevi Central and has not shifted control back to Tillington. There is no word from the ship-aijiin. We have no word from the Mospheiran shuttle. They are communicating only with ground control while Central communications are currently in Ragi."

The Ragi-Mosphei' switch was operation as usual: so was the Mospheiran shuttle's reliance on ground control during periods when Ragi was the language in Central, the same as the atevi shuttle relied on ground control during Mospheiran control of Central. And there was a station-based ops, not subject to a clock-based rotation, but working so long as a shuttle was in flight. The system usually ran very smoothly, ops—which until lately was all atevi teams—handled most of it, and opposite-language technicians were always on call.

But Geigi was not going to switch control back to the Mospheiran crews in the immediate future, and not until that incoming shuttle was safely docked. Geigi had the advantage, unassailable once active control had been switched to his boards. Ogun was apparently off-shift. Jase and Sabin were likely exhausted, sleeping as they could, to recover from their own standoff with Tillington. The fourth captain had not been heard from. But *Phoenix* had indeed repositioned herself before they'd arrived, free of the mast, accessible only by shuttlecraft, and likely Riggins was there.

"The kyo?"

"Lord Geigi reports there is no change. Lord Geigi says he will not relinquish control nor release his staff from duty until he hears from you or the dowager, and he says he would be surprised to receive such an order until some time after the next shuttle has docked. He is prepared. He has set up his staff to stay on duty and eat and sleep there in shifts."

Two could play Tillington's game. "Messages from anyone else?"

"There is none. The dowager is requesting information, but she is querying Lord Geigi in Central."

The odds that anyone in Tillington's system could crack courtly Ragi spoken by two very literate adepts were low. Vanishingly low. Without Jase or himself to translate, it was as good as code.

So the overall situation was not that bad. Except for the exhausted Mospheiran techs, who had to be fraying at the edges. And Tillington, camping out in a non-functional control room.

"You requested to be informed of any change in Central, Bren-ji. I shall turn out the lights again if you wish. You might go back to sleep for another hour."

Tempting. But there was so much to do.

Including talking to Tillington, who *might* be in a better mood, though it hardly sounded like it. Tillington was apparently sending demands to Geigi for a turnover. Geigi, flexible fellow that he was, would understand quite a bit from whatever

Tillington said, but Tillington would not get a word of Mosphei' out of him, not this morning.

And Tillington had to have expected that. He was just going through the forms. Doing his duty. Being where he was technically supposed to be.

Couldn't blame the man for that. It could be a good sign, Tillington's showing up where he was, by the clock, supposed to be.

Give the man a graceful out. Cheap, counting the alternatives. There were Mospheiran offices that would never intersect atevi. Ever. Shawn could park him in one of those, *maybe* pay him enough to keep him away from politics.

"I shall dress," he said. "But if Narani and Jeladi are sleeping, Jago-ji,—"

"They will come," Jago said, and went out to bear that message.

The dowager didn't send an invitation to breakfast. He had halfway expected, being up at dawn, that she would ask him to report the news.

"She is well, is she not?" he asked of Bindanda, who had appeared with the breakfast fish. He trusted Bindanda to be tapped into every shred of gossip in their section. And he wanted to know things were in order and that he had all the information he could get, before any meeting with Tillington.

"One understands, nandi, that, Lord Geigi being absent, and you being engaged with human problems, the dowager is taking a day of rest and quiet, along with the young gentleman."

So Ilisidi was officially expecting him to solve the human problems, while she was keeping Cajeiri close—a good idea, given the situation with the Reunioners.

Breakfast was more than palatable. Fish—real fish—was a standard fare up here, with a dry hot spice, an efficient item to ship. There was bread, but one did not ask made of what. The space program had necessitated a few exceptions in the ancient atevi tradition of season and appropriateness. And in the notion of what constituted food.

But the morning was not without messages. "Riggins-aiji called," Narani said, just as he exited the little dining room, "and the phone indicates he wishes a call."

Pavel Riggins.

Fourth Captain. Ogun's man, appointed by Ogun in the absence of Sabin and Jase. And *possibly* in charge of the ship, at the moment. And possibly under-informed, for that reason.

He'd queried Jase on Riggins' character, during those recent holiday conversations. Jase had described Riggins as in his thirties, a bit cautious in changing anything, voting consistently with Ogun, but honestly trying to get along with Sabin.

Not a bad report. Good man, Jase said, on systems coordination; intelligent where it came to supply and distribution, a man who'd gotten a fast and scary education in atevi protocols when the coup had happened on Earth and he'd had to work with Geigi to deal with shortages.

Ogun had made a unilateral appointment to fill that fourth captaincy—though Riggins had been too close to the late and unlamented Pratap Tamun for Sabin's liking. Jase said that, too, but said he had no complaint.

Well, Pratap Tamun and all history aside—Riggins was what they had in charge this shift. And Riggins was handling everything by remote, not even on the station deck.

He put his coat on, prepared for the day, and finally made the call through the atevi system, which got him, not unexpectedly, ship-com. "This is Bren Cameron. Captain Riggins, please."

That took a moment.

"Mr. Cameron." A new voice. *"Welcome aboard."*

"Thank you, sir. Pleased to meet you."

"I understand there's a problem with atevi Central refusing to carry out the shift change."

"You understand correctly, Captain. Tillington's staff exceeded its own shift considerably and exhausted itself. Mr. Tillington left last night. At that point, I'm sure you are aware, Mospheiran Central switched control to Lord Geigi at Captain Graham's instruction. I understand Mr. Tillington is back in Mospheiran Central this morning, but quite frankly, Captain, that turnover will not happen with Mr. Tillington in his present emotional state."

"You are not qualified, Mr. Cameron, to make that judgment."

"Most respectfully, Captain, I am here at the request of the aiji in Shejidan, *and* the President of Mospheira, who has authority over Mr. Tillington. My immediate business is preparing to deal with the incoming visitors. Securing the station, and particularly Central Operations, against a territorial dispute is within my instruction. I am working with an atevi administration competent, cooperative, and incidentally operating *in the language* in which we will contact the visitors. The inbound Mospheiran shuttle will be obliged to rely on ship-com as well as ground control for any non-operational matters during approach tomorrow. I trust you will be able to provide any needed assistance."

There was a moment of silence. "I have received no such request."

"You are now receiving it, sir. I am sure you will also receive it from the inbound shuttle, and I thank you on their behalf, in advance."

Another silence. Then:

"I have to consult."

"Please advise me if there will be any difficulty."

"I'll communicate as my own command directs, Mr. Cameron."

"Understood, sir. Please notify me of any problems, any change in the kyo situation."

"I report within my own chain of command, sir."

"Thank you, Captain."

Well, that was not the best first conversation he had ever had with an official. But counting the way things had had to work during Ogun's long cooperation with Tillington in the ship's absence; and counting Ogun's year-long feud with Sabin since, he could understand that many instructions to Riggins had probably begun with, *Take no action.*

Riggins was in charge until Ogun woke up. Which was probably a good time to take on problems and get an update on the kyo.

He needed to go to Central and try to calm Tillington down, preferably before Ogun or Sabin became involved again.

He called his aishid. He sent word to Ilisidi where he was going, and sent word by Guild runner to Lord Geigi, to advise him what he was doing.

Forewarning Tillington did not seem like a good idea.

The message came during breakfast that Lord Bren was going to go to Central to talk to Tillington-aiji.

Because Tillington had shown up to demand control back.

"Annoying man," mani said of the situation, which, if it were back on Earth, would not promise well for Tillington.

Probably it was true up here, too.

Cajeiri fretted his way through the eggs in sauce, wondering about his associates, hoping they were all right, and wondering if, once Tillington's replacement arrived, they could open the section doors.

He dared not say anything. Or mope, which would invite a sharp question. So he would have tried to be cheerful, except mani had agreed to receive nand' Bren's message right in the middle of formal breakfast—and he could tell she was not happy, either.

He did not dare ask why she was unhappy. Lord Geigi had not shown up at breakfast because he was holding on to Central, so there was no news to be had. He could only guess there was about to be trouble.

The kyo ship was still coming in, and signaling with their names, mani's name and nand' Bren's and his. Antaro had heard that, and told him so before breakfast.

That was a good thing.

And the Mospheiran shuttle was coming in, too, tomorrow.

So good things were going on, too.

But people in the Reunioner section right now were not happy. They were probably scared that with Tillington in charge, there might be some sort of political deal, and that very bad things would happen—not just getting shipped off to Maudit, but being handed over to the kyo in some sort of deal to save the station. People always believed the *worst* things. And he knew there were reasons they had closed those doors.

But he wanted nand' Bren at least to assure his associates that they were here and that everything was all right.

Nobody could take time for a handful of children.

But nand' Bren was more patient than most adults. Nand' Bren would not tell Great-grandmother he had asked a forbidden question. And if *anybody* could slip a word through the locked doors, nand' Bren might.

At least it was worth trying.

If only nand' Bren would have paid mani a visit this morning.

But nand' Bren had had to go deal with Tillington, who had started the day with another problem.

Heading into the Mospheiran section, where security was under Tillington's command, brought objection. Banichi wasn't at all trusting of Tillington. So Banichi sent for one of Geigi's men as a guide, and roused out Cenedi's second, Nawari, before breakfast, so that he could get firsthand information back to the dowager.

Then he'd called up all four of the Guild observers—so, Banichi said, that those four might witness their dealing with Tillington, the manner of it, and the outcome.

Bren rather doubted there would be a physical problem. But security was Banichi's call. Listen to your aishid, Tabini had said, and meant it.

"If you think it a good idea," Bren had said, regarding calling in the Observers. Their company assembling in the corridor presented an intimidating show of black uniforms. The Guild had also unpacked, and this time had not brought just their sidearms.

He did consider suggesting they leave the rifles, though it was standard procedure to carry them in a similar situation on Earth. He hardly wanted shooting in a room full of controls, instruments, and innocent techs.

But, he thought, while atevi universally understood that he represented a certain force, maybe it was a good idea for the human side of the station to get the same picture.

When they took the lift to the vicinity of Central, Mospheiran workers stopped what they were doing, stopped talking, except a few quiet mutters. Those in their path moved back to the walls.

And if Mospheirans caught the notion that atevi officials had firepower to match a ship's captain, that might be salutary in itself.

They passed into Central's area. Human security, in green fatigues, and carrying only sidearms, looked uncertain, and one urgently used communications, reporting their presence, one surmised, and hoping not to be told to stop it.

The door to Central itself turned up shut when they reached it, with two armed Mospheiran security in front of it.

"Order of President Tyers," Bren said. "Open the door."

The crew there didn't look confident. Didn't move, at first.

He read the name tags. "Mr. Reeves. Ms. Kumara. Order of President Tyers, open the door. I will report names of the noncompliant, and I will report them to the President. *Please* open the door."

Reeves quickly punched in a code. The door opened.

Bren walked ahead with Jago and Banichi in the lead. The observers split into two teams as his aishid team did, either side of the door. Geigi's man and Nawari entered with him, into a wide room lined with displays and consoles—while the two guards outside came inside, looking upset.

Techs at their stations looked in his direction and froze, evidencing unease and alarm as Guild took up station with crisp precision. Bren gave a very little nod, still watching hands, and put on a neutral expression. "No problem, ladies and gentlemen. As you were. Is Stationmaster Tillington here at the moment?"

There were nervous looks at that question. Some few looked at each other; most looked at him, and two people independently and very slightly nodded toward the administrative office at the rear of the room.

A second little nod. "Thank you. Please carry on." He said in Ragi: "Banichi, Jago, stay close with me. The rest please wait. The technicians themselves are complying. There are, however, a few buttons in the administrative offices." And again in Mosphei': "Be at ease, everyone, please. Please stay in your seats. Thank you."

He went to the office, knocked on the door, and with no answer pushed the button.

It didn't open.

"Mr. Tillington, open the door, or any damage will be laid at your account. I have come up here at the President's request as well as the aiji's. Open the door. What I have come to say to you this morning is not that unpleasant."

The door opened.

Tillington sat at his desk, an ordinary-looking, middle-aged man in shirtsleeves, looking greatly upset.

Banichi and Jago positioned themselves on either side of the door, inside. Bren gave a little bow. "Stationmaster Tillington. Thank you. And good morning."

"What is this armed intrusion?"

"Atevi security accompanies me wherever I go. It's a regulation. And it's useful for them to understand the current situation here so they can convey correct information to the aiji-dowager, among others."

"You're scaring hell out of my workers. This intimidation is not appreciated."

"I'd suggest, sir, that we carry on a quiet conversation, the two of us, and it would be far better conducted here, quietly. I would much prefer that. If you would like your own security present, that would be perfectly agreeable, and we can wait for you to call them."

Tillington stared at him, not moving.

"I know you oppose my presence as a Mospheiran official," Bren said. "That's nothing I take personally. It's your right. I would like to uphold the dignity of your office on principle, and I would like to support you in my reports to the President and to the aiji. You've done a good job. You kept the station going through very difficult times. You deserve respect for that. Now we have a different situation, and the President has found it necessary to bring additional resources to bear. I am certainly one of them, at your disposal, if you would view it in that light. The president is also sending a personal envoy aboard the incoming shuttle, with emergency powers. At that point, you will be dealing with the President's representative, and I'll be concerning myself primarily with the kyo situation."

"You arranged these aliens coming here! You arranged the whole mess we're dealing with!"

"Stationmaster Tillington, the kyo declared they *would* visit. We had no means to prevent that, and we have none now, but certainly keeping their visit quiet and pleasant is in all our best interests. Dealing with these visitors will be entirely an atevi responsibility, initially, since the language of choice during the initial contact was Ragi, and the persons with whom the kyo chose to speak were atevi."

"No way."

"Sir, you have no means even to speak to them."

"We will not be excluded from negotiations!"

"The Presidential envoy will deal with that question, sir. And Mospheira will be *consulted* during negotiations. But atevi Central will be the operations center until the envoy arrives to take command."

"No. No, this will not happen!"

"I ask your cooperation in the meanwhile, sir. And the more cooperation we receive, the more we will give."

"Damn you, no!"

"Sir."

"You have no right to be here. No right! The same two captains who set up this situation come in here and quarrel with my staff, second-guess my orders. *Sabin* is the reason we have this situation. Sabin is the *last* person who ought to be directing anything to do with this! And you've been right there with them!"

"I'm sure Captain Ogun makes command decisions, sir, within the Captains' Council. I don't. The President of Mospheira has asked me to represent Mospheiran interests in the negotiations, and I will do that."

"Get out of my office!"

"Listen to me. This is in no wise Sabin's fault. From the moment we entered Reunion space, the kyo, already sitting there, watching the station, had absolute ability to track the provenance of the ship. They used the station for bait. They were waiting to see what humans would do. Our choice in this last encounter was to communicate. And they responded. Our choice now needs to be to communicate. We need to take up the conversation we left off at Reunion, and demonstrate that we have no ambitions to be a problem to the kyo. I am exceedingly sorry that we could not have had this conversation between ourselves in advance and in detail, but we could not guarantee the security of communication within the station prior to our arrival, and we had no wish to generate panic aboard the station. The information was held within ship command. We've done our planning through ship channels until we docked here, and you can ask Captain Ogun to confirm the nature of it."

"No."

"Mr. Tillington. Stationmaster Tillington. The Presidential envoy is arriving to make decisions on the Mospheiran situation. The envoy will take charge of Mospheiran operations, and what your own relations may be with that person is for you to determine. I would advise cooperation."

"Tell that to Braddock and the Reunioners!"

"I intend to."

"Fine. Then start there. And get the hell out of my office!"

"Stationmaster Tillington."

"*These* are the people that started the whole problem. *These* are the people that we couldn't live with. *These* are the people that stirred up trouble with God knows who out there, and now we're all in danger!"

"Let me inform you officially, sir, that the Reunioners *are* going to be removed from the station and resettled as soon as possible. But that is a future we cannot visit until we have dealt with this crisis."

That caught Tillington's attention. *"Removed."*

"Removed, sir."

Sharp attention. "Is that what these visitors want?"

"I don't think so. Out there, they had the Reunioners at any time they wanted them. I doubt they want them, or you, in any sense."

"So what *do* they want?"

"Likely to find out what we are, what we wanted in building in an area they consider their territory, and whether we're a threat."

"So *then* they attack us."

"If they do, frankly, sir, we'll be in a lot of trouble, because *we* have no weapons."

That brought a shocked look.

"We don't," Bren said. "They *do.* So I suggest diplomacy as a solution. Cooperation."

"Tell that to Braddock!"

"Stationmaster Tillington, I *want* to do something about Braddock. I can't do it while the Reunioners are in a state of distrust and panic."

"It's their *fault, dammit!*"

"I'm not debating you on the matter, Mr. Tillington. And fault is nowhere in my list of considerations. I need one thing from the Mospheiran establishment. Quiet. I agree that the aishidi'tat and Mospheirans have a treaty. I agree that, excepting the ship, which is its own authority, this station and *any* station must be equally divided between Mospheiran occupants and atevi. I agree that the Reunioner presence puts that out of balance. I agree that station occupants should pass screening. We are in *complete* agreement on these issues. The aishidi'tat is unwilling to tolerate the population imbalance. The aiji will also be arguing to a resolution, a rapid one. But we cannot solve it now, and we are not helped by measures that put the Reunioners in fear and discomfort."

"You don't touch those doors!"

"I agree. I would not have ordered the closure, but now that the doors are shut, this is not the time to try to resolve the problem."

"I saved the station from riot. And I'll tell you this, Mr. Cameron: if this ship wants the Reunioners handed over I'm not willing for Mospheirans to die to protect them."

"I doubt the kyo can tell the difference between humans at this point, and I greatly doubt they'd care. We will deal with the Reunioner issue when we get through this. In the interim, I want your agreement, sir. I'd like access to Reunioner records, and I'd like an assurance of adequate supply over there."

"You're worried about *their* supply. We've had shortages the last whole *year,* Mr. Cameron."

"I'm aware of that. I'd like to see the records."

"You'd like. You'd like me to give you what you damned well *know* you've no authority to deal with. I'm not letting you meddle with the Reunioners."

"I'd like to preserve Mospheiran authority on this station, and not agitate the situation beyond easy remedy."

"*Agitate* the situation? Mr. Cameron, you *agitated* the situation when you picked those three kids to go down to be the aiji's guests! Now they're Reunioner *royalty!* They're a *cause!* Keep the politics quiet? Not give Braddock a platform? We've got politics run amok over there, because they know *those kids* have atevi backing!"

"You have my interest in *that* matter, sir. Is that Mr. Braddock's claim?"

"Of course it is! The *kids.* The damned *kids* get to go down to the planet, the *kids* get themselves a landing spot, and they get the aiji's backing. What do we conclude about *that?*"

If there was a way to construe anything Reunioner as a threat, Tillington seemed determined to find it.

"I'd like to hear your theory, Mr. Tillington. What on earth would Tabini-aiji do with five thousand Reunioners? Understand, I have to get special permission for my *brother* to visit the coast."

"The kids get in with the aiji's son, the kids get a wedge into the atevi court, and the *Reunioners* get the aiji's backing."

"Which would do exactly *what,* Mr. Tillington?"

Tillington gave him a surly stare. "I think you can figure it. Five thousand technically adept humans spilling every technological step the aiji wants."

Well, that was an interesting jump of logic.

"It's very unlikely he would want that. Mospheira *has* the Archive. It's always *had* the Archive. The knowledge has always been down there. We just had a coup on the mainland because the technology necessary to get shuttles up here destabilized the atevi economy, and put pressure on old regional grievances. The last thing on earth Tabini-aiji would want is a flood of humans violating the social rules, which, believe me, are what makes civilization civil down there. And it's damned certain the aiji would not take Mr. Braddock for an advisor. Please appreciate that atevi don't *want* any such intrusion. Atevi don't *want* the whole continent to look like the station corridors. Modernity on the human pattern is not what they want. It's not what they ever want."

"Geigi does well enough having his little kingdom up here."

"Geigi does his job up here out of loyalty. He had rather have his fruit orchards and his antiques. He had rather go sailing. No, sir, your scenario does not apply. Tabini-aiji has no desire to let these children establish residency."

"Tell that to Braddock. He's raised expectations. Mightily."

"I wish he had not. Which is not to the point, Mr. Tillington. What is to the point—is that we cannot shape the encounter with the kyo around Mr. Braddock or the Reunioner issue, which I am relatively sure plays no part in what the kyo want here. What we need most is *your* cooperation."

"Fine. Then get your people out of my office."

The man had one theme.

"I still am asking, Mr. Tillington, to be assured we don't have a crisis developing while we're occupied with the kyo. I want to know that supplies are flowing, that we *have* communication within the Reunioner . . ."

"No."

"A little cooperation, Mr. Tillington. *Where* is Mr. Braddock?"

"Somewhere in 23."

"Where are the children?"

"Hell if I know. In 24. Mostly."

"Mostly."

"The girl's in 23."

"I take it the doors between 23 and 24 are still open. Or aren't they?"

"Why are we talking about three *kids,* when we've got a ship bearing down on us?"

"Because *you* brought up the kids, sir, and in your general lack of information, I'm wondering if you have any *idea* what's going on in the sections you walled off with fifteen minutes' warning. I'm wondering what your communication with the Reunioners is *like,* and how often you undertake to inform them what's going on."

"They get regular news, along with everybody else."

"Do they get it now?"

A shrug. "I suppose they do."

He swept a gesture back toward the outer room. "All those buttons. Sir. I trust you know what they do."

"I trust you *don't.*"

"We are not coming to a good conclusion, Mr. Tillington."

"So leave."

"Mr. Tillington. I am not here to oppose you. You've served through a difficult period . . ."

"Of your making!"

"Sir. I ask you—I *ask* you, I do not demand—that you cooperate in this situation. I don't know what you've theorized the kyo are, but *knowledge* of these people resides in *me,* in Sabin, and in the team that dealt with them last. I believe we can get us all out of this safely, given cooperation—"

"You have no authority!"

Disappointing. Extremely. He could order the man arrested. Detained.

Shot, for that matter. The Guild would oblige without hesitation.

But it wasn't a choice.

"If it's your choice to take that position, Mr. Tillington, I am exceedingly sorry. I have alternatives I don't want to invoke. And you're leaving me no choice."

Tillington's stare went past him, instantly, to Banichi and Jago.

"You're out of office as of this moment, sir, and you're removed from all authority on this station. You'll be returning to Earth on the next shuttle. I'd like not to make that evident to your staff at this point. I'd like not to have any embarrassment to you. I'd like you to walk quietly with me out of Central, and then let's call *Phoenix* security, so you can go talk to Captain Ogun about this, as I'm sure you'll want to. Tell him I'll talk to him about it at his convenience."

"Damn you!"

"Nadiin-ji, contact Jase. We need ship security to come here. The gentleman apparently declines to go with us, and I have no wish to have a machimi in view of his staff."

"Nandi," Banichi said, and Jago took up her pocket com and made a call, in Ragi, to Jase.

Bren just stood there.

Tillington clenched his jaw. "My own security's coming."

Button under the desk edge, one was quite sure.

"That will be fine, sir. Unfortunately nobody out there speaks Mosphei'." He changed to Ragi. "Jago-ji, trade with Tano. Tillington-nadi has called his security. Advise Nawari and communicate peacefully with Mospheiran security, if they come in before ship security does. Advise Jase-aiji to contact their command and warn them."

"Yes," Jago said, and went out into Central. Tano immediately came in.

Tillington's look was anger and extreme unease. His eyes followed the movements.

"If you should have a firearm in that desk," Bren said, "I very strongly caution you not to use it. I think a conversation with Captain Ogun would be far more helpful to you. Please don't make a spectacle for staff out there. Let's just take a walk outside. Shall we?"

"I'll protest this clear to the legislature."

"I'm sure you will. I'm even sure you'll find support. Please live to get there."

Tillington's chin wobbled.

"Take a walk, sir?" Bren asked quietly.

Tillington got up slowly.

Bren made an inviting gesture toward the door.

Tillington walked, slowly, out into the middle of operations. Stopped.

Turned. Clamped his jaw, sucked in a breath and said, loudly:

"You're being taken over. We're being taken over. They're setting us up!"

Bren rolled his eyes. Caught a senior tech's shocked look and held it.

"No," he said, and shook his head slowly as Tillington went on yelling about takeovers and conspiracies. He turned to catch stare after stare. Shocked, worried techs sat, some with chairs turned about, some looking at him, some looking at Tillington. One tech got up, and thought better of it, freezing in place.

"Please," Bren said, as that tech looked his way. He made a small gesture for the man to sit down. The man felt back for his chair, and sank into it.

Tillington made a sudden move toward the boards.

Jago stepped into his path. And if Tillington didn't know it, that was the most dangerous person he could have challenged. Tillington stopped. Cold.

"Stop," Bren said sharply, in a sudden silence. "Stop right there, sir. Everybody stop." He took an easier stance and said, to the room at large. "Mr. Tillington has called Mospheiran security. *These* are atevi security. We've called ship security and they're coming. We're up to our *elbows* in security. Everybody please just stay seated and we'll sort this out. Understand what's going on. The President has instructed Mr. Tillington to defer to a Presidential envoy, who's arriving on tomorrow's shuttle."

"Some bureaucrat who's got no idea what goes on up here!" Tillington shouted.

Bren raised his voice, swept a wide gesture. "We have a ship out there that's capable of destroying us where we sit! I suggest that we all calm down and consider what we're going to do."

"Do?" Tillington shouted. "Do? Maybe you should go out *there* and talk to them!"

"As I will, at need! But you've done enough to complicate this situation, Mr. Tillington."

Mospheiran security showed up in the doorway. Guild immediately shifted, Tano, Algini, Nawari, Geigi's man, and the four Guild Observers all facing them, while Jago held her arm still outstretched, still barring Tillington from a move toward the boards. Banichi alone stood watching the techs in stony, forbidding silence.

"Arrest him!" Tillington shouted. "Get him out of here!"

Mospheiran security, three in number, with two already in the room, didn't look supremely confident in that order.

"Security!" Bren said sharply in Mosphei'. "Stand your ground! Mr. Tillington is removed from command by order of the President."

"He has no authority!" Tillington shouted.

Mospheiran security didn't move. Guild didn't move. And quick footfalls in the hall said another force was on its way.

Kaplan and Polano, in blue fatigues, entered the room, armed with rifles and focused on the five Mospheirans. Immediately behind them, Jase Graham arrived in the doorway, ship's officer, with two more blue-uniformed ship's security behind him.

"Captain Graham," Bren said quietly, in great relief. "Will ship's security take custody of Mr. Tillington? I suggested that he take his complaints to the senior captain. I think the offer should still stand. He can wait in custody until the senior captain comes on-shift."

"That can be arranged," Jase said. "Sir. This way."

Tillington hesitated, eyes darting.

"Sir?" Jase repeated.

Tillington found the power of movement. Walked toward the

door, then snapped at Mospheiran security. "Don't leave! Witness what goes on here! I want a record!"

Jase accompanied Tillington out the door, and gave quiet orders to security outside.

Then came into the standoff again.

"Mr. Cameron. I understand Lord Geigi retains the handoff."

"Yes. He does. And will." Bren swept a look around the boards, where shaken, upset techs sat backed by dead screens, boards that wouldn't work until Geigi pushed a button in his section. He raised his voice. "Gentlemen. Ladies. We have absolutely no fault to find with you as a team. Please understand that. We need you to stay just a little longer. Please. Is there a way to communicate with Lord Geigi's office?"

Silence for a moment. Then one of the techs centermost nodded.

"Is there a way to bring a few of these boards live?"

"There's the handoff mode," that man said. "Theirs and ours."

"So I understand," Bren said. "Good." He looked around, as Guild, Mospheiran security, and Jase's bodyguard stood a little easier, but still watching each other, watching him, watching Jase.

"I came in here," Bren said in a low voice, as Jase joined him, "to try to make peace with Tillington. Clearly it didn't work."

"Wasn't likely to. Tillington already suspected he's on his way out."

"Ogun said as much." It was a large room. They were surrounded by Guild security, out of earshot of any human not amping the sound. Which might happen. A little caution was in order. "Tillington could have called the President to ask. Maybe he did. Maybe he didn't like what he heard. Do we have any assessment what conditions are, over in the sealed sections?"

"We're technically in charge," Jase said. "*Ship* is. We've taken control of communications to those sections, at least. The emergency seal wasn't what we'd have done. But there *is* provision for doing it. There's water, sanitation, emergency supplies for considerable duration; and there are personnel refuges, but we're keeping all those resources locked for now. For one thing, we don't want the psychology of resorting to those supplies. Ship personnel have been successful getting water and supply in: that's never been disrupted. And we don't want the emergency supplies used up, in case we have any worse problems."

"Opening those doors, however—"

"No." Jase drew a deep breath, staring at the techs across the room. "That wouldn't be the best move. What happened, Bren, when the news got out about the kyo—there was a report of a panicked mob in one Reunioner section, 23. The distribution center, mid-corridor, tried to shut down because the crowd was pushing in. A riot broke out, we scrambled security, and Tillington reacted with an announced closure on all section doors. I can't say it was a wrong decision—given the situation. But panic set in all over the station. People at work took out running, trying to get to family and friends. Reunioners definitely panicked. People tried to get out, and *in,* and people ended up hurt. All three distribution centers were looted, to the walls. People were putting water in every container they could find and emptied the tanks for 23 and 24. We did get security in through the personnel locks, we caught the runners and put them back into their proper sections in small groups—we kept a list, but just put them back. So that's where we are now. All the other doors were opened again within a few hours. But the Reunioner residency sections are still shut down. The two adjacent sections are open to each other. The other, 26, is closed at both ends. Water's working, supply's getting to distribution centers. We've kept the public address going, and we've told them you're here and that the closure is temporary, for safety, and that you're optimistic, all that. We've tried to reassure them. And they *are* stationers. They're not tearing up things, except the initial mess. We're getting things through three freight accesses straight to the distribution centers. We put goods in on the Mospheiran side of the passage, roll a carrier through, offload, retreat and unlock that that door. The distribution people take the load in, we lock the passage at their signal and search it and lock it up again at both ends. Nobody's tried to exploit these points . . . so far. And people are respecting the armor guarding the doors. They're scared of it and we want it that way. That's what we've got."

"Where's Braddock?"

"We haven't heard from him. That's another worry. We don't know where he is."

"The kids?"

"I don't know that, either. At one point, about eight days after we got back, I called Gene's apartment. I talked to a woman I think was his mother, but she didn't want to talk to me. Fact is, by the time we got back, the parents wanted their kids, and they wanted not to talk to us. There'd been the delay. That was understandable. I gave it a little time. Frankly, I was busy debriefing, one conference after another. I brought up the matter, expressed the worry that the families might be pressured. Consensus was, even with Sabin, let the situation alone, give it time, there's no urgency. Two days later the kyo showed up. Right then I proposed going in, moving the kids and their parents out, and word was hell, no, we don't want to stir the Reunioners up. That went along until Central got the signal and word went all over the station. I don't know whether that broadcast was an accident or not. I don't know, just as I don't know what part Reunioner politics has played in the parents' reactions, refusing Geigi's invitations, refusing to talk to me. I haven't liked the reaction. I haven't gotten clearance to pursue it. But asking for the kids now—"

"They could become hostages."

"Exactly."

"Can you get people in there?" Bren asked.

"Can *I* get people in there?" Jase rephrased that, which one took to mean—taking it on himself. "We have people in there, between you and me. We get reports. We still aren't finding Braddock. We also have the distribution accesses in our control. How important is it, to request the kids again, right now? As far as we know, they're safe, they're supplied, they're with their parents."

Jase had his constraints. Ogun and Sabin weren't unanimous. The station was in precarious balance.

He had his own . . . the kyo inbound, which overrode all other priorities—including time he was spending right now, trying to deal with the Mospheiran breakdown. And the kids were indeed with their parents, who presumably *could* take care of them. He understood Jase's position. It was also, reluctantly, his.

"I'll mention it to Sabin," Jase said, "that we *should* have them somewhere in our planning, if there's a security breach. If it becomes critical."

He thought about it, pros and cons. And what could go wrong . . . which was everything. "Mention it, if you can. The kyo situation tops everything. It has to. And if that situation can stay quiet, let it." He cast a look past Jase's shoulder, at the blank screens, the techs who'd been waiting, not patiently. "Meanwhile we've got a tired staff who's not sure who's taking care of their interests. I'd like to get that question answered. Can you stay with me for a bit?"

"I'm missing Tillington's meeting Ogun," Jase said wryly. "But that's probably a good miss. I'll stay here."

Bren drew a deep breath, and with Jago and Banichi, who were bound to shadow him, he walked over to the half-circle of overtired techs, who probably expected—and dreaded—a dismissal from any control over the situation.

Mospheirans. As he was. And if they resented him, they resented everything they saw in front of them—his dress, his manner, his whole history, not to mention the massive atevi presence that had overwhelmed the room.

"Gentlemen, ladies," he said quietly. "Who's senior tech, here?"

A man at the end console half turned, looking dubious, then slowly stood up.

"Will you come here, please, sir, so everybody can hear, and answer a few questions?"

The senior tech came, close-clipped hair, rumpled, many-pocketed jacket, career man in a field that hadn't existed when he'd started university, that hadn't been defined when he'd left everything and come up here. It was the story of most of them who'd come up to the station.

But this man would be all that *and* a supervisor.

"You need authorization for what's happened," Bren said. "And I want to get it for you. Can we get communication with the incoming shuttle?"

"If Geigi's lot gives us communications."

"I understand there's a handoff mode. Board linked to board."

Head nodded slowly. Mouth stayed set.

"There is."

"With that, with Geigi's boards and these boards both live, we can get communication with that shuttle."

Eyes flickered, passing thought. "Ops handles shuttle-com, but we can get that link."

"They'll have a passenger. They *should* have a passenger. They held the shuttle to launch right behind us for that reason. President Tyers has sent somebody—somebody with direct Presidential authority, and technical knowledge to go with it. There's been a secrecy issue, getting organized and getting up here as fast as we have, for fear there *would* be panic. But the reason for secrecy is past and the kyo certainly aren't going to understand the transmission. Can you get us a connection with the shuttle?" He read the name on the badge. Okana. And resolved to remember it.

Communications with the shuttle *might* have gone through ship-com with far less fuss.

But right now it was important for Mospheirans to have their hands on the connection, and it was important to bring Mospheirans and atevi operators onto the job. Rumors had flowed from this room, from someone's indiscretion. Let them flow again.

"Yes, *sir,*" the answer was. Mr. Okana started giving directions, and some of the techs, who had sat worried-looking and idle throughout, swung around to the boards and started to work. Others watched.

"When it comes," Bren said, "put the volume up, so the whole shift can hear it."

"Young gentleman," mani said. Mani sat in her most comfortable chair, with her cane at hand, and a small, untouched plate of pastries. "Nand' Bren has successfully ejected Tillington-aiji." Mani sounded very satisfied about that.

Cajeiri felt the same. He had sat studying his kyo notes for some time, keeping mani company, but his thoughts kept straying. He wished he might have gone with nand' Bren, but that had not been likely, so he had not asked. He wished he might have added Antaro to the people with nand' Bren, so he would get an account of what was going on. But he had not dared ask that, even.

So Antaro would have to get what she could from Nawari when he got back, if Nawari was permitted to say anything.

Tillington-aiji and Lord Geigi had been feuding about control of Central, he understood that extremely well; and Tillington was not behaving respectfully where it came to Lord Geigi, or reasonably where it came to the Reunioners.

And Lord Geigi had sent his letters over to the Mospheirans to be delivered, because that was the way things were supposed to work, but no answer had come back from them.

Which meant his letters were somewhere and not in the hands of his associates, he would be willing to bet on that. And that was Tillington's fault. So whatever else Tillington had done wrong, he had also disrespected his father's order and nand' Bren's arrangement.

And *that* was not smart.

"It is good," mani said. "We are rid of that influence, or at least, rid of him in an administrative capacity. Tomorrow we shall be dealing with some different person, who, we trust, will have more common sense."

"One is glad, mani."

"What are you reading?"

"My notes on the kyo, mani."

"Are they productive of such consistent frowns?"

He had let his face show things. And lying to mani was never a good thing to do. So he shrugged and told the truth, not pertly. "I was thinking of my associates, mani. One hoped they would be safe in all this. One is glad Tillington is gone."

"He *will* be gone. Count nothing certain until then. But you have business before you."

"Yes, mani. One does."

Mani frowned. "We are relieved, be it known."

"Might one ask, mani—could my associates be moved?"

"Should they be taken from their parents?"

"One would ask their parents be moved, mani, if we could."

"And their relatives?"

He understood then what mani was saying. But he had already understood that. He and his associates had talked about it, and wished there were a place, if all the Reunioners were to be shipped to Maudit, the way Tillington wanted. They had talked about how they would solve that. And solving it needed mani's help, at least. "Still," he said, "*they* are in everybody's thoughts. They cannot be ordinary people. They understand that. And one is worried."

"I have not brought up a fool." Mani frowned, but she was not unhappy with him. He sensed that. "Nand' Bren believes that they are safer where they are at the moment. Nand' Bren is in charge of Central, Tillington is gone, and the doors that seal them in also seal out the Mospheirans, which may be a good solution for the next number of days."

"Do they know we are here?"

Mani nodded. "We understand they have been told. The guards at the doors have passed that word, and they have announced it."

If they had said that, then they knew he was here. He had told them very definitely that nand' Bren and mani and *he* would come to deal with the kyo should they come to visit.

They would know he was here, and they would know he would speak up for them, and track what was happening to them. They would trust nand' Bren. And mani. It was on him, now, to be sure they were safe.

"Cenedi believes," mani said, "that until we can lay hands on Braddock the doors should stay shut, and until we can lay hands on him, it would not be prudent for us to ask for your young people—since Braddock might then decide to bargain over them. And we will not, as a matter of policy, bargain with this man."

"One understands, mani."

"We *are* paying attention," mani said, "and we do not fault your concern, Great-grandson. And this you may know, but forget you know. Nand' Bren is working on a solution which will bring *all* Reunioners to live on Earth—not on the continent, be sure, but still, on Earth. The Presidenta's agreement *and* the agreement of the legislature are required. Politics may still arise, and if it arises because someone has spoken too soon, it would make a settlement of your young associates very much more difficult."

His heart had picked up its beats. "They will live on Mospheira?"

"Now I have told you something you absolutely must not tell them, young aiji. You can greatly harm their prospects if you tell this to them before nand' Bren is ready to tell the Reunioners as a whole—and *this* will be when we have concluded all that we have to conclude with the kyo. So you, young aiji, have a secret to keep. And understand that anything which brings the Reunioners into conflict with Station authority could make this impossible. I rely on my great-grandson. I rely on him for discretion, and following instructions, and making no moves to contact these young people. This is a test. Are you of a disposition to be aiji? Prove it in this."

He found nothing to say for the moment. It was the best outcome he could ask, the very best, coupled with disaster if he made a mistake and the notion got out.

"I shall not be a fool," he said. "I shall not be a fool, mani."

She nodded slowly. "I have every confidence you are not, Great-grandson, or I would not have told you. And I suggest that you consult us at any time common sense says you should consult, where it regards your young associates. Do not think your silence protects them. Ever."

He so wished he were still young and stupid. Growing up left one looking at far too many sides of a thing.

If he had known they would one day be here, the way things were, would he have dared explore the ship-tunnels with strange humans he had just met?

What he knew now would make him afraid.

But he hoped he still would do it, someday.

He *definitely* still would do it. And they would get to ride again, together, at Lord Tatiseigi's estate. And sail on nand' Bren's boat.

He just had to grow smarter and tell things the right way. Mani was telling him when and how to manage, and what politics he had to look out for.

He had to learn those things. Fast.

It took a bit in Mospheiran Central, arranging things with Geigi, bringing a section of communications up, then getting a handshake with the inbound shuttle, which indeed had been aware of a crisis on the station. Then they made a handoff link with one of Geigi's boards.

Jase had absented himself, heading over to atevi Central to consult with Geigi and advise him what was going on, besides, through Geigi's boards, querying ship-com, extracting information on conditions in the Reunioner sections.

There was video monitoring to which the ship and now Geigi had access. A few installations had been put out of operation in 23 and 24, but most worked. That word came through.

Ship-folk armor units maintained video surveillance from the doors. Lights there had gone to twilight, but nothing so dark the armor's eyes couldn't see everything that moved.

There was, as Jase had said, an uneasy peace in the Reunioner sections. They kept the lights dimmed for all but a few hours a day, to encourage people to keep to their own quarters, and to conserve supplies.

It might easily have been worse. Things functioned. Supply arrived steadily, food and medicines. Water flowed. Heat kept people warm. Fans moved air, and scrubbers kept that air clean. Vid provided endless entertainment and offered at least some news in a handful of functioning gathering places—the food distribution stations. All of these might have malfunctioned. And hadn't.

"Yes, ma'am," Bren heard the tech say. "The atevi rep, Mr. Cameron, is here. He wants to talk to you."

There was an answer. Bren came close and put a hand on the seat back. The tech took off his own single-sided headset and handed it over. Bren slipped it on. "This is Bren Cameron. We're in good condition here. I hope the same on your end."

"Yes, sir."

"I trust you've got a passenger."

"Yes, sir. Do you want to speak to her?"

"I'd like to, yes."

"Stand by, sir."

That took a moment. He heard the background noise of the cockpit, a question from someone asking what was going on with Central, and an *"I don't know. It's the paidhi. Cameron. He says it's all right now, but he didn't say why they're off schedule. He wants to talk to the envoy."*

Shuttle expected human-language operations at certain hours, which they had not yet gotten. They should have been able to get station news, talk to Tillington's office, set up anything ops didn't cover with its numbers and diagrams. Instead—atevi voices had prevailed, right into what should be a Mospheiran shift.

Now human ones again, but not in the mode they expected.

And they were in space, at the highest speed the shuttles could safely use, past the point of no return, and bound for dock. It was reason for them to worry.

More thumps and clicks and rattle of gear came over the com, combined with a steady ping from somewhere.

"Bren?"

He knew that voice. Lighter, higher, and not Kate Shugart's. "Is that *Gin?"*

"It's Gin. We've been a little concerned here. Everything all right?"

Virginia Kroger. A complete surprise. But not a bad one. Far from a bad one.

"Everything's better. No emergency. Good to hear your voice. Surprised. I thought you'd be Kate. I didn't know they could pry you out of Northern Dynamics."

"Kate broke two ribs rock-climbing. She's mad as hell she's not up here."

Rock-climbing. At her age. God, that was Kate. And yanking Gin out of the Mospheiran shuttle program . . .

A year and two rolled backward, rife with images of life on the ship, Gin's ready smile, wry humor, steady nerve—a small, wiry woman well over the edge of fifty by now—high-level project manager, degree in engineering. She'd taken over the robotics program and built it, literally *built* it from Archive records and the ship's know-how and capabilities. She'd pushed crews hard, but with no fatalities, and she'd led, as much as pushed. If there was a human being alive besides bluff, no-nonsense Kate he'd have wanted up here in charge of a nervous Mospheiran workforce at the moment, it was Gin.

"You're beyond welcome, Gin. I've officially asked Tillington to step down. He was highly exercised. I'm asking you to step in as of now. Can you do that?"

"I copy. I'll be arriving tomorrow, and I'll take over as of now. Give me the details, bring me in touch with the situation, and get me people."

"I'm going to hand you over to Mr. Okana, who identifies himself as the senior tech in Central, this shift, and he'll be able to give you more detailed information. Tillington locked down the Reunioners in sections 23, 24, and 26. The ship has continued supply to the sealed sections, and ship command feels that the situation in there is stable and safe, but there are ongoing issues, mainly that Reunioners and Mospheirans have no certainty about their situation up here, and Reunioners are scared. If you'd kindly take over command of Mospheiran Central and give Captain Ogun a call in that capacity, I'll be greatly obliged."

"I copy all that clear. Do what you can. I'll be getting a briefing from Mr. Okana, fast as I can."

"Anything you need, Gin." He took the headphone off. "Mr. Okana. If you would. This is Virginia Kroger, robotics, head of the shuttle program. You know her reputation."

"Yes, sir."

"Good. She's President Tyers' envoy, she's taking over as Mospheiran-side stationmaster, and she's going to be in charge. Personally. She'll show you all the credentials you can want when she gets here. She'll bc taking over that office. And right now you're her second in command."

"Sir," Okana said, and took the headphone and settled it on, with a very sober expression. The tech at the board vacated the seat and Okana sat down, with: "This is Central, Ms. Kroger. This is Shift Captain Okana."

Okana listened, then. And started answering questions. Rapid ones. *Yes. No. Yes, ma'am. No. We can.* And said to the tech beside him: "She wants the log, everything since the morning of the contact. Send it."

Gin. Thank you, God. Thank you, Shawn.

He had backup. Sane backup.

Get contact with Ogun, now, and explain it all? Gin would handle that.

Ogun was having a busy hour, if Tillington had gotten his interview.

And Tillington's outrage wasn't going to trump relations with Shawn Tyers, who controlled vital food supply to the station, or with Tabini-aiji, who controlled both food and critical materials and processes, not to mention Tabini's owning all but one of the shuttles that carried everything up there.

Nor would Ogun fail to recall that Gin Kroger, cooperating with Lord Geigi *and* the Captains' Council, had captained the operation that *built* the robotics critical to the station, the robotics that had kept it going when the shuttles weren't flying. Kroger, Lund, and Shugart were names everybody on the station knew.

"Gin-nadi," Banichi remarked, near at hand. Banichi likewise sounded satisfied.

"Gin-nadi. *Gin-nandi,* as of right now. And, one is very sure, still Gin-ji. Kate-nandi broke ribs while rock-climbing."

Banichi was quietly, wryly amazed and amused at that news. So was he, still, given that Shawn had sent them the best alternative. Gray-haired Kate. Rock-climbing, probably in the park near Mt. Adams. Would she want to come up here now? She was probably beside herself—and *might* find a doctor's permission and a shuttle berth in the next rotation.

Kate's style of management would have been rougher, more

blunt when she waded in. He'd somewhat looked forward to Kate encountering Tillington.

Gin typically applied charm, humor. Which Tillington at the moment wouldn't appreciate.

He'd meet the other side of Gin, then, which he definitely wouldn't like.

Ask for the log, while she was still hours from arrival?

Everything Tillington had allowed to be recorded, along with things the systems had automatically recorded. Gin could read those auto-records with an expert eye, figure what the sequence of things had been, and she'd hit the deck with a good grasp of the technical *and* the political situation—things Tillington wouldn't have had time to cover.

Oh, there were questions *he* wanted to ask.

She went on asking Okana questions. Okana kept answering, rapid-fire.

News was spreading, too, to the Guild Observers. Nawari and Algini had been conducting a very quiet flow of interpretation, and the Observers listened, watched, absorbing every clue around them—learning how human authority worked, first-hand, and how the Presidenta's authority worked.

It *wasn't* an atevi way of solving things, over there among the techs, with Gin inbound and taking over and Tillington kiting off to Ogun instead of demanding to talk to his own chain of command, in the President's office. To atevi ears it would sound less like a struggle for power between aijiin and more like an internal clan dispute, with a clan lord whose quarrels inside the house had suddenly outnumbered all his allies . . . so he went out-clan, looking for an ally.

Classic machimi, in its strange way. He had a notion most of his aishid read it exactly that way . . . except maybe Jago, who knew enough to understand that machimi wasn't an entirely reliable guide with humans.

Mospheiran security in the room had begun to get the word, too, audio amped so they could overhear Okana and the techs—

even *his* ears could hear the spill from their audio. They wore no less worried looks than they had come in with, still stood clustered in a far corner, observing, outnumbered and still not happy about that, while their command was mutating by the minute.

But the chance that someone would set something off by a wrong move was diminishing. Now endurance began to matter more than authorizations.

Conversation between Okana and Gin ended, with the link left available. Okana talked to a cluster of techs, some of whom left their seats to join the group.

"One requests us to hold here a little longer, Nichi-ji," Bren remarked.

"Yes," Banichi said quietly.

Bren clasped his hands behind him and avoided the impulse to flex his shoulders. Court etiquette. One stood. One flexed small muscles, and kept outward appearances.

Gin made another call to Central, talked to Okana and then asked to speak to Bren again. He went over to the boards and took up a headphone.

"Talked to the Senior Captain," Gin said. *"We completely agree on points of security, and I'm officially asking you to ask Geigi to change the access codes and then hand them to you, so you can be his backup and my surrogate until I get there and log in, at which point I'll make another code change, so I won't burden you with that, politically speaking. I'm going to be reading the log. I'll also be making suggestions for the empowerment of a Reunioner council, for accuracy of communication—their choice, anybody but Braddock and his crew."*

"I'm sure the atevi sector will back that."

"My next call is going to be to Sabin. I trust you to call Geigi and get that code change made. I am not going to request my predecessor vacate his apartment until he's able to board a shuttle, so I'll be looking for a residence—tight as things are, I may be bedding down in Central tomorrow night."

"I'd offer you space on our side, but I'm sure you'll prefer otherwise."

"Politically speaking—not so good. But I appreciate the spirit of the offer. A dinner invitation, now . . ."

"Whenever you need anything, just ask. Dinner's on offer whether I'm at home or not. My staff would be honored. Did Ogun mention the whereabouts of the other captains? Jase is off in atevi Central, Riggins is aboard *Phoenix,* and I'm not sure where Sabin is. I doubt she's sleeping with all this going on."

"Appreciated. How long do you look to remain where you are?"

"As long as I can be useful here."

"Don't wear yourself out, but if you could personally stay in Mospheiran Central at least long enough to get a good read on who's in charge of second-shift, I'd feel better."

"I'll do that. No problem. Are we keeping full schedule on this shift?"

"No. I'm going to hold this shift until I'm satisfied I've done all I need. I'll call second-shift on for an hour or two so they can understand what's happened and understand my orders. Then I'll give them an early night. I'll ask Geigi to stay in place through my docking, tomorrow. I want all active control on his side of the wall, including communication with ops, until I get there to take formal charge into my hands. I'll be working my way through the log, and I'll appreciate any log updates outside routine, if you'll arrange that."

"Understood." Communications was the only aspect of Central even marginally in human hands right now, and while that didn't involve life-support systems and locks all over the station, it was still worrisome so long as human hands were involved. Gin was right. They needed to be sure that only Geigi could push the buttons. "No problem at all. I'll convey what needs conveying to Geigi on the code change. And trust him to deal with the technicals. He'll put the shuttle crew through to ship-com at their request."

"I'll be reading the log, meanwhile."

"Gin, you're a jewel."

"Flattery, flattery. You definitely owe me dinner."

Long haul, then. Through this shift and into the next. It occurred to him there was one place he might personally gain a little rest from waiting. Tillington's office.

But that, he decided, wasn't a good appearance. Or a good idea.

Politics.

Legal matters.

He went to the doorway of the office, looked about. Typical desktop. Files. Keys.

Drawers. A lot of drawers.

He called Okana over.

"I want you to witness," he said to Okana, "the condition of this office now. You know I haven't entered it since Tillington left."

"Yes, sir."

"I'd like to close this door, now, and lock it, and I'd like you to provide orders to the next shift that they not enter this place, because they won't want the responsibility. I'd like for you and the next-shift chief to assure Gin Kroger that nothing in this office has been touched, by me, or anybody else, until she arrives."

"Yes, sir," Okana said. "Understood."

"Meanwhile," he said, "I'm going to send my own bodyguard off, group by group, for a short break. I take it there's somewhere close."

"Adjacent room, sir, number 12. Not big, but it's got the comforts."

"Appreciated," he said.

It would be. It was shaping up to be a long day. No outsiders got to see atevi Guild or a lord of the aishidi'tat in anything but official form. Gin called for shift-end, and a shunt over to Geigi.

Gin's contact went over to ship-com, through which he also had Jase.

"You with me?" he asked Jase.

"Still holding out," Jase said. *"Tillington is sulking in his apartment. He's tried to call the President. He doesn't have that authority right now, does he?"*

"Actually no, he doesn't. He did. But right now he'll have to do that through Gin."

"That's what we thought."

"Gin's letting him stay in his apartment until he leaves. You can tell him that."

"When he asks," Jase said.

"This is going to be a short shift, next. Just informational. We hope. Everything's quiet."

"Do you need relief over there?"

"I'm all right. A couple of hours. We're going to be briefing the new shift, getting an understanding."

That was the hope at least. A request to Geigi brought a screen live, a read on the kyo transmission, on a screen tucked away in the corner. One part showed, as Bren tried to make sense of it, the course plot. Another was a clock ticking down the expected arrival of the next kyo signal.

Another was another clock, which one guessed marked the time to their automated reply, a few minutes on. The clocks counted off as he watched, a note popped up on the fourth quarter of the display, and the clocks reset.

That was the exchange with the kyo. Measured. Identical. Proceeding while human authority had a relatively quiet upheaval.

It stayed even, measured, identical, for which one was duly grateful.

So did the course, which one suspected, though had no knowledge to prove it, led toward the station.

Okana dismissed his people, who quietly left. The place was deserted for a moment. Then second-shift arrived by ones and twos, anxiously so, people eyeing the weapons, warily settling into place at dead boards. A few had exchanged a word or two with Okana on the way in, and people leaned together, to say in low voices, things like, "Tillington's out. *Dr. Kroger's* coming in." And: "It's all right. We're doing all right. They're not touching the doors."

Meaning—barriers weren't coming down. Angry people weren't coming in contact. What Tillington had set up wasn't being undone.

Okana caught Bren's eye, then quietly left.

"Thank you for coming in," Bren said. "I'm Bren Cameron. Everybody you see is somebody's security; don't be anxious. You may have heard that Mr. Tillington's been relieved, and his office is now locked pending the arrival of a Presidential envoy. President Tyers has asked Dr. Virginia Kroger to come up here to handle Mospheiran affairs in the kyo situation—she's experienced, she was with the expedition when we met the kyo, and she's arriving with current knowledge of the situation. We're holding everything as we found it, meanwhile, taking advice before we change anything—" He saw that brought visible release of pent breaths. "In short, you'll have a stationmaster who has experienced the kyo. We expect to meet with them, exchange scientific information, assure each other of good will, and part company for another number of years. So far, so good. We're communicating exactly as we did in the last meeting. It's certainly an exciting event. But no reason for panic. We'll get the station through this, and we're going to be taking some precautions for your safety, but we really don't anticipate a problem. I'll be retiring over to the atevi side of operations as Dr. Kroger assumes command here, and we've assembled the team that met the kyo the last time. We somewhat expect they've done the same, and that we'll have a pleasant, maybe a productive encounter. I can't answer more than that, except to say that they promised to come visit, and they have, to firm up agreements, and they'll likely go away again to their own territory. So bear with us. We'll be feeling our way through this, but there's no sense of alarm about it. Who's shift-captain here?"

A hand went up, at Okana's former seat.

Bren beckoned. The man got up and walked over to him. Put out a hand.

"Jim Harris," the man said. "Port Jackson. Met your brother more than once."

That was an unexpectedly pleasant meeting. A lord of the aishidi'tat in public and on official business stayed properly formal, but there was personal conversation, how Toby was, where Toby was. Mospheira was, in many ways, astonishingly small. Everybody had lived where they lived for generations, and if you were in any social subset—like boat-folk in Port Jackson—people knew people who knew you. It was a thoroughly strange conversation, Port Jackson, Toby's boat, and bilge pumps, here, in the troubled operational heart of the station, but two authorities talking together eased everyone's nerves. People began to talk among themselves in the background, with occasional curious stares at atevi—whom they might never have seen at such close range, over such a long time—though, as Geigi said, crew could say—also—*We talk. We show each other pictures.*

I know four or five whole words of Ragi.

It was all going very easily, very smoothly.

Then Tano had a call on com, and the look Tano wore changed. Fast.

Mani declared that the hour would be what the hour was in the Bujavid, and that had meant supper while the time felt like the middle of the afternoon, and bed before what was ordinarily supper.

Mostly Cajeiri suspected it was because mani was tired and sore and wanted to go to bed. She absolutely would not let anyone see her limp—much—but she had worn a constant frown, saying that the flight was certainly necessary, but that there were a great many inconveniences in the process.

Not to mention, she said, the cold of the mast, which had gotten through the cloak quite uncomfortably and made her bones ache.

So the whole house went to bed, and he lay abed, trying to persuade himself it was night, even if, up here, there was always night outside, and always day for somebody, inside.

He was a little worried about mani, that she had had such trouble, and ached, and now had so little appetite. He worried about her going to bed early, but if mani said it was night, it was night for everybody in the household, and that was that.

Lord Geigi had said everything was all right, that Tillington was gone, that the codes were all being changed, which in this place was the same as changing all the locks to everything, and it could be done very fast, in the blink of an eye.

That was what Lord Geigi had said.

Changing the codes was fast, but it confused a lot of things, Lord Geigi had said that, too. And there was no prospect of Lord Geigi getting back to his own apartment until tomorrow.

Which might mean nand' Bren would not be coming back either.

He wished they would; and he punched the pillow with his fist. He wished they could all have dinner and then brandy with mani. He wanted to listen to the serious talk and learn things.

But that was not going to happen.

It was too early, and his mind was wide awake. His aishid was learning to sleep whenever they had a chance to sleep, but it was a knack he had not learned yet.

And if he stayed up past mani's hours now, then mani would be up and about things in what she declared was morning and he would be too sleepy to think tomorrow. And he would be cross. Which was never a good thing to be, in mani's household.

There had been excitement today. There was going to be excitement tomorrow, too, with the new station-aiji coming.

Well, and he had gotten one exciting bit of news, too, from Lord Geigi's call, which was that the new aiji would be Gin-nandi.

He hoped he would get to see her soon, before the kyo came and everything started. Gin-nandi was the best. Gin-nandi had been on the ship with them, and she had built the robots the station used for mining, and she would be *fair*. Unlike Tillington.

And she would talk to *him,* if he got to see her. He was sure of it.

And if he got to talk to her, the furtive thought came to him, he could ask her to please be sure his associates were all right. Mani would not be happy about his saying anything.

But he would do it. And Gin-nandi would do something to be sure they were safe. He had every confidence she would.

He just had to plan how to get to talk to her.

When she came, Bren-nandi would not have to stand guard in Central. But she would be there, and Mospheiran Central was on the Mospheiran side, where he was not supposed to be.

Maybe, however, mani would ask her to dinner.

That was likely. If Gin-nandi came to dinner, then when mani was talking to somebody else, he could get a quiet word with Gin-nandi, lean close and say, really fast, *My associates are trapped. Please get them out!*

That was about as fast as he could say it, in as few words as he could say it, and it would make mani really mad.

But sometimes one just had to go ahead anyway.

And a whole lot of things were bound to happen to occupy mani's attention before they all got home.

When they did get home, however, as surely as the sun rose, mani would not have forgotten: she would find some way to make him remember he had gone against a promise to her.

He was too old now for her just to thwack his ear and tell him to mind.

And if he was wrong—if something went badly wrong because of it—

Mani had given him an order. She was not going to discuss it. Not likely. He could ask, but *he* was upset, and that was never going to go well, if he began talking to her.

Nand' Bren was the one who would talk to him, and tell him things.

That was who he had to talk to.

As soon as he could get to nand' Bren. Which was not easy, not being able even to leave the apartment.

There was a stir in the house. He listened to it, wondering if perhaps something had happened to get Guild attention. Or maybe nand' Bren or Lord Geigi had finally come back home, across the hall, or down. When nand' Bren got home, Cenedi at least would want to talk with Nawari, who had been out all day with nand' Bren, where he was.

Then there was a stir in the *back* of the apartment.

And a light went on under the door of his bodyguards' rooms. His aishid had waked. He heard them stirring, and he sat up in bed, shoving his hair out of his face.

"Nadiin-ji," he said, as their door opened, no longer with the light on. "Is something going on?"

"I shall go see." Jegari had hoped to slip out, clearly. A message had come through. All his bodyguard was up and dressed. And Jegari left to go ask questions.

It was probably just nand' Bren, who would send Banichi over, likely.

But Jegari came back with somebody who turned the room light on. Cenedi himself had come, and that was scary.

"Is mani all right?" was Cajeiri's first thought.

"She is," Cenedi said. "But, nandi, one of your young associates is in custody of ship security. Lord Geigi is going there."

"I shall go!"

"No, young aiji. Not without your great-grandmother's order. She is dressing. She will be in the sitting room shortly."

Mani would never permit his going. He was sure of that.

"*Which* of my associates, nadi? Who has escaped? Is this person all right?"

"As yet there is no word of the circumstance, young gentleman. One expects it momentarily. Will you come to the sitting room?"

He had to. If he was to gain anything, he had to dress, and go wait, and stay calm.

He felt a shiver coming on in the cool air. But he tried not to let Cenedi see it.

18

A child had crossed the line from section 23. It was possibly one of the young aiji's guests, Geigi's second-in-command had said, but they were not sure. Jase had gotten a call, given orders in ship-speak, and Geigi and Jase had left Central together in haste.

"They will contact us when they know," Bren said, scanning the room full of anxious Mospheiran techs and Mospheiran security.

Calling Gin to take over seemed the only help. And that took a process. He asked for that connection, stood patiently, waited until Gin came on, a thin, remote presence in the headset.

"I've got a call from Lord Geigi," Bren said into the mike. "Something's evidently happened with one of the kids, one of the three who visited the mainland. One may have ended up outside confinement. But no one's sure. Captain Graham has gone to investigate. I'd like to. Can you take over with Mr. Harris?"

"No difficulty," Gin said on the link. *"I'll handle whatever needs handling. Put Mr. Harris on."*

"Mr. Harris," Bren said, and handed him the headphone.

Harris took it, settled it on, gazing into the distance. "Yes, ma'am," Harris said. "I'm here. We'll stay on. Yes, ma'am. —She wants us to stand by. She says she wants a report when you can, sir."

"I'll give it as soon as I have it," Bren said. "Thank her." He was anxious about leaving the situation and withdrawing from hands-on control of the area. But it was Gin's job. Gin's authority, now.

They *did* need him wherever the child was. *Something* had happened, involving a Reunioner kid. Something needed to be found out. Questions needed to be asked. Fast.

"We shall go," he said in Ragi, and a second thought said maybe he should talk to Mospheiran security as he left, but, no, that was Gin's job, too. He wasn't operating as a Mospheiran official. Not once Gin took over.

He walked toward the door with his aishid forming up around him. The others came right behind them, and Guild talked to Guild in a quiet mutter of relayed queries, finding out locations, whatever details they could get.

The lift system was the first thing they needed. They reached it, and there Geigi's man, Sakeimi, on the verge of pushing buttons, stopped and took on a preoccupied look for a moment, listening to something remote, then said: "There is word from Jase-aiji, nandi. Jase-aiji ordered the child brought out. Ship-folk security delayed long enough to query Ogun-aiji on the matter. Ogun-aiji has now set the child in Jase-aiji's hands, and says, nandi, as Jase-aiji translates, Please deal with this urgently."

One strongly suspected that was a very loose translation of what Ogun had actually said.

"Where shall we find him?"

"Jase is going to the main interface. He has ordered the child brought there."

That was the central and largest of the three lift stations that had, on one side, the atevi side of the station, and on the other, the Mospheiran area. One passed through it, going in either direction, to deal with the other side. But getting off there—there was a very small shared zone. Administrative and shipping offices that had their backs to each other. And a checkpoint.

"Then we shall go there," he said. It was *not* a place most people saw, except shuttle crews and people employed in cargo. "Tell him we're on our way. Which child?"

"I shall ask, nandi." Sakeimi punched the lift call. It arrived fairly quickly. They all entered, and Sakeimi quickly put in the numbers.

"We are in communications silence," Sakeimi noted. But that was no news. Guild communications, not going through Central, was an issue in certain places, and the lift system was one such. Sakeimi had asked. But there would be no answer until they actually arrived.

It was a dogleg turn and ascent before it slowed and stopped. The door opened in the human zone, beyond which was a simple security gate of rotating bars, and a window on either side that gave a panoramic view of the other side's offices.

There was, uncommonly, an atevi presence on *this* side besides their own: Lord Geigi had arrived with Jase, both with their bodyguards.

"Who is it?" Bren asked Jase first-off.

"I'm not sure. The description is dark-skinned, not as dark as atevi, dark hair—speaks Ragi, won't respond to questions."

Smart. Presented a quandary that required a command decision—

"They called up to command," Jase said. "I ordered the kid escorted to the atevi side. Ogun—the man's getting no sleep—first intervened to object, then cleared it. He wants an answer."

Other lifts had opened around them, discharged a few humans, who looked sharply toward a gathering of atevi Guild, a ship's captain, and two atevi lords, and avoided their vicinity.

Then a lift opened right next to them, disgorging ship security, and a smaller figure in atevi riding clothes. Hair dark, close-clipped as no ateva would wear it . . .

That hair had been gold. Abundant and glorious, on a brown-skinned child.

Now it was black, slicked down tight.

That dress, that dignity and a fluency in Ragi, *could* pose an enigma to ship-folk who'd never seen an atevi youngster close-up. Irene had the bearing of an atevi lord.

She saw them and started walking. "Wait!" one of the escort said, and Irene never flinched, never reacted as if she understood, clever girl. She just walked toward them, and the man who'd made to stop her—didn't touch her.

She stopped at a proper distance. Bowed quite solemnly and properly.

Bren bowed. Geigi did.

"Irene-nadi," Bren said quietly in Ragi. "Come. You may come with us now."

She bowed slightly, perfect manners. She came forward. Banichi and Jago let her through. Then Guild in general closed ranks, so that no passersby could see.

"Dismissed," he heard Jase say to the escort. "Go on back. We're fine, here. Good job."

"Sir," the answer was, smartly. And that was that.

"Irene," Bren said, and in ship-speak: "You're all right now. We've got you."

There'd been no crack in her demeanor. None. Now Irene sucked in a deep breath and hugged her arms about her as if chilled to the bone.

An atevi lord didn't hug a person in front of witnesses. But he could hold a wounded one. He flung an arm about her, hugged her thin frame. What colored her hair was a hazard to a good coat, but he had no care for it. "Good girl. Where are the others?"

"I don't know," she said. She held to his arm, shivering. "I was so scared. I was so scared."

"Let's go to the atevi section," Jase said. "Get her entirely out of Mospheiran reach." He changed to Ragi. "Let us go to the residency, Geigi-ji. Never mind crossing the interface. We shall take a car from here."

"Gin Kroger is in voice contact with Mospheiran Central, Geigi-ji," Bren said. "Harris-nadi is in charge in Central."

"Harris-nadi is sensible," Geigi said, "and most control still rests in my boards. I trust my lieutenant. Let us all go to the residency. Introduce me to this pretty child."

"This is Lord Geigi," Bren said, as Jase went to use his override on a lift call.

"Nandi," Irene said, half out of breath. "Thank you. Thank you. Thank you."

"One is gratified," Lord Geigi said. "But one believes you have done very well for yourself, nadi."

A lift arrived, the door opened, and Guild escorted them safely inside, as Geigi's escort keyed in numbers.

Then the door shut and the car immediately began to move. "Now we are officially in atevi territory," Lord Geigi said, "and under the aiji-dowager's authority. You are entirely safe, Reni-nadi."

"Nandi," Irene said, and started to shiver as she pushed away from Bren. "Your coat," she said in ship-speak. "I'm sorry."

"It's all right. It's all right. Where are the boys?"

"I don't know. Bjorn. Bjorn's father came. He said Bjorn was at classes when the tunnels shut. He didn't get home. His father wanted to ask me and I wanted to help. But my mother sent him away and I couldn't talk to him. Bjorn's father's com wasn't working. He said nothing is working. I'm scared. I'm *scared* for them."

"Could he have tried to come back in the tunnels?"

"He could have. They *all* could have gone there when things went crazy. Cajeiri said—he said, if anything ever goes wrong, get to Lord Geigi or Captain Jase. They might have tried to go. They might have tried— Damned hiccups. I always do that. Sir. Sorry."

"It's all right." He set a hand on her shoulder, felt her shoulder heave. "Do *you* ever go in the tunnels?"

"No, sir. I can't. I couldn't." She swallowed hard, fighting hiccups. Stammered, "Mr. Braddock's there."

"Where?"

"My mother's apartment. They're—"

"It's all right. He's in your mother's apartment?"

A nod. A grimace, fighting her reactions. "My mother. Was with this Bocas. Braddock's lieutenant. But since the doors shut—Braddock. Braddock showed up. With this woman. They moved out the people next door. Braddock and this woman moved in. And they asked me—they came over to our apartment. They asked me. Asked me where Gene was, first off. I didn't know. They asked about *Gene.* That was all." A tremor shook her voice. "They didn't *ask* about Artur. Or Bjorn."

Which could mean they already knew where Artur and Bjorn were. It wasn't good. It wasn't good at all. "Braddock's living next door to your mother."

Nod. "But he sleeps. In our apartment."

The lift slowed, changed directions, sideways. Jase had been keeping up a quiet, running translation of the details for the company.

"Didn't ask about Artur and Bjorn," Irene repeated, teeth chattering, and swallowed hard, trying to get the hiccups under control. "Didn't have to ask—about me—either, did he? They knew where I was."

Smart kid. Very smart kid.

"We'll do what we can."

"In the tunnels," she said, teeth chattering. "They could freeze. I'm so scared. I'm so scared."

"There's emergency kits, emergency shelters," Jase said grimly. "But how kept, in the *old* tunnels? I don't know."

Damn. Damn it all.

He pressed Irene's shoulder carefully, gently. "We'll do what we can. We'll try. Think of all the information you can. We need addresses, accesses, any information you can think of."

She reached into her coat, pulled out folded paper. "My notes," she said, and handed it to him, a wad of information, everything she had.

A charge. A trust. A responsibility handed to him he didn't

have time for, with the kyo situation advancing and the human situation poised on a knife's edge of old history and suspicion. They didn't have a way to extricate the kids, even given the addresses, without the possibility of stirring up problems that might *threaten* the kids and put them in the center of a riot. And they couldn't bet on *any* schedule of operations: they were utterly dependent on what the kyo decided to do.

And to stir something up that might not be finished by the time the kyo ship decided to dock . . .

But what in *hell* was Braddock doing moving in on Irene's mother? They didn't ask about Artur and Bjorn, but they asked about Gene?

And *They knew where I was . . .*

Braddock didn't want Irene's mother, he strongly suspected. He wanted those kids, and if they took action, they were going to force Braddock's hand. Otherwise Braddock would pick his own time to stir up a problem, to gain leverage, involving—what was Tillington's phrase? Those kids being *Reunioner royalty?*

It didn't take a gift of prophecy to figure Braddock's intentions once the kyo showed up and the pressure was on.

He'd already shifted his priorities long enough to deal with Tillington. Conscience on one side said no, the kyo problem had to take over his attention at this point. Let Jase deal with getting the kids out. Let Gin. Let people who didn't have a unique skill on which all their safety depended.

The kid's hand clenched his, chill and desperate. He didn't find the resolve to look down at her as the door opened in their outside hallway. He was telling himself it was damnably irresponsible to involve himself in Braddock's moves, that the kids' lives weren't likely in danger.

Their sense of justice might be.

And Cajeiri's.

And the value of Tabini-aiji's protection.

Damn it.

Promise this kid? He couldn't.

But try his damnedest in the time he had left, before things went critical? He could do that, at least.

Irene was coming. Cajeiri sat, dressed in his second-best coat, waiting. And mani was waiting. Mani had ordered tea, but Cajeiri was too anxious to drink more than a sip.

Only Irene was coming. Irene was the last of them he would expect to try to reach them. Irene was scared of things. Irene was terrified of flying. Her mother was the strictest, besides, and supervised everything Irene did.

And where were Gene and Artur? And Bjorn, for that matter? Bjorn hadn't been allowed to come down to visit. But he was trapped with the others, likely, on the other side of the locked doors.

And only Irene had escaped?

He heard the sound of the main door opening, and he heard an exchange in several voices, Jase-aiji and nand' Bren among them. And what sounded like Lord Geigi. That door shut.

The quiet disturbance reached the door of the sitting room, and Cajeiri stood up as first nand' Geigi came in, and then nand' Bren, and a dark-haired human boy in fashionable riding clothes, with Jase-aiji behind.

Except it was not a boy. It was Irene—who was not gold-haired any longer. Irene had not very much hair at all, and what she had was stained dark, still looking damp, and plastered very close to her head. The clothes were the coat and trousers and boots she had worn when she boarded the shuttle.

"Reni-ji," he said, and stood up.

Irene drew in a deep breath, then flicked a glance at mani and bowed very, very properly before she said anything.

Then it was: "Nandi. Nand' dowager."

"What is this?" mani asked sharply. "Paidhi, what has happened?"

"Braddock," nand' Bren said, "has taken up residence in Irene-nadi's apartment, aiji-ma, with her mother. Irene-nadi disguised herself and slipped out during twilight. She approached the ship-folk guards, speaking only Ragi. They suspected she was not atevi, surely, but they had no way to solve the puzzle she posed, so they brought her through and called Jase-aiji, who told nand' Geigi. She has no knowledge where Gene and Artur may be. She says the third boy, Bjorn, was at his lessons when the doors shut and he has not come home."

"Clever girl," mani said. "Clever. Come here, child."

"Nand' dowager," Irene said very faintly, and came closer—scared, Cajeiri could see it. But proper. Proper, with everything she had learned in Lord Tatiseigi's house.

"Excellently done," mani said, looking her up and down. "What shall we do for you, child?"

"Find Gene and Artur and Bjorn, nand' dowager. *Please.*"

Mani heard that, and took on that look that said she was truly calculating now, not just politicking, and Cajeiri took in his breath, prepared to go take hold of Irene's arm if he must, to moderate whatever she did when mani spoke.

"The tunnels the youngsters have used are locked, aiji-ma," nand' Bren said. "The boys may be together in the locked sections, or not. Bjorn's father came to Irene's apartment to ask whether Irene knew where he was, but Irene was not permitted to answer."

Irene nodded. "Yes."

"We have the ship-folk for allies," mani said. "We hear the stationmaster will be Gin-nandi."

"Yes," nand' Bren said, "she is, aiji-ma. Gin-nandi has already taken over."

"Then arrest Braddock," mani said with a flick of her hand.

Everybody took in breath. Except mani. Except Irene, who stood there expecting just that. And there was Cenedi, who, right along with nand' Bren's aishid, would arrest Braddock this instant if they had Braddock near at hand.

"This man has been a nuisance long enough," mani said. "Now we know where he is. And is not this station, like the ship, penetrated with service passages which you say are locked. Surely we can unlock them."

Bren-nandi and Jase-aiji were not immediately against it, Cajeiri saw it in their faces. But there was sober consideration there, too.

"If it is an atevi operation with Gin-nandi's consent," Jase said, "my governing consideration is not leaving hostages, or having damage. I may not have heard about this in any timely way to prevent the move. Once it begins, I shall back the ship's allies."

Sometimes Jase-aiji's Ragi was a little confusing. But not this time, Cajeiri thought. He understood perfectly that Jase was standing back and saying mani and Gin-nandi could do what they liked. Cajeiri had his hands clenched behind him, trying to restrain himself from saying anything that would set things wrong. But:

"I have maps," he said.

"You," mani said immediately, "are *not* going."

He understood that. He longed to go. He desperately longed to do something. But he understood. If they were concerned about Gene and Artur and Bjorn being hostages, they would certainly not want *him* in Braddock's reach, in any sense. And he could not impress them by saying otherwise.

"Yes," he said, "but I have the maps, mani. All the places. All the routes. Irene-nadi helped me draw them."

"Nand' Bren has my map, too," Irene said. "With *my* section. Where my mother's apartment is."

The notebook was indeed in code. A fairly effective code, at least to Bren's eyes, as they clustered around the dowager's dining table.

"Freight tunnel. F24-01," Cajeiri said. "Is that not how Bjorn would go, Reni-ji?"

"Yes," Irene said. Proprieties or not, they had hot tea and cakes at the formal dining table, which had become the center of business, with Cajeiri's notebook and Irene's folded notes spread out. Lord Geigi sat consulting a handheld device with a station schematic, which provided the precise location and address, given the children's notes. Bren translated, where vocabulary met gaps, in either direction. Jase simply observed, officially not seeing a thing.

"If he was trying to get home from his lessons," Irene said in ship-speak, which they had insisted was the best for the purpose, *F24-09* is where we all would meet. And M298 is how you get between 23 and 24."

"M298," Geigi said in Ragi, "is an old and generally unused maintenance tunnel from the original station construction. Even a tall human must guard his head in such places. They are rarely inspected."

"But they retain pressure," Tano said.

"Yes," Geigi said. "When the doors shut, likewise the section's tunnels are locked and sealed. Heat and pressure continue, as with the rest of the section: they fare as it does."

"And, Reni-nadi," Cenedi said. "*Your* apartment."

The dowager had retired to her office, having made her demands. Guild—his aishid, the dowager's, Geigi's, and the Guild observers, as well as Cajeiri and Irene—clustered about the dining table which the dowager had not hesitated to provide. They took notes from Geigi's diagrams and from Cajeiri's notebook and Irene's . . . quickly so, in the theory, as Banichi put it, that they had an unguessably short time before Braddock woke up, realized his first hostage had fled the apartment, and sent his people to look for Irene in the logical places—notably Artur's apartment and Gene's, over in 24, which was not sealed from 23. Braddock's people might have already taken Artur: they had not asked about him. They might have taken Bjorn. There was no knowing. Moving himself and his lieutenants closer to the section 23 door, only a hallway away from that vital checkpoint, Braddock had put himself in a prime position to assemble a mob, make his demands by way of the ship-folk guards at the doors, who had communication with exactly the people Braddock would want to reach, and in the same move, he had *had* Irene under lock and key, secure, with no fuss—until Irene had stolen the key and finessed her way into ship-folk hands.

"This is the master key, the one that can override everything in the apartment." Irene had reached in her pocket and laid the red card on the table. "My mother's. I was very quiet leaving. The main door makes very little noise. I locked it when I left. But they have to call Central to open it, without the master key. And the com is out."

Irene, in her element, had unsuspected qualities, Bren thought. Where had she kept the clothes? Behind her nightgown, deep in the closet. The stolen makeup and the scissors? Under her mattress. The boots—hardly the sort of item to conceal under a mattress? "I wore those. I liked them."

Had she planned it? Likely she'd started thinking about escape when the doors closed, when Bjorn's father came, when she'd found reason to worry about the others.

And when word had gotten out that the shuttle had arrived, when she hoped she'd have high-level help if she could get out, she'd disguised herself, working fast, opened the apartment door and locked it.

And if they were extremely lucky, Braddock might still be asleep, oblivious to the fact his prime hostage had escaped.

They had Irene's address, in A-level, very near the section 24 doors. And they also had the mother's master key.

That key, that unlikely square of plastic that locked and unlocked everything in that apartment, was an inspiration.

"Geigi-ji," Bren said, "we do not really *need* this key to get in, do we?"

"No," Geigi said. "Not while we maintain control of Central." Geigi's face, ordinarily genial, was very different in this deliberation. "More, nandi, what is not generally known, Central can lock or unlock *all* apartments in a section at once, and set the code so that this key will not work."

"All locks?" Bren asked.

"All locks of a given category in a given section can be unlocked or locked—or have their codes changed—from our boards."

"Could Mospheiran Central do this?"

"That is a question," Geigi said. "Within a single section, a single category, such as section 23 residency, all lock codes *could* all be set to zero one, which no extant keycard can then open. Once all set to zero one, the entire category can be completely recoded. It was a setup procedure, not used since, that we can tell. Currently if a person *is* accidentally locked in or out, procedure is that the resident calls Central, produces the correct account number, which is read through the lock, and the command is sent to that lock. But that is the only part of the recovery procedure that is currently in operation. We found the category reset feature years ago, during setup on the station. We were never sure Mospheirans knew it, but we did not find it useful to mention when they wrote the modern manuals. So when it came recently to the issuance of keycards to the Reunioners, we let our human counterparts handle that operation, and watched with curiosity what they *would* do, with such a large number to process. They worked quite hard at it, card by card, with long lines and some altercation. So we believe we know something they do not."

No, Lord Geigi, discovering such a drastic capability under his hands, would certainly *not* hasten to advise the Mospheirans. Trust had not run that deep.

"How long would it take?" Cenedi asked.

"The set to zero one is instant," Geigi said with a shrug. "The reset goes at a computer's speed. One believes we can set to zero one and then back out of the situation, restoring the old codes from the backup files just as quickly. If that fails—" Geigi shrugged. "We can equally well unlock all those doors at once. But that would be a reluctant choice."

"Is not communication shut down," Ruheso asked, the senior Observer, "so these people cannot call for help?"

"Tillington mandated a communications shutdown in all the Reunioner sections, excepting only official announcements. We can likewise restore that service at any time, and if the backup fails, it would seem to be a good time, indeed. Tillington's act also shut down *relays* we might wish to use, and shut down worker communication inside the tunnels. If we restore one—we restore all. But I believe the Guild can actually manage without those, until we choose to restore communication with the residents."

"*We* can," Geigi's Guild-senior said. And Hanidi, of the Observers, likewise nodded.

The Guild could indeed manage a detail like their own communications. That went with them, one of those details on which the Guild generally didn't comment.

"A Guild operation entirely," Bren said, "would be my choice."

It *was* a political question—*which* security organization would go in after Braddock. Mospheiran security nominally had sole control of the Reunioner sections, but Gin was still en route, and even if she could trust officers whose most recent commander was under house arrest, they were not the ones to go into Reunioner territory to arrest Braddock, not with the political situation Tillington and Braddock had set up.

The Captains were maintaining order by holding the sections shut and guarded, and by seeing to supply through the distribution centers. They had access. Armored personnel could easily walk into that hall, as physically close to the doors as that apartment was, and retrieve Braddock with no harm to themselves.

But using armor units posed a political problem of its own. Jase was the captain on duty for now, but very soon fourth-senior Riggins would take over. "Promise me asylum," Jase said, not entirely facetiously. "Four units, battle armor, kitting up for shift-change right now, and walking right through that section door if you want them. Short and sharp and done."

"No," Bren said, "we need you politically safe." He changed to Ragi, which everybody present understood. "Fault me where I am wrong, nadiin. First step is to disable all Reunioner residence keys in 23 so we do not have a crowd running the halls in panic. We access the two apartments in question. We arrest Braddock and his lieutenants, who will be locked in, and extract Irene's mother. Simultaneously, we search the tunnel Bjorn Andresson and the other two boys might have used and bring them out if we can find them, while the first team questions Braddock and his lieutenants about the boys. Second step, with or without success in the tunnels or with Braddock, is three teams entering the boys' separate residences by the nearest service passages and extracting anybody we find there to a safe location. At that point, barring further information, we restore public address in the Reunioner sections, ask them to protect the boys wherever they are, advise the other commands what we've just done, and, we hope, reset their locks to work. One cannot believe Ogun-aiji will be that unhappy to learn Braddock is in custody. We hope not to disturb 23 and 24 too much in the operation. Section 26 need not be inconvenienced in all this, but if they must be, nandi Geigi, do as you must, whatever you think prudent to stop a crowd forming."

"You need me to translate," Jase said in Ragi. "I am already in this. My bodyguard will get no blame for following my orders. And their suit systems can communicate with others, if they have to. One asks we operate as much within my watch as we can . . . and my time is running out."

"Let us identify the tunnel accesses in question," Banichi said. "And memorize the maps."

"In that matter, search teams may use this unit," Geigi said, handing the unit with the schematic display over to his own Guild-senior. "It is not dependent on transmission."

"Are you going into the tunnels?" Irene asked from beside Cajeiri, a young human voice, in Ragi. "Please let me go. The boys will *answer* me."

Unconscionable—under other circumstances; but finding one boy—or three—who wanted to stay hidden, in a tunnel with countless machinery installations and storage . . . Irene's was the one voice they *would* believe. "Yes," Bren said, and saw Cajeiri start to speak. "You, young gentleman, know your responsibilities. No, you should not."

Lips closed. Hard.

"Nor can *I* go," Bren said. "In some situations my presence is an advantage. In this one I would endanger everyone. You, young gentleman, have a mission with the kyo, the same as I do." He *wanted* to go. It was always hard when he had to send his aishid into harm's way, and wait. And wait.

But there *were* things he could do meanwhile.

"Get permission from your great-grandmother to go with me. I shall oversee this operation from the vantage of atevi Central, where there *will* be information. If you wish, you will be able to see everything there."

"Yes!" Cajeiri said, and hurried.

"Nawari and I claim Braddock," Cenedi said quietly, having attended something coming through his earpiece. "Sidi-ji will very likely come to Central, to answer any questions of authority."

"One would be grateful," Bren said fervently. Treaty law, and a step toward removal of the Reunioners, was the only thing that might quiet Ogun's objections. "Banichi-ji, the search of the likeliest tunnel. Can we undertake that, simultaneously with the move on Braddock?"

"*Your aishid* can undertake it," Banichi said sternly. "Irene-nadi, however, will be an asset."

"My workers," Geigi said, "will gladly assist."

"We shall need a translator in the other searches," Jase said. "If we get nothing from Braddock, my personal bodyguard and I will move into the tunnels with Banichi."

"Let us go, then," Cenedi said. "Time is running. It will take half an hour to position ourselves, with the workers' assistance."

"On your signal," Geigi said. "I shall call senior workers to meet you. Service tunnels penetrate the divisions at certain points, and you will be able to go and come as you wish, with their help."

"Call them," Cenedi said. "And let us move quickly. Sidi-ji will arrive in Central with an escort. Nandi, how soon can you lock the doors?"

"Within a few moments after I reach Central, nadi. I have written down the sequence of commands in a manual *I* keep. I wish to be sure of them."

"Let us go, then," Cenedi said. "Sidi-ji and the young aiji will arrive as she pleases."

"Sakeimi," Geigi said to the fourth of his aishid, "you will stay to escort the aiji-dowager. Let her meet no inconvenience."

"I'm signaling my bodyguard," Jase said, "to armor up and meet me at the interface. Best we hurry. Once Riggins starts asking for my handoff, he's going to be highly frustrated."

Bren translated that for the others, rose and put a hand on Irene's slight shoulder. "Irene?"

"Sir?"

"Go with Banichi, stay with him wherever he goes and if there should be trouble, hide in a dark place and trust we'll come back for you. We *absolutely* will come for you. Captain Graham's going along to be sure your mother is safe. And if you and Banichi can't find anybody in the tunnels, our next step will be the addresses you gave us. And if they're not there, we'll keep on 'til we find them. Got it? If you get separated from my bodyguard for any reason, don't call out, don't try to catch up. Get into one of the maintenance shelters, get into a cold-suit, and wait. If you absolutely have to, exit on the Mospheiran side and ask for Gin Kroger. Understood?"

"Yes, sir," she said in a small voice, and got up from the table. Everybody did, and Hanidi said quietly, "Wherever we can be of service, nandi."

"We shall be searching in two sections," Cenedi said quietly. "Attend Jase-aiji. His bodyguard does not speak Ragi, and they will be guided by atevi workers once he leaves us. Stay with him wherever he goes, and be sure he understands his guides."

Jase, Cenedi and his men, and the Observers took the first lift, Banichi, Jago, Tano, and Algini, with Irene, immediately took the second, and Geigi's man Haiji pushed the button to call a third.

"The dowager is coming," Geigi said then, just as the car arrived.

"Hold for her," Bren said. Ilisidi was coming, and with her, Cajeiri and Cajeiri's young aishid, at the dowager's pace. They held long enough for the lift to advise them, in a mechanical voice, that long holds inconvenienced others.

The clock was running on Jase's shift. Distances and procedures—a simple traffic condition in the lift system—could run their margin closer. Not to mention what happened to their timing if Ogun woke up and wanted to talk to Jase.

Promise me asylum, Jase had said. It was Jase's sort of levity. But it was also dead serious. Ogun could well cast blame on Sabin if the operation against Braddock failed. Ogun could take over the operation if it worked.

But if it failed, if it came to a contest between Sabin and Ogun, with Jase's future in the balance . . .

Riggins would have been negligible in the whole game—except Riggins sat out there, Ogun's man, in possession of the ship . . . and ultimate ship-folk power.

At his own suggestion, that was the hell of it. It had seemed a sensible idea at the time.

Ogun certainly wouldn't have *Gin's* assistance if Ogun went against Sabin. And Ogun damned sure wouldn't get the aiji-dowager's approval.

But that sort of standoff was by no means the situation they wanted to get into.

Ilisidi arrived at the lift, with her company, and Cajeiri and his. She leaned heavily on the cane as she walked, not her habit, and gave a deep, discontented sigh as she joined them.

"Go in, go," she said with a wave of her hand. "We understand there is an urgency."

She hurt like hell, he guessed. The long trip and hiking about the long halls had been hard on her. But she knew exactly what she was doing, and she well knew what her presence was worth, in politics, representing the government that was the station's major source of critical supplies. Be damned to those who thought an atevi request for compliance was of minor import.

God, he loved this woman. Loved. He had been thinking human for hours.

Tillington was down, having crossed Geigi.

Braddock had had the bad judgment to cross the dowager's great-grandson.

Would Ilisidi order Cenedi summarily to remove the man from further troubling them? On Earth, that required a Filing.

Up here, under the Guild Observers' direct witness?

One had no idea what sort of signal she might have passed to Cenedi.

And, though he had a little twinge of conscience, he conscientiously didn't ask.

The lift let out again a short walk from atevi Central. A man and a woman in Guild black guarded the shut doors to Central operations. And two men in workers' green waited there. Geigi signaled them, excused himself to speak to them, a hasty delivery of instructions before he hurried after them.

The dowager with her bodyguard, Cajeiri with his own, continued. Bren followed Cajeiri, with two of Cajeiri's young guard behind, and none of his own. He had not been without his aishid, waking and sleeping, in—in what length of time he could not remember. It was a strange, a frightening feeling, as if he were hyper-extended, part of him headed clear across the station, at great risk, if things went wrong. The tunnel environment itself held dangers.

He was not going to let things go wrong. There was little he could do, from here, in the detail sense. But if his aishid or any of the others found themselves in trouble—he *would* act. He would act if it took calling down every influence he owned or could borrow.

As they entered Central, techs at their stations, realizing their presence, began to rise.

"Sit!" Ilisidi thumped her cane against the deck, instantly stopping all such movement. "Please attend your duties, nadiin! We need you to pay attention there!"

Geigi, entering his office briefly, ordered a padded chair brought out, providing Ilisidi a place to sit. When he came out again, he strode into the center of the room, with an open notebook in hand, and began giving rapid-fire orders to this and that station.

Locks and codes were at issue. Geigi gave step by step directions, reviewed instructions with certain stations.

And meanwhile a pot of tea, ordered from the adjacent service area, arrived at Ilisidi's elbow.

Bren stood and watched the screens, such as he could. Listened, for what he could gather of their units' progress.

Cajeiri stayed close by his great-grandmother, talking to her, watching anxiously as Geigi moved from section to section of the boards, giving orders.

Twenty-nine minutes gone, since they'd arrived in Central. Jase's duty was about to end. Riggins would be due to take over.

The suspended screen above, triple-faced, changed from numbers to an image of darkness, a green glare on machinery.

Banichi? Bren wondered. That camera was body-mounted, possibly borne by one of Geigi's men, moving in haste, within one of the tunnels.

Then he heard, on speaker, voice contact from Jase. And unmistakable behind the moving shadows, as the camera-bearer turned, two white figures, large as atevi, glared ghostlike in the dark.

That was Cenedi's group on screen. Jase, with his bodyguards, Kaplan and Polano. And the Guild Observers. The move was underway, headed for Braddock.

Geigi meanwhile, continued up and down the row, giving orders, supervising what had to be a tight sequence of events.

There was nothing for the rest of them to do right now but stay out of the way, and cling to that murky image, that distant mutter of voices, one of the two operations currently underway. Cenedi's team was moving very fast, presumably with Geigi's workers leading. Occasionally a green-lit girder flared into visibility, and slipped away, distorted at the edge of sight. *12,* Mospheiran numbers said, on a girder.

At what stage his own aishid was in their operation, he had no word. There was no contact with them, yet, that he could tell. But Guild didn't seek contact with directing authority until the Guild-senior in charge decided a report was due.

There was one resource, and Bren hesitated to resort to it. It had been for other contingencies, other emergencies—in case. It breached regulations. He reached into his coat pocket, felt the presence of that Guild com, told himself he could do damage if he resorted to it. This wasn't the time. His aishid didn't need his interference. He would embarrass them if they knew he was holding on to it like a superstition, a surrogate presence. But he was. As if wishing *could* help them.

The image on the hanging screen shifted then, flicked to another, larger, area with tanks and pipes casting strange shadow in a moving light.

A young human voice called out, *"Bjorn? Gene? Artur? If you're here—come out! It's all right! It's me!"*

That *was* his aishid, with Irene, underway in their search

just about the time Cenedi's group was prepared to move into the apartment corridor.

The white readout in the sidebar next to that dark image said six past the hour.

Six past. Into next shift. Riggins was in charge—except Jase was not going to be handing off with a report any time soon.

"Doors in the residencies in 23 and 24 have now reset," Geigi said quietly, the first report from him, in his close attention to the boards. He was talking to someone, likely his own workers. And the apartment doors were all locked. The master card for Irene's apartment was in their hands. And if that household had waked, they would not spend long before realizing Irene was missing. And that the master key was missing.

"Nandi," one tech said, turning. "Riggins-aiji seems to be asking for Jase-aiji."

Good *guess* Riggins was looking for Jase.

Everybody was going to be looking for Jase-aiji in a few minutes.

"Mospheiran Central officially shut down all operations half an hour ago," Geigi said. "Gin-nadi has handed all control back to us. We shall decline to answer Riggins-aiji."

"Nandi," the tech said, and simply pushed a button.

Ship-com was going to be asking a lot of questions.

Meanwhile all apartment doors, throughout sections 23 and 24, were *supposed* to open from the inside, using the master cards, but those honest souls who had not had their master cards stolen were now finding that *their* cards wouldn't work.

And their com service had been cut off days ago. That was very a scary situation, and they could not maintain that for too long before people became completely panicked.

"Bjorn? Gene? Artur? Come out! It's all right! It's safe!"

The display had switched again. Cenedi's, Bren thought. For a few moments the display was green-lit pipes, and blackness, and shadows.

Then a white-lit wall flared bright. A door opened. Camera view adjusted to low corridor lighting.

"Retain the first thread, nadiin!" Geigi said to his techs. "Hold on that source."

Over audio came Cenedi's voice, in Guild code. The video image jolted, veered to the right, to a broad, deserted expanse, a low-light image dimmed by distance and motion.

Then the view jolted repeatedly and turned right again, in a flare that momentarily washed out the image, then reestablished it as another station corridor. The camera jolted, suddenly shoved aside by a trio of Guild at a run, someone saying, in Ragi. "This way!"

"Station One," Geigi said, "Unlock A113 and A112 in 24. Now. *Cenedi!* The doors are unlocked."

"One hears," Cenedi's voice came back, jolted by running. Bren became aware that Ilisidi was levering herself to her feet, using her cane. He moved to assist as Cajeiri did.

"Pish!" Ilisidi said, shaking them off. Her attention was for the screen.

Guild in the lead stopped, became a black wall between the camera and a door. The door slid open. A woman cried out in alarm and indignation, an outcry culminating in a series of shrieks. The camera caught up, jolted, showing furniture, a flailing arm.

"Hold her," someone said, and audio had the sound of crashing furniture. Image became suddenly a second, interior door, and a struggle, two fast moves, and human voices, male, at least two in number, angry screaming.

Screaming became ship-speak words. *"Stop! Stop! Stop!"*

And Jase's voice. *"Drop the knife. Drop it! You're under arrest! If you want to be under ship authority and not atevi, drop it now."*

One wouldn't translate the reply to that. Bren stood still, holding his breath.

"You're theirs," Jase said, to which there was a stream of profanity, and something hit the wall.

"Two men are in custody, Braddock and one injured," Cenedi's voice said. *"Irene-nadi's mother is safe."*

Then a second voice, Nawari's, Bren thought: *"Unit in 112. We have two more in custody, one male, one female."*

"Search both premises for records," Cenedi said. *"Addresses and contacts. Take the prisoners to the tunnels."*

"What's he saying?" an angry voice asked in ship-speak.

"Mr. Braddock," Jase answered that, *"he wants the location of those kids. And if you don't answer him, I won't be sympathetic. Where are they?"*

A leather-clad arm reached past Jase, grabbed Braddock by the collar, and yanked upward. Braddock flailed, yelled, grabbed at an implacable grip and gained nothing.

"Where are they?" Jase asked.

"You want them, let me go!"

"Let him breathe," Jase said. *"Talk, Braddock!"*

"The girl ran! Dammit, you're choking me!"

"That's one," Jase said, dead calm. *"Where are the others?"*

"We don't have them! We assumed you did!"

"The parents?"

"They're under guard. Safe."

"In their own premises? Or yours?"

"Theirs."

Good and bad news. Jase translated, rapidly for Cenedi, which served for the dowager and for everyone in Central. The dowager said, quietly, into the unit she was holding. "We claim custody of them. Bring them."

Cenedi said quietly. *"Aiji-ma."* Then: *"Take them to the tunnels and secure them. Wari-ji, if he will walk, let him walk. So with the others. But do not release them for an instant."*

"No!" came from Irene's mother, several times repeated. *"Let me go! No!"*

The whole company began to move. A shriek. Several

shrieks. Presumably Irene's mother was moving with the rest, with no choice about it.

Curiously there had not been one question from the woman about her daughter. Not one query.

That was information, too . . . which he hoped not to mention to Irene.

"Nandi," Geigi said. "We have an inquiry from Ogun-aiji."

One was not entirely surprised. And Ogun would certainly not improve with waiting.

"Aiji-ma," Bren said, excusing himself toward the indicated console. He took up the offered headphone, slipped it on.

"Captain? Bren Cameron."

"I'm suddenly missing a captain, Mr. Cameron, and 24 and 23 are in the middle of an incident. Doors are locked with people wanting in and wanting out of their premises, and in a fair panic about it, including people we do communicate with off the main system, with a riot starting in the B24 barracks. Would you know anything about that?"

"The aiji-dowager has just extracted Braddock and several persons connected to him, without bloodshed. The operation is continuing. We've taken custody of one of the children Tabini-aiji asked be under special protection, with one of the parents, and we're in the process of locating the others."

"You didn't rescue that kid. You got him from perimeter security!"

"*Her,* sir. Yes, we did."

A moment's silence.

"Mr. Cameron."

"Sir."

"Where *is Captain Graham?"*

Damn. Jase had apparently shed his locator. Or Jase was going to claim malfunction.

"A moment ago, within 23, sir, he was extracting Mr. Braddock and his aides. That group's now gone back into the tunnel system to ask Mr. Braddock some questions. Three of the children are missing and presumed to be in danger from Mr. Braddock's people, whether as hostages or attempting to hide from searchers. The aiji-dowager asks your cooperation in this action, Senior Captain. The loss of those children would have a severe effect on atevi relations."

"Tell the aiji-dowager—" Ogun began. But he left it there for a long moment.

"Captain Graham has not wished to burden you with what could be a failed effort, sir. I believe that was his reasoning. If it goes wrong, you will be able to say it didn't happen on your watch."

"That, Mr. Cameron, is unmitigated crap."

"In point of fact, sir, with the kyo heading toward us, this would not be a time to have ship command tainted with a failed operation and a breach with the aiji-dowager."

"I told you I don't take threats."

"I assure you the aiji-dowager doesn't issue them. We will not be *in* that situation, sir, since we intend to find the children and extract them and their parents to safe-keeping. We hope to have those locks reset within half an hour. A public announcement from ship-com that the lock reset process is now underway will calm the sections."

"Mr. Cameron." There was another lengthy pause.

"Captain. We protect our allies. This is *why* we will protect you."

"Your planet-bound *authority is making decisions with people the history of whom you damned well don't know, Mr. Cameron."*

"An authority that's spent two hundred years learning how to communicate with foreigners. With each other, sir. There have been tense moments, and there have been quarrels. There have been moments when we've each pursued our extreme self-interest, but if we forgive each other our necessities, sir, we do get along. I'm asking that. I *am* asking that wisdom of ship command right *now,* sir."

Lengthy, lengthy pause. On the hanging screen, Banichi's

search was proceeding. A young girl's voice continued to call, *"Gene? Artur? Bjorn? Can you hear me?"*

"Mr. Cameron, I'm going to go have my breakfast. When I finish my breakfast, I'd like to hear that the door locks on a major slice of this station are well on their way to a fix, that the riot in 24 is under control, and that Captain Graham has finished his foray into an area that is due to become a purely Mospheiran concern when the shuttle docks. I want the principal troublemakers isolated and I want those three locked sections to stay locked *until I get the last of the problems off this station on a priority basis. Will you convey that request to Ms. Kroger when she arrives?"*

"Thank you, sir. I will do exactly that, and I'll recommend your advice."

"Don't mess this up, Mr. Cameron. You stirred this up. You fix it. And don't push your luck!"

The contact clicked out.

"Is Jase-aiji in danger?" Geigi asked.

"One has offered Ogun-aiji the certainty he can collect credit if Jase-aiji succeeds," Bren said. "He understands he can shed the ship's responsibility for the children, succeed or fail, and he has been able to express his displeasure to me without involving Sabin. He is probably not entirely unhappy, at the moment. But I need the public address. I need to tell these people that the malfunction is in process of being fixed."

"Indeed," Geigi said. "We can enable that. If you will make the statement, we will broadcast it, Bren-ji. Come."

God. What to say. How much to say. The operation was ongoing, and they hadn't gotten all of Braddock's people, hadn't gotten the parents out—the less information Braddock's people got, the better.

Things broke. It was a lot to say something had broken that locked up an entire section of the station, with all its fail-safes, but it was the best story he had.

He took up the mike. He said, "Citizens. This is Bren Cameron, speaking from atevi Central, which is at the moment in process of fixing a local computer problem that has affected the door locks. Please be patient. Technicians look to have this problem solved very shortly, and we apologize for the inconvenience. We retain the ability to open all doors, but in the interests of your personal security and privacy, we prefer to restore keycard function. Some changes are in progress, and you may look forward to having Mospheiran Central back in full function tomorrow, with the arrival of a new stationmaster, who will be working closely with the atevi stationmaster and the Captains' Council. We are in contact with the approaching kyo ship and believe that we can manage a peaceful exchange with them. Their visit is not unexpected, and we expect it will be a confirmation of the understandings we have already reached with them. Please be assured, your safety and your future are not a matter of negotiation. The President of Mospheira considers you his citizens, along with those born to the planet. There will be more news once the new stationmaster has arrived. Meanwhile please be patient. Whether you are locked out, or locked in, please allow us about an hour, perhaps less, and be patient. There is no general malfunction. It is limited to certain locks. Thank you."

No promises. No wider statements. He returned the headset and drew a deep breath. He *hated* having to speak cold. Especially to people who'd been damned well put upon and hammered down and pushed to the limit for the last decade and more.

No one in the room with him knew what he had said, or what he had promised those people.

Well, perhaps one had understood a lot of it. *Cajeiri* was at the dowager's side.

And Geigi himself understood a lot more than he ever admitted.

"Bjorn? Artur? Gene?" he heard from the speaker, a shade more desperate than before.

Then: *"Bjorn!"* he heard Irene say, and he looked up at the screen overhead. *"Bjorn, it's me!"*

He turned, looked up at the image on the screen—a place undistinguished from the rest of the tunnel they'd been searching—girders, machinery, ducts, and a narrow walkway. The camera wasn't picking up what Irene had seen—then did, as a lumpish shadow lumbered toward them.

He heard something. If there had been an answer to Irene's call, the mike didn't pick up.

"It's all right!" Irene called out. Someone knocked into pipe, raising echoes. *"It's me! It's nand' Bren's people with me! It's all right! Keep coming!"*

Cajeiri arrived at Bren's side, for the closest possible view. "Can they hear me, nandi? Can I talk to them? Can they see me?"

"They cannot hear or see you, young aiji, but they will be coming here." There were two cold-suited figures in the light now, a tall boy and a shorter, younger one, whose freckled face suddenly showed clear as the light swung over them. The boys flinched, and shielded their eyes and the light traveled past.

"Artur!" Cajeiri exclaimed. "Is Gene with them?"

"Nadiin," Banichi's deep voice said, within the pickup, *"you are safe. Is Gene-nadi with you?"*

"Gene. Not here," Artur said in Ragi. *"Not see."* And in ship-speak. *"He never got here. Bjorn almost didn't make it. We met at the rendezvous, but Gene—Gene didn't get here."*

The two had reached the tunnels before the shutdown—had run *for* them at the closure warning, met and hid together. They'd managed to get cold-suits, at least, likely from one of the emergency shelters, maybe emergency rations and water that wasn't frozen . . .

"Gene would not be caught," Cajeiri said. "He would be hardest to catch."

"What would he do, young aiji? If Braddock's men came, what would he do?"

"He would hide. He would take care of his mother and he

would hide. Once everybody heard the kyo were coming, he would know we were coming. I *told* everybody we would come."

If anything went wrong, if there was any trouble, they were to go to Lord Geigi or nand' Jase. That was the pact the kids had made. Irene had gone. Two of the boys had had the tunnels close on them before they could make it out.

Gene *might* have gotten caught before he could get there. The next part of their operation, before they released the locks, was to reach the kids' parents; and that *might* turn up Gene.

Or he could be in the same predicament, but not in the same tunnel system.

There was some sort of tunnel access in Gene's apartment complex. Cajeiri's notes and Irene's had said it was accessible. And if Gene had taken longer than fifteen minutes getting from it to the new tunnel system, if concern for his mother had delayed him, or if Braddock's men had moved faster . . .

"Attend your great-grandmother, young gentleman. I shall advise Jase."

Geigi stood over near the boards, and Bren went there, quickly, said, quietly. "Bjorn and Artur are safe, but Gene did not reach them, and Ogun-aiji reports rioting in 24. I need your workers to continue to search the modern tunnel all the way to its end, in case Gene has used another shelter. We need to contact Jase-aiji."

"Sit," Geigi said, and ordered a contact with the workers with Jase.

Cenedi and Nawari had Braddock, presumably on their way out of 23 and headed toward a lift that would get them to atevi Central. Jase and his bodyguard were moving to join up with another team, consisting of one atevi worker and two of the dowager's men, who were en route to Bjorn's residence, closest to Irene's, to extract Bjorn's parents and any of Braddock's people they found. A second such team, heading for the edge of section 24, was setting up to move in on Artur's apartment, with no translator, but with the hope of finding Artur, who *would* translate.

There *was* a third team moving toward Gene's residence at the far side of 24, a small apartment next to a section of barracks and a food distribution point, one of the sections of old station tunnels and storage areas, where distances meant more exposure of the team and more risk . . . and that was where the trouble was. That was where their lockdown hadn't prevented trouble breaking out, trouble possibly *because* of the lockdown.

And Gene, of all of them to be missing, the kid who'd mapped the tunnels on the ship.

They'd planned their action logically, by the architecture of the area, starting from 23, Braddock first, then Bjorn, then Artur, as nearest, both those very quickly.

But Bjorn's father had come to Irene's apartment looking for his son. And since Bjorn hadn't been in Braddock's hands, Braddock had known right then that one of the kids had slipped his reach. He might have gone straight for Artur and Gene at that point.

Then he'd have discovered he'd missed Artur, as well.

That would have left only Gene, the boy neither ship security nor station security had been able to contain.

Everybody who'd made a move on the kids so far had gotten it wrong.

Only hope they'd gotten it wrong with Gene. And that Gene was as resourceful in the tunnels as Bjorn and Artur.

"Bren," Jase said. *"How do we stand?"*

Contact made.

"We have Bjorn and Artur safe," Bren said in Ragi. "Gene, however, was not with them, and I understand order in 24 is breaking down. I think get down to 24, meet up with Cassimi, get Gene's mother out, find out what she knows, and pick up the families in 23 when we can. I'm worried about the situation down there if we delay the reset."

"Excellent on getting the kids," Jase said in ship-speak. *"Not*

so good in 24. Getting word of a breakout and disturbance somewhere around 18-main—some looting, traveling bands."

Eighteenth cross-passage on the main corridor. Gene's apartment was in block C18, at 21.

"If you can get to the area—"

"I'm going. Moving now." Jase's voice carried, hard breathing and the sound of movement around him. *"But those apartment blocks in the twenty-four eighteens? Aren't like the ones here in the twenty-three. Worker with us says the main corridor in the twenty-fours is reskinned old construction center, two hundred years old, and they're not sure armor can get through those tunnels, because there's ladders. Apartments on our map they say are all temp paneling, bolt-to-frame, sixteen to twenty units per area. Atevi can make it but we may have to go in without armor."*

Damn. Ad hoc planning, and a scaling map.

They'd had no choice. Had none now.

"There is no cover from the freight access to that address," Bren said, "but you could go in with armor. That's tunnel's got to be a level run."

"We've got disturbance in the eighteens, there." Jase was breathing hard, still moving. *"Getting that word from the door watch. Freight access is good, but we've got a hundred, hundred fifty meters of exposure from the freight access to Gene's address. It's right in the middle of the disturbance. We don't want to use weapons."*

Listen to your aishid, Tabini had said. And his aishid had strong words for him when he involved himself in tactical matters.

Tell Jase to turn back? Give up on Gene—who probably would have taken cover? Braddock's people were no more likely to find Gene than Jase was.

"Keep going," Bren said, and turned and looked at Cajeiri. Beckoned.

A word to his great-grandmother and Cajeiri started toward him at a run that turned into a fast walk.

"Young gentleman," Bren said, "Jase says Gene-nadi's residence is not like Irene's. There is trouble in the area. The place is not secure. What would Gene-nadi do, if he could not get through the tunnel?"

"He would hide, nandi. He would hide. Gene's access—there is no lock. There is a panel. Where the conduits come in *from* the big ones. *That* is Gene's tunnel. A very little one."

"We need the official map," Bren said. "Nand' Geigi."

Geigi gave orders, and the console went to area map, the area of 2418.

"The address is number eight in 2418-A12," Bren said, resisting the impulse to touch the display. "We are looking for a passage, an access—a service panel."

"At the back. At the lavatory," Cajeiri said, "in the inside wall, nadi."

"Deeper, nandi," Geigi said to the tech controlling it. "On the service access." Focus went deeper, to colored lines. "The blue is potable water. The black line is recycling."

Lines going to a larger bundle, that reached, via a symbol Bren didn't recognize, to what seemed a conduit, joined by other lines, blue, black, green, and red.

Cajeiri quickly pointed to a symbol on the display and said, "Here."

"The hose access," Geigi said, and reached to touch his stylus to the master diagram. "How does this join, nadi?"

"Bren?" Jase asked, on the earpiece.

"We're working on it," Bren said. "Keep going as you are."

"Hose." Geigi drew a deep breath. "We need one of the maintenance workers," he said, and gave an order to one of the techs.

"Gene said he climbs," Cajeiri said at Bren's shoulder. "He said once he climbs. He gets there outside most timcs. But he says there is this way, too."

Vocabulary in the kids' interface was sometimes sketchy, but it was thus far bearing out. Two routes. One outside, reaching the freight access, which was somewhat more exposed.

And a second one, that was not on the chart.

"Maintenance is also looking at this map," Geigi said, holding his own earpiece close. A red line appeared on their display, a rough stylus mark, tracing from the lavatory through several bends, and stopped. The stylus mark circled that.

"Water is pumped to section 24," Geigi relayed the information, "from a tank in the freight tunnel, at bulkhead 18. There are such service accesses at all endmost water sources, and there is a small transverse passage for a supply hose behind the section wall, which serve various installations on this level. The area is pressurized and heated enough to prevent freezing. It comes from a meter and valve assembly *in* the adjacent freight tunnel. There *is* a service access in the freight tunnel."

"Are such accesses locked?"

"Nadi," Geigi asked of his remote contact, "will these have locked with the lock reset or with the general section seal?" A moment. Then: "There is no containment except the freight access lock, which is an independent system, but it will lock and unlock with the freight access lock. A freight access can unlock from the inside *if* the section seal locks are not engaged—as they are, now. It shares security, heating, and pressurization with the general area.—Nadi, a man cannot, but could a child do this?" Geigi listened, and relayed, "A child, Bren-ji. Or a human."

"Jase. Gene's area freight access. Go there."

"Copy that. What am I looking for?"

"Gene, if we're lucky, if he's gotten out. He couldn't get out either end, and that tunnel's not been opened since."

"It terminates in the Mospheiran area," Geigi said. "I can open that end with no difficulty, at Jase-aiji's request."

"I'm doing my best," Jase said. He was running. Bren heard that.

He sat there, with Cajeiri at his shoulder, feeling they were so close, so very close to getting all the kids safe, at least, and the adrenaline was running out of him. He didn't want it to. He just felt it go.

And they *still* had the parents to extract. Units were moving on that . . . with no translators.

"May I talk to Banichi, nandi?" Bren asked. Geigi relayed orders, and a distant deep voice said,

"Nandi?"

"Banichi-ji. We are working to reach Gene's area. Are you able to talk to the units in 23?" Meaning those moving on Artur's and Bjorn's addresses. "Can the children translate for them, on com?"

"We are in contact, nandi," Banichi said. "The children are providing information and words the parents will understand, and are available on com."

"Understood." Trust Banichi to handle the details. Wishing Guild to stay safe was itself an order, as his aishid had dinned into his human sensibilities, and he refrained from giving it. "Baji-naji, we are making progress. Ending."

Jase's input was back in his hearing. They were moving at a steady pace, armor using its assists, by the sound of it. He didn't trouble Jase with chatter. Jase was getting directions from the workers guiding him.

And it was going to take time to get positioned, while unrest might well seek to breach that freight access as a way out.

"Go attend your great-grandmother, young aiji," he said to Cajeiri. "Get her sugared tea if she will have it. She must be exhausted. This will not be immediate. But we are working on it. I shall advise you when we are in reach."

"Your hand is shaking, nandi."

"One confesses to anxiety." It was embarrassing, to have the boy notice it. Likely everyone else did. "But not to dcspair. Go. See to your great-grandmother. She is far too tired."

No reply. Cajeiri went away, and Bren sat where he was,

lacking the will to get up, the coherency to assemble thoughts on what to do next. Jase kept the contact open and he sat there, hearing Jase's running footsteps and the action of the armor near him.

Then the opening of a hatch and Jase's hard breathing. *"Going to cut you out now,"* Jase said. *"I'm entering 24. I'll be coordinating with my units."*

"Got it," Bren said, and the contact switched out.

A cup of tea arrived beside him. Geigi had ordered two. He picked it up and took a sip, and it was strong tea, sugared to the point of syrup. He winced. He hated the type. The sugar hit his stomach, a questionable moment.

"Nandi," one of the techs said, down the row. "Nandiin, we have a variance in the kyo signal."

Mental whiteout. Panic. He picked up the tea, took another sip, spilled some onto his hand, if not his coat. He set the cup down, a carefully controlled action.

Drew a deep, deep breath.

The brain was here. It had to be *there.* Fast. Accurately.

"Bren. Ilisidi. Cajeiri." It was a voice like rocks clashing. *"Prakuyo an Tep. Speak."*

"Give me contact," he said. He was numb for the moment. His heartbeat jolted, it was that strong.

"Contact is established," Geigi said calmly. "Proceed, nandi."

"Prakuyo an Tep," he said, clearing his mind of dark tunnels and lines on a chart—summoning up the mental image of a huge, gray presence, a voice that, strange as it was, held a reassuring familiarity. "Bren-paidhi." Counting the pause, he took another sip of tea. Swallowed it with difficulty. "Come."

He'd done it. Issued the come-ahead. *Dock. Meet us.*

"What is our time lag on that," he asked, "from them?"

About ten minutes, was Geigi's answer.

Approximate. But close enough.

Ten minutes before Prakuyo could hear him. Ten minutes,

twenty, thirty . . . he was obliged to hold up, keep his wits about him, *think,* if the kyo handed him a problem.

God, the sugared tea was making him sick.

"Artur!" he heard from across the room. *"Bjorn-nadi!"*

Cajeiri had made contact of his own. But he could not divert his attention.

He was not wholly surprised, however, when a living shadow came up behind him. Banichi and Jago, Tano and Algini had turned up at his back, having delivered three of the youngsters to atevi care.

"The kyo are talking," he said to them without looking around. Vision fuzzed, fixed on the schematic that had turned up, this time with a moving dot. Jase was there, somewhere.

He heard another approach near his seat, light footsteps, a quiet presence.

"Nandi." Irene's young voice. "We could go to Jase-aiji. We could *help."*

Explain that the situation was dicier than that? That they weren't sure of anything? That it wasn't safe, where Jase was? Cajeiri had filled them in. Told Ilisidi, as well, what was going on.

"Bren?" he heard from the earpiece. Jase's voice. *"Bren. Got some good news. The crew in the freight tunnel . . ."* Out of breath. *"Got him. Got Gene. And his mother."*

"Got them! Thank God. Are they all right?"

"Cold and thirsty, need medical, maybe. But they got out. They're out. They don't need me at this point. They're in atevi custody. Ship-com isn't answering. I'm on my own. So I'm delivering them to the only authority that's talking to me."

"You've got the dowager's backing. Mine. Geigi's. Gin's, for that matter. Get back here."

"Soon as I get a report," Jase said.

He took an absent-minded sip of the awful tea. Swallowed. "You're on."

A second sip, still staring at the screen, waiting.

"Meanwhile," he said in Ragi, "I am speaking with Prakuyo

an Tep. He has made contact. He will likely answer my invitation in a moment. And I shall answer him. Then, likely, we shall have a little time." Two measured breaths, with the sounds of young voices trying to be quiet, in the heart of Central. "I think, nadiin, the dowager definitely should wish to rest now. Tell her I shall deal with the kyo. I thank her for standing by us. Beyond that, beyond that—I think I shall have to shift my attention to the kyo ship."

A weight descended on his shoulder . . . Banichi's hand, rare gesture from an ateva. "Understood," Banichi said. "Do as you need to do. We are here. We shall be here. Gin-nandi will provide relief, and deal with Ogun-aiji. And we shall deal with the kyo when they come."

They had gotten all the parents, and Cajeiri met them—everybody's parents but one. Everybody had gathered in Lord Geigi's sitting room, being served tea and cakes, retelling their adventures, how they had hid, and were afraid even to turn the com on, until it came on by itself, and they had heard nand' Bren telling people he was there, and they were safe.

Then they had gotten up and headed out, because nand' Bren had said he was there, and they were going to go down to the exit and try make themselves heard. Gene had heard, too, and headed up to the joining with 23.

Now Gene and Artur and Bjorn were all going to spend the night with their parents, in Lord Geigi's beautiful guest quarters. The parents were all happy and relieved to have them safe, and absolutely overwhelmed at the quantity of food and the beautiful furnishings and Lord Geigi's hospitality.

Everybody but Irene.

Irene had told her story, but solemnly so, without the excitement or the laughter—how she had cut and stained her hair, stolen the key and just walked out; and how she had gotten the guards at the doors to take her to Lord Geigi. Irene did laugh a little, because she *was* glad to be safe, and to have everybody out, and Cajeiri was glad about that. But Irene made a silence around her story. The other parents put arms about her and thanked her, and told her they were grateful.

But Irene's mother was not with them. Irene's mother was still with ship security, and ship security might not let her go right away. Nand' Bren had said he was going to ask Gin-nandi to get Irene's mother out. Tomorrow. And meanwhile Irene's mother was safe, and the ship-folk would see she stayed safe.

So Irene said she was glad about that.

But now Irene just sat in a chair in the corner, looking tired and sad, now that the excitement was dying down and the others were helping Lord Geigi's servants talk to their parents.

Cajeiri went over to her and pulled a chair over close to hers. "Nand' Bren will do what he said," he told her. "And your mother will get here."

"She can go away," Irene said quietly, and drew a deep breath. "She will not be happy with me."

"You will not be obliged to see her, if you wish not."

"I wish not." Her eyes shed water that trailed down her face. "I wish to be in Tirnamardi. I wish to be at Najida. I wish us all to be at Najida."

"You shall be," he said. He was determined about that. "I shall make it happen."

She wiped her face and clamped her lips together. "You will try."

"I shall *do* it."

That brought a very small spark. A slight smile. "*Here* is all right." The smile died. "If the kyo do not attack."

"Nand' Bren will fix things," he said, and added: "And there is good news! Nand' Bren says it is definitely Prakuyo an Tep, and I shall be glad to see him! He said he would come to see us, and I shall talk to him, right along with nand' Bren and mani, and solve everything!"

It was a little immodest, if it had been under less scary circumstances. But Irene took courage from it.

Nand' Bren and mani had both gone to bed. Mani had simply dismissed them all to Lord Geigi's care the instant she reached her apartment, saying she had given instruction for her own dinner. Jase-aiji had gone off duty—well, he had *been* off-duty since the whole search of the tunnels began, but now he had to explain everything to Ogun-aiji and Sabin-aiji, who were not necessarily on the best of terms. So Jase-aiji was not having a pleasant evening, and they had not seen him at all.

Lord Geigi, too, had disappeared with his aishid a little while ago, and one rather suspected he had gone to bed, because he had been on duty in Central and only sleeping in small naps for days.

Now their party was winding down in exhaustion. They had not that much energy left. Mani's physician, nand' Siegi, had had a look at everybody who had been in the tunnels, and patched the cuts on Gene's fingers—Gene had gotten them bending a piece of metal out of the way, so he could pull his mother up a very difficult ladder. Gene's mother was a very little woman, who by no means looked strong, but she had made it. And she had had one little glass of vodka, that was all, and nand' Siegi had said he wanted to see her tomorrow morning.

They were all strangers, all to get to know.

And Gin-nandi was coming to help them, on the shuttle that was coming in. Gin-nandi would talk to the Mospheirans *and* she would talk to the Reunioners and calm everybody down.

Secretly there was a plan by which *everybody* could come down to the world. But he was strictly warned not to mention that.

He wished he could tell Irene more than he had said, but he had already pushed the edge of what he could say.

"When everybody goes to bed," he said to Irene, once people began to talk about going to their rooms, "come with me to mani's apartment. We shall be very proper. There is a room for you, next to mine. Veijico will give you her bed, and Veijico and

Antaro can take Jegari's and Lucasi's, and Jegari and Lucasi can sleep with me. Everybody will be glad if you come."

Irene thought about it a moment. "Will your great-grandmother be upset? Or Lord Geigi?"

"By no means. Come. Tomorrow mani will sleep late, and likely nand' Bren will sleep until Gin-aiji comes; and Lord Geigi will go back to Central early, because his people are still holding on there—they have to do that until Gin-aiji can call the Mospheirans back to order, and until they get all the door locks proper again. But Lord Geigi told nand' Bren that is almost done. Come stay in mani's apartment and we shall come back here for breakfast with everybody."

Gene came over. And Artur. And Bjorn, who was with them for the first time.

They were all together, all worried about Irene.

But Irene was going to be with them, and right then he made up his mind he was going to see to it that, whatever Irene's mother wanted, or whatever her associations turned out to be, none of it ever separated them.

Nand' Bren would say exactly the same. He was absolutely sure of it.